PSi

INVADERS

J. PATRICK CONLON

America Star Books
Frederick, Maryland

First printing

All characters in this book are fictitious, and any resemblance to real persons, living or dead, is coincidental.

America Star Books has allowed this work to remain exactly as the author intended, verbatim, without editorial input.

Softcover 9781680908435
PUBLISHED BY AMERICA STAR BOOKS, LLLP
www.americastarbooks.pub
Frederick, Maryland

Dedicated to our Future

We choose to go to the moon. We choose to go to the moon in this decade and do the other things, not because they are easy, but because they are hard,

John F. Kennedy, 35th President of the United States

TABLE OF CONTENTS

PROLOGUE

EXALTED IMPERIAL COMMANDER, THIS SCOUT 45Y43T5 HAS DETECTED A NEW SUN THAT HAS IGNITED OUTSIDE OF THE SYSTEM AT COORDINATES JX45682 ARC THREE. THIS SCOUT DOES NOT SPECULATE AS TO WHETHER THE IGNITION OF THE SECOND SUN IS SIGNIFICANT. WE HAVE ALSO DETECTED ARTIFICAL SPACE BORN CONSTRUCTS. CLOSE EXAMINATION OF A DEVICE OUTSIDE THE SYSTEM INDICATES THERE IS ONE PLANET THAT CAN DO OUR BIDDING. IT WILL REQUIRE A HEAVY FORCE TO SUBDUE. THE THIRD PLANET FROM THE SYSTEM'S SUN IS RADIATING ENERGIES THAT INDICATE A GREAT DEAL OF THE MINERALS AND OTHER MATERIALS WE REQUIRE ARE AVAILABLE. REQUEST SENDING A SPECIAL FORCE TO SUBDUE AND TRAIN THE PLANET'S SPECIES AS SLAVES. SCOUT 45Y43T5 AWAITING INSTRUCTIONS. MAY THE SANDS OF LIFE EVER BE WARM.

SCOUT 45Y43T5, YOUR REPORT IS INCOMPLETE AND INCONCLUSIVE. CONTINUE OPERATIONS, SUBDUE THE LOCAL SPECIES USING THE TELEMENTAL TRANSMITTERS, SEND A COMPLETE REPORT WHEN WE MAY ENTER AND HARVEST THIS SYSTEM. YOUR REPORT THAT YOU HAVE ACCOMPLISHED YOUR MISSION IS EXPECTED IN THE NEXT NINE OF NINES KEKS OF THE SANDS. EXALTED IMPERIAL COMMANDER.

With many of the corrupt governments removed from the world scene, earth has turned into a hothouse of progress with the construction of more space habitats underway, business opportunities abounded. The one drawback is that much of the well-educated highly motivated and adventurous population is migrating into space to the habitats, moon, Mars, and the other planets. Most of the planets have at least a research station now manned by intrepid scientists, and their robots, who are pursuing esoteric researches. One such station is a galactic observatory just outside the orbit of Pluto.

Much of what remains on earth for the world's governments to deal with are shysters, crooks, gangsters, terrorists, corporations who are exercising every method possible to control the world economically, and people desperate to make their lots better but cannot because of a multitude of issues. Diseases run rampant through these populations killing nearly as many people as gangs do.

Anyone with a gun, who is mean enough or ruthless enough can form a gang and be slightly better off than those he terrorizes. Most of the honest and otherwise have only a basic education, if they have any at all. Along with starvation, drought, and disease, gangs are forcing many people into slavery. They rounding up the unfortunate and using them as forced labor. When the gangs finish with them, they often execute them in lots that make the Rwandan Civil War of 1994, look like a tea party. Several hundreds of thousands of people have died this way. Africa, South America, and many of the island nations of the Pacific Ocean and Southeast Asia fall into this category.

The United States had its own problems resulting from Wendy Winston's mind trio diverting the Jupiter-body away from our sun. In addition, the invasion of Chinese armies bent on capturing Wendy and her team, plus terrorist and religious fanatic armies who wanted to destroy the trio before the Jupiter-body's diversion added to the countries damages. In the United States, repairing the damages was happening because the government was using mentally checked military forces to control the criminals and assist in rebuilding the nation. After six years of rebuilding the nation and many of the Western Nations are looking towards the future with goals that include assisting Third World Nations and expanding even further into space.

Scientifically the partial cancellation of inertia in spacecraft has become full cancellation and getting to Mars is a day trip, Pluto is less than a week from earth. The abilities of robots have grown as well and those who look after Wendy Stevens, Katherine Warren, and Aiko Esteban are always among the most advanced robots on earth or off. The three women now have two sets of young triplets apiece. The first sets from artificial insemination. The younger sets resulted because the programming to activate women's mental powers altered their DNA in a way that causes triplets to be conceived. They live with their husbands in the small village of very large houses that has grown up around a place called Central, which is South of Des Moines, Iowa. Life is idyllic almost pastoral if raising six Psi capable children with the help of the practical joking robots can be considered such. At least that is how it was until Secretary General of the United Nation visited them and the aliens started tampering with the children's minds.

A HIGH LEVEL BACKYARD MEETING

Patrick Riley Dugan, once of New York, now from Iowa, walked out of the patio door to his house. In his very large backyard, eighteen children were playing a game of telekinetic, no hands dodge ball. Along the sides of the playing field, some of the ever-present family robots were refereeing the game. The robots' bodies were footlocker like boxes placed on end. They are a little over a meter and a half tall, half a meter wide and two thirds of a meter deep. They have four tires similar to those found on small lawn tractors. There is a camera on each side near their top and a double camera on a swivel in the middle of their top. There are two radio antennas in diagonal corners on top. They have arms with claws, much like a lobsters, on the same sides as the tires. There is a computer screen and cargo shelf on what is considered their front.

The children the robots were supervising were making fantastic jumps and other moves. There were constant small booms as a child would teleport him or herself or another player out of the way of one or more of the six balls which moved at startling speeds and changed directions in midflight seemingly of their own will because the children were using their telekinetic powers to throw them at one another.

Under the shade of a large patio awning Pat's wife Carroll and his guests the Stevens, Warrens, Estebans, and Vasquezs were seated or reclining on various pieces of lawn furniture chatting about the things they would be doing in the next few days. Jackie Vasquez's three eldest children who were in their late teens were listening to the adult conversation quietly.

"We're going to take my kids up to Tank Circuit One on Monday, Katherine's Tuesday, and Aiko's on Wednesday," Wendy Stevens formerly Wendy Winston told the group.

Pat bent, kissed his wife then asked, "Both sets of triplets?"

"Just the oldest ones this time," Wendy replied, as she watched her children with motherly pride, "We'll take the others up when they are a little older."

Eduardo Vasquez asked, "Are you popping up or flying?"

"We're flying," Katherine Warren, former President Kenneth Jordan's daughter, answered. "They need to understand how the rest of the population has to do things."

One of the robots left the dodge ball game and rolled up to Katherine. It typed, "Your father just landed at the air field."

"Thank you Jennifer," Katherine replied, "Do you know why?"

Jennifer typed, "I do not know but he has President Harper and another person with him. They will be here in ten minutes."

Wendy asked, "Did Gustov give any hints?" Jennifer beeped twice.

"Perhaps they are just dropping by to say hello," Aiko Esteban said wistfully.

"Boy, are you ever dreaming," Jackie replied.

Secretary General to the United Nations, Kenneth Jordan, President of the United States Percival Harper, and Ms. Jeannette McDonald Director of the International Aeronautics and Space Administration appeared from the side of the Dugan house and Katherine asked, "What's wrong dad?" Several robots arrived with the three new comers and stationed themselves about the Dugan's patio. As she got up to hug her father, Katherine asked one of the robots, "Gustov, what has he gotten into now?" A robot beeped twice. "Please, have a seat can you be served something to eat or drink?"

"Can't I show up for a visit without you assuming there's a problem? Let me introduce you to President Harper and this is Ms. Jeanette McDonald, Director of IASA." Then with a sigh he continued, "Unfortunately dear daughter you're right, we are here about several problems that we're hoping all of you can solve for us," Kenneth said as he gazed at the youthful activities in the yard.

Wendy asked, "Does one of the problems have to do with something in space?"

Ms. McDonald replied, "One of the problems is in space but it isn't of our making."

"That sounds like another Jupiter-body problem," Wendy stated.

"I don't think this will be that easy. I have a data chip if you have a way to play it," Jeannette answered.

Robin rolled up to her and typed, "My name is Robin and I can play your data chip." She handed the robot the chip and a holographic image appeared above the robot, of events that occurred at the location of the Pluto observatory forty Astronomical Units from earth. "This is an optical record sent by one of the monthly supply ships to the observatory. Something destroyed the Pluto observatory and it looks like every scrap of material from the observatory was absorbed by whatever that is. A short time after that the ship stopped reporting also."

"How long after those events did you receive the information?" Aiko asked.

"It takes about five and a half hours for a laser com report to reach earth. That was three days ago.

"Okay so we have something going on in space we need to look at," Wendy said. "Mister President, what issues are you laying at our feet?"

"Piracy, both at sea and on land," President Harper replied. "Some of the pirates have acquired what look like old warships from someplace. They sail into a port accompanied by a cargo ship demand that it be filled from a list they provide, and then blow the harbor to pieces as they leave. This has happened to Portland, Oregon and Charleston, South Carolina and I've received requests for help from several other coastal countries."

"You said that there were also land based problems as well," Katherine prompted.

"There are and we think that these attacks are linked to the sea going ones because they are mostly close to the coast," the

President said. "One attack was on the military ammunition storage facilities in Alabama. The army repulsed that raid. The worst attack was on Mexico City. They took foodstuffs, destroyed several jewelry stores, and used artillery to blow open bank vaults. In many of these raids, they are also taking women."

"Anything else?" Carroll asked.

"That pretty well sums up my woes," President Harper replied.

"Then that just leaves you dad," Katherine said, "So what's bugging you?"

"The piracy problem seems to be an extension of what I've got along with civil wars, famine, and droughts," Kenneth answered. "The civil wars are turning out to be over things like diamonds, and tantalum which have been discovered in several new regions of Africa and South America. Africa, and the Southeast Asian islands are experiencing famines and massive disease problems. In Africa its drought, Southeast Asia flooding. The UN doesn't have enough resources to handle everything."

"So two of the questions are; how are the pirates getting information on where to strike, and are the land based pirates part of the same group as the ocean going ones?" Katherine stated thoughtfully.

"Are any of the pirates tied to any of the civil wars?" Freddy, Jackie's eldest child asked in an exceptionally deep base voice.

There was a pause in the conversation and Kenneth said, "That's an ugly thought, I hope not."

Jackie asked her son, "What made you ask that, Freddy?"

"War costs a lot of money and the faction with the most has the best chance of winning," Freddy replied soberly.

The dodge ball game ended suddenly and groups of triplets ran to their mothers and Arielle one of Wendy's red headed girls said, "Mommy, somebody is trying to get into my brain." Several other children nodded and told their parents the same thing.

Wendy looked at the children and said, "Let us see what they were trying to do, dear." Wendy and her children went into momentary blank stares. Aiko and Katherine did the same thing with their children. Wendy's eyes began to smolder as she read what she found implanted in her children's minds. Wendy linked with Katherine and Aiko her mind partners, and saw that they had found the same thing in the minds of their children. She took a deep breath and said aloud, "I thought that we had defused the religious fanatics when we deflected the Jupiter-body."

"This doesn't have the same flavor. I wonder if it was really them or if they were a tool for the E.T.," Katherine commented thoughtfully. "Children, we need for all of you to sit down and relax so we can fix what has happened to you." The children all sat on the patio, the trio linked, and one by one the children all laid down asleep.

An hour later Clarence Stevens walked into the Dugan's patio and asked, "What has happened to the kids?"

Carroll answered, "Someone or something implanted a time bomb in all of our children's minds that would have turned them into slaves at the appropriate time."

"You said someone or something?" Clarence asked.

Jackie said, "Robin, show him what Ms. McDonald brought." The robot rolled to where Clarence stood and activated its holographic projector.

The scene played through and Clarence asked, "So you think that this is responsible for what was done to the kids?"

Jackie replied telepathically, "*Yes*," then she showed him what had been implanted in all of the younger children's minds.

"I see," Clarence acknowledged, "Jason, pass the field information we've been working on to the other robots." Clarence's robot, Jason beeped once and typed, "Done!" Clarence continued, "The field was designed to give Wendy and me a little privacy from nosy kids. When they are done cleaning our kid's minds, we'll turn it on. That means that none of us should be able to use telepathy and that no outsider should be able to intrude either."

Secretary General Kenneth Jordan asked, "Will that affect their ability to link, and what about the other teams? I know that some of them don't have robots."

"I have a feeling that we may need to build some planet sized generators and then hope that our power trio here can deprogram all of our human spaces through them," Clarence replied.

"Through what dear?" Wendy asked having just come out of her link trance.

Clarence said, "Jason, activate the field." Clarence continued telepathically, "*Through a thought screen dear.*"

"I saw you go blank but I didn't hear anything," Wendy said. "Did you try to send me a thought?"

"Yes I did, which means the screen is working," Clarence replied.

"Can it be tuned to prevent the ET from putting things in human minds," Katherine queried, "And still allow us to communicate and link?"

"We just got it working so I haven't played with it to see if I can make it tunable," Clarence replied.

Jason rolled to where Clarence could read its screen and typed, "Your shoes are untied and I only blocked your thought to Wendy. When we were designing the field I discovered that it could be tuned."

"Katherine," Clarence said, "Would you reprogram this tin box into something like a lawn sprinkler."

Wendy asked, "Did Jason strike again and your shoes are untied?"

"That's what it said, along with telling me that it had blocked my thought to you," Clarence replied. "It seems that this tin smart aleck determined that it is possible to target specific thought frequencies and block just those. Jason, if you don't want me to start disassembling you then the ET had better be blocked and the rest of us had better be able to communicate telepathically." The robot beeped twice and backed away from Clarence.

"I've watched Clarence take things apart, Jason," Pat said, "So if I was a robot I'd do as he says. Have you developed any thoughts on how we should handle this pit of snakes, Katherine?"

Katherine asked, "Jackie how good are your three oldest kids?"

"Freddy's a trio with Naomi Judson and Winona Bright-Feather, two of the original fifty women," Jackie replied smiling at her son. "Look at him blush."

Teasing Katherine asked, "Tell us Freddy, have you found out about the birds and the bees yet?" Freddy turned a brighter pink and looked like he wanted to hide."

Jackie asked, "What did you have in mind?"

"If we saddle them with some electro-mechanical chaperones," Katherine responded, "I was thinking that maybe they could grow some crops using the technique Wendy, Aiko, and I used to restore the area around here."

"How about rain to keep the crops growing?" Kenneth asked.

Edna, Jackie's senior daughter asked, "Are there fresh water wells in the drought area?"

Everyone looked and Kenneth who asked, "Would one of you electronic surveyors, map and display the water availability in Africa?"

Jennifer turned on its projector with a map of Africa showing regions of blues and browns. On its screen was typed, "The wells themselves don't show on the maps. This is a map of the water table levels in Africa. Some of the water is mildly salty with over use but data is not accurate on where those areas are."

"If the countries in question will let us bring in our army," President Harper said, "They have portable desalinization units that could be used for drinking and irrigation."

"Maybe we could talk some of the farmers around here into taking their plows and such to Africa," Wendy inserted, "To prepare the land like they do here. Freddy, Can your team link with generators?"

"Yes Ma'am, at fifty-eight hertz so we can use almost any alternating current source," Freddy rumbled. "How do we keep the peace and feed the populations until the crops can be harvested? Also, what about thought screening the habitats and settlements on the moon and Mars"

"Your child is full of good questions today," Wendy told Jackie.

"Yes, and he has a very good point," Jackie replied. "I think that not only are we going to have to feed them we're going to have to train them to grow their own food as well."

"I think that those two items fall into my realm for solutions," Kenneth said. "As head of the UN, I need to get the Security Council and General assembly to come up with a resolution to let us do what you've all been suggesting. I'd also like to hit them with a complete package that includes all of the problems except the aliens."

Katherine asked, "Why not the aliens, Dad?"

"I'm not sure that would be a good idea in view of everything else. I think that using some miss direction might work better in this case. We don't want to scare them into inaction."

"In that case," Wendy said, "How do we end the piracy and the civil wars?"

Katherine asked, "Jennifer, do you have any surveillance of the pirate ships?"

The robot beeped twice and typed, "I have been checking satellite surveillance but haven't found the ships yet."

"Is it possible that the pirates are disguising and using flags and markings of legitimate ships?" Aiko queried.

Jennifer beeped once and typed, "I will factor that into my search."

"While Jennifer searches," Wendy asked, "How can we stop the civil wars and how many are we talking about?"

Silence followed as everyone thought about answers to those questions then Carroll said softly, "It's been a long time since Wendy got mad and her doppelganger took a walk."

"What was that?" Pat who was sitting next to her asked.

"I was just thinking out loud," Carroll replied.

"About what?" Wendy asked.

"The last time that you got mad and your doppelganger went for a walk," Carroll replied.

"You know, I've been wondering how the brothers Pan have been doing of late," Katherine said. "But I don't think the same technique will work in Africa or any of the other problem places.

Around the patio, young children began to stir and Carroll's son, Caleb, asked, "Mom, I'm hungry and can we go swimming later?"

"Rebecca," Carroll asked her robot, "What do we have that we can feed a school of hungry young sea monsters?"

The robot typed, "We have prepared a picnic style meal for all of you that includes hamburgers, hot dogs, fried chicken and all of the other things the children like. There is cake for desert provided they eat properly first."

Pat said, "Then lead them to it and bring the rest of us some as well. Kids, follow Rebecca and Robby to the goodies." The entire crowd of young children got up and ran after the robots trying to be first in line to get their choices. "I'm surprised that they didn't all pop over to the food." Next to him, there were three loud bangs as Jackie's teenagers did just that. "Me and my big mouth."

The rest of the adults laughed at him and Aiko asked, "Do we need to watch our adventurers that they don't try to handle the alien on their own?"

"I hope not," Jackie replied thinking of her three teenagers. "I think I'll have a talk with them later to make sure."

"I have a feeling that she was thinking of ours, Wendy's and Katherine's oldest triplets," Hiro Esteban, Aiko's husband said. "Right Wendy?"

A few moments later Wendy came out of a blank stare and asked, "What did you say, Hiro?"

"I asked if we were going to have to watch our young adventurers so that they didn't try to take on the alien by themselves," Hiro replied.

"I was just checking on that very thing," Wendy told the group, "And yes we will because they were planning a midnight raid on what seems to be an alien scout. They seem to be a bit put out that it put things into their brains that would make them hurt us."

"How are they planning on doing it?" Katherine asked, "And do we let them and stand by to bail them out or do we block them?"

Wendy replied, "They seem to think that the thoughts were mechanically generated so they want to break its machines and then teach it a lesson in how leave us alone by wrecking the ships weapons."

Kenneth asked, "Are they powerful enough to do that?"

"All nine of them together," Katherine responded, "You'd better believe it."

President Harper asked, "Can all nine of them link into a single unit?"

"Remember the dam collapse in Tennessee last year?" Katherine asked.

"There was something strange in the water flow as I recall," Kenneth replied, "The kids had a hand in that."

"They kept the flow inside the normal banks of the riverbed for about two hours with nothing but news cast images," Wendy replied. "Then fatigue got to them and they hollered for help from Jackie's teens."

"So that's why every generator around here went to full load when that happened," Jackie said. "Did the triplets know how to interface with them then?"

"Not then," Wendy replied, "Your three tapped the generators and shoved power at the youngsters. Remember the geyser that popped up in the middle of all of that? Well that was all of that power hitting all three sets of triplets. The 'Water Tube', as the news called it, was them forcing the flood through the air over the shortest route to the Gulf."

Kenneth Jordan asked, "So you think that they can help with our problems here on the surface?"

"The problem will be limiting them to things that won't bite back too hard," Katherine answered.

"I have a feeling that Pat, Jackie and I will be babysitting while you three deal with the alien," Carroll said.

Several robots arrived with trays laden with plates heaped with picnic foodstuffs, which they distributed to everyone. Robin rolled near Wendy and typed, "The oldest triplets were discussing how to defeat the alien scout before it can do more damage. They are planning to do it tonight."

"That might not be a bad idea," Clarence said. Wendy gave him an angry look and he continued, "Let me finish before you blow your carrot top. If the alien gets the impression that humans aren't that powerful then they may underestimate our capabilities. Besides, we'll kind of ride along to make sure that the aliens are the only ones that learn lessons. Think about it for a few minutes, if unaided kids can mess up their works what could full power adults do to them?"

"As the mother of three of those children," Aiko said, "I want to protect them but as Clarence said our children must learn that they can't always succeed."

"I guess I agree but I don't want to do it in the middle of the night when I'm dead tired," Wendy admitted. "Robin, do you know when they plan to do it?"

The robot typed, "Tonight right after you, Katherine, and Aiko have gone to bed.

Katherine who could see Robin's screen as well said, "You know I've been really tired lately, I think I'll go to bed early. Dad, I'm sorry that we're not paying more attention to your problems but I think that when our youngsters get boxed around a bit we will be able to use them more constructively to handle the other issues."

Kenneth said, "That sounds a bit cruel to the children. Can't you just stop them?"

"I understand your feelings," William said, "The problem is twofold. One, the development of PSI abilities is fastest and to the highest levels with stress. We try to use constructive stress as much as possible with things like that dodge ball game earlier that had six balls flying around instead of one. The second thing is that those nine children are very powerful already and have a tendency to do things on their own mostly without telling us."

Wendy entered the conversation with, "If I hadn't listened in or Robin hadn't told us about their plans we could have been caught cold with hurt or burned out children, especially since they will probably try this stunt without power assistance to keep from waking us up."

Aiko closed the argument by telling the visitors, "We don't like it any better than you seem to but if we don't let them try then they will find another way or not develop fully. Besides we will be watching over them, secretly we hope so that they don't come to harm."

"And speaking of those same children here they come," Wendy said. "You nine look like you have something on your minds, would you care to share it with us."

Arielle responded, "Mom, we were talking about the alien and what it did to us and we would like your help."

"That sounds ominous," Wendy replied, "Go on."

"We want to see if we can throw the alien off track by attacking it. We each have been having flashes of memories or something of things like the aliens eating humans alive and if they are we want to do something about it."

"That's mighty profound for a six year old," President Harper said in a low voice.

Wendy smiled at him and said to her daughter, "Show me the visions, honey." Arielle and the other eight children went into blank stares and Wendy said, "Everyone link to me. You too Kenneth." Everyone linked, and saw constantly shifting images of the aliens doing things to include eating live humans. After a few minutes, Wendy broke the link and asked her daughter, "What is it that you kids want to do to the aliens."

"We want to invade their ship and destroy their mind machines and if we can save any humans still alive," Arielle replied. "We want to do it alone and without power so that the alien gets a wrong idea of what you and dad can do to them."

The IASA director asked Pat quietly in astonishment, "These are six year olds?"

"Yes," Pat replied, "Six years going on sixty I sometimes think."

"What school do they attend," President Harper asked, "I want the department of education to study how they do it."

"They all have the ability to interface with computers," Carroll told him, "And the robots handle school and all things educational. Jackie's three oldest kids had to have connectors like ours installed to be able to do that."

"Connectors?" Jeannette asked.

Pat bent forward so that she could see the back of his head and Carroll replied, "Yes connectors. See the square patch on the back of Pat's neck at the base of his skull? Under the cover is a connector that allows him to hook himself to a computer. Jackie's three oldest kids and we adults have them. Wendy, Katherine, and Aiko also have two other interfaces as well that don't need wires but are limited in range and scope."

"Do the younger children have connectors?" President Harper asked.

"No," Carroll answered, "They are all naturally PSI active and only need temple contacts."

"Naturally PSI active," Jeannette asked, "Do you mean that the rest of you aren't?"

"Exactly," Pat inserted, "The installation of our connectors allowed us to be programmed so that our PSI abilities activated."

"Then how did your children do it?" Jeannette asked.

Carroll answered, "When our powers activated, it changed our genes so that the PSI genes are dominant in our children."

"How did everyone end up with sets of triplets?" President Harper asked.

The oldest ones were artificial insemination. Vice-President Wellington, who we called the boss, set that up except for mine and Pat's," Carroll replied. "Pat is a triplet so ours were conceived the old fashioned way."

"Clarence," Wendy said, "Katherine, Aiko, and I are going up to tank circuit one. Would you three guys link with the kids and watch them while they go hassle the alien scout?"

Clarence looked at his wife, saw the anger in her eyes, and replied, "Certainly, Love." Three booms followed his reply and the women were gone. Clarence told the children, "If you're going alien hassling you'd better get at it." Nine six-year-old girls sat on the Dugan's patio in a circle and joined hands. In the alien spacecraft a cloudy something appeared, tendrils reached from it to machines throughout the ship and they exploded or melted into hot metallic pools on the ship's deck. The cloudy something broke into three smaller ones and began destroying other things in the ship. One of the somethings entered a compartment that was blood coated and a group of aliens was tearing a live human man to pieces with their claws and teeth. The man was screaming in agony. The something touched his head and he died. Then the something reached tendrils towards the aliens grabbed them and slammed them together then dropped them. An hour later the Clarence, Warren, and Hiro cloudy something that had been watching the smaller somethings told them, *"Okay kids, that's enough, we think they've gotten the message."*

Back on the patio, three booms signaled the return of the children's mothers and Wendy's children got up and ran to their mother crying. Wendy sat on a chase lounge and hugged them all. Telepathically Wendy asked Clarence, *"What happened?"*

Clarence replied, *"They killed a man who was being torn apart and eaten alive, then they killed about half the crew of the scout ship. Some place I read that some cultures did what was called a mercy killing, "Giving Grace". You might try explaining it to them that way."*

Wendy looked at her husband bleakly and nodded. She asked her children, "What has upset you so much?"

Arielle the spokesperson for the trio replied, "The man was in so much pain that we murdered him."

"Tell me the rest of it," Wendy coaxed gently.

"Then we picked up the aliens and banged them together and killed them too," Brenda answered.

Wendy asked softly, "Would you have been able to save the man if he was injured so badly?"

The three girls thought for a few moments then shook their heads no, and Arielle said, "But we're not supposed to kill mama and we did."

"Way back in history some of the cultures did mercy killings when soldiers were so badly wounded that they would not live for very long," Wendy explained to her children. "It was called "Giving Grace" or sending the person home to his or her God. I think that what you did for the man was give him grace and while it is not something to be happy about in this case it was needed. As for the aliens, I probably would have banged them together too."

"So it was okay to kill him?" Brenda asked.

"In this case and only in this case, it was alright," Wendy replied. "You were right about there being other humans in that ship?"

Melinda, one of Katherine's blond haired girls replied, "We looked and looked for more humans, where did they go?"

"Aiko, Wendy, and I wrapped them in a force shell of thought and put them in the big hospital on the moon," Katherine answered. Her triplets went blank for a moment then their looks of concern changed to satisfaction. Katherine asked, "Didn't you rascals believe me?"

"We just wanted to check on their status mom," Melinda answered.

"And how are they doing, Minx?" William asked referring to Sarah the one redhead in his and Katherine's eldest trio.

"Four are in a decompression chamber and six are still in surgery the other fifteen are in intensive care," Sarah replied authoritatively which sounded very strange coming from a six year old girl.

"Good," William said, "Then you don't need to worry about them anymore do you?"

"No, Papa," Sarah replied and crawled into his lap, "They are in good hands, but I do have a question."

"What's that?" Katherine asked.

"The aliens have to use thought generators to do their dirty work," Sarah said as if she were thinking out loud, "Is it possible to turn the tables on them and do we want to just make them leave us alone or do we want to destroy them so that they can't do this to a different star system? Oh, can we use a projector to make the pirates and other bad people behave and turn themselves in and deprogram the rest of the humans."

"That's five questions," William replied smiling at his daughter, "But you have touched on some very good points two of which we will have to discuss. Clarence, can your thought screen be turned around and projected?"

Clarence replied, "I would think that if the aliens can do it then we should be able to as well. The idea of using it to deprogram our population could save us a lot of effort too."

"Could we use it to train farmers in Africa?" Wendy asked.

Kenneth Jordan answered, "I think that something like that should be used in conjunction with real humans because the uneducated can also tend to be very superstitious."

"I'll look into it," Clarence said.

"Dad," Brenda Stevens, the quieter of Wendy's first triplets said, "I got a really good look at the machine's insides if that will help."

"I don't know how much help it will be, Brenda, but let me look," Clarence her father replied. The two did momentary blank stares and Clarence continued, "You weren't kidding about getting a good look, kitten. I think we can deduce their basic method, which will save a lot of trouble. You did very well. In fact all nine of you did very well, just don't get swelled heads."

"If we did the robots would play a joke on us that would make us feel really dumb for being tricked," Arielle told her father.

IASA director McDonald shook her head and said to no one in particular, "Listening to your children makes me feel like Alice at the Mad Hatter's Tea Party."

EXALTED IMPERIAL COMMANDER THIS IS TENDER OF THE MACHINES REPORTING FOR SCOUT 5Y43T5. THIS SHIP WAS ATTACKED BY SEVERAL ENTITIES WHO DESTROYED THE TELEMENTAL TRAINING PRO-JECTORS AND SEVREAL WEAPONS. THIRTY-FOUR OF THE CREW INCLUDING ALL OF THE CONTROL COM-MANDERS ARE DEAD. THE REST OF THE CREW DROVE THE ENTITIES OUT OF THE SHIP. RECOMMEND VOLI-TALIZATION OF THE THIRD PLANET IN THIS SYSTEM TO PREVENT FURTHER ATTACKS. AWAITING INSTRUC-TIONS.

PLAYING SEA SERPENT AND MORE

SCOUT 45Y43T5 YOUR REPORT IS INCOMPLETE AND INCORRECT. YOU DID NOT DRIVE THE ENTITIES FROM YOUR SHIP. THEY LEFT ON THEIR OWN. YOU ARE DE-MOTED TO WIPER OF THE DECKS. REPLACEMENTS WILL BE SENT. EXHAULTED IMPERIAL COMMANDER.

After class a few days later Arielle, the most outgoing of Wendy's six-year-old triplets, asked Robin, "Has Jennifer found the ocean going pirates yet?" The robot beeped and Arielle continued, "Show us a map and an image of one of the ships, please."

Robin turned on its holographic projector, showed a map of the portion of the Pacific Ocean near Catalina Island off the coast of California, and the picture of a ship that was only about a hundred and fifteen meters long, and appeared to be a very old design. Sharron asked, "Where did they get that relic, from a museum?" The robot beeped and typed, "The source is unknown. Specifically it appears to be a Fletcher class destroyer from the World War Two era."

"Those burned oil to run steam turbines didn't they?" Brenda asked. "Where are they getting fuel for it?"

Robin replied, "The emission signature indicates that it is using a fuel cell and is actually a little faster than the original design."

"What has to be even more amazing is that the main guns look like they work," Sharron said, "Or did they replace those too, Robin?"

The robot typed, "Unknown."

"I wonder what else we could discover about the ship," Arielle mused. "Do you remember when we woke up at Ms. Carroll's and she asked Robby what there was to feed hungry sea monsters? Why don't we make like a sea serpent and see what we can add to the available knowledge about them?"

Sharron said gleefully, "Why not?" Brenda nodded her head affirmatively.

The three merged and a small something appeared in the sky high above the destroyer. "*How should we make the approach?*" the Brenda part of the something asked.

"*It looks like they are heading for Catalina or California and there's a cargo ship following it,*" the Arielle part replied. "*Should we foil their plans?*"

"*Maybe we can make a big splash to get their attention,*" the Sharron part replied, "*What shape should make the biggest splash?*"

"*A wide 'V' shape should do it and probably better than a flat shape,*" the Brenda part thought. The something darted towards the water at a very high speed. As it moved, it changed into a wedge and entered the ocean a short distance from the ship. Huge waves rose on the broadsides of the wedge and rushed away from the impact. The wave on the side where the ship was nearly capsized it. The crew was tossed about and many went overboard. Under water, the something changed into a long snake like monster with a Raptor's head and long octopus like tentacles. Its tentacles wrapped around the crewmen then rose to the surface and put them back on the ship's deck. The sea serpent wrapped its tentacles around the barrels protruding from the ship's gun turrets and they bent towards the ship's deck. Some of the crewmembers backed away from what they saw while others attacked it with anything they could find at hand to no avail.

The ship's captain stood on the bridge yelling at his crew to destroy the sea monster he saw attacking his ship. The serpent finished bending the ship's five-inch gun barrels and turned its head towards the captain. The end of a long tentacle picked up the captain and drew the luckless wit towards its head, which tilted to examine him closely with one of its broadly spaced eyes. In his mind he heard in little girl voices asking, "*Who is your boss? Who are you working for?*" The man screamed insanely as the sisters drove deeper and deeper into his mind until they found the information they were after. Having gotten what they wanted, the sea serpent put the captain down gently on the deck of the destroyer, and dove back into the ocean and disappeared.

The three came out of their link trance and discovered their father standing near them and he asked, "What have you three been up to that Robin told Jason to get me?"

Answering for the trio as usual Arielle said, "We were investigating a pirate ship and we know who is responsible for that ship's activities, Dad."

Their father, Clarence Stevens, sat in a chair next to his girls and asked, "How did you make sure that you didn't give yourselves away?"

"We remembered Ms. Carroll calling us a bunch of sea monsters so we used that as our disguise. Do you want to see?"

"That might be a good idea," Clarence replied, "But on a small enough scale to fit here please." A sea serpent many times smaller than what they had been before appeared in the room and its head moved to a couple of inches from Clarence's face. "I get the idea," he said.

A little girl voice that sounded like Sharron issued from the serpent that said, "We never talked out loud so they didn't hear any voices to go with this." The serpent disappeared and Arielle asked, "Would you like the information now?"

"You three need to start clearing things with me or your mother before you jump in too deep and get hurt," Their father told them. "Yes I would like to have the information."

"Robin told us about Doctor Janice being hurt in something called the Singapore Brush War," Sharron said. "I was curious about it so I looked it up. It turns out that Elec Corp, one of the three companies that started that war is involved with the pirates and the civil war in Guyana."

"According to the destroyer's captain the loot they get in the Pacific is fenced through Somalia and several other small country ports," Arielle added to the report, "And the money is used to provide weapons, drugs, and other materials to their mercenary led armies. The women that are kidnapped are used by the crews of the ships and some are sent to the mercenaries for their pleasure."

Clarence noted that all three of his children's eyes smoldered in a controlled rage that was very like their mother's as they told him this. He asked, "Is there anything else I need to know about this particular operation?"

"No, Dad," Arielle replied in a tone that showed just how angry she was about what had happened to the kidnapped women.

"Thank you, you have done very well but," the girl's father told them sternly, "Don't try to deal with this on your own. Let's hold a team meeting with your mother's team and organize things so that you can participate in ending this mess." His girls got up from where they had been sitting on the floor, and attempted to all climb into his lap at once causing him to fall out of the chair he had been sitting in. In the power of the hug that followed, none of them noticed that they were all on the floor. After a few minutes the hug turned into a wrestling match the girls all ended sitting on Clarence's chest then he began tickling them making them fall off him laughing.

Wendy, the girl's tall slender auburn haired mother, who the girls thought was very beautiful, appeared at the door to the family classroom and smiling asked, "What are all of you up to?"

"These three went on a fishing trip after class today and Robin sent for me," Clarence replied. "We were just discussing what they caught."

"Dad," Arielle interrupted, "I just realized that we learned something else too."

"What's that Squirt?" Clarence asked.

"The destroyers all came from the Xiamen shipyard in China," Arielle replied seriously, "And the captain knew about six other ships."

While Arielle added her information the sea serpent that they had shown Clarence appeared behind Wendy and tapped her on the shoulder. Wendy turned to see who was there, screamed in surprise. In six-year-old Brenda's voice the sea serpent said, "Hi Mom."

Wendy looked at the apparition, tried unsuccessfully to suppress her laughter at the sight, and asked, "Where did this come from?"

The serpent answered in Sharron's voice saying, "This is what the crew of the destroyer we visited saw only a whole lot bigger. We didn't say anything out loud to the crew."

"From what I gather," Clarence told his wife, "They got all of their information from the captain's mind and then dived back into the sea and disappeared."

"You know this size is cute," Wendy said, "I can imagine what the crew saw and felt. Did you do anything else?"

"We bent the ships gun barrels down to the deck," Arielle answered.

Brenda asked, "Is it supper time yet, mom, I'm hungry."

Wendy replied holding out her hand to take her daughter's, "Why don't we go see what has been prepared?"

In the family dining room Clarence asked, "What is for supper Jason?"

In its typical robotic humor, the robot typed, "Nails, snails, puppy dog tails, and crab grass for desert."

Non-pulsed, Clarence said, "Sounds good, serve it up and let's eat."

The family sat at their dining room table, and the robots served them a meal of fried chicken, corn on the cob, mashed potatoes with gravy, and apple pie with ice cream for dessert. During the meal, the conversation stayed on topics such as when the next backyard picnic would be held and at which family's house.

After eating, the family adjourned to a spacious family room and Brenda climbed into the overstuffed recliner, squeezed beside her mother, and asked her, "Do you think that the kidnapped women are still alive?"

"Which kidnapped women are those, baby?" Wendy asked. You haven't told me what you three found out."

"Sorry Mom," Brenda replied, "Can I show you instead?"

Sensing that her daughter was upset, Wendy said, "Certainly," and both did a momentary blank stare. Wendy looked at the children's father and asked, "Have you notified Secretary Jordan about the China connection?"

"Not yet," Clarence replied, "Jason, contact Ivan and tell it to ask Secretary Jordan to contact us via a secure method."

The robot beeped once in acknowledgement then typed, "Done." Several minutes later Jason beeped and typed, "The Secretary will arrive here around noon tomorrow. He will explain the reason for a face to face meeting then."

"That doesn't sound good," Clarence said. "Kids, have you figured out how to make the link thing be invisible?"

"We haven't tried to do that Dad," Arielle responded. "Is it important?"

"I have something in mind that it would be a good idea for," her father said.

"What's that dear?" Wendy asked her husband.

"Snooping around that shipyard to see what is going on that we may need to deal with," Clarence replied. Neither parent noticed their children go into blank stares and suddenly Clarence oofed and his stomach collapsed visibly. Sharron's voice issued from thin air saying, "Surprise!"

Clarence groaned, "Lighten up," and sighed in relief when the weight on him lifted.

The three came out of their trance and Arielle said, "We can be invisible. What did you want us to do?"

"I would like for you to let me link with you and then go look at that shipyard," her father told her.

"I'd like to go to if you think we can all link together," Wendy said.

Brenda twisted next to her mother and said, "We should be able to do that but we should probably practice first to make sure we can do that and be invisible too."

"You're right," Wendy said, "Robin, detector mode visible, monitor for the something." The robot beeped once and typed, "Ready."

"Is everybody ready?" Clarence asked and when heads nodded said, "Link!" A five way something came into being and then faded until it could not be seen. A voice that sounded like Clarence's asked, "Can you detect us Robin." The robot beeped twice.

Wendy's voices said, "Then let's go to China."

"Alright kids," Clarence thought, *"You discovered the shipyard information so you get to be the investigators."*

Arielle thought, *"That ship is a British modified 'Battle Class Destroyer'. Where are they finding such antiques, Dad?"*

"I don't know, this ship looks new," Clarence thought. *"I wonder if they're building them from scratch or on hulls for other types of ships. How come you know so much about military hardware?"*

"We soaked up the Naval Academy library after pirates were discussed at Ms. Carroll's house," Sharron thought. *"There's the manager's office."*

In the manager's office, a very angry man was standing behind a large desk shouting at two underlings. Arielle thought, *"Mom, you speak Chinese, can you get him to make those two leave so there are no witnesses when we read his mind?"*

"Let's let him rant a little longer," Wendy thought, *"I think he is about finished and I can give you Chinese."* Several minutes later, the underlings scurried from the manager's office closing the door behind them. The manager sat in his desk chair and his eyes bulged out as the three youth's minds penetrated his. A band of invisible thought forces covered his mouth preventing him from screaming and more forces held him immobile.

"Who contracted for these ships?" the three thought at the man and bored deeper into his mind with a ruthlessness that belied their few years of age and experience. *"How are the ships to be used? What are their objectives? What are their targets?"* Their thoughts continued to bore into the manager's mind until they had all that he knew. They withdrew from his mind and the family left the man shaking and sweating in his office.

Back in their family room they all came out of their trances and Robin typed, "You have been gone for two hours do you need a snack?"

Wendy replied, "I think that would be a good idea then these three need to take their baths and go to bed. Girls, you did very well and I think we can put an end to Elec Corp's mischief tomorrow when your Uncle Kenneth arrives."

When the snacks had been eaten and the girls gone for their baths Clarence said quietly, "Jason thought screen us from the girls."

The robot beeped once and typed, "The screen is on."

"Dear," Clarence continued, "Where did those three learn to be so ruthless?"

Wendy moved from her chair to the one her husband reclined in, snuggled into his lap and said softly, "I don't know, maybe they inherited it from me. Watching them interrogate that manager was frightening. We're going to have to watch that they don't lose control of themselves."

Clarence told Jason, "Jason, contact Doctor Janice and ask her to visit us sometime tomorrow morning." Then he sighed and added to his loving wife, "What do you say we get some sleep too?" Then with a mischievous grin, he slid his hand to her thigh and pinched it.

Wendy yelped, slapped him lightly on the arm, and said, "You didn't have to do that." Then she got out of his lap and they followed their children to bed.

EXHALTED IMPERIAL COMMANDER, THIS IS SCOUT 45Y43T5. THIS SHIP HAS BEEN REPAIRED. TELEMEN-TAL PROJECTORS ARE IN OPERATION AND THIS SHIP IS RESUMING THE MISSION.

SCOUT 45Y43T5 HOLD POSITION A NEW WAVE FORM HAS BEEN DETECTED INDICATING THAT TELEMENTAL PROJECTORS ARE BEING BLOCKED ON THE PRIMARY FREQUENCY. CHANGE TO SECONDARY FREQUENCY. EXHALTED IMPERIAL COMMANDER.

Shortly after two in the morning, there were six loud bangs in Wendy and Clarence's bedroom and both sets of triplets were wide eyed with fear. Arielle yelled, "Mom! Wake up the aliens are trying to put things in our heads again." Both of the family robots came charging through the bedroom door, clacking claw hands raised for combat.

The noise was so loud that Clarence yelled, "Quiet!" In the sudden silence he said, "Tell us again Arielle."

Arielle gulped twice and repeated, "The aliens are trying to put thoughts in our heads again."

Hugging Samantha and Elizabeth two of the younger triplets, Wendy said, "Show me dear." Rodger the third child of that set of triplets sat wide eyed beside his father on the big bed acting as brave as only a four-year-old boy could. Arielle and her mother blanked for a moment, then Wendy sighed and said gently, "Go get in your favorite sleeping positions in your beds and your father and I will fix things. At least some of us will get a good night's sleep that way." The children scattered to their beds and were put to sleep by Wendy and Clarence as they removed the alien programming.

Clarence told his robot, "Jason, raise the thought shield frequency until I tell you to stop." A moment later he said, "Stop! Alert every one and have them change frequency also. Notify the government that we are going to produce more screens that will handle multiple frequencies simultaneously and a modification kit for the existing ones. See if you can come up with a preliminary plan for me to look at later this morning."

Wendy and Clarence settled back down to return to sleep. Wendy asked, "I wonder why it's the children who seem to be the alien's targets for mind control?"

"Sleep on it dear," Clarence replied as he pulled his wife close to him and closed his eyes.

The next morning Wendy and Clarence arrived in the family breakfast room yawning and rubbing sleep from their eyes. They discovered Doctor Maryann Janice already seated there drinking a hot beverage. Next to her sat a broad faced dark haired woman that the Stevens had not seen before. Doctor Janice said, "Good morning. I had one of my medical robots consult with Robin and Jason so I have a general idea of what you want to talk about. Socrates also contacted the other robots that are in families for more data about the problem. So let me introduce Doctor Elana Wallace who is a psychiatrist and who has been studying us Psi capable humans looking for problems. She came along to talk to your three rascals if that's okay."

"Pleased to meet you Doctor Wallace and forgive us we're not really awake yet," Wendy replied, "We had our night's sleep interrupted. Maryann you said us Psi capable humans, did you activate?"

"Yes," Doctor Maryann Janice answered, "With a range of skills that let me fix things that would normally require surgery."

Wendy and Clarence had seated themselves during this conversation and Robin served them their breakfasts. Wendy started to explain, "Doctor Wallace…" when six noisy children burst into the room and upon seeing Doctor Janice ran to her and gave her hugs before noting the other woman seated beside her.

Arielle bowed slightly to Doctor Wallace and said as she pointed at each of her sisters and brother, "I am Arielle and these are Sharron, Brenda, Samantha, Elizabeth, and Rodger. How do you do?"

Doctor Wallace replied, "I am very well are you always so polite?"

Arielle giggled and answered as she sat in her chair, "In the presence of a robot, you'd better believe it."

Doctor Wallace turned to Wendy and said, "I would be happier if everyone called me Elana. What part do the robots play in the children's up bringing?"

Wendy replied, "The robots are their primary teachers for all school type things. They are also our house keepers and have a fair range of other responsibilities."

Maryann said, "What we'd like to do if it's all right is have Elana stay with you here for about two weeks observing."

Elana added, "More like being nosy and prying into your family and personal lives a whole lot. I'm trying to determine if the geneticists and programmers that designed your modifications for the Boss left anything out or put too much in."

Wendy asked, "Are you able to connect to a computer?"

"Alas, no," Elana sighed, "I'm not one of those who can accept the surgery and have it work. If you want to do a security check the fingers on my temples will work. Maryann told me that and said you might want to."

Wendy replied, "If you don't mind," then continued as she rose from her chair and went around the table, "We've had too many attempts on all of our lives for me to be comfortable not checking.

"Check away," Elana replied.

Wendy placed her fingers on Elana's temples for a moment and then instructed her robot, "Robin, see that Elana's things are moved into the guest room. Kids, you have classes in fifteen minutes so you'd better get with it." Having finished their breakfasts, the children left the table. Wendy asked, "Can you use temple contacts, Elana?"

"I get a nasty headache when I do," Elana replied, "So I tend to shy away from them."

Clarence said, "There is something we need to show you that can best be done with thought."

Elana sighed, "You think there is a problem with some or all of your children. Is that why you dismissed them before telling me about it? Okay, I'll get my contact set." The Doctor started to get up when Robin rolled back into the room with a box on its cargo tray. Elana took the box from the tray and thanked the robot.

When she opened it Clarence asked, "Where did you get that antique? Jason, get the good doctor a new contact set. No wonder you get headaches."

Jason rolled out of the room and reappeared a minute later with a very small box that contained a new set of contacts and their interface device. Elana opened the set and put on the contacts and Jason plugged the interface into a computer connector in the edge of the table. Wendy and Clarence pulled cables from the edge of the table and connected themselves. In flashing thoughts, they explained their concerns about their children and showed her the interrogation of the shipyard manager.

When they finished, Elana whistled softly and said, "I understand your concerns and I'll certainly look into it."

Wendy said, "Thank you. Do you need something for a headache?"

Elana looked surprised and replied, "Amazing, I don't have a headache."

"Maryann," Clarence asked, "Wendy is due in Tank Circuit One in a little bit can I drop you someplace or are you staying awhile?"

"Actually," Doctor Janice replied, "I can get around like you do now days but thank you for the offer."

Wendy held a hand up towards the door and said to Elana, "While they sort out who is going where and how they are getting there, let me show you where your room is and then I do need to leave."

"Thank you," Elana said as the two women left the room, "I was afraid I was going to have to deal with a joker or two before I found it on my own."

Wendy chuckled and asked, "So you know about our robots?"

A little after noon an executive jet landed on the airstrip near what had become the town of Central, Iowa. A limousine and a delivery truck waited for it to stop. When the plane's hatch opened the Secretary General to the United Nations stepped out and got into the limo and several robots exited the plane's cargo hatch and boarded the truck. The two vehicles drove to the Stevens residence. Clarence greeted Secretary Jordan asking, "Did you have a good flight?"

Kenneth Jordan replied, "Yes, thank you. Where are the kids?"

Clarence laughed and asked, "Is that the reason you wanted a face to face meeting, so you could play with the kids?"

"I wish it were," Kenneth replied sadly.

A loud triple boom occurred and Wendy, Katherine, and Aiko were standing a short distance from the two men. Katherine walked to her father, hugged him, and said, "You look troubled dad."

Wendy added, "Why don't we all go inside, have lunch then discuss the various issues that seem to be present."

When they had entered the large Stevens house, both sets of triplets appeared along with Doctor Elana Wallace. The kids all rushed to Secretary Jordan and hugged him and asked what he had brought them. Clarence told his children sternly, "Your uncle Kenneth just got here and he doesn't have to bring you anything so leave off."

Kenneth Jordan smiled at the children and said, "This time I didn't bring anything for you, you greedy lot."

Arielle replied saucily, "That's all right Uncle Kenneth, we love you anyway."

Wendy told her children, "Go wash up for lunch and meet us in the dining room. Kenneth, this is Doctor Elana Wallace a psychiatrist who is studying us PSI types for aberrations and such for a couple of weeks. She has been cleared so it is okay to discuss things in front of her."

Elana stepped toward Kenneth, offered her hand, and said, "How do you do Mister Secretary."

Secretary Jordan replied, "Pleased to meet you and anyplace outside of the UN please call me Kenneth."

Elana nodded and replied, "Fine and call me Elana, I get rather tired of being doctored all of the time."

Kenneth chuckled as the adults entered the dining room and Clarence told his robot, "You can begin serving Jason." The robot beeped and rolled away to the kitchen.

The lunch conversation revolved around the work that Elana was doing without mentioning Wendy or Clarence's concerns about their children. Elana commented, "One of the strangest things, to me anyway, was six-year-old kids doing college doctorial level math and liking it."

"Math is really fun especially the simul-tant-ious solution ones," Arielle said stumbling over the big word.

Wendy asked, "What did the problems have to deal with, Arielle?"

"Putting something into a stable orbit in space," Arielle replied.

Kenneth Jordan asked, "Do you solve those kinds of problems as a unit?"

"Oh no, Robin won't let us," Sharron answered. "It gets really upset with us if we try to link to solve a problem."

"What happens when the robot gets upset," Elana Wallace asked.

"It gives us a lecture and then gives each of us separate problems that are lots harder to do," Arielle replied. "Mom, can we go swimming this afternoon?"

"I think we need to have you three present at our meeting honey," Wendy replied, "But we'll see if there is enough time afterwards."

"Jason, tell Maud that it can clean everything up in here," Clarence instructed the robot "You and Robin need to attend the meeting also." Then to everyone else he said, "Shall we adjourn to my office and conduct our meeting?"

Katherine asked, "Won't we be a bit crowded in your office?"

"Yes," Clarence answered, "But my office is shielded from electronic eavesdropping. Robin, fetch Elana's contact set and kids you need to get yours." With that, Clarence stood up walked to Wendy's place and offered her his hand.

Wendy said smiling, "Thank you kind sir. Kids scatter get your contact kits." The children left the dining room followed by everyone else.

In Clarence's office, the adults found chairs and the children sat or sprawled on the floor in comfortable positions. Those with connectors in the base of their skulls plugged in and the rest connected with temple contacts. Clarence told his robot, "Jason turn on your thought screen, block everything." The robot beeped once and typed "Done." Clarence continued, "Kids this may be a new technique to you but everything goes over wires for this meeting. Kenneth, why don't you start?"

Secretary General to the United Nations, Kenneth Jordan, began, <The UN has run into a problem with setting things up so that Psi capable people can help solve problems. Specifically in several countries, Psi manifestations are considered witchcraft. One country has taken a page from our own Salem Witchcraft Trials and is using dunking stools and burning people at the stake.>

Wendy asked, <How long ago did this start, Kenneth?>

<It seems to have started before you deflected the Jupiter Body,> he replied.

Arielle asked diffidently, <Which regions of the world, Uncle Kenneth?>

<That's the problem. It's happening all over the world and religion seems to be driving it,> Kenneth replied.

<Is it possibly the alien's mind control machines?> Katherine asked her father.

<No,> Kenneth replied, <We've had people secretly check for that and it isn't there.>

<Uncle Kenneth,> Brenda asked, <Is there any information available on the average educational level of the populations in general and of those who seem to be driving this?>

Kenneth looked at Brenda stunned, then asked Wendy, <Why is it that the kids in this part of the world ask the thorniest questions? The answer Brenda is that I don't have any definite information on that but I agree that it is important.>

<I guess that they ask the questions because they have learned to do some serious thinking,> Wendy replied, <So how do you think that is going to affect us in both the short term and long term?>

<There is legislation to make you illegal being considered in several additional countries and the crusaders seem to have gained a new cause,> the Secretary answered. <Some are advocating witch hunting, which pretty much explains why I wanted to come and talk to you. I also talked to President Harper about beefing up your security. What do you have that I need to know?>

<Arielle, Sharron, and Brenda went looking for information on the piracy problem,> Wendy replied. <Girls, tell him what you found.>

Arielle began, <Doctor Janice told us about being injured in the Singapore Brush War so we looked it up to see what it was about. We checked what appeared to be an old World War 2 era destroyer near Catalina. We discovered that one of the companies involved in the civil war in Guyana was behind at least one group of pirates and is using a shipyard in China to build or at least rebuild antique war ships for piracy. The captain of the ship knew of six others. Later with mom and dad, we went to the

shipyard and interrogated the manager in charge of constructing the ships. According to him the former Chinese dictator, Lao Pan, is involved with Elec Corp and they are responsible for three other civil wars and are using piracy to finance them.>

<Do you have proof that will stand up in court?> Kenneth Jordan asked.

<We made brain records of what we found out from each man but that may not be enough considering what you just told us,> Sharron replied, <Especially if the people behind the pirates and civil wars are involved.>

<She's right,> Clarence said, <If they can brand us as witches and discredit us they can get the courts to throw out anything we have.>

Kenneth sighed and said, <I guess I'll have to make a trip to China to talk to Premier Sang.>

Katherine said, <Since Elec Corp can't publically admit to the war ships, maybe we can at least stop that part of things by putting the ships we know about into a small lake or something. I don't think we would need to touch the cargo ships.>

Brenda added, <Leave the cargo ships alone so they can run home to tell Elec Corp that their covers have disappeared mysteriously.> Her eyes gleamed as she added, <That sounds like fun.>

Wendy chided her child saying, <That would be a bit of a challenge for three unsupported six year olds I think.>

<Not if we link with generators mom,> Sharron said. Her eyes gleamed also. <Perhaps we could work our sea serpent into the deal.>

Doctor Elana Wallace entered the discussion by asking, <What makes the three of you think that you have the power to pull off a stunt like that?>

Arielle responded saying, <Robin, pass everyone our unlinked and linked power ratings please.> The robot beeped once and the information appeared in everyone's minds.

Clarence chuckled and said, <Alright Minx, we'll give you a shot at it but only with Freddy's team as a backup. Jason, contact Jackie and ask her to come and bring Freddy with her.> Clarence's robot beeped once. He continued, <Where do you girls think you should put them?>

<How about the Caspian Sea?> Arielle asked.

Kenneth chuckled and inserted, <I think the Caspian Sea is a marvelous place because it will upset people in governments I think are involved.>

<We can interrogate the ship captains and see what else we can find out,> Sharron added.

Wendy shivered slightly and said, <Let us adults do the interrogating please.>

<Why mom?> Arielle asked, <Is it because hearing little girl voices in their heads makes them think they've gone crazy?>

<That and we want to make sure they haven't been programmed by the aliens,> Wendy replied.

<And do a little programming of our own,> Aiko who had been silent until now added.

Clarence asked, <Does that wrap things up for now?>

Heads nodded and everyone disconnected from the network and Kenneth asked smiling, "Ivan did you fetch the packages I had on the plane with me?" Secretary Jordan's security robot beeped once. "Thank you, please give the kids theirs and give the other packages to their mothers."

"You told us a fib, Uncle Kenneth!" Arielle told him in an outraged voice.

"Yes I did," Kenneth replied, "But isn't this more fun?"

Wendy opened her mouth to say something to her child when Arielle said, "It is more fun but you shouldn't lie. Thank you for the gift." Then she got up from where she had been sitting Indian style and hugged him. Doctor Wallace hid a smile behind her hand as she watched what went on.

Jackie Vasquez and her son, Freddy, arrived and Freddy's team's Mission was explained. When the explanation was done

Jackie said, "I was right; Carroll, Pat, and I are going to be babysitting while you big guns clean up everyone else's messes including the aliens.

SCOUT 45Y43T5 TO EXHALTED IMPERIAL COM-MANDER, EXAMINATION OF SEVERAL LOCATIONS CONTAINING THE LOWER LIFE FORM SLAVES INDI-CATES THAT THE TELEMENTAL PROJECTORS ARE NOT PRODUCING THE REQUIRED RESULTS.

SEA SERPENTS, CRUSADERS, AND PIRATES

SCOUT 45Y43T5, YOU ARE BEHIND SCHEDULE. EX-
PIDITE SLAVE TRAINING. PLANET BORES HAVE BEEN
DISPATCHED AND WILL BEGIN OPERATIONS ON THE
TWIN SUB PLANETS NEAR YOU IN FOUR KEKS OF THE
SANDS. EXHALTED IMPERIAL COMMANDER.

Two days after Secretary Jordan had visited, Sharron asked
her father, "Dad how can we figure out an unknown time unit
and convert it to minutes and such?"

"That's a strange question," Clarence replied, "What have
you discovered?"

"I guess I'm sensitive to the alien's communications
machines," Sharron answered concernedly. "I picked up
something in my sleep about planet bores arriving in four Keks
of the Sands and I was wondering how long that was in case we
have to build something to stop them."

"I thought I was just having a dream but I got that too,"
Arielle told her father. Clarence looked at Brenda who nodded
indicating that she had also.

Wendy asked, "Rodger, Samantha, Elizabeth did you dream
too?" The three younger children shook their heads no, Wendy
continued to Arielle, "Can you show us your dream?"

Arielle frowned and went into a blank stare with her mother
for a moment. Wendy asked, "Can you show me yours Sharron?"
Sharron blanked then Wendy asked, "Brenda?" After a moment
Wendy said, "You each got most of the same thing but from
different points of view." She frowned then went on, "I put
the parts together to see if I could make anything from them
and was able to pull an image together of the messenger and
its surroundings. It looks like they are using some kind of hour
glass to tell time." She pulled a cable from the edge of the table,
connected, and said "Robin, Jason, see if you can build a model

of the hour glass and determine how long it takes a grain of sand to move from one end to the other."

Clarence said, "That won't do much good dear. We would need to know several other things as well, like the gravity the sand is in, the size of their home planet's orbit and such. Then there are things like its rotation and diameter and if it has moons."

Wendy wrinkled her nose and said, "Nuts, I thought it would be less complicated than that. Well I'll store this in case the other information shows up. Now the question is do we want to block things so these three can't have dreams about them anymore?"

"Or let them continue to eaves drop?" Clarence asked. "I think that programming could be done to our children that way if the aliens figure out that they are being monitored."

Doctor Wallace asked, "Can I make a suggestion?" Wendy nodded for her to proceed and she continued, "If the robots can monitor their dreams in a pictorial manner, have the girls sleep with their temple contacts on and record them."

Clarence looked at Jason and said, "Contact Jennifer and ask it to ask Katherine to contact us as soon as possible." The robot beeped once and typed, "Done."

Aiko appeared in the hall leading to the dining room with a bang and asked diffidently, "Can I come in? I think we have a problem."

Wendy replied, "Please come in and have a seat. Let me guess, your older trio is having dreams about the aliens, right?"

"Yours too, huh?" Aiko replied.

Another boom occurred and Katherine said, "You called?"

Clarence replied, "Yes I did. We're trying to decide how best to use dream espionage and not let our kids become slaves to the aliens at the same time. Elana suggested having our kids sleep with their contact sets on and having the robots monitor, them but I don't think their programming is capable of that."

"You're right, their programming can't do that." Katherine replied, "It would take some fancy programming to accomplish it. The other problem is that I don't know enough about the human brain, especially the brains of our children, to do it either."

Elana asked, "Have your robots been blocking the thought frequencies of the aliens at night?"

"We thought so," Wendy told Elana. "Evidently our kids have a wider range than is being blocked."

The doorbell rang and Jason rolled out of the dining room to answer the door. Wendy asked no one in particular, "I wonder who that is?" An explosion crashed through the house causing large chunks of wall to knock everyone out of their chairs. Clarence was shoved into the table edge injuring him further. Robin turned its force shield on to protect the adults and children from further harm. Suddenly the room was full of armed and masked people and one of them shouted, "Kill the witches!"

Arielle looked at her brother and sisters and said, "Let's play tag. Knock them all out." The room was suddenly filled with the loud bangs of teleporting children, and gunshots from the attackers' guns as they tried to kill them, and crashing noises from breaking furniture and dishes. The two sets of triplets disappeared and then reappeared behind the attackers banging them on the head with whatever they could lay their hands on until each attacker went down unconscious. Robin pushed clear of the derbies that had buried it and began shocking assailants rendering them unconscious also. In the space of a few short minutes, twenty attackers were scattered around the room out cold.

Sharron said as she banged an attacker who had moved, "Robin, check mom, dad, and the others and make sure they are okay, get Doctor Janice, and security." The robot beeped once.

Arielle asked, "Where is Jason?"

Elizabeth answered, "It went to answer the door and then there was the explosion. You're bleeding pretty bad sis."

Arielle looked down to discover a long splinter of wood sticking through her right leg. "Oh," she said and very carefully sat down in the one remaining undamaged chair in the room.

Arielle asked her younger siblings, "Can you guys pile these people in one place where they can be watched easier? Just make sure they don't have any weapons or more bombs." The three younger triplets mentally lifted the attackers and dumped them all against the remains of a wall. The two older girls mentally removed the attacker's weapons at the same time.

Ten minutes later Central Security arrived followed by Doctor Janice and several medical robots. She looked at Arielle and asked, "Can you hold out for a couple of minutes while we look at your parents and the rest?" Arielle nodded grimly.

The captain in charge of the security detail looked at Arielle and asked, "Can you explain what happened?"

Arielle replied, "The doorbell rang, one of our robots went to answer the door, there was an explosion, and these guys came charging in trying to kill us. We teleported around them hitting them with whatever we could find that was hard. When you take them to jail you are to undress them search their insides for more weapons and bombs and hold them undressed for our parents or Ms. Vasquez or the Dugans to interrogate."

The look that Arielle had on her face despite her pain made the captain gulp and say, "yes ma'am." The captain turned to his people and said, "You heard the lady let's get it done and move some of that garbage out of the hall for stretchers."

Sharron said, "One of our robots answered the door, please find it or any pieces of it and bring them in here."

The captain replied, "Yes ma'am," with the respect he normally would only have accorded an adult woman.

The children's parents, Katherine and Aiko, and Doctor Wallace were taken to waiting ambulances and Doctor Janice asked, "Are any of you besides Arielle hurt?"

The children looked at themselves and each other and Sharron replied, "It looks like mostly scratches but we could be hurt inside."

"Okay," Maryann said, "Let me get Arielle situated and then load all of you up and check to make sure you're okay."

Three security officers entered the shattered room with a metal footlocker sized box and several smaller pieces, which they laid on the dining room table which miraculously had suffered no damage. Arielle looked at it and asked, "Robin can you tell if Jason's core is okay?"

The robot rolled up to the table, extended its claws out on each side of the box for a moment, then withdrew them and turned its screen to Arielle and typed, "The core is intact but is completely depowered."

Arielle slumped in her chair and Doctor Janice said, "Robin, contact the maintenance people and have them pick Jason up to see if it can be rebuilt. Now young lady," she said to Arielle, "Let's get you to the hospital."

Several hours later Doctor Janice pushed Arielle, who sat in a wheel chair, into her parent's room. The other five children followed quietly behind them. Wendy and Clarence were awake and Wendy asked, "Are you alright Baby?"

"She had a half a meter long piece of wood stuck through her right thigh," Doctor Janice said.

"I'm sore but I'm okay mom," Arielle answered. "We fixed the creeps that did this and security has them until Ms. Jackie or the Dugans can get to them." Arielle rolled her chair to her mother's bed, took her mother's hand and said, "I was afraid that they had killed you and daddy."

"They would have if Robin hadn't gotten its shield turned on," her father said from his bed. "That stopped some of the damage to the dining room. What did you do to stop the attackers?"

Rodger answered proudly, "We played tag, daddy and hit them on the head with pans and stuff from the kitchen."

Doctor Janice chuckled and said, "They were still holding an assortment of skillets, and a rolling pin when I got there. One of the attackers started to move and Rodger hit him a good whack on the head and put him back out. Seven of the twenty attackers have serious head injuries and are locked in the security center's ward. They all have concussions but the rest are locked in separate cells with our local FBI agents interrogating them."

Wendy asked, "What about us, how are we?"

"Clarence got busted inside and will need to spend about two days here while his innards knit," Maryann Janice told Wendy. "You, Katherine, Aiko, and Doctor Wallace will be able to leave tomorrow but you're going to be sore and need to rest for a couple of days."

Lieutenant General Thomas Gregory knocked on the hospital room door and asked, "Can I join this crowd?"

Wendy replied, "Certainly General, how have you been?"

"I've been fine but you didn't need to blow your house to pieces to get me here," Gregory answered. "When Secretary Jordan talked to the President, I was ordered to bring my Airborne Corps back here and to build a permanent military installation because you all can't seem to stay out of trouble." Then the General chuckled and added, "Did you have anything to do with a Fletcher class destroyer with bent guns being hauled into the San Diego Naval Station or the Tsunami that brushed Hawaii?"

Wendy said, "Our three oldest ones played spy yesterday and messed up the destroyer but nothing has been said about a Tsunami."

Arielle said, "That could have been us mom because we dove into the water as a huge wedge to make a big splash. Was there any damage in Hawaii, General, Sir?"

"Fortunately no," Thomas Gregory answered, "It hit the new island which is still too volcanic for people to live on. Made a huge steam cloud I understand. You can call me either General or Sir but not both together please."

Arielle tilted her head and asked, "Which do you prefer General or sir?"

"Sir is usually enough," the General replied, "Are all of the kids around here always this polite?"

Sharron giggled and answered, "If we're not and a robot finds out then life gets pretty miserable until we apologize for being rude."

The General grunted and then said, "I remember that your robots are practical jokers too. The main thing I wanted to do is let you know that we are here permanently. The other is that my Corps Engineer got a look at your house and told my Chief of Staff that the army would be living in tents for a couple of days longer than planned because he was going to rebuild your house first."

Clarence asked, "What is the new post going to be called?"

"Congress wants to name it Fort Miller after Major Glenn Miller a musician who was born in Iowa," General Gregory answered. "The soldiers are already unofficially calling it Camp Wendy."

Wendy blushed and said, "Oh dear, please dissuade them from doing that I'd rather keep a very low profile."

"Good luck," the General replied. "Well, I wanted you to know we are here and as usual I have a few million things to do so I'll see you later." With that, the General waved and left.

Arielle asked, "Mom, are we going to keep the schedule for Operation Swimming Pool?"

"What is Operation Swimming Pool?" Wendy asked.

Sharron answered, "It's what we decided to call moving the pirate ships to the Caspian Sea."

"That depends on what Doctor Janice has to say," Wendy replied.

"I'd like for all of you to take it easy today and rest because the blast rattled your nervous systems pretty hard," Doctor Janice told the girls. "Why not do it first thing tomorrow when you're rested?"

Arielle did her characteristic head tilt as she thought about what the doctor told her and said, "That should work. It's not pushed so far off that the pirates think they will have a free hand.

I think that it might be interesting if we could plant a little fear of sea serpents in the crew's minds too."

Wendy asked, "Why do you want to do that, Arielle?"

Arielle asked, "Dad, how many main gun rounds can a destroyer carry for each gun?"

"You're the one who soaked up the Naval Academy library," Clarence replied, "Suppose you tell me."

Sharron answered, "As near as we have been able to determine they can carry over six hundred rounds per gun. Those guns can shoot a little over thirty kilometers. What we want them to do is waste them trying to kill sea serpents rather than firing on the coastal villages and towns."

"That makes sense," Clarence told them, "But it would be more effective to disable the guns."

Arielle asked, "How do we do that, Dad"

"Katherine, her father and mother had to defend Los Angeles from the army before you were born. They did it by removing parts from the army's vehicles," Wendy explained. "Why don't you research how the guns work and just take out some key parts?"

"We didn't know that was possible," Arielle said. She sighed and continued, "I still feel there is a reason for the sea serpent to be there. Do you have any ideas?"

Wendy smiled and said, "Pirates are in general cowards who will probably try to leave their ships to keep from being caught. The sea serpent could put them back on their ships until the local law enforcement agencies can take charge."

Jackie entered the room and said, "But not Iran's."

"Why Iran, Ms. Jackie?" Sharron asked.

"Because that is where your assailants came from," Jackie replied. "They were part of a crusader organization bent on ending Christianity in the Middle East and were recruited for this Mission. You six get to spend the night at my house so let's go so your parents can rest."

"Thank you, Jackie," Wendy said feelingly, "We really appreciate this."

"You'd do it for me so don't worry about it," Jackie said. "Your house will be completely repaired by tomorrow evening. On top of that Freddy wants to discuss the plan with these three and introduce his two ladies to them."

"Has that turned into some kind of romance?" Clarence asked. "They seem to be spending more time together then working requires."

"Any mention of him marrying one of them?" Wendy asked.

"I think they cornered him," Jackie chuckled, "They're both pregnant and have told me that he's the father. Both women are having triplets again also. If there is a marriage I think he will marry both women at the same time."

Clarence started to laugh and then grimaced in pain and Doctor Janice said authoritatively, "That's enough for today. Kids go with Jackie so your parents can rest."

Arielle asked, "How are Ms. Katherine and Ms. Aiko?"

"Resting which is what your parents need to do now scram," Maryann Janice said smiling.

Wendy added, "Go to Jackie's and get rested for tomorrow."

The next morning at Jackie's house should have been shear bedlam with two extra sets of triplets and three teenagers to egg them on, but such was not the case. Jackie and Eduardo Vasquez rose at their normal time to discover that the army had set up several tables in their back yard and that they were ready to serve the adults, twelve children and Freddy's mind partners. Robin, Wendy's robot, Virginia and Stanley, the Vasquez's robots were busy checking everything. Edna called, from the kitchen, "Mom, what are we having for breakfast, nothing is started."

"Come out on the patio, Edna," Jackie replied.

Edna stepped onto the patio and asked, "What is all of this?"

Her father replied, "I think it's the army's way of telling us how much respect they have for Wendy and the rest of us. Go get the rest of the herd so we can eat."

Edna stepped to the patio door and yelled, "Come on everyone breakfast is served." Eduardo shook his head at his daughter's teenage method of getting everyone.

The Vasquez triplets charged out the door and screeched to a halt as three robots confronted them. Virginia typed, "Is that the proper way to behave when we have guests?"

Veronica, the tomboy of the trio replied, "But we're hungry."

Wendy's six children arrived next with Arielle moving somewhat stiffly and she said, "Good morning Ms. Jackie, Mister Eduardo, how are you today?"

Next out the door were Tim and Freddy. With Freddy were two young women and Jackie asked, "Good morning, Naomi and Winona are you hungry?"

Naomi answered, "Yes ma'am, I left home this morning before the kids were awake so I haven't eaten yet. Mom and dad said they'd take care of them today."

Winona added, "The same for me."

Tim asked, "Are they ready or are we going to stand around and talk all day?"

The army sergeant who had been supervising the setup of the food and tables approached the family and said, "Sir, Ma'am, We're from General Gregory's headquarters dining facility. He sent us to help this morning, so if you'll all be seated well take your orders and get your breakfast served. Oh, your robots have approved everything and everyone."

While everyone was eating Jackie asked, "Freddy, Have you six worked out how you're going to upset Elec Corp?"

"We've worked things out," Freddy rumbled, "And scheduled the use of generators one, two, and three."

"You don't need more than that?" Eduardo queried.

Arielle replied, "We're going to do the sea serpent unpowered and only tap Freddy's trio as needed. The idea is to keep the bad guys guessing about our strengths. Mom and dad are going to interrogate the ship captains with help from their mind partners."

Jackie asked, "What is the sea serpents roll in all of this?"

"To make sure that none of the pirates jump ship, ma'am," Sharron replied.

The army sergeant who had been managing their breakfast stepped up and asked, "Anyone need fifths or sixths?"

Jackie looked around the table and replied, "I think we're okay for now. Please thank the General for us."

"Yes ma'am," the sergeant responded, "Can I ask a question?"

"How can we eat so much and stay so slim?" Jackie asked. The answer is that when we use our Psi powers we burn calories faster than you would if you ran ten kilometers in full combat gear every day for a month. That and the fact that we all use our powers every day. Believe me we burn every calorie we eat."

"Well then if everyone has had enough we'll pack up and head back," The sergeant concluded, waved and turned to his soldiers to begin clearing away the remains and their equipment.

The triplets, Freddy and his team, and Katherine's robot, Jennifer, arrived at the generator site and Winona asked Arielle, "Do you need to prop your leg up while you work?"

Arielle responded, "This control room has some nice carpet and some pillows, so I think I'll just lie on the floor." Suiting her actions to her words Arielle went to a pile of pillows in a bin in a corner of the room, pulled out several of them, and laid down on the floor.

Sharron said, "Flip around so we can lie head to head and we'll join you." Arielle moved, the other two lay down, and Sharron continued, "One sea serpent reporting for duty."

Everyone else laughed and Freddy's team settled in the recliners in front of the generator controls. Freddy rumbled, "Let's do it. Jennifer, put up the ship locations on screen one and the Caspian Sea on screen two, please."

Arielle added, "Please put a satellite image of the Caspian Sea on screen three and update as changes occur."

Scattered across the earth's oceans the captains of the pirate cargo ships watched as their gunship covers disappeared. The gunships appeared in the Caspian Sea with very confused captains and crews. Various law enforcement organizations and the news media that had been notified in advance moved in. The guns on the pirate ships swiveled and pointed towards the law enforcement ships and news boats but nothing happened after that. The captains of the ships raged, ordered, cajoled, and threatened their crews to get them to fire guns that were missing their firing mechanisms. In desperation, the captains ordered their people to scuttle their ships to prevent their capture. For some reason the ships wouldn't sink so the captains tried detonating hidden bombs only to discover they couldn't do that either.

Then Wendy, Katherine, and Aiko arrived invisibly and the captains found they couldn't do anything to their ships. The trio read each of the twenty plus ship captains minds and then implanted a compulsion to tell the truth. When that happened all attempts to destroy the ships stopped and the crews surrendered to whichever law enforcement boat arrived. The news media, which arrived along with the police forces, were allowed to interview the captains and their crews for several hours before the crews were taken into custody.

Back in Iowa, three six year olds stretched hugely and Arielle said, "I'm glad mom finally showed up. I wonder what kept them."

Winona Bright Feather replied, "Well, since we've killed the morning playing navy why don't we go eat and ask?"

Jennifer beeped for attention and typed in its screen, "Arielle, your mother said to bring Freddy and his team with you and to teleport." When the line of type was read, six bangs occurred leaving the robot by itself. It emitted a series if beeps that sounded forlorn in the empty control room then it disappeared with a bang.

Everyone, except Clarence Stevens who, was still in the hospital, gathered in the Stevens' newly rebuilt dining room, where Robin and Yoshi, Aiko's robot, served them lunch. Katherine asked, "Where did you girls get the sea serpent idea? It was cute."

Wendy's triplets giggled and Arielle replied, "Do you remember Ms. Carroll calling us a bunch of hungry sea monsters at our last picnic?" Katherine nodded and Arielle continued, "We did too and decided to put the idea to use."

Wendy said, "I thought that you were only going to be one serpent."

Sharron told her, "There were too many pirates jumping off their ships at once. At one time we were using power from Freddy and had sixteen sea serpents fishing people out of the water."

"The biggest problem we had," Freddy said, "Was keeping the captains from blowing up their ships and sinking them."

"We discovered that Elec Corp had told the captains about an explosive device in each ship," Aiko told the group. "Those have been dismantled."

Wendy added, "When the press started interviewing the crews and Captains, Elec Corps' board of directors tried to disappear but got arrested and are now awaiting trial so I think that is one problem solved and a bunch to go."

"So what do we do next mom," Arielle asked her mother, "Civil wars or the starvation problem?"

"You have school to do yet today," Wendy chided gently, "But we'll let you know so you can help."

"Actually," Katherine said, "You've made my three a little envious because you worked on one problem and came up with solutions that worked."

SCOUT 45Y43T5 TO EXHALTED IMPERIAL COMMANDER THIS SCOUT HAS DISCOVERED THAT THOSE THAT HAD BEEN TRAINED HAVE BECOME UNTRAINED. THIS SCOUT IS UNABLE TO DETERMINE THE REASON FOR THIS.

SCOUT 45Y43T5, YOU ARE TO CEASE ALL OPERATIONS. YOUR REPLACEMENT WILL ARRIVE IN TWO

KEKS OF THE SANDS. EXHAULTED IMPERIAL COMMANDER.

Wendy looked at Arielle, frowned, and asked, "Arielle, are you still with us or do you need a nap before school?"

Arielle snapped out of her dazed look and said, "What mom, Oh, I just discovered that I can tap the alien's communications by staring off into space." Wendy's six-year-old daughter giggled and asked, "Guess what?"

"What?" her mother asked.

"The alien scout that has been putting stuff in our heads is being replaced because it is so far behind in training us to be slaves."

Aiko said, "You know, it seems that we have the makings of a little competitiveness between our older sets of triplets. Mine have been trying to figure out solutions to problems too."

Jennifer beeped and typed, "Linda, Melinda, and Sarah have been planning something but they stop when one of us robots comes near."

Katherine asked, "Can you handle three more for lunch, Wendy?" Wendy nodded and three bangs occurred in the hallway so recently destroyed by a bomb. Katherine continued, "Come have lunch and tell us what you three have been plotting that you have to keep it a secret from the robots."

Melinda answered, "We've been studying oceanography, mom. In particular we've been studying the salinity levels at various depths and lat..., what's it's, and we've discovered something interesting."

Katherine asked, "The word is latitude and what did you discover, dear?"

"The water at different depths and at different latitudes has different levels of saltiness," Sarah replied. "Some of it is almost fresh because the salt level is so low. It seems to depend on where the water is and what its temperature is. We haven't figured out an effective way to get the rest of the salt out of it yet."

Doctor Wallace shook her head in amazement that a six year olds would have such knowledge but Aiko asked, "What kinds of salts are you needing to remove?"

Melinda asked glumly, "Is there more than one kind of salt? We didn't know that. If it is all dissolved in the ocean water how do we separate out the harmful ones?"

"Hey guys," Clarence said from the dining room door where he stood leaning on crutches.

"Clarence?" Wendy asked as she got up and went to her husband to give him a hug. "I didn't think that Maryann was going to let you out until tomorrow."

"Take it easy with the hug," Clarence said grimacing in pain, "I'm out on good behavior but I still have to rest and take it easy."

Solicitously, Wendy escorted him to his chair and asked, "Have you eaten yet?"

Clarence queried, "How did the pirates like the Caspian Sea?"

"They didn't," Katherine replied chuckling, "But yours and Jackie's kids did very well. In fact they've stirred a little competiveness between mine and Aiko's triplets which is what we were discussing."

The wall video phone chimed and Wendy asked, "Who is it?"

The screen lighted with the face of General Gregory who said, "Good afternoon, My G-2 and G-3 offices have just had some of the strangest queries. My people tell me that young girls are asking specific questions about how certain types of weapons work. Are some of your youngsters up to something I need to know about?"

Wendy laughed, turned to Aiko and said, "Now we know what your three are working on." Then she turned to the phone screen and continued, "They are most likely Aiko's oldest triplets and they've decided to see how to end the various civil wars, I guess by disabling the weapons of the combatants."

Aiko added, "Tell your people that it is okay to give my kids the information. Now that I know what is up I can monitor things."

"Well I'll be darned," the General replied. "Say did you have a part in what went on in the Caspian Sea?"

Wendy replied proudly, "My triplets designed that plan and then they and Freddy's team executed it. Has it made the news channels already?"

"Yes ma'am, in a big way," the General replied, "The Elec Corp executives are all screaming foul and trying to get the interviews discredited before their trials start. Well, since it's okay," the General concluded, "I'll instruct my staff to provide your kids with whatever information they ask for. Thanks for the confirmation. I'll keep in touch."

Clarence said into the silence, "Never a dull moment around here is there?" Then he stepped slowly to his place at the table and sat with a sigh.

His wife asked, "Have you had lunch dear? You didn't say when I asked before." Clarence shook his head and Wendy continued, "Robin, would you bring Clarence some lunch please?"

"Dad," Arielle said, "Melinda and her sisters are working on one of the problems and they have a problem. Can you help with some information please?"

Clarence asked, "What sort of information do you need, Melinda?"

"We need to know how to take the dangerous salts out of ocean water and leave the good minerals and such in," Melinda replied.

Clarence grunted and said, "You don't want much do you? Let me think about it while I eat lunch. Besides I haven't heard about how things went today."

"From what the General told us just now," Wendy replied, "Things went better than we expected them to."

Aiko said, "I need to do some domestic things and make sure my three do school, so if you'll excuse me."

"Certainly," Wendy and Clarence replied together. Freddy and his mind partners took that as their cue and excused themselves.

Katherine said, "Girls, you have school this afternoon also and Clarence can pass any suggestions he comes up with over the robot network. Say good bye and let's go."

Clarence and Wendy told their guests good-bye and then Clarence said, "Jason, you can come out of hiding."

A robot in a shiny new silver box rolled into the room and typed, "Man, what a headache!"

Wendy said, "Being blown up can do that to you Jason."

The robot typed, "Is that what happened. I thought I was out with the guys and drank too much. It is good to be back in one piece. My shield could not handle that much explosion so close."

"I'm glad you're back in one piece too," Arielle told the robot.

Jason typed, "You were hurt. I can see the bandages on your leg."

"We were all hurt some," Clarence told his robot. "I want you to contact the army and find out if they have a portable desalinization plant. If they do, ask them to take one to the Warren's house and send along someone who can explain how it cleans the salts out of the water."

The robot beeped once and typed, "Done," on its screen. Then it turned to Arielle, Sharron, and Brenda and typed, "You're late for class." Sharron stuck her tongue out at the robot as all three girls left the table.

Doctor Wallace, who was quietly observing all that went on, chuckled and said into the quiet room, "I don't think I've ever seen such a bunch of stubborn people in my life. Even if they are only six years old."

Wendy asked, "Why is that, Elana?"

"They don't give up," Elana replied. "Just because they hit something that stumped them, they keep on picking at it until something happens. Most six year olds I have encountered would give up very quickly. The other thing I'm noticing is that your children don't seem to play nearly as much as non-Psi capable children do. Tell me when was the last time you took your kids on an honest to goodness vacation?"

Wendy replied, "We've never gone on a vacation. We've always been so busy that I don't think it ever occurred to us to take a vacation."

"With what's going on right now," Clarence interjected, "I don't think we could really take one at this time either."

"I think that the closest we've come to a vacation," Wendy added, "Are the weekend picnics we hold at each other's houses."

"Then you need to take yourselves and your kids to a big noisy amusement park like the one in Florida for a week or two," Doctor Wallace said emphatically.

Jason typed, "Clarence, the General is on the phone for you."

Clarence sighed and replied, "Put him through."

General Gregory's face appeared on the wall monitor and he said, "Good afternoon, I've got several kinds of news for you."

Wendy asked wearily, "What disasters are befalling us now?"

"Man, do you two look beat. When was the last time you had a vacation?"

Doctor Wallace replied, "We were just discussing that. I think I'm going to prescribe a vacation for the Stevens family and make them take a couple of weeks off."

"We may not be able to do that because of the security we need all of the time," Wendy said.

General Gregory asked, "Where would you like for them to go, doctor?"

"One of the big amusement parks like the one in Florida," Elana Wallace replied. "In fact I'm extending that order to all five families since I know that they haven't been out of town either.

"Give me a couple of hours to see what can be arranged," the General said. "Clarence, My G-4 has assigned a desalinization unit to the Warren household with its crew for as long as it takes her kids to learn what they need to. Tomorrow at ten hundred hours, all of your families are invited to a groundbreaking ceremony for Fort Glenn Miller. Lastly, one of our security patrols got into a firefight with a bunch of crusader terrorists trying to sneak into Central. That is also a good reason for us to get you out of the area for a while. I'll call back in a couple of hours and let you know what I've worked out."

The screen blanked and Elana asked, "What are you doing sitting here go pack."

"Can I finish my lunch first?" Clarence asked.

Wendy turned to her robot and said, "See what you can do about packing clothing for a two week vacation for the family." Robin beeped once and left the room.

Four hours later General Gregory called back and said, "Everything is set. You're all going to Florida for two weeks. Colonel Glenn Loren will be flying your C-7 in tomorrow and two additional planes are joining it for the security force I'm going to saddle you with." The General chuckled and continued, "The resort isn't too happy about that but I understand that President Harper was rather insistent."

Wendy wrinkled her face at that and said, "I hate living in all of this super security stuff."

Clarence replied, "It beats being dead, dear."

"Which doesn't mean I have to like it," Wendy replied acidly.

General Gregory closed saying, "The other families have been notified. The planes are scheduled to depart here at noon after the groundbreaking ceremony. Catch you all later, have fun."

At Central's, air strip the next day, three C-150 Galaxy 7 cargo jets sat with their loading bays open. Two had vehicles and a large numbers of soldiers filing orderly into them. The other had two people standing at the base of its ramp when five busses followed by five delivery trucks, drove up and stopped. The lead bus stopped in front of the ramp, Wendy stepped out of it and said, "Hello Glenn, I see that you got drafted to chauffer us around again."

"I didn't get drafted," Colonel Glenn Loren replied. "The word came down to my office that three planes needed to be diverted here for a special mission so I started asking questions. When I found out it was you, I told that paper shuffling General at the pentagon that you wouldn't tolerate anyone that you hadn't already checked mentally near you or your family. In fact, I got Lieutenant Colonel Alan Sheffield as the pilot for one of the other planes and his old copilot as pilot for the third."

Clarence joined his wife and the Colonel and said, "And I suppose you just couldn't wait to get back on flight status either."

Glenn Loren grinned sheepishly and replied, "How'd you guess? I get rather bored with desk jobs like I had scheduling planes for places around the world and being stuck inside four walls all the time." Then he waved a hand towards the interior of the plane and continued, "Let's get your vehicles loaded and get you on the way. By the way I have someone upstairs I'd like you to meet."

"We have a lot more vehicles than last time," Wendy inquired, "Will they all fit?"

"That's for my loadmasters to worry about," Glenn said, "Come on, let's get out of their way."

The upstairs passenger compartment of the Galaxy C-7 looked the same as the plane that Wendy and the rest of her companions had used when rescuing fifty kidnapped women. Wendy asked, "Is this the same plane that we used before?"

"Yes it is," Colonel Glenn Loren replied grinning broadly, "Welcome home." Then he smiled even wider, went to the entrance of the plane's cockpit, reached in and drew a dark haired petite woman into the passenger compartment. "Ladies and gentlemen, I'd like to introduce Sally Loren." Leading the woman to Wendy he said, "This is Wendy Stevens otherwise known as 'Fearless Leader'."

Wendy blushed and responded, "I haven't been Fearless Leader in a long time. Tell me did you have to trip him and hog time him to get him to the alter?"

Sally laughed her voice like a tinkling of chimes answered, "Actually I kicked him in the shins several times and while he was bent over rubbing them I pushed him the rest of the way over."

"She was wearing combat boots at the time too," Glenn, added sourly causing the adults to laugh.

Wendy asked, "Are you part of the crew also?"

Sally replied, "No, I'm a stowaway. Since Glenn is playing chauffer, we are getting what amounts to a two-week vacation. Glenn said that you would need to do a security check on me so shall we, then get this joy ride underway?"

Wendy asked, "May I place my fingers on your temples?"

"Sure," Sally replied and leaned forward. Wendy placed her singer on Sally's temples and she collapsed onto the plane's floor.

Wendy told Glenn, "The alien's programming had been implanted in her. She will wake up in about an hour and I'll explain what happened to her. Would you guys please put her in one of the rooms so she can rest comfortably? Glenn, why don't you get us in the air?"

"Sally'll be alright?" Glenn asked worriedly as he and William Warren picked his wife up.

"She'll be fine," Wendy, told him then turning to her husband she continued, "She's the first adult we've had to deprogram, we'll have to look at that."

Clarence turned to his robot and said, "Jason, remind me to look at creating thought projectors for deprogramming whole populations when we get back and work out some design ideas based on what Sharron gave us about the alien machines." The robot beeped once in acknowledgement.

Sally woke an hour later and what happened to her was explained. A little later, the three planes landed in Florida to the consternation of airport officials who were not used to having such large planes on their runways nor having their security people denied any part in the care of those planes by the army. The busses and delivery trucks drove out of one plane and a large number of soldiers with their combat vehicles from the others. Most of the vehicles formed smartly into a convoy and left the airport.

After a short drive, the convoy caused a near riot when it pulled into the driveway of the amusement park hotel. Bellhops with visions of huge tips dancing before their eyes were disappointed when robots appeared to handle the luggage of the families and soldiers ordered them away. The Stevens, Warrens, Dugans, Estebans, and Vasquezs walked between rows of soldiers that had materialized between the busses and the registration counter as if this were an everyday occurrence.

The hotel manager stepped up to a Major, and said, "I have the keys for the suites for your charges. The floors above and below them have been cleared for military use. May I escort our guests to their suites?"

The Major looked at a sergeant and said, "Search him," in a voice that caused the manager to swallow twice.

The sergeant removed a device from a pouch on his belt and ran it over the manager's body, then said, "Clean, sir." The Major waved for the manager to proceed.

The manager stepped past the major and said, "Ms. Stevens, if your group will come with me we'll get you to your suites."

Wendy replied, "Thank you." Then to the rest she said, "Come on gang, let's go see our rooms." The soldiers shifted so that there was now a cleared corridor to the hotel elevators.

Clarence noted the acid look on his wife's face, wrapped an arm around her shoulders, and said, "Come on dear, they're just doing their job," and nudged her towards the elevators. Wendy grumbled but started moving.

Once everyone was in their own suites, their robots presented the families with an itinerary and Wendy exploded, "Why do I feel like I'm in a prison and being punished because I have an ability that makes everyone afraid of me? Why can't I just go for a walk without anyone watching out for me?"

Robin beeped and typed, "This is from Jackie, 'I saw the look on your face downstairs. Quite fretting about it and enjoy things despite the Boy Scout attitudes of our jailers.'"

Clarence laughed, sat on a sofa, pulled his wife onto it with him, and said, "Follow Jackie's advice dear and live large within the confines of the jail. Believe me as a billionaire I had to learn the same lesson. Granted you're a bit more sensitive subject as a national resource which makes the guards a bit more intrusive but you can live with it." Much more was said until Wendy had calmed down enough to accept the situation.

"Mom, Arielle asked, "This place has a huge swimming pool downstairs, can we go swimming?"

Before Wendy could reply, Clarence answered, "Do it sprite but no sea serpents we don't want to scare the other guests."

Arielle replied, "Thanks dad," and popped out of the room with a small thunderclap to tell her brother and sisters.

Wendy started get up and go after her errant child who knew she wasn't supposed to pop about in the family living spaces but Clarence held her and said softly, "Leave it this time. Robin, tell the kids not to display their powers in any way that can be connected to them in public." The robot beeped once and rolled out of the room. Clarence pulled his wife into his lap and kissed her. After a moment, Wendy relaxed and responded whole-heartedly to his ministrations.

"*Mom, Dad,*" Arielle thought, "*There's a woman here who is in a lot of pain. We peeked inside her and she is having a heart attack. There isn't anyone from the hotel here can you send help.*"

Clarence yelled, "Jason, send the house doctor to the pool area!"

Wendy sighed and said, "Come on dear, we'd better make sure things stay under control." When they arrived at the pool,

Sharron and Brenda were performing CPR on a woman who appeared to be in her twenties. Arielle was standing beside them and Wendy noted the glassy eyed look in her daughter's eyes. She took a telepathic look and discovered that Sharron and Brenda were putting on a show while Arielle was telekinetically keeping the woman's heart under control.

The house doctor arrived but before he could approach the woman, Clarence pulled him aside and whispered earnestly in his ear. The doctor looked at Clarence in shock, then nodded his head and went to the woman to check vitals. He told Sharon and Brenda, "Good work girls, keep it up while I prepare this injection for her." In a louder voice he said, "Someone call the front desk and have them send for an ambulance."

Wendy sat in a chair near Arielle and whispered, "Good girl, let me take over and rest a minute." Arielle leaned back against her mother and nodded. Wendy picked up where her daughter had released the woman's heart then said, "Doctor, don't." The doctor looked at her and started to ask why not, when she added, "You know who we are and we have the ability to detect things. She's been drugged or taken an over dose of something and your injection will kill her."

An army captain and several medics arrived and the captain asked, "Have you got stuff for an IV in your bag?"

Startled the doctor said, "Yes."

"I checked the security video of this area when I was informed that the children were coming here and discovered that a man with a snake attacked her. We've brought anti-venom. Kids, can you scan the area for a snake?"

The girls went into a blank stare and a Rattlesnake floated in the air above the woman. Arielle said, "It was over there in a sunny spot. What do you want us to do with it?"

Clarence said, "Let me take it from you, girls. Corpsman, find me a box or cage or something this can be put in then call the nearest zoo to come get it."

Jason rolled up to the snake, took it gently in a pincher, and typed, "This is a Mexican Green Rattle Snake that lives in western Mexico." Then it held up its other pincher and typed, "Hang the IV and anti-venom on my hand."

The doctor stared at the robot and then sat back too stunned to move. Another corpsman knelt and dug in the doctors bag removing the needed items to set up an IV, put the needle in the woman's arm, connected the bags of solution, then checked the doctor, and said, "The good doctor is in shock but he should be alright in a bit. The ambulance should be here shortly."

Clarence asked, "Who told you guys we needed help?"

The corpsman replied, "A robot named 'Ivan the Terrible', number something."

Wendy asked, "Did you kids at least get a chance to get wet?"

"No mama," Sharron answered.

"Then do it while we tend to the woman," Wendy said, "Just be careful of which direction the splashes go." All six children ran and dove into the water so smoothly that they would have made an Olympic high diver jealous. Wendy stood and walked to Jason and said, "Release your data cable for me please Jason." She connected for a moment then disconnected and added, "Put that picture out to our security, the army, and the police please." The robot beeped once and on its screen appeared the word, done.

Clarence told his robot, "Jason, get the hotel manager down here and have a search conducted for more snakes and the life guard that is supposed to be here." Jason beeped and the word, done, appeared on its screen a second time. Several minutes later paramedics arrived with a stretcher and took the woman away. Then the manager arrived followed by the corpsman that had gone for a container for the snake. The snake was put in the container, the soldiers saluted, the Stevens, took the snake and left.

Jason beeped, turned its monitor so that the children would not be able to see it and typed, "The lifeguard has been found," then it showed an image of the lifeguard and a young woman who were very actively involved with each other.

The manager asked, "Where?"

Jason typed, "Private dressing room #1."

The manager took out his personal phone and dialed a number. Then the phone was answered said, "Swimming pool private dressing room one. Tell him he's fired, escort him to his locker, and then out the door, and off the property. Get the woman's room number and tell her she has one hour to check out." Then he hung up, dialed another number, and said, "I just fired the lifeguard. Get another one down to the pool now." He hung up, put his phone away, and asked pleasantly, "I apologize for not checking on my lifeguards more often. How can I be of assistance?"

"You just fixed one concern," Clarence replied. "My other concern is that I would suspect that this pool would have more people at this time of day, why doesn't it?"

"You're right," the manager, "I'll have to check into that."

"Do that," Clarence told him, "My kids need to interact with other people's kids. If I find out that someone has been deflecting people because of any of our families, I will be most unhappy." Two lifeguards arrived and Clarence turned to his wife and said, "Come on dear, we were interrupted in what we were doing." Clarence took Wendy's hand and walked away from the manager. As soon as they were out of sight of anyone, he teleported them both back to the couch in their suite.

EXHAULTED IMPERIAL COMMANDER THIS SCOUT JJ4536FD HAS RELIEVED SCOUT 45Y43T5. SCOUT 45Y43T5 IS RETURNING FOR DISPOSITION.

EXHAULTED IMPERIAL COMMANDER THIS SCOUT 45Y43T5 IS RETURNING.

The next morning the Stevens family gathered around a huge breakfast buffet and Arielle said, "Mom, dad, the new alien scout is on station so we can expect more attacks again."

"Thank you dear," Wendy replied, "We'll wait and see if it tries anything new while we enjoy ourselves."

Arielle responded, "Okay, Jason, what are we doing today?"

The robot typed, "You are going to sample the part of the park that has the castle, ride on the rollercoaster and do the other things that are there."

"That looks like you need to eat a good breakfast," Arielle's mother told her smiling, "So you'll have lots of energy."

Breakfast was finished and all five families met in the hotel lobby. They boarded a monorail train that was only moderately full. Some of the passengers were soldiers in uniform with their weapons. The families pretended the soldiers weren't there but the other passengers kept giving them and their weapons worried looks.

When they arrived at the castle area of the park Wendy gathered everyone's children and said, "You're here to have fun. The military and the robots will do their best to protect you, but keep your mental shields up, especially when you are on the rides."

"We'll meet here at noon for lunch," Katherine added.

Clarence thought to everyone, *Keep your powers under wraps. Don't let yourselves be connected to your powers if you do use them.*"

Jackie added out-loud, "I suggest you stay in teams just in case. Now scatter and have fun."

Wendy chuckled as all of the children got in line for the rollercoaster and said thoughtfully, "I wonder if any of them will have problems with motion sickness," as she leaned on her husband's shoulder. "What should we do first?"

"Let's go through the castle, then take a snack break in one of the restaurants," Clarence replied. "That should give the kids plenty of time to get into mischief." The couple strolled away from the rest of the parents without saying another word.

Jackie shook her head as she watched Wendy and Clarence walk away, then sighed, and said, "Pick a direction dear and let's follow their lead."

EXHAULTED IMPERIAL COMMANDER THIS SCOUT JJ4536FD HAS DETERMINED THAT A SMALL GROUP OF SLAVE BEASTS IS REMOVING THE TRAINING IMPLANTED IN THE MINDS OF OTHERS OF THEIR KIND. RECOMMEND THAT THIS GROUP BE DESTROYED BY SPECIALLY TRAINED SLAVES.

SCOUT JJ4536FD YOUR REPORT IS INCOMPLETE AND INCONCLUSIVE. ACTION WILL BE CONSIDERED. STEP UP TRAINING AND MAINTAIN YOUR ASSIGNED SCHEDULE. EXHAULTED IMPERIAL COMMANDER.

The alien scout left the five families alone for the rest of their vacation and worked on a way to destroy them using those around them. Unfortunately, for the scout, Clarence had spent a few odd moments looking at the designs that Jason presented to him and had refined them into a machine that was already being constructed and put into operation to detrain humans on a very large scale. At the end of the two weeks, everyone reluctantly boarded the Galaxy 7s and flew back to Central airstrip in Iowa.

ENDING A REVOLUTION

When three Galaxy 7 cargo planes arrived over Central, it was evident that things on the ground were anything but normal. The runway was pockmarked with holes made by explosions. Several houses, the generator station, and maintenance buildings were on fire. Colonel Loren sent for Wendy. When she arrived he said, "We're diverting to Des Moines airport. I can't contact anyone on the ground here."

"How long can you stay in the air?" a young voice asked from behind Wendy.

Wendy turned and asked, "What are you three doing here?"

Arielle replied, "We looked out the plane's windows and saw the mess, so we did a little peeking. The army is fighting people who've been programmed by the aliens including some of their own, mama. We need to deprogram them to make them stop."

Wendy looked at Glenn and asked, "Well now we know what is going on, can you loiter for an hour?"

Glenn replied, "An hour, no problem. I have a suggestion, check the other planes and make sure they are still friendly, then send them to Des Moines, so they can reinforce the friendly forces down there."

"That's a good idea," Clarence, who had followed his children into the cockpit. "Let's go link up with everybody and see if we can stop this destruction."

Back in the passenger compartment Wendy explained, "There is a war going on down there because of the aliens and their programming. We're going to all link together and try to deprogram everybody friend and enemy just to make sure we get everyone. I want you kids to feed your power to your parents and we'll do the rest. Everyone ready? Link!"

In the other two planes, a few people passed out but on the ground, everyone in a ten-mile circle around Central's defenders went to sleep. The families came out of their link trance and

Wendy returned to the cockpit. "You can head for the airport, Glenn," she said.

He replied, "It's a good thing because that took you a little over two hours and we're getting low on fuel." He turned the plane out of the circle he had been flying in and lined up on a heading to the Des Moines, airport. "The guys from the other planes have radioed and said the enemy is waking up and is very bewildered."

Wendy asked, "They're not still trying to fight are they?"

"No, it seems that the soldiers who you deprogrammed are disarming and rounding up the rest of what was the enemy."

They landed and joined the other jets near the IASA hanger. When it had parked, the families' busses and trucks drove down the ramp, joined a column of army vehicles and left the airport, and drove south toward Central. When the convoy arrived at Central, they were stopped at a checkpoint that had been erected on the highway. A lieutenant approached the lead vehicle spoke with the soldiers in the vehicle for a moment then signaled for them to proceed. When the convoy reached the houses, belonging to the families the convoy broke up and the families all stopped in front of the Stevens house.

General Gregory stood in front of the Stevens' home and greeted them by asking, "Did you enjoy your vacation?"

"Hello to you too," Wendy replied, "And came back to put a stop to your war. How bad is the damage?"

"Actually the shield robots stopped a lot of the damage, Gregory replied. "Most of what you saw inside the town was caused by our own people who were under alien control. The problem is that there are more on their way here."

Clarence asked, "Jason have you finalized the generator design?" His robot beeped once and he continued, "General have you got an estimate of how long and how many?"

General Gregory sighed and replied, "I wish I really knew and I don't really want to slaughter masses of people who have just been mind altered by the aliens. If you have something in mind, then do it as quickly as possible."

Katherine looked around while the conversation was going on and asked, "Where did our kids all disappear to?"

Jason beeped for attention and typed, "They have all gone to the patio and Robin says that they are sitting in a circle holding hands."

"I have a feeling that we'd better join them," Wendy said and started walking hurriedly towards the back of her house.

When the adults arrived on the Stevens's patio, the children let go of each other's hands and Arielle said, "Now let's see how long it takes them to figure out that we've reversed their machines."

Wendy asked, "What did you do Arielle?"

"We gave dad some time to work on his machines by changing the way the alien machines work, mama"

Clarence asked, "How did you go about that Squirt?"

"We tied some information we collected from them together and determined that they don't used electronic computers like we do," Sharron answered. "They are using a patch cord system like the Eniac computer that was made back in the early 1900s."

"So we figured out how to rewire the insides instead of moving the patch cables," Melinda said picking up the explanation, "And set them to deprogram everyone and to program a block into everyone's minds so that they can't be reprogrammed."

Clarence asked, "Did the aliens detect you while you were doing the work?"

"We did it invisible and kept the amount of the something as small as we could," Arielle answered. "Would you believe they are using vacuum tubes instead of solid state devices like we do?"

Hiro asked, "What good is a tube with a vacuum in it?"

Karlita, one of his daughters replied, "They are made of glass and have several elements in them that have connections on the outside that they can apply voltages to, to do work like our solid state stuff does."

"We think we've also figured out how long a Kek of the Sands is," Arielle added smiling. It works out to just under two weeks."

"We appreciate what you've done," Clarence told the children sternly, "But didn't we tell you to clear things with us so that you didn't end up getting hurt?"

"Yes Daddy," Arielle replied in a sorrowful voice but her eyes held a gleam that indicated she wasn't sorry at all.

"Good, please remember that from now on," Clarence, admonished.

Wendy said, "General, I think that your expected invasion may fizzle but we could end up with an extreme tourist problem instead."

"I'll have my staff work on crowd control planning," General Gregory sighed, "So that we don't have to close the park and we can keep them out of mischief in other areas."

"When we were landing," Aiko said, "We saw what looked like burning houses, how many families were hurt and displaced?

"Three families had some minor injuries and two houses received some fire damage," The General answered. "The grounds keeper robots put the fires out before much damage was done. I'm very happy that the hospital is underground because of that. Well, I need to get back to work so I'll catch you all later."

As the General departed, Robin rolled onto the patio, beeped, and typed, "Lunch has been prepared for everyone and is set up in the dining room." The children yelled "Hurray!" and scrambled into the house.

Doctor Wallace who had appeared a moment before chuckled and told the parents, "Now that's more like kids should act."

Wendy replied, "I'd be willing to bet that they are all behaving themselves inside."

Elana Wallace asked, "Why is that?"

Aiko answered laughing, "Robots."

Elana looked dubious and said, "I think I need to see this phenomenon."

Wendy said smiling, "Come and eat with us and see for yourself."

The adults followed their children to the Stevens's dining room where the children had lined up and were politely serving themselves from a buffet style lunch that was on the dining room table. As they moved along the table, Karlita, one of Aiko's triplets asked, "Pecos, did you compile the weapons data we asked about before we went on vacation?" The robot beeped once and typed, "I will display the information after you have finished school for today. Colonel Sanders will arrive at that time to discuss the information with you as well."

Karlita replied, "That will be helpful, thank you."

Elana shook her head in amazement and asked the children, "Did you kids enjoy your vacation?"

Arielle answered, "Yes ma'am, we enjoyed everything but the snake."

"Snake?" Elana asked.

"Our kids stumbled on an attempted murder our first afternoon there," Wendy replied. "They saved a woman's life. The killer had the snake with him and caused it to bite her. The police have him and the woman is recovering."

Discussion about the trip continued throughout the rest of the meal. When everyone had finished eating, good-byes were said and the visiting families went to their homes.

Karlita, Mika, and Hana Esteban finished their school lessons for the day and Mika asked, "Pecos can we see the weapons data now?"

The robot beeped once and turned on its holographic projector. On its screen it typed, "This is a list of the typical weapons being used by the rebels in the four civil wars you are interested in. Colonel Sanders is here and he has brought some of his staff with him."

Karlita said, "Please ask Yoshi to escort our guests here and provide some refreshments for all of us. Mika, Hana, let's clear the table so we have room to work." Pecos beeped once and Karlita and her sisters began removing things from the table where they usually studied.

A few moments later, Yoshi escorted Colonel Sanders and his staff members into the room. The three girls bowed and Karlita said, "Good afternoon Colonel Sanders. I am Karlita and my sisters are Mika and Hana."

Good afternoon to you also," Colonel Sanders replied, "These are Major Winfield and Captain Jones."

"Please, everyone be seated," Mika, said indicating the adult size chairs that were at the study table. "Did General Gregory explain what information we are seeking?"

Colonel Sanders replied, smiling to find himself discussing highly classified information with three six-year-old girls, "Yes he did and we have most of it available here. The rest is what we call compartmentalized data and can only be viewed and discussed in special facilities. Captain Jones would you tell them about the weapons and tactics the rebels in Guyana are using."

Captain Jones looked somewhat dubiously at the three girls and began, "From the intelligence that we've been able to assemble, the Guyanan rebel commander is a Colonel Jim Drago. We don't have a current picture on him," The Captain said as he slid a photograph out of a folder. This was taken when he was a private in the Peruvian army."

Pecos beeped and the weapons listing image was replaced by the image of a darkly tanned man. The robot typed, "I obtained this picture from the National Security Agency in Washington."

The Captain chuckled and said to the girls, "It appears that your intelligence gathering works better than ours."

Karlita replied, "I don't think that's the case. I think that what happened is that Pecos was able to find a newer picture because you had the old one." Then she turned to Pecos and asked, "Would you please print a copy for the Captain?" Pecos beeped.

"One beep means yes," she told the officers. "Yoshi should bring the print in a few minutes. Continue please."

The Captain shook himself and said, "Colonel Drago has a force of approximately four thousand people. He has a cadre of fifty other mercenaries who are his…" The Captain continued for another fifteen minutes explaining everything known about the Guyanan rebel forces tactics and operational structure. The girls listened attentively and asked very intelligent questions until they had gleaned every bit of information the Captain had to offer.

When the Captain had finished, Yoshi the other family robot rolled in with a tray of drinks, snacks, and the picture for the Captain. Major Winfield said, "That must mean it's my turn. I saw a weapons listing being displayed when we came in can that be brought back up, please?"

Pecos beeped and the holographic display changed showing the list of weapons. Major Winfield examined it for a moment then asked, "I gather that you want to remove or disable the weapons that the rebels have at a point in time that will allow the Guyanan military forces to capture them, is that correct?"

Hana replied, "Yes ma'am, but we aren't sure at this point which would be best because we don't know what munitions could be converted to bombs or other weaponry allowing the rebels to escape or continue. We aren't sure even if all of these weapon types are in use in this particular situation."

"We would particularly like to round up the mercenaries and hand them over to the Guyanan government," Mika added.

"Okay," Major Winfield said, "From reports of some of the attacks that have taken place we know that they have mostly semi-automatic rifles in several calibers that fire solid slug rounds. That's what most or the rebels are using. The ammunition for those doesn't convert to bombs very well. The mercenaries however are using American made combat rifles similar ours." The Major took a box from a bag she had brought with her. "This is a combination magazine and power pack. It contains five hundred rounds and a onetime use battery." The Major passed the magazine to the girls and continued her briefing.

"Girls," Aiko, their mother said from the classroom door, "You've been at this for two hours don't you think you should take a break."

"Colonel Sanders," Karlita asked, "If mom says it's okay would you join us for supper?"

"We'd be happy to have you," Aiko said.

Colonel Sanders replied, Thank you ladies, we accept."

"Dinner will be ready in about fifteen minutes," Aiko said, "Which should be enough time for you to fix your boot laces if the robots had the opportunity to tie them together."

Major Winfield chuckled and told Aiko, "General Gregory got us a special issue of boots with zippers ma'am. So that shouldn't be a problem."

"Then be sure to check that you haven't been fastened down some other way before you stand up," Mika added. The three officers slid their chairs back from the table and discovered that two of them were fastened to their chairs with plastic tie fasteners. As they stood and the triplets got out of their chairs Mika continued, "I think that Yoshi and Pecos must want to become moving targets for your corps artillery when it has gunnery training, Colonel."

Colonel Sanders smiled and replied, "I'll see what can be arranged."

In due course dinner was finished, the officers and triplets completed their discussions, and the officers departed. Karlita asked, "Mom, do you know if Freddy and his team are committed tomorrow or the next day?"

"I haven't checked their schedule," Aiko replied, "Why don't you three explain what you have in mind and then we'll see if they can be available."

"With the information that the Colonel gave us, we think we can stop the rebels weapons from working right when they are about to be trapped by the Guyanan army. We'll have to arrange things so that they actually walk into the trap to do it, which is why we need to have Freddy's help."

Hiro, their father asked, "How are you thinking of arranging for the rebels to enter the trap?"

"We will have to plant information for them to discover about a treasure or something," Mika answered as she climbed into her father's lap. "Then we would need to tell the Guyanan army where to set the trap and at the right time fix the rebel weapons so that they won't work."

Hiro asked, "Have you considered that there might be rebel spies in the army?"

Mika shook her head and said, "No daddy, how do we find out if there are?"

"Why don't you think on it while you sleep?" Aiko asked gently. "Besides it is time for the three of you to take your baths and to go to bed."

"Okay mama," Mika said, hugged her father, got down from his lap, and all three girls disappeared to their baths and beds.

Hiro said quietly, "Pecos, I have a mission for you."

The robot rolled into the family room and beeped, and a question mark appeared on its screen.

Hiro continued saying, "Contact Gustov and ask Secretary Jordan to arrange a meeting with Guyana's president and top military commander as quickly as possible. Our children would like to end the civil war he is dealing with."

The robot beeped one time and typed, "Message sent." A minute later, Pecos beeped and typed, "Secretary Jordan said he will see what he can do in the morning."

At the Warren home after the triplet's school Captain Ferguson was explaining, "The desalinization unit uses ionization to remove all of the impurities from the water fed into it. What we get out is chemically pure water."

Sarah asked, "Isn't chemically pure water acidic? We don't want to make the soil worse by leaching away what few minerals are still in it."

The Captain replied, "That's true and it also has no flavor so we have to add some minerals back into the output. That's what is in these canisters over here. We add Calcium and minerals like niacin, some phosphates back in, in extremely small amounts. Those canisters will process about five million liters of water."

Melinda said, "What we want to do is create one kilometer square lake beds that are a hundred meters deep then fill them with fresh water and fishes from hatcheries for several of the drought areas in Africa."

Sergeant Brady whistled a long low whistle and queried, "You don't want to do much do you?"

Captain Ferguson asked, "Have you calculated how much fresh water that is and what are you going to use as your source?"

"We looked at the oceans and decided that the best place to get the water from, red headed Sarah replied, "Is either the North Atlantic or from around Antarctica. We did some research and discovered that the saltiness of the water varies depending on temperature and depth."

Sergeant Brady asked, "Did you consider using snow or ice from The Arctic or Antarctic?" When it is melted it should be much purer than ocean water and shouldn't take as much effort to clean up."

Linda answered, "We considered it but it isn' we don't want to damage the ecology of those places and there are things trapped in the snow packs that would be as difficult to clean."

"Then why not use icebergs?" the Captain asked.

"That would upset the ice harvesting industries," Melinda said, "And affect some companies that make their living giving tours of icebergs that have unusual shapes. There's also the problem of things trapped in the ice."

"Why not look at the ice that is in the shipping lanes north of Russia?" Private Herschel asked. "You might have to take the ice over several days but it should work."

"We actually looked at that but pancake ice," Melinda responded, "As it's called has a lot more salt trapped in it than liquid ocean water." Melinda tilted her head to one said and continued, "That might work though. We'll examine that closer. The big problem is the cleaning process."

Captain Ferguson asked, "Are you planning on lining the lake beds to prevent the water from seeping into the ground under them?"

Sarah shook her head and queried, "No, why?"

"That would put water back into the water table that is fresh and because it is pure it would dissolve the minerals in the soil and carry them with it," the Captain replied. "If you are planning to scoop out a hole and pile the dirt around the edges you could be inviting a flood too."

Linda asked, "How would you resolve that issue?"

"Line the sides with something like a plastic sheet," the Captain said, "And only partially line the bottom so that most of the water is retained in the lake but so that the water table is also reloaded with fresh water for the wells in the area."

Sarah put on her temple contacts and said, "Jennifer would you please start your projector in drawing mode." The robot beeped once and a blank holographic image appeared. A three dimensional image of a lake appeared and Sarah continued, "Something along these line?"

The discussion continued and like at the Esteban house the soldiers were invited for supper, and departed after more discussion that evening.

Katherine asked, "Have you three figured out how to solve the water shortage in Africa?"

"We think so," Melinda responded, "But we're going to need help if Freddy's team is available."

"You missed out on Freddy's team by about five minutes," their mother said. "I just finished talking to Aiko. She was checking to see if you three had already asked Freddy."

Hiro asked, "Didn't I hear that Edna had found her frequency matches?"

"I know that Lin Kwong tested as a match for her," Katherine replied, "Who is the third?"

"What I heard is that Edna was out running errands before we went on vacation," Hiro said, "When she supposedly stopped to look at a vehicle that had been wrecked and discovered him about half dead from dehydration and other wounds in the back seat. It seems she was using her powers to see if he was alive when they linked."

"Jennifer," Katherine told her robot, "Please get Jackie on the phone for me." Jennifer beeped and the phone panel brightened to life. When Jackie appeared Katherine said, "I understand that congratulations are in order."

"Yep, we have another trio in the family," Jackie replied chuckling, "Provided that Edna and Lin let him up for air once in a while. They're doing their best to get him nursed back to health as quickly as they can."

"Was he hurt very badly?" Katherine queried.

"He had several wounds," Jackie answered. "A couple of them were bad enough to kill him if Edna hadn't found him but he's out of the hospital and staying here. I noticed that the robots are building new houses so I think that my partnered kids are going to get their own places to live very shortly."

"With king size beds in the master bedrooms I'll bet," Hiro said chuckling. "I wonder how the various religions are going to handle marriage triangles."

"The other side of that is that most state laws prohibit polygamy too," Jackie added.

"That sounds like a job for our illustrious President," Katherine replied. "Do you think Edna and her partners can link well enough to help my kids with a project?"

"They probably can," Jackie chuckled again, "Let me see if I can get them to come up for air." Jackie turned to Virginia, and said, "Please go get Edna and tell her she needs to talk to Katherine." Jennifer beeped and rolled out of the room.

A minute later Edna appeared and said, "Hi Ms. Katherine, whacha want?"

"My three need some help with a project they're working on and I was wondering if you and your partners could help," Katherine replied."

"We can try," Edna, replied, "We aren't the strongest team yet. What time and where?"

"Tomorrow about two after they have finished school," Katherine answered. "I think generator four is available if you need it."

"Edna said, "Okay, we'll meet at your house and go to the generator station from there. Have your kids got everything figured out?"

"They probably do since they were asking for power help," Katherine replied. "It would be a good idea for you get a briefing before you start."

The next afternoon, Edna Vasquez, Lin Kwong, and Stuart Evans, a very tall slender young man on crutches, arrived at the Warren house. Jennifer greeted them at the door and led the trio to the triplets.

Edna said, "Hi kids what's up?"

Melinda replied, "Water."

Lin asked, "Do you mean like in that old poem? The one that goes, 'Water, water everywhere, and all the boards did shrink. Water, water everywhere nor any drop to drink…'"*

*From the *Rhyme of the Ancient Mariner* by Samuel Taylor Coleridge.

"Sort of, but I don't think there are any shrunken boards to worry about," Melinda responded. "We're thinking about how to fix the fresh water problem in Africa. Please have a seat and we'll explain." Everyone sat around the children's school table and Melinda continued, "We're thinking of creating several artificial lakes."

Sarah picked up the explanation with, "We plan to dig ten; one kilometer square lakebeds that are a hundred meters deep then fill them with ocean water that we've cleaned."

Stuart asked diffidently, "How many people are in the areas where you're going to put the lakes and how superstitious are they?"

"We're planning to use areas with very low populations," Melinda answered, "But we haven't considered superstition. Do you think it will cause a problem?"

"Have you contacted the countries," Lin queried, "Where you're going to build the lakes?"

"Why would we need to do that?" Sarah asked.

"Because it is the proper thing to do," Edna answered, "And the governments probably have a better idea of where to put the lakes and they can move people out of harm's way."

"Then I guess that we'd better talk to grandfather," Melinda said in a very serious voice. She turned to her mother's robot and asked, "Jennifer, would you contact Gustov and have it explain to grandfather what we need please?" The robot beeped once and the word, done, appeared on its computer screen.

"While we wait for an answer," Stuart said, "Why don't you show us how you plan to pull this off?"

Melinda said, "If you'll all connect up we'll be happy to show you what we have planned."

Stuart picked up an interface cable and started to plug it into his neck. He flinched in pain and Linda said, "Here let me help you," as she took the cable from his hand and connected him. "Our parents told us that for those who have to be connected this way that the area around the connector stays sore for a couple of weeks."

"It certainly is that," Stuart replied, "And I'm not sure which way to turn the cable to get it plugged in yet either. Thank you."

"You're welcome," Linda replied. "Pecos, bring up the images of what we planned please." The robot beeped, plugged its connector into a computer connection, and started its holographic projector.

In flashing thoughts, the Katherine's eldest triplets explained what they had planned. Edna's team examined the plan and made suggestions refining the plan even more. An hour later, Jennifer rolled into the room with refreshments, beeped several times, and typed, "Anyone thirsty?"

Edna said to the robot, "After discussing water for the last hour, yes and I have another need too."

The robot typed, "Second door to the left down the hall. I have a message from Gustov. Secretary Jordan will bring several ambassadors here the day after tomorrow."

EXALTED IMPERIAL COMMANDER THIS SCOUT JJ4536FD IS ON SCHEDULE WITH MIND TRAINING SLAVES.

SCOUT JJ4536FD YOUR REPORT IS INCORRECT. SLAVES ARE NOT BEING TRAINED. YOUR TRAINING MACHINES ARE NOT SENDING THE CORRECT TRAIN-ING. REPROGRAM YOUR MACHINES IMMEDIATELY AND GET ON SCHEDULE. EXHALTED IMPERIAL COM-MANDER.

Two days later a business jet with the United Nations emblem on its tail landed at Central's airstrip. Two limousines and a small cargo truck met the plane and took its passengers to Central's main underground conference room. Waiting in the conference room were two sets of triplets, two robots, Katherine and Aiko. When everyone was seated, Katherine said, "Good morning ladies and gentlemen. For those of you with civil wars in your countries Aiko's girls want to discuss how they can help your countries end them. For those of you whose countries are suffering droughts my girls wish to explain how they can reduce your water shortage problems and allow your farmers to use irrigation to water their crops."

Ambassador Santiago from Guyana asked, "How can little girls solve problems?" Then he demanded, "Mister Secretary why have you brought us here to waste time?"

Karlita stood and said, "Mister Ambassador, we propose to use the powers of our minds to end your civil war." Then her eyes narrowed and the ambassador began to float in the air still sitting in his chair.

Aiko told her daughter, "Put him back down, dear. If he doesn't want to end the civil war in his country then perhaps he's part of the problem."

"Yes momma," Karlita replied unrepentant and Ambassador Santiago sank back into his place at the table.

The ambassadors looked worriedly at each other and Secretary Jordan said, "I brought you here so that these children could explain how they can help your countries so that you can tell your governments, and if needed your military. Please let them explain what they have in mind. After that it is up to you to do what you feel is right."

The ambassadors turned back to Karlita with doubt in their eyes, and she said, "Pecos, please show the Guyanan rebel commander's image." The robot started its holographic projector and displayed the image of Colonel Drago. Karlita continued, "This is the leader of the rebel forces in Guyana. He is a Peruvian."

The conference room door opened suddenly, four security robots rolled into the room, and stopped behind the Guyanan ambassador. A fifth robot rolled to Secretary Jordan and typed, "The President of Guyana states that he has evidence that his ambassador is responsible for providing weapons to the rebels in his country. The President also states that if there is something that can be done to stop the civil war he would like it done as quickly as possible."

Kenneth said, "Thank you Gustov. Katherine, I think we need to find out what else Mister Santiago might be involved with."

"I've contacted Wendy," Katherine replied, "Her three have developed the ability to interrogate people very completely. They should be here in a moment."

A loud bang occurred in the hall outside the conference room, then Wendy and her three oldest triplets entered.

Wendy walked to the front of the conference room and sat in a vacant chair. Arielle, Brenda, and Sharron looked at Ambassador Santiago and he stiffened his eyes bulging as they entered his mind. The other ambassadors watched not understanding what they were seeing. A few minutes later Ambassador Santiago sagged in his chair and Arielle said, "You can escort Mister Santiago to Security now. Mama we don't have contact sets can you connect so we can pass the information to you?"

Wendy pulled a cable from a slot in the conference room table and connected. The remaining ambassador's eyes bulged in amazement as they watched. A moment later she said, "Gustov, please collect the printout for these gentlemen." Gustov beeped and rolled out of the room.

Ambassador Urillio of Kenya asked, "How are you able to do these things are you witches?"

"No," Wendy answered, "We adults were changed by having surgery done to us." Wendy held up the computer cable and continued, "The surgery gave us new abilities and also made it so that our children were born with the new abilities. Our children are already stronger in many areas than we are."

"I have had the same surgery as Ms. Stevens," Secretary Jordan added. The ambassadors looked at him stunned and he continued, "Shall we continue with what we came here to accomplish?"

Ambassador Urillio shook himself and replied, "Please, by all means." His eyes glowed in understanding that the young girls could really help his country, "My country has both a civil war and a very severe drought."

Arielle said, "Since those are areas that our friends have worked on we will return to our studies. It has been nice meeting you ladies and gentlemen." Arielle and her sisters left the conference room.

Karlita stood up and said, "Now that, that issue has been resolved let us continue. Ambassador Urillio, We have discovered that in your country that the rebels are actually gangs hired by a mining consortium that has discovered several very large Tantalum deposits. They are attempting to gain control of your country so they can have exclusive control of the metal." Karlita finished her briefing and the Warren triplets explained their solution to the drought problems in the affected countries. The ambassadors asked questions until they had satisfied themselves that what they were hearing from the children would actually work. When they had satisfied themselves, they asked if they could speak with Secretary Jordan privately.

When they arrived back home and completed their studies for the day Karlita asked, "Yoshi, would you please get General Gregory on the phone please?" The robot beeped and the wall screen brightened.

The General's aide, Lieutenant Colonel Chandler, answered the phone and she asked, "What can I do for you ladies today?"

"We'd like to talk to the General about setting up a secure call to Guyana," Karlita responded.

"The General is in a conference right now," the Colonel replied, "I also think that Colonel Saunders, the Corps signal officer can probably set that up for you."

Karlita said, "That would be fine. Could you forward us to him?"

"Certainly," the Colonel answered, "Just a moment."

A few seconds later the face of a middle-aged woman wearing the collar insignia of a full colonel appeared and asked, "I'm Colonel Saunders, How may I help you?"

Karlita responded, "I'm Karlita Esteban and these are my sisters Mika and Hana. We need to make a secure call to General Demerara in Guyana. It would be best if he could go to our embassy there for the call. Can you set that up for us?"

"I'm at a loss," Colonel Saunders answered, "Who is General Demerara?"

Mika replied, "He's the commander of the Guyanan military forces."

"Ah," the Colonel said, "It could take a little over a day to set this up. What time would you like to speak to him?"

"We finish school for the day at two," Karlita answered, "So let's say about two-fifteen or so."

"Okay I'll get it set up," Colonel Saunders told the girls, "Is there anything else I can do, today?"

"Thank you," Karlita answered, "I think that's all for today." Colonel Saunders added a good bye and disconnected.

Two afternoons later, a lieutenant and a sergeant arrived at the Esteban residence with several pieces of electronic equipment. The equipment was connected to the family's phone. The three girls gathered in front of it and the Lieutenant dialed a very long number. The screen brightened and three men looked out of it at the girls. The sandy haired man sitting in the middle said, "Good afternoon ladies I am John Sebastian the Ambassador to Guyana. On my left is President Trujillo," Then indicating a man in a military uniform he continued, "This is General Demerara. I will translate if it's needed."

Karlita replied, "We're pleased to meet all of you, I am Karlita," indicating her sisters, "And these are my sisters, Mika and Hana." Karlita pointed at her father's robot and continued, "This is Pecos one of our family robots. Pecos please project a map of the area South of Bartica." The robot rolled to where its projected image could be seen by those on the phone and turned on its projector. The three girls put on temple contacts and an area in the map changed color. Karlita said, "We know that this area has some large chromium deposits that are being mined so we plan to use one of the mines as a trap. The Paco Company open pit mine has a large shipment of chromium about ready to go. We're going to convince Colonel Drago that the shipment is tantalum instead and that the army is there to defend it. Mister Ambassador, do you have print capability on your end?"

"Yes, I do," the Ambassador, replied.

"Pecos, please send the maps of the defensive positions to the Ambassador's printer," Karlita said. The robot beeped once and typed, "Sending," on its screen. Karlita continued, "Mister Ambassador, have you received a fairly large crate?"

"A large crate was received this morning," the Ambassador replied.

"Karlita said, "Good when this call is finished please turn it over to the General. General the crate contains body armor for forty people, which is a platoon in your army's structure. Please choose your most reliable platoon to act as a combination of look out and to draw Colonel Drago and his forces into the mine."

Ambassador Sebastian stood and said, "Excuse me a moment." He stepped out of the phone pickup's view and returned a moment later with a stack of paper that he handed to the General.

Hana said, "General, the maps show where to put your soldiers and also the route for your lookout platoon. The reason that platoon needs the armor is because we can't act until all of Colonel Drago's forces are in the mine and the way out has been blocked. Then all of his weapons will stop working."

Karlita asked, "General, How long do you think you will need to prepare your soldiers for this?"

The General thought for a moment and then replied, "The problem I have is that I don't have a way to know how many of my soldiers are loyal."

Karlita asked, "Would it be possible for you to assemble your soldiers that will participate in one place?"

"I can do that," The General replied, "May I ask why?"

"Our parents can check your soldiers," Hanna answered, "And can tell you who is loyal from a distance. If everyone is in one place it makes things easier and faster."

The Guyanan Ambassador asked, "Just because you have stopped their weapons doesn't mean the rebels will stop fighting. How will you handle that?"

"After their weapons are broken," Karlita answered, "We're going to let them mill about long enough for the mercenaries to be identified and then we'll put everyone to sleep."

Hana added, "You'll be able to send your soldiers in to collect their weapons. We will continue to monitor what is going on just in case."

"I will have my soldiers on the parade field at my headquarters for an inspection at eight tomorrow morning," General Demerara said with a grim smile on his face. "Thank you. I would have never thought that children could have the power to end the destruction in my country," He added.

The girls bowed to the screen and Karlita replied, "We are happy that we are able to help. We will be ready tomorrow."

"I will accompany the General tomorrow with a secure phone see you then," the Ambassador added and the broke the connection.

That evening at supper Aiko asked, "Did you get everything arranged girls?"

"Yes Mama," Karlita answered, "But we discovered that we're going to need some adult help too."

"Explain," Aiko said.

"General Demerara asked if we could help him discover who is disloyal in his army," Mika replied picking up the explanation.

"So," the girl's father asked, "What kind of help did you offer?"

"We told him that was something our parents had to do," Karlita answered.

"The Ambassador told us that he would go with the General to his headquarters with a secure telephone so that we can explain anything that needs to be done," Hana added.

Hiro asked, "Did you check our schedules to see if we are available?"

"Oops," Mika said ducking her head, "I guess we kind of forgot to do that. Are you busy tomorrow morning?"

"I am part of the morning," their mother said, "What time?"

"Eight o'clock, Mama," Mika answered.

"Yoshi, get Wendy on the phone please," Aiko told her robot with a sigh.

Yoshi beeped, the family phone screen brightened. "Hello Aiko what do you need?" Wendy asked.

Aiko replied, "My youngsters received a request from General Demerara to check his soldiers for loyalty by remote control and they agreed without checking with us. Can we shift the first mission to say ten so we can do this?"

"How about we go up as planned," Wendy replied, "And check the General's army together, then let your kids carry on from there? That shouldn't delay us more than about thirty minutes that way."

"That sounds reasonable to me," Aiko replied. "Kids, what else do we need to know to do this?"

"General Demerara said he would have his forces out for inspection on his headquarters parade field at eight in the morning," Karlita answered.

"All in one place will make it easier," Wendy said, "And faster. I think the three of us could do that quickly enough not to be too far behind scheduled."

The triplet's father asked, "Girls, do you know how many soldiers the General will have?"

"It's not really a true army Dad," Hana responded, "It's more of a national police force with heavy weapons. There are fifteen hundred nationwide and only about nine hundred are at headquarters."

"And their taking on how many?" Wendy asked from the phone screen.

"As near as we've been able to determine fifty mercenaries and roughly four thousand locals," Karlita replied. That's why we want to ensure that the entire rebel force is in the trap when we disable their weapons and put them to sleep."

"It's also why we spent a lot of time on choosing defensive positions for the Guyanan forces," Hana added.

"Who have you got helping you?" Wendy asked.

"Freddy's team is going to help us on this mission," Karlita answered, "We'll have to see who is available for the other wars when we get to them."

"Then it sounds like things are under control," Wendy said, "So get a good night's sleep and we'll do it in the morning."

"Thank you, Ms. Wendy," Hana said and the phone screen blanked.

Karlita asked, "Yoshi, are we having desert tonight?"

"What makes you think you should have dessert?" appeared on the robot's screen.

Karlita asked in a slightly aggravated voice, "Where did you come up with the concept that I expected dessert daily? Especially with you electromechanical nurse maids managing our lives."

The robot rolled backwards a few feet and typed, "There is Baked Alaska for dessert." Yoshi did not answer Karlita's question.

Karlita said with all of the adult authority she could put in her six-year-old voice, "Thank you, however you haven't answered my second question and you would not let us get away with that so I'm still waiting."

Hiro burst out laughing and Aiko said, "She is correct Yoshi, so perhaps you should answer her question."

Yoshi typed, "She is a child and all children seem to want sweets all of the time without an understanding of what they are asking. I wanted to find out if that was true. Unfortunately these children do not fit the normal pattern."

Hana snapped up straight in her chair, looked at Yoshi, and said rapidly, "Yoshi, bravo one, bravo one, bravo one, Zulu execute."

The robot's arms snapped into their storage position and the word, "Running," appeared on its screen. Aiko asked, "Why did you trigger a self-check, Hana?"

"Curiosity is outside the programming parameters that Ms. Katherine created for the robots," Hana replied. "If the self-check doesn't show anything then Ms. Katherine should probably look at the heuristic changes occurring in the robots to make sure we haven't got a problem."

Hiro asked, "Have you been studying programming?

"I've just gotten started, Papa," Hana replied.

Yoshi beeped three times and a list appeared on its screen. Hana looked at the list for several minutes, pursed her lips and said, "We need Ms. Katherine to see this." Hana pulled the computer connector from the robot's claw and plugged it into a connector on the edge of the dining room table, and then she said, "Yoshi Print Bravo One, to file Yoshi Bravo One, execute." The robot beeped, and then Hana continued, "Reboot and self-check."

The robot emitted a long string of beeps paused and then beeped one last time. On its screen the message "Self-test complete," appeared and Yoshi came back to life.

Hana asked, "Mama, would you ask Ms. Katherine to check that file when she has a chance?"

"Certainly," Hana's mother replied, "Is morning soon enough?"

"I think Mama," Hana said thoughtfully, "Yes."

"Good," Hiro said, "Yoshi, bring the dessert please." Yoshi beeped and rolled away. A few minutes later, it returned with flaming baked Alaska.

After everyone had gone to sleep, Yoshi rolled up to Pecos, connected to the other robot and turned it off. Then Yoshi opened Pecos's access panel, removed a circuit board, installed several new ones and some other components, then it turned Pecos back on, and copied several programs into it.

The next morning Karlita, her sisters, and Freddy's team met at the generator station's master control room. Everyone looked around in disbelief because the room was a shambles. Everything was broken. The six young people and two robots looked about in wide-eyed disbelief. After a few minutes Mika said, "Yoshi, we need security here and tell Pecos to let dad know about this." Yoshi beeped and the word, "Done," appeared on its screen. A minute later, a double boom occurred as Clarence and Hiro arrived. In the distance, sirens wailed.

Clarence asked, "Has anyone touched anything in here?"

Freddy shook himself as if he were coming out of a daze and replied, "I think we've all been too stunned to touch anything, sir. But we've all been here before if you're thinking of finger prints."

"I was more concerned that one of you may have been injured," Clarence answered. "Security will be interested in fingerprints and DNA. One of you robots contact General Gregory to come here."

"I'm already here," the General, answered from the control room door. "Anyone have any ideas as to how this happened?"

"No sir," Freddy answered. "Kind of looks like someone got past security."

"Sir," a sergeant wearing a military police brassard on his left arm said, "We just found the security detail. They're dead, sir"

General Gregory looked at the sergeant grimly and replied, "Get the crime investigators over here ASAP and don't let anyone else in." He continued waving his hand towards the children, Clarence, and Hiro, "These are the only people to be allowed to leave." Turning to the children he asked, "Were you kids here to work on a mission?"

Mika replied, "Yes sir. Do you have some other generators someplace we can use?"

"I think we can find some, little lady," the General answered holding out his hand to her to lead her from the damaged control center.

Mika cocked her head, took the General's hand, and asked, "What frequency are the generators?"

"They're sixty hertz which is close enough for Freddy," Gregory replied as they walked out of the damaged room.

Fifteen minutes later in the General's conference room, Clarence who had joined them said, "I've notified Wendy of the delay and why."

Karlita replied, "That will work, sir but we will need a secure phone to the Guyanan Ambassador so we can tell him about the delay."

"That's Lieutenant Herschel," the General said pointing to a young man seated at a control panel in a corner, "He will place the call and take care of anything else you need. If you'll excuse me, I'll get on with my own work." Having said that, General Gregory nodded to everyone and left the room.

Karlita went to the conference room table and wrote the call number on a pad that was laying there. She tore the sheet from the pad, handed it to the Lieutenant, and said, "This is the number to the Guyanan Ambassador. Please place the call in secure mode."

The conference room communications screen brightened and Ambassador Sebastian looked out from it and said, "Good morning ladies, I understand you had some problems."

Karlita replied, "Yes sir a little, is the General ready?"

"He's walking through the ranks checking equipment to kill time while he waits for you."

"This is Mister Clarence Stevens, Ms. Wendy's husband," Karlita said, "He will contact her when you're ready to start finding out who is disloyal. What will happen is that the disloyal soldiers will lay down their weapons and march to the front of the formation and wait."

"I'll tell the General," the Ambassador answered, "Go ahead and start."

Karlita turned to Clarence and asked, "Mister Clarence, will you ask Ms. Wendy for them to begin?"

Clarence contacted Wendy then replied, "They will begin in two minutes when they finish transferring supplies to the base on Mars."

The Ambassador turned from the phone pickup, watched the formation for a moment, then turned back and asked, "Do you have three friends who can do things to people's minds?"

Clarence asked, "Can you show them to me?"

The Ambassador's phone pickup was turned to show three red headed young girls standing, facing the formation, and holding hands. "Those are my oldest triplets," Clarence said, "I think the determination of loyalty is underway under no uncertain terms. I'll be there in a moment." A loud bang occurred in the conference room and Clarence disappeared. When those in the conference room next looked at its screen, Clarence was standing a couple of meters behind his daughters.

In the formation, people began to lay down their weapons and walk jerkily towards the triplets. It was obvious that they were under some sort of compulsion and were fighting to stay away from the girls. In ones, twos, and threes the soldiers knelt in front of the girls and placed their hands behind their heads. When all of those soldiers had arrived before the girls, there were twenty of them. General Demerara completed his inspection, hastily walked to where the girls were, and asked, "Who might you three ladies be?"

Arielle replied, "I am Arielle Stevens, and these are Sharron and Brenda. And this is our father," She concluded waving her hand towards her father.

Sharron stepped beside her sister and said, "General, seventeen of these people are traitors. These two are murderers," Sharron continued.

Brenda, who was wearing heavy hiking boots, walked to the last kneeling soldier and kicked him squarely between his legs. The man screamed in agony and collapsed in a heap. Brenda said in a very angry voice, "This one has been raping and abusing his mother, sisters, and some of the other women in his town."

General Demerara turned to a colonel who had been following him and said, "Place these men in custody and do not let them communicate with anyone not even each other. Send a team of doctors and nurses to this one's town to find all of his victims. Have them taken care of then bring them here."

The colonel snapped to attention, saluted, said, "Yes sir," turned and departed to carry out his orders.

While everyone waited for the Colonel to return, Clarence walked up to his children, and Sharron asked, "Hi dad, did mom tell you what happened?"

Clarence replied, "No she hasn't and she's so focused on something that I haven't been able to ask, so why don't you explain."

"We'd been doing our school work for about an hour," Sharron explained, "When mom telepathed and told us what to do. Then she sent us here. Other than that we don't know anything."

While the triplets explained their presence to their father, a truck and several military police got out of it. The sergeant in charge saluted the General and stated, "We have been instructed to arrest prisoners that you are to point out to us, sir."

"These who are kneeling are to be arrested," the General, answered. "Keep them separated and do not let them talk to each other."

Ambassador Sebastian joined the group and said, "General the young ladies who are to help capture the rebels want to know if you are ready to depart."

The colonel had returned from his mission and the General turned to him and said, "We have held these people up long enough. Get everyone loaded up and ready to move out in five minutes." Again, the Colonel saluted his General and ran towards the formation waving a hand in a circle over his head. All across the parade field soldiers scrambled into trucks that were waiting nearby.

Sharron turned to her father and asked, "Dad, when we get home can we go swimming for a while before we finish today's school stuff so we can cool off?"

"Mister Stevens, I want to thank you and your children for what you are doing for my country," General Demerara told Clarence.

"On behalf of my children and the Hiro triplets," Clarence replied profoundly, "You are most welcome. The children are the ones who have actually planned and are carrying out those plans for your benefit. As their parents our concern is that they don't get hurt doing what they've planned but we must be going because these three have school yet today."

Forestalling anything further, Ambassador Sebastian said, "Let me add my thanks also and we'd better catch up with your army, General." The General looked across the parade field, turned to the three red headed children, gave a quick bow, and signaled for his staff car.

In a moment the General was gone and Clarence said, "I guess you can swim for an hour when we get back, let's go." A multiple bang echoed across the parade field and the triplets and their father were gone leaving only a cloud of dust to mark where they had been.

Back in General Gregory's conference room, in Iowa, Mika mumbled disgustedly, "'bout time."

"Yes," Karlita replied, "Keeping the rebels asleep is getting boring. We should have anticipated that they might try to steal the shipment before the army got there. The question is how did they find out before we were ready?"

Hana replied, "That makes me think there is a leak here in Central someplace or else one of the other ambassadors we talked to."

"It could be someone on Ambassador Sebastion's staff to," Mika added.

"We'll have to get Arielle and her sisters to look into the issue," Karlita replied. Addressing the communications screen she queried, "Mister Ambassador are you still with us?"

"Yes we are," the Ambassador answered, "We've just arrived and are dispersing to get ready."

"There's been a change in plans," Karlita informed him. "The rebels are already in the quarry and we have disabled their weapons and put them to sleep. It seems that there was an information leak possibly at our end. Tell the General to send his people in to collect the rebels."

"He heard and said to tell you all thank you," was the Ambassador's response. "He also asked if you could stay on watch for another hour to make sure he gets all of the rebels rounded up."

Mika said, "I'm getting hungry."

Lieutenant Herschel said, "I'll get lunch sent in for all of you. What do you like best?"

The triplets told him but before the Lieutenant could make the call the conference room door opened and Yoshi and Pecos rolled into the room with food warmers on their cargo shelves. Pecos beeped and typed, "Is anyone hungry?" on its screen.

Yoshi typed, "Your mother said to tell you that there was a cave in on the moon in one of the main tunnels which is why they sent Arielle and her sisters to Guyana."

Mika asked, "How many were hurt?"

"They are still being rescued," the robot replied as the girls sat at the conference room table. "Lieutenant, we have brought lunch for you as well."

The Lieutenant said, "Thank you," and joined the triplets Freddy and his mind partners at the table. The conference room, communications screen showed some soldiers collecting weapons from sleeping rebels and others waking them and herding them into trucks.

Hana looked at the screen and commented, "Looks like they've just about got that wrapped up."

"I wonder how Melinda and her sisters are doing with their lakes," Mika mused quietly.

Pecos beeped and typed, "They had a delay and will not be able to build the first lake until the day after tomorrow."

GETTING THINGS WET

Three days later General Gregory's aid escorted the Warren triplets, Edna and her partners through headquarters. They stopped at the Chief of Staff's office and introduced Brigadier General Rowe, a short stocky man with piercing blue eyes, to the Warren triplets, Edna and her partners. General Rowe said, "Welcome to headquarters." Then looking around for an adult he asked, "Who is in charge of your group?"

"My sisters and I are," Melinda replied.

"And you are?" the General inquired.

"I'm Melinda Warren and these are my sisters, Linda and Sarah." Then indicating the older three she continued, "These are Edna Vasquez, Lin Kwong, and Stuart Evans our power assistance for today."

General Rowe looked at Colonel Chandler in confusion and asked, "Are we giving tours to youth groups?"

The Colonel replied, "I wasn't aware that you hadn't been briefed on the families yet, sir. Then addressing the children she continued, "General Rowe has only been here a few days." To the Chief of Staff she added, "The generator station these people normally use has been damaged badly and its guards were killed. The engineers have brought two, hundred-kilowatt generators for them to use. There is a meeting in the conference room and the General said you have a large table and asked me to bring them here. He also said he would appreciate your helping them with whatever, they need. I'll also tell the G-2 you need to be briefed."

"In that case, kids come in and let's get you started," General Rowe said waving his unexpected guests into his office. Once everyone sat, the General asked, "Since I'm not familiar with you or your mission could you give me a thumbnail briefing?"

"You are probably more familiar with our mother and her mind partners, at least by name," Melinda replied. "Our mother is Katherine Warren and her mind partners are Wendy Stevens and Aiko Esteban."

"Yes," the General responded, "I'm familiar with the names and that gives me an idea of what your abilities might be. So what is your mission for today? Was it you or the children of the other families that put all the war ships in the Caspian Sea?"

"That was Ms. Wendy's oldest triplets, Arielle, Sharron, and Brenda," Sarah answered. "We're going to build a lake in a drought area in Uganda."

"I'd have thought that Sudan would have been a better choice," The General said thoughtfully.

"It would have been," Linda said picking up the briefing, "But the current government is corrupt and they have also passed a bunch of laws that declare us witches and the penalty for their people interacting with anything done by witchcraft is death. That means that the population could not use any lake we make in Sudan. Uganda doesn't have any such laws."

"I wouldn't have thought that Uganda would have a water problem with Lake Victoria and several other lakes in and around the country," General Rowe commented.

Melinda replied, "They have been in extreme drought conditions for the last fifteen years and much of their wetlands have disappeared. This should help them be able to keep what has survived and perhaps help them revive more of it."

"Why not refill the lakes?" the General asked.

"That would be beneficial to some areas," Sarah replied, "But wouldn't put water where it is needed or back into the water table."

"That makes sense," General Rowe said thoughtfully, "And I hadn't considered recharging the water table. Okay, what do you need from me to get started?"

"A secure phone call to the U.S. Ambassador in Uganda," Melinda responded sliding a piece of paper toward the General. "Our Grandfather has arranged for several U.N. camera crews to be there to give us images of our work area."

"Your grandfather must be a really important man to be able to do that," Rowe said amazed.

Linda giggled and added, "He's the Secretary General of the U.N."

General Rowe said, "Hmm," and turned to his phone to dial the number Melinda had given him.

The General's phone screen lit and a dark skinned man wearing a khaki shirt looked out of it. When he saw the triplets at the table, he smiled and said, "Hi kids. Your work area is clear of people and animals. The camera crews are in place. We had a few wild herds that delayed us some but their out of the area now."

"Great," Melinda replied, "This is General Rowe who got saddled with us unexpectedly. He's the communications person on this end today. Warn everyone to put on their goggles, hearing protection, and masks. We'll start in five minutes."

Edna asked, "General Rowe would you tell the engineers to start the generators and set them to seventy-two hertz please?"

The General rose, walked to his desk, pressed a button on his intercom, and said, "Tell the engineers outside to start the generators and run them at seventy-two hertz." The generators started and after a couple of minutes settled into an idling rumble. Edna held her hands to Stuart and Lin then nodded at the triplets who had also joined hands. All six looked at the phone screen then the General watched a glow appear around the older three that connected itself to the younger ones. Outside the generators rose to a mighty roar as power was drawn from them. General Rowe looked at the phone screen and gasped. A large something that glowed brightly was scooping earth into ridges twenty meters high and nearly as wide. The something pushed in several directions at once so that the earth was piled up forming a wall around a vast one hundred meter deep pit. When the digging was done the something settled onto the wall and moved along it leaving a glowing and smoking glassy surface behind. Then it began to rain in the hole at a rate of meters per second. The General looked at the six children then noticed the hair on his arms was standing straight up. He rubbed them but the hair remained standing. He shook his head trying to clear the strange feeling of stuffiness he had. He looked back at the screen and chuckled as he watched fishes, and seaweeds being put into the new lake. Finally, the generators wound down and the children returned to life shaking themselves.

Melinda stretched mightily and said to no one in particular, "Boy am I hungry."

General Rowe chuckled, pressed the intercom button on his desk, and said, "We need some food in here for six starving construction workers."

Melinda asked, "How long did that take us General, sir?"

The General looked at his desk clock and replied, "You should be starved to death that took seven hours."

On the screen Ambassador Matthews was laughing, and pointing at the lake, saying, "I hope all of those people are good swimmers." The camera crews and the Ugandan military that were in the area were jumping into the lake. The Ambassador continued, "General get those kids fed and President Museveni says thank you. I'm disconnecting now."

There was a knock on the General's door then it opened and three robots rolled in with food cocoons on their cargo shelves. The cocoons were distributed and the General was pleasantly surprised to discover one placed before him as well.

Jennifer beeped drawing the General's attention and typed, "It has been seven hours since you ate last, enjoy."

The General lifted the lid on the cocoon smiled at Jennifer and said, "Thank you."

Before anyone could eat, there was another knock on the door and General Gregory walked in and asked, "How did it go?"

"From what I was watching," General Rowe replied, "It went very well."

"General Gregory," Melinda said, "You're going to lose General Rowe for several days."

Gregory asked, "Why is that?"

"He's going to get the connector surgery and programming because he's PSI able," Melinda replied. "If we'd needed another hour he probably would have activated completely on his own."

"Is that why," General Rowe asked, "I don't remember much other than the hair on my arms standing up? That and a fuzzy feeling in my head."

Edna answered laughing, "That's the best description of telekinetic usage anyone has come up with yet."

General Gregory said in a no bones about it voice, "General Rowe you are on detached duty to Central while they get you situated." Then he asked, "Melinda, can anyone be programmed?"

"Not everyone," Melinda answered, "But since you have the connector you probably can be. Some of the things required to make the connector work are also, what can enable your Psi abilities. Jennifer please schedule both Generals one at a time, just in case." Jennifer beeped.

"You know sir," Sarah said thoughtfully, "I think it would be a very good idea to test all of your officers."

General Gregory asked, "Why is that?"

"Because of something that just surfaced in my mind about the aliens," Sarah replied. "It seems that they not only have the ability to mess with our minds but with our electronic communications as well."

"Ah," Gregory said, "So you are thinking that the more of us who are telepathic the more effective we can be in combat against them."

"Precisely," Sarah answered.

General Rowe whistled softly and said, "Man what a force multiplier that would be. Jam proof communications." His eyes were gleaming when he looked at his boss and continued, "I like that idea."

Gregory asked, "Who would do the checking or do my officers need to go to the hospital to be checked?"

Linda said, "Jennifer contact Robin and have it ask Ms. Wendy if Arielle and her sisters can do the check."

Jennifer beeped and typed, "Done."

General Rowe shook his head smiling, asked sir, "How old did you say these kids were?"

"The young ones are six going on sixty I think," Gregory replied smiling. "These older ones are in their teens and twenties. The triplets have younger brother and or sister triplets as well."

Jennifer beeped for attention and typed, "Ms. Wendy wants to talk to General Gregory at his earliest convenience about what you are requesting."

"Since I see you've finished eating," General Gregory said, "Let me drop you off at your houses and I'll go have a chat with Ms. Stevens.

After General Gregory and children had left, Sergeant Major Smith knocked on his General's door and asked, "Will the generators be needed further today, sir?"

Coming out of the reverie he had fallen into, General Rowe shook his head and replied, "I don't think so, why?"

"The crews say that they are in very bad shape," Smith answered. "It seems that they were running at absolute maximum output the whole time and need some serious maintenance because of it. Sergeant Kennedy told me that those are not the generators that started the day and that they've worked with these kids before and they never pulled power that hard. She said it was as if there was another person drawing power also."

"Well I'll be," Rowe said in awed wonder, "That was, me. I was doing it too." Then he looked at Sergeant Major Smith, became excited and repeated, "I was doing it too!" Then General Rowe seemed to come back to earth and continued, "I'll be out of the office for the next several days on a mission for General Gregory. Here are the letters of commendation for the guards that were killed at the generator station. Tell Sergeant Kennedy, I intend to commend her for thinking about spare generators and having them on hand today."

Sergeant Major Smith replied simply, "I'll let her know sir."

General Rowe smiled and said, "I think we can all go home for the day too." Reaching for his beret he added, "Let's go."

When they reached the Warren home Melinda told General Gregory, "Tell Sergeant Kennedy that we weren't trying to burn her generators out."

"What happened," Katherine asked as she joined the General and her children.

"General Rowe, the Chief of Staff has started to activate momma. It was hard keeping him under control and finishing our job too. The generators got overloaded and they had to change them as we worked."

"I thought there was something funny in the way they sounded," General Gregory said. "Well he's reporting to the hospital in the morning for a connector and programming, so that should solve that problem. I need to go see Ms. Winston, so if you'll excuse me."

"I know that Jennifer fed you but your father, the boys, and I are just sitting down to eat," Katherine said. "So why don't you three come tell us the details of your day."

At the dinner table, Sarah said, "That looks good. Bennett, could you bring me a small portion." Bennett beeped and rolled out of the dining room. A few minutes later, it returned with three small plates of pizza. During the meal,ral Gregory.meal the triplets explained what happened and the problem they had with General Rowe and what they suggested to Gen the triplets explained what happened, the problem they had with General Rowe, and what they suggested to General Gregory.

That night after everyone had gone to bed, Yoshi and Pecos quietly left the Esteban home. Yoshi went to the Stevens home and Pecos went to the Warrens. In each house, they deactivated the family robots, made the modifications that Yoshi had made to Pecos and installed the new programs. Then they returned to their own family.

EXHAULTED IMPERIAL COMMANDER THIS SCOUT JJ4536FD HAS DETERMINED THAT THE BEASTS ON PLANET 3 ARE OF A VERY HIGH ORDER AND ARE COUNTERING OUR EFFORTS TO PROGRAM THEM. REQUEST THAT A SPECIAL MISSION BE SENT TO NUETRALIZE THE BEASTS THAT ARE RESISTING.

At breakfast the next morning, Bennett rolled into the dining room and beeped for attention and typed, "There is a call from Brigadier General Wallace."

"I wonder what the army is up to now," mused William. "Put the call through Bennett." The phone screen lit and a craggy faced man looked out of the screen. "I'm William Warren," Katherine's husband said, "What can we do for you today?"

"Good morning, I'm General William Wallace the Corps engineer," the man on the screen replied. "I'm calling to let you know that the generator facility has been rebuilt and at General Gregory's insistence has been enlarged to handle three times its previous capacity. Also, there is improved security and restricted access. A messenger will arrive at each of the family's homes with a package containing an access pass for every member of your family. There is also a disc with access codes for your robots."

"You certainly rebuilt the station in record time," Katherine responded, "Thank you."

"You're most welcome," the General replied. Then he looked at the triplets and asked, "Were you the three in General Rowe's office yesterday?"

"Yes sir," Melinda answered.

"I thought you might like to know," Wallace continued, "That Sergeant Kennedy is now Chief Warrant Officer Kennedy and is in charge of the station's maintenance program."

"We will congratulate her when we see her," Melinda replied.

"Good," the General said, "While I'd like to talk to you some more I still need to call the Estebans and Vasquezs. Good bye."

The triplets, father asked, "Where are you building the next lake?"

"Either Zambia or Chad depending on which country grandfather gets us clearance for first," Sarah answered. "If it is Zambia it will be two lakes."

"Why two lakes?" their mother asked.

"One of the lakes will be like the one we did yesterday," Melinda replied. "The other one will be made to soak in really quickly to recharge the water table because much of their available water is salty from overuse."

"I can see where a trillion liters of water would recharge the water table," Katherine said, "But how does it solve the salt problem?"

"The salty water is heavier than the fresh water," Linda, answered, "So the fresh water floats on top. The wells in the area will gradually freshen as a result."

Bennett beeped a gain and the message typed on its screen said, "There is a call from Wendy."

"Put the call through," Katherine responded. "Good morning Wendy, what can we do for you today?"

"I'm sending out a warning," Wendy replied from the screen. "My alien eaves droppers have intercepted a couple of messages stating that a special team of humans is being trained to come after us."

Katherine looked at her three and asked, "Did you three get any messages?" The three girls shook their heads. Katherine looked back at the screen and asked, "Have you notified General Gregory yet."

"Yes," Wendy replied, "And he was most uncomplimentary about greedy aliens."

"I suppose that your three want to go alien hunting again," William said, "And want help to do it."

"Not that I know of," Wendy replied, "And while I'm grateful they are handling earth bound problems, I think that identifying programmed humans is a different situation. Well I need to call Jackie and Pat to so I'll meet you in Tank Circuit One in a bit."

Three days later General Rowe was in his office with a bandage wrapped around his neck. Seated in an easy chair near his desk was a petite woman with straight black hair that disappeared down her back. She was wearing a burnt orange coverall that was belted at the waist accenting her very womanly figure and tanned complexion. She also had a bandage around her neck. General Gregory knocked on the doorframe and said, "Sergeant Major Smith said you were in this morning. How are you?"

Before General Rowe could answer the woman said, "Couldn't you have found him someone cute enough to chase around a desk instead of that stodgy old Sergeant Major?"

General Rowe sighed and said, "General Gregory, meet Sylvia my wife. Sylvia, behave yourself."

Gregory laughed and replied, "I'm pleased to meet you, Sylvia. As for cute things to chase around desks Sergeant Major Smith was already here and the G-1's personnel section makes the assignments not me."

Sylvia responded, "Oh well, Jerry." Then smiling wickedly continued, "At least I tried to get you someone prettier than Smith."

"Sergeant Major Smith is going to be retiring in about nine months so perhaps you should try again then," Gregory told Sylvia. To General Rowe he continued, "There has been a new development with the alien invaders that I need to brief you on." Then noticing the bandage on her neck he continued, "And your wife too since she seems to have become a lodge member."

"You can't imagine the shock I got," Jerry Rowe, said, "When I got home the other day and she told me, 'I see you finally figured it out' telepathically. I took her to Central hospital with me the next morning."

"Arielle Stevens came to the room we were being programmed in and told us about the alien mischief," Sylvia said. "Are they just trying to kill the families or anyone with Psi capability?"

"As far as information available," Gregory replied, "They're out to harvest the entire solar system and use humans and all the other animals as food. They seem to be able to use machines to implant information into human minds. Clarence Stevens has been devising electronic counter measures to each new thing that they try, so they are after the families first then the rest of us."

"And so far dear it has been three sets of six year old triplets that has saved our bacon," General Rowe told his wife, "By alerting their parents to whatever the aliens try."

"I've been watching the news," Sylvia said thoughtfully, "And if they're that powerful as youngsters, what are their adult abilities going to be like? By the way, have you thought about retaining any officers who test out as Psi capable and how about their careers and promotions?"

General Gregory looked at his Chief of Staff and asked, "Are you sure she's a civilian?"

"She's been hobnobbing with the army for twenty-six years," Jerry Rowe replied. "She has to have picked up a few pieces of information here and there. When are you going for your programming?"

"Tomorrow," Gregory replied, "Since I don't have an exec currently you'll be holding the fort down for two days from what I've been told. If something happens, call one of the families for help because chances are the people have been conditioned by the aliens."

"I'll keep that in mind," General Rowe replied, "And I'll try not to have anyone killed in the process. I hate unnecessary killing."

"I remember the nightmares you had after the Singapore Brush War," Sylvia said quietly.

"A lot of us had nightmares after that idiocy," General Gregory responded, "Come to my office at two and I'll brief you on everything you will be up to for the next two days. I'll also send a message about promoting in place any Psi soldiers we have." The General waved at the two and left the office.

"Bennett," Sarah said in thought, "Please get with Jason and see if there is a way to detect if a mind has been altered by an outside agency such as the aliens."

The robot beeped and typed, "Done," on its screen. Several minutes later Bennett beeped again and typed, "Jason said that it would need more specific information before it can consider any such project. It would like to know if you have put any research time into such a project."

"Tell it not yet," Sarah, replied, "The thought just occurred to me. If it has any information to contribute I would appreciate it without any hassles or jokes." Bennett beeped once.

Jennifer rolled into the room with Sarah's contact set and typed, "Jason is ready to pass what information it has." Sarah put on her contact set and plugged it into Jennifer's communications connector closed her eyes and activated her contact set.

Fifteen minutes later Sarah's eyes snapped open and she commanded, "Tell Jason to show this design idea to Mister Clarence for modification and approval, then schedule it for construction."

"What did you come up with, sis?" Melinda queried.

"Something to help the army stop programmed people before they can do damage," Sarah replied.

"You were thinking so hard," Linda, said in a worried voice, "That you shut us out of your mind."

Without answering her sisters Sarah said soberly, "Bennett, please get their contact sets." The robot turned without a sound and left the room. When Bennett returned and her sisters had connected, Sarah continued, "Show them the philosophy and the circuits please Jennifer."

While Sarah and Jennifer were showing her sisters what she had created, Jason connected and Clarence thought to them over the network, <Good afternoon girls. Can the three of you come to my office and bring both robots with you?>

<Let us clear it with mom,> Melinda replied, <And we'll be there as soon as possible.>

Clarence thought, <Okay, and don't discuss Sarah's brainstorm with anyone outside of my office please.>

<I asked Doctor Janice a couple of questions about how the mind works,> Sarah said. <You might ask Brenda to join us since a lot of the information for the machine design came from what she saw in the alien scout ship.>

<I'll see to the security of the others,> Clarence told Sarah, <Just don't discuss it outside my shielded office.>

An hour later, Clarence looked up from what he was studying on his desk and said, "Come in kids and find a seat." After everyone was seated he continued, "Sorry about all the security stuff but I've discovered that we have a problem with telepathic spies who seem to be under alien control. We got the jump on the aliens with the projectors but if they find out what we did they can develop a counter to it."

Sarah queried, "Does that mean that we are going to see an increase in attacks directed at us?"

"Unfortunately," Clarence replied, "That's exactly what it means."

"So we're going to have to be much more effective in what we do to protect our populations," Melinda responded in thought, "And our first step is to get them cleaned of programming and build in prevention."

"That's two steps," Clarence replied, "But essentially, that's what we need to do."

"I also think we need to use this to our advantage," Sarah said.

Clarence prompted, "How so?"

"Unless we can stop the aliens in space," Sarah answered, "We'll be fighting them on earth, probably by ourselves. If that happens, I don't see us winning."

Linda added, "The people of earth need to become one massive army just in case."

"Not only that, dad," Brenda added, "I think that the aliens are stepping up the power on their machines to get at us which is going to make things worse."

"What makes you think that, Squirt?" Clarence queried.

"Two things," his daughter replied, "One, we're seeing more attacks directed at killing us, and two, we've learned how to monitor them without being programmed but it is getting harder to keep the programming out of our minds." Shrugging her shoulders she continued, "After all we have to sleep sometimes."

"What I haven't figured out is why they haven't attacked you adults," Melinda told Clarence.

"That is a very good question," Clarence stated, "Do you have any ideas?"

Melinda cocked her head in thought then asked, "Has anyone with a connector been attacked?"

Clarence sat up straighter in his chair, looked at Melinda, and then said, "Jason, contact the medical records computer and get a list of those with connectors at central. In addition, I want you to access whatever or whoever is necessary, to get a list of everyone in the world who has a connector. Robin contact General Gregory and ask him to come here immediately."

Robin beeped and typed, "General Gregory is in Central hospital being programmed. General Rowe the Chief of Staff is on his way."

Sarah added, "Jennifer, we need Doctor Janice also." Both robots beeped.

When Doctor Janice and General Rowe arrived, Clarence explained, "Sarah, working with Jason came up with a way to detect humans who have been programmed and we've been discussing things. We hit two points; one is that no human who has had connector surgery seems to have been programmed, at least so far. The other point is that we need to find out how many people have had the connector surgery and if there have been attacks on them."

General Rowe grunted and asked, "Don't want much do you?"

"I know that it can be difficult," Clarence said, "But we need to prevent as much bloodshed as possible. Unfortunately, at this point we also need to continue to keep the aliens secret."

"Doctor Janice," Sarah said, "We need to know more about where the connector contact points are in the brain. One or more of those places seems to be involved in the aliens programming efforts."

"Find the points and permanently block the aliens," Doctor Janice replied nodding her head. She turned to the nearest robot and asked, "What's your name?"

It typed, "My name is Bennett."

"Please contact Socrates and have it bring the needed diagrams here."

Bennett beeped and typed, "Done." A minute later, Bennett beeped again and typed, "Socrates is in surgery and can't come at present. It is sending Gregor Mendel with the information."

Melinda said, "I see that your medical robots are named for historical medical researchers and philosophers. That's kind of like our defense robots. Are there ten or more of each?"

"I've never heard or seen any of them address themselves with a number on their name," Maryann Janice replied. "If we can identify which portion of the brain turns the aliens off, how can we apply that knowledge to the population as a whole and how long will it take?"

"We'll still have those who are programmable despite whatever we can do to them," Brenda added.

"True," Clarence replied to his daughter, "But anything that cuts the size of the opposing force is worth the effort."

General Rowe added, "Amen to that."

"Dad," Brenda asked, "Why can't we just put a large nuclear bomb into their mother ship and end this?"

"William, Hiro, and I wondered that also," Clarence replied. "We think that the aliens may have been attacked that way before. Their mother ship is compartmented and reinforced so much that the biggest nuclear bomb we could build wouldn't do much damage."

"My thought is that if we can build force shields they probably can too," General Rowe added. "Or if they couldn't, this meeting makes me think that they may be able to now."

"Which strengthens what you were saying," Sarah added. "I can also see that we need to stop them from stealing our technology in general or we won't stop them."

"Since we seem to be the ones designing the defenses General," Linda injected, "How hard would it be to shield our dad's offices and our family rooms as a minimum?"

Clarence spoke up, "That's a good idea but it would probably be easier to shield an entire house."

General Rowe added, "I'll send my engineer to see you for the specifications and start a program to shield the families while you work out a shield field for the whole town."

"The problem with a field," Melinda stated, "Is that it can be analyzed."

Jennifer beeped once and typed on its screen, "Secretary Jordan says that Zambia has accepted the agreement for two lakes. He also said that he will be coming to Central the day after tomorrow with several ambassadors for project discussions."

Sarah replied, "Thank you Jennifer." Then she tilted her head and started giggling, took a deep breath, and asked, "Do we know if there are any parasites that the aliens have problems with?"

Melinda looked at her sister, smiled sinisterly, and said, "Fleas! Their ship must have to ration water usage so several infestations might slow them down at least."

"I wonder if we could inflict any successful amount of biological warfare on the aliens," General Rowe said in thought. Then he shook himself and continued to Clarence, "I'll get my G-3 to look into it as soon as we shield Headquarters and get your girls to come check everyone working there."

"General," Sarah asked quietly, "Do you think it would be a good idea to shield the generator station and the tank circuits? I have a feeling that the aliens could attack us while we are concentrating on some project."

Clarence answered, "We'll have to see if we can work through the shielding first but after what happened to Wendy, Aiko, and your mother I think it will be a priority to find out."

General Rowe added, "I'll have the engineer plan on doing it as soon as we can stop the peeping Toms just in case. What about this gizmo Sarah brainstormed? How soon will I be able to use it?"

I haven't had a chance to finalize the design yet," Clarence replied, "I needed to ensure that the information didn't get leaked."

A CONCERT AND OTHER THINGS

Charging into the family's Kitchen Edna asked in her usual flippant way, "Mom, there's a concert at the stadium in Des Moines that Lin, Stuart, and I want to go to. Do you think we'll need guards?"

"It doesn't really matter whether you need guards or not," Jackie answered, "The army would have a fine case of high dungeons if you tried going without them."

Edna sighed and replied, "Do you think we can at least get them into civilian clothes and concealed weapons?"

"Why don't you call the Security people at headquarters and see?" Jackie responded. "You're old enough to do your own planning."

Edna hugged her mother and said, "Thanks mom, I'll do that."

Jackie returned her daughter's hug and then held her back at arm's length and asked, "How long have you been pregnant? You glow."

"Since I got Stuart into bed with me," Edna replied blushing.

Jackie pulled Edna close, hugged her again, and instructed, "You can also go get Doctor Janice to check you out."

"Yes mama," Edna replied meekly.

Jackie snorted and told her daughter, "You have never been able to do meek so stop trying." Edna grinned, stuck her tongue out at her mother, and then skipped out of the room.

That evening an army bus arrived at the Vasquez home and twenty young soldiers in civilian clothes got off. The family bus and another civilian bus pulled up to the curb behind the army's vehicle. Edna, Lin, and Stuart came out of the house and boarded the family bus. Some of the soldiers joined them and the rest boarded the other bus then both busses left and an hour later the group was seated for what had been billed as the concert of the year. As the concert progressed, the audience's behavior began to change from fun and frivolity to something ugly and directed. Many of the soldiers began looking about worriedly.

Stuart leaned to Edna and said, "The aliens are using the band and music to program the crowd. We need to get out of here." Edna nodded and told the lieutenant sitting next to her that they needed to leave. The Lieutenant gave a signal for the group to leave when a bottle sailed out of the crowd hitting Edna in the temple. Edna tumbled across the seat in front of her hitting her head on another seat. A loud snapping sound occurred where her left leg had become tangled in the seat she had been sitting in. The back of the seat she had fallen across broke and her abdomen was cut open by the remaining piece.

As if on cue, the crowd erupted into violence chanting, "Kill the witches!" Then it attacked. While Stuart and Lin attempted to help Edna, the soldiers formed a defensive wall trying to protect the trio. Three little girls the Lieutenant recognized as the Vasquez triplets, appeared next to Edna with a bang, and lifted her free of the seating. Looking at Stuart and Lin one of the girls commanded, "Teleport her to the hospital. We'll take care of this." Then she turned, joined hands with her sisters, and faced the crowd. The crowd faltered and seemed to become extremely tired. The attack slowed, people began milling around and sitting or lying down and going to sleep. Twenty minutes later, the three girls let go of each other's hands and Teresa said, "Lieutenant Jackson, Let's get out of here while we have the chance."

The Lieutenant waved her hand and commanded, "Let's get out of here people." The soldiers moved into the aisles and toward the exit. Veronica stumbled over something in the aisle then squealed as one of the soldiers caught her and swung her to his back. Two other soldiers picked up Teresa and Tabatha. A few minutes later, the busses were loaded and driving towards Central.

In the bus, the Tabatha said wearily, "That made me tired, I need a nap." She suited her actions to her mood, slid down in her seat and closed her eyes. The sergeant who had carried her onto the bus smiled then turned to look out the bus window. Tabatha's sisters joined her in slumber for the ride back to Central. At the Vasquez home, the sleeping triplets were carried into their worried mother and put straight to bed.

Jackie asked Lieutenant Jackson, "How did you end up with my triplets when you left here with my oldest daughter and her companions?"

"The character of the crowd changed as the concert progressed," the Lieutenant replied. "My people noticed it and so did Edna. She told us we needed to leave and when she stood up to go, she was hit in the head by a bottle. She fell across the seat in front of her and suddenly your young ones were there. They untangled Edna from the seats, told Stuart and Lin to teleport her to the hospital and then they joined hands and put the crowd to sleep."

Virginia rolled into the room and typed, "Doctor Janice is calling."

Jackie replied, "Put her through please." When the screen lit she asked, "How is Edna?"

"She has a concussion and a broken leg," Doctor Janice replied, "But the main issue is that she may lose her babies. According to Lin, when she fell across the seat in front of her it broke. The seat cut her abdomen open caused her uterus to be torn. The surgeons are working on that."

"If needed could her babies be transferred to host mothers?" Jackie asked worriedly.

"That's probably what will happen but only if Socrates can't put her back together well enough to continue carrying them."

"How long will she be in surgery?" Lieutenant Jackson queried.

"Probably another thirty minutes," Janice replied.

"We'll bring Jackie and her husband to the hospital right away," the Lieutenant responded.

Doctor Janice replied, "Thank you."

Lieutenant Jackson ordered two of her soldiers to stay in the house in case the children woke and needed something then loaded Jackie and Eduardo onto the family bus.

Two hours later, Edna opened her eyes and Jackie worriedly asked, "How do you feel Baby?"

"Mom?" Edna asked weakly.

"Doctor Janice says you're going to be alright," her mother said softly in a worried voice.

"What's wrong mom?" Edna asked alarmed and more alert

"You were hurt and the surgeons had to take your babies out," Her mother replied.

"Out, mom," Edna asked, "What do you mean?"

From the door, Doctor Janice answered, "When you fell across the seat in front of you it broke and your abdomen and uterus were torn open. The surgeons had to take your babies out and move them to host mothers before they could repair you."

"Does that mean I can't have babies now?" Edna asked.

Maryann smiled and answered, "It means that you are going to need lots of rest and yes you will be able to have more babies." Jackie sat in the chair that was next to the bed and held her daughter's hand and the doctor instructed gently, "Let's all leave Edna and her mother alone for a while."

After everyone had left Edna said, "Mom, I'm sorry. We tried to leave. We, we…," then she burst into tears.

Jackie held her daughter's hand to her cheek and smoothed her hair with her other hand and responded, "I know Baby. It's all right, your safe now." When Edna had calmed down Jackie continued, "It seems that someone may have called your little sisters and they rescued you and put an end to the riot as well. They were so tired that your escorts carried them into their beds sound asleep."

Edna asked in confused wonder, "Terry, Tabby, and Vera, how did they find out?"

"We're not sure yet. We'll ask them in the morning. Close your eyes and sleep now, I'm right here." Edna closed her eyes and her mother sat back in her chair with a slight frown on her face.

When the triplets arrived at breakfast, Tabatha asked her father, "Where's mom at?"

"She's still at the hospital with your sister," their father replied. "Are you three awake enough to tell me how you found out about what was happening at the concert?"

"That's easy dad," Veronica answered, "Stuart let us peak at the concert through his eyes. We saw the signs of programming and watched Edna get hit in the head by the bottle." She shrugged a shoulder and continued, "The rest you know."

Eduardo nodded then turned to his head and said, "Stanley, please contact Clarence and tell him about what happened at the concert." The robot beeped once and typed, "Done," on its screen.

Stuart knocked on the breakfast room door and asked, "Can Lin and I come in?"

Eduardo replied, "Certainly. Have you had breakfast?"

"Not yet," Lin replied. "We mostly wanted to thank Teresa, Veronica, and Tabatha for saving us last night. I think when Edna was hit in the head we panicked a little. Stuart told me when we got her to the hospital that the kids had been enjoying the concert through him."

"Tabatha responded, "You're welcome. Won't you join us for breakfast?"

Stanley beeped and typed, "Jackie is calling."

"Put it on screen," Eduardo said

The screen cleared showing Jackie sitting next to a hospital bed with a very awake Edna who said, "Hey twerps, Thanks for fishing us out of trouble last night."

Veronica stuck her tongue out at her big sister and answered, "You would've done the same for us fish face. So don't sweat it."

"How are you doing," Eduardo and Stuart asked at the same time.

Jackie responded before Edna could deny any pain, "The robotic medical staff has her doped to the gills with pain blockers. Doctor Janice said that she will be here on total bed rest for a couple of weeks." She chuckled and continued, "The robot surgeons were very adamant about that. They don't want any stresses on her uterus or abdomen while they heal. Maryann also told me that they want a swimming pool built down here so that they can put Edna in it to do therapy and to treat other people who need it."

"Do we need to call the army engineers," Eduardo asked, "Or is Maryann doing that?"

"Maryann already did that," She answered entering the phones pickup area. "Your wife can stop being a bedside leach and go home for some sleep."

Jackie smiled wanly and said to Edna, "I'll be back later."

Stuart added, "Lin and I will be in to see you in a little while after we eat."

Edna chuckled, holding up her arm so that IV tubing was visible saying, "I'm on a liquid diet for a while. Only problem is that it doesn't have much flavor. See you when you get here."

Jackie said wearily, "I'll be home in a bit dear. We need to discuss the shenanigans our kids are pulling with Wendy and Clarence."

"I agree sweetheart," Eduardo said, "We'll see you shortly."

When the call ended, Virginia beeped and typed, "You three need to finish your breakfast it's school time."

Freddy entered the room, seated himself, and asked, "How did the concert go? Where's Edna and mom?"

"In the hospital," his father replied. "Edna was injured when the crowd was programmed by the aliens and it attacked them."

"Are they okay?" Freddy asked.

"Edna was injured very badly and your mother spent the night with her," Eduardo replied. "She should be home shortly."

"Dad the robots have told Naomi that they have a house ready for us," Freddy said changing the subject. "We'd like you and mom to come look at it with us later today if that's possible."

"We'll see if we can work it in," Eduardo responded. "It will depend on everything else going on."

An hour later Freddy, Naomi, and Winona arrived in Edna's hospital room. Freddy announced their presence saying, "Hi sis, couldn't you have found a better way to goof off?"

"I didn't intend ending up here," Edna replied, "Who would have figured that the aliens would use a concert to program a crowd."

"The aliens?" Naomi queried.

The conversation continued until a robot nurse came and informed the trio that they needed to leave. On their way back to the Vasquez home Naomi became very quiet. After returning and settling into Freddy's room, Winona asked her, "You've gotten very quiet, what's wrong? Why so somber?"

Naomi replied very angrily, "I'm going out there and stop them. They have no right to hurt us. All we've done is deprogram people and that's not enough."

"Hey girl," Winona said, "Were on your side but you've seen the data. That leviathan is bigger than all of us together can do something to."

"But we can't just sit here and wait for them to kill us," Naomi moaned.

"No," Freddy interjected, "But perhaps there is something we can do to at least slow them down until a solution is found."

"Like what?" Naomi demanded her anger still present.

"Like maybe disable or destroy the planet bores they have sent to Pluto."

"Their ore scows too," Winona added seriously.

Freddy said, "We'll need to wait until mom and dad have looked at the house the robots have built for us so that we won't get interrupted."

"Or stopped," Naomi added.

A robot rolled into Freddy's room. It stopped in front of Freddy and beeped. On its screen was typed, "My name is Simon and I am assigned to you. Your parents informed me that they would be available to look at your new house at two this afternoon."

Freddy looked at his bedside alarm clock and said, "Let's go ladies, we have ten minutes to get there before mom and dad." A thunderous bang occurred as the three teleported to the new house. Freddy said, "Change the frowns to happy faces; we don't want my parents discovering what we're planning."

The Vasquez family bus pulled up in front of the new house and Freddy's, Naomi's, and Winona's parents all got out. Jackie looked at the house and called to her son, "Freddy, this isn't a house it's a barn or a barracks, or such."

"The first time I looked at it," Freddy replied, "I thought it was an airplane hangar."

"It's not that large," Naomi said in an exasperated voice.

"It does look large enough for the size family we three have though," Winona added looking thoughtfully at the house. "After all with six kids already and six more on the way, one thing we'll need is space."

"How many robots is it going to take to help keep things straight?" Jackie asked.

"Right now we only have one," Freddy replied. "At least only one that I know about."

Eduardo asked, "Where did the one come from?"

"It rolled into my room at home and said it was assigned to me," Freddy replied. Then turning towards the front door he continued, "Come on inside and look the place over with us."

Inside they discovered a fully furnished home. After they had looked at the dozen bedrooms and other areas of the house and returned to the huge family room, the front door opened and a string of robots rolled in with children and all of their possessions. One of the robots handed Winona a large piece of paper, which turned out to be a layout of the house with names neatly, typed in the bedrooms.

Laughing Jackie said, "It looks like you just moved in."

"So it would seem," Winona answered then called to the children, "Come here kids so I can show you where your rooms are."

One of the robots rolled up to Winona and typed, "My name is Nan-Yi Hi, and I am assigned to you. The children's names have been put on signs next to their bedroom doors."

"We already know mama," Peta, one of her children responded. "The robots showed us."

"Then go check them out and arrange your stuff the way you want it," Naomi said. "All right robots, which one of you is mine?"

A robot rolled up to her and typed on its screen, "I am Beatrix Potter and I am assigned to you."

Jackie asked, "I know who Beatrix Potter was but who was Nan-Yi Hi?"

"She was a Cherokee woman who became a Cherokee tribal war chief and later married a colonial era trader," Winona responded. "She was also known as Nancy Ward."

Eduardo stepped out of the kitchen and said, "I think all of us parents should leave and let these three get used to domestic life."

After the three sets of parents had left Naomi asked, "Beatrix, have the kids done school today?" The robot beeped twice and Naomi continued, "Then get them gathered into the classroom and get started."

"Do we do it now," Freddy asked, "Or after the kids are in bed?"

"Now!" Naomi and Winona said together. Suiting actions to their words the two women shoved some overstuffed chairs together, sat down, joined hands, and held their other hand out for Freddy to take. Freddy looked at them, shook his head pushed his own chair in front of theirs and joined hands with them as he sat down.

In orbit around Pluto were two huge machines. Winona thought, *"God what monsters, how big are those things?"*

"More importantly," Naomi thought, *"How do we destroy something that huge?"*

"I think we need to look inside," Freddy answered.

When the invisible something tried to enter one of the planet bores, they bumped into an invisible wall and stopped. *"What is that?"* Winona thought.

"Offhand I think it is a force field shield of some sort," Freddy thought in answer.

"Does that mean that we can't get through it?" was Winona's thought.

Freddy's replying thought was, *"It means that we go fess up to Mister Stevens and tell him about this and see if he thinks there is a way through it."*

Bringing themselves back to their living room Naomi said, "Whether there is a way through the field or not, we need to go on the offensive. Beatrix, come here please." The robot rolled into the room and Naomi continued, "Please contact Mister Stevens and see if we can see him right now."

The robot beeped once and typed "Done," on its screen. A few moments later the robot beeped again and typed, "Mister Stevens can see you in his office now." A loud bang sounded as the three teleported to Clarence's office.

"Good afternoon Mister Stevens, Thank you for seeing us so soon," Freddy said without preamble. "Did you know that the alien's planet bores have force shields around them?"

"I take it that you've been looking for a way to destroy the planet bores because of what happened to Edna," Clarence replied. "Am I right?" The women looked at him stunned and Freddy blushed and looked at the floor. Clarence continued, "I thought so. We discovered that they have made some humans into spies and are stealing our technology."

"But we need to go on the offensive now," Naomi stated emphatically, "Not when they're down to finishing us off."

"I agree Naomi," Clarence replied, "But we need to be sure that when we attack that we win. I feel that destroying the planet bores is a good idea, however we need to know how to penetrate their force fields first."

"So we need to analyze them somehow," Winona stated thoughtfully, "And do it without actually transporting any equipment out there."

Freddy added, "That means doing it with thought somehow."

"Jason," Clarence said, addressing his robot, "Can your systems detect and analyze a force field?" The robot beeped once and Clarence continued, "Could you join a telepathic trio and detect and analyze a field through them so that they will know the information?"

Jason typed, "That kind of link has not been tried so I don't know if it will work. Yoshi has some additional circuits that may be able to do what you are asking."

Clarence activated his phone and called the Esteban home. When the screen was answered, Hiro looked out of it and asked, "Hi Clarence, do you need something?"

Clarence replied, "I'd like to borrow Yoshi for a little while if I may."

"I have a feeling that it will be a while before I can send it," Hiro responded. "The kids are up to something as usual and have it wrapped up in a link with them." At that moment Karlita, Mika, and Hana entered the room and squealed joyfully to find their father home. He turned and said sternly, "Can't you see I'm talking to Clarence? Where are your manners?"

"We're sorry Daddy," Karlita said in remorse that was over shadowed by joy, "But we wanted to tell you that the planet bores blew up just now."

Clarence asked, "How did you get through the force field screen?"

"We were doing some wave analysis problems in school." Karlita answered, "And Yoshi showed us what some of the wave forms in the house looked like. We asked it if it was showing them in real time and it said yes. We discovered a long time ago that with our contact sets we could join it to our something, so we went to see what we could do."

"What about the ore scows?" Naomi asked.

"We didn't do anything to them," Karlita responded, "Because we were tired after blowing up the planet bores."

Freddy, Naomi, and Winona joined hands and went into the blank stare of telekinetic energy use. "I think they are being taken care of right now," Clarence told Karlita over the phone. "Hiro, I'd still like to borrow Yoshi for a while if it is convenient."

"No problem," Hiro replied, "I'll send it over."

Twenty minutes later Freddy, Naomi, and Winona came out of their link trance. Robin, Wendy's robot rolled into Clarence's office with a tray of snacks and drinks. It typed, "Would something to eat help?"

Naomi replied, "Yes please. Mister Stevens, the ore scows had shields too."

"I suspected that they might," Clarence responded, "And you all can call me Clarence."

"It didn't do them any good," Freddy stated as Robin served him a sandwich and drink. "They were in a line so we stopped the leader and pushed the others into it from behind. There's a big ball of scrap in orbit around Pluto now."

"Good," Clarence said with satisfaction. "After I've talked to Yoshi and probably Hiro's kids I'll let you know how to defeat their force shields. At least until they change them."

"Thank you Clarence," Naomi replied. "We'll get out of your hair and wait for the information."

"Don't discuss anything outside of a shielded space," Clarence added, "We've discovered that the aliens are using mentally adjusted spies to steal our technology."

Back at home, Naomi slumped into an easy chair and closed her eyes. Ten minutes later her eyes snapped open and she said, "I'm going for a walk," and stalked towards the door.

Winona asked, "Would you like some company?" but Naomi didn't seem to hear her.

"Let her be alone for a while," Freddy told her. "I think all of this is overwhelming her a little."

"I hope that's all it is," Winona replied. "She's still pretty angry about Edna."

Naomi walked in thought not paying attention to her surroundings. As she passed by a wooded area, a group erupted from the trees yelling. "Kill the witch!"

Naomi stopped and her anger exploded in a telekinetic surge that knocked all of her attackers back into the trees. She yelled at them, "Leave me alone!" Then she disappeared with a bang and appeared outside the generator station where another group tried to attack her. The army security people there opened fire with special guns that stunned the attackers. Naomi put her access card in the door slot and went inside to one of the control rooms. She stood for several minutes then nodded and said aloud, "This has to end." Then she sat in a chair, and activated the rooms control panels. When the meters showed that the generators were all operating she drew their power and launched her something into space toward the alien scout ship. Inside the scout ship, Naomi's something was attacked by aliens using a machine that fired bolts of electricity at it. In the control room Naomi screamed in pain.

The duty officer for the station and his runner came running into the room and saw her body arched in her seat. The duty officer yelled, "Call the Stevens and tell them we need help now." The runner dashed back out to make the call. A minute later Freddy and Winona exploded into the room on each side of Naomi. Then each grabbed one of Naomi's hands. In space the scout ship exploded. Naomi's body went limp and her mind partners fell to the floor unconscious.

Wendy, Katherine, Aiko, and Doctor Janice appeared in the room with their own loud bang. Doctor Janice asked, "What happened?"

"Ms. Judson came in about fifteen minutes ago and turned on a generator pair to do something," the duty officer replied. "Then she screamed and we found her body arched in what looked like a great deal of pain. Her partners appeared, grabbed her hands then she went limp and all three passed out. Also the generators haven't dropped back to idle since the three passed out."

Robin rolled into the control room and beeped for attention. Wendy asked, "Yes Robin?"

The robot typed, "Arielle told me to tell you that the alien scout ship isn't there anymore. She and her sisters think that it has been destroyed."

Doctor Janice put her fingertips on Naomi's temples for a moment and said, "She isn't here so I suggest that you three go see if these three are still out in space like happened to you when you diverted the Jupiter Body."

"Robin," Wendy said, "Contact Virginia and have it tell Jackie to meet us in Tank Circuit One." Robin beeped. "Doctor," She continued, "Keep them here and make sure they keep holding hands. If you can move the other couches to put Freddy and Winona on do that."

"I notice that they aren't connected," Doctor Janice answered, "Do you want them connected up?"

Wendy shook her head no and replied, "We don't want to change the parameters of their link, so don't. An IV if you think it's needed but nothing else."

A loud bang followed as the three women teleported themselves to the tank circuit control room. Jackie appeared right after the trio. Without preamble she asked, "Do you think there is a chance they are out there?"

"We're about to find out," Katherine replied, "Get comfortable and link with us so we can go see."

At the site where the alien scout ship had been the four women's something discovered four slowly expanding clouds. The largest they determined was the destroyed ship so they ignored it. Wendy thought to the others, *"We'll have to spread and surround them, then compress them back into a single something."*

"Were they joined or did Freddy and Winona come out here afterwards?" Jackie's thought replied.

"That's possible," Katherine thought, *"In any case we need to get them compressed before we lose them. Why don't Wendy, Aiko, and I compress them first and see what happens."*

The something split into four parts and surrounded the drifting somethings compressing them. Jackie thought, *"Bring them closer together and let me insert a tendril into them to connect them."* The Jackie something inserted the tendrils and in the tank circuit her body arched in pain. In space the tendrils became rigid rods.

Wendy's thought asked, *"Jackie are you okay?"*

Jackie's screamed thought was, *"Fire, dear God help, I'm burning up, I can't get away from them."*

Katherine sent a thought to earth, to her husband, *"William, we need help. Bring Eduardo too and join us from tank circuit two. Hurry!"*

Suddenly a large heavy something and two smaller somethings appeared in space. The smaller somethings darted to the something that was their mother and disconnected Jackie's tendrils from them. The smaller somethings seemed to merge with the stricken somethings. The Eduardo something joined with Jackie and the tendril that was in the Freddy something grew and became more substantial. After what seemed like an eternity Jackie/Eduardo something withdrew from the Freddy's. Two new tendrils, one from each of the stricken women's somethings shot out and joined the Freddy something. All three somethings disappeared.

The Clarence something thought, "*I just got a thought from Maryann, they're back in their bodies.*" All of the somethings, large and small vanished.

In tank circuit one Wendy asked, "Jackie are you alright?"

"I have the worst headache you can imagine and can't seem to focus," Jackie replied, "Everything is spinning."

Aiko got up from her couch, placed her hands on Jackie's temples and said, "Sleep my friend." Jackie was asleep in the space of a breath.

Wendy said, "Thank you Aiko. Let's get her to the hospital so Maryann can make sure she's okay."

Wendy, Katherine, Aiko, and their husbands sat in Central's main dining room drinking coffee while they waited for Maryann's report. A nurse robot rolled into the room and beeped for attention. It typed, "I am Clara Barton. Doctor Janice said to tell you to all go home and sleep. She also said that you are not to work tomorrow, that you are to rest. She will explain why tomorrow afternoon."

"Whose kids were those?" Clarence asked.

Clara Barton typed, "Naomi Judson's and Winona Bright-Feather's."

"Are they alright?" Katherine asked.

The robot beeped and typed, "Go rest."

"Come on dear," William said, "We're being evicted and I'm tired." Everyone got up and walked out of the dining room.

The next afternoon everyone was assembled in the main conference room. Maryann entered with a very tired look on her face. She sagged into a chair and said, "Good afternoon."

Wendy asked, "How are they?"

Maryann Janice sighed, pulled a cable from the table and activated the room's projector. An image appeared and she said, "I entered Naomi's mind and found this image. They used some kind of weapon that shot an electric charge at her when she first entered the ship. It burned her mind badly but with several weeks of absolute quiet mentally she will recover. I built a block into her mind and literally turned her off for now. The other two were hit by the weapon also but not as badly. I've turned them off too just to make sure. Their kids should be okay with a couple more days rest. They absorbed a lot of the pain their mothers were feeling. I think the power of love is the only reason their mothers are still alive."

"What about Jackie and Eduardo?" Wendy inquired.

"They are both doing okay, although I think Jackie should rest more…"

"She's rested enough for now," Jackie said from the conference room door. "I saw images of how they destroyed the scout ship while I was connected to them and if the good doctor will allow me to, I will connect and show you what happened."

Maryann asked, "Are you sure. Your mind was stressed very badly by that union." Jackie nodded grimly and the Doctor continued, "Let me set the computer to record then show it one time." Jackie nodded again and connected. The attack on the alien scout ship played itself out and then Jackie slumped in her chair holding her head in pain. The doctor disconnected Jackie, placed her hands on Jackie's temples and put her to sleep. The conference room door opened and robots with a gurney entered. Clarence and Hiro helped lift Jackie to the gurney and she was taken out.

"Well at least we know that they have a weapon that can hurt us badly," Wendy sighed. "What other secrets are you keeping Maryann?"

"Mostly that their kids will be up and about tomorrow," Doctor Janice replied, "But their parents are going to be kept asleep for at least a week. Their grandparents aren't PSI capable, which is good for now. The kids will need to be brought back into their powers slowly to make sure that they don't reinjure their minds."

"How about you?" Katherine asked, "How are you holding up after being into all of their minds?"

"That's why I wanted to talk to all of you," Maryann answered, "I need another human Psi capable doctor here to help. First because I need to rest my mind after treating everyone and secondly because this community is getting too big for me alone."

"Have you asked General Gregory for help?" Wendy asked.

"I sent a request to him but he said that currently he doesn't have any such doctors," Doctor Janice replied. "He also stated that they are contracting most of their medical care out to doctors in Des Moines. All the army has at the moment is a clinic with six non-Psi doctors and support staff."

"Clarence," Wendy said, "I think that we need to get some Presidential help."

"Or maybe some U.N. help," Katherine added.

Clarence nodded, pulled a cable from a table pocket, connected himself and went into the blank stare that indicated he was communicating with someone.

"What about Doctor Wallace?" Aiko asked while they waited for Clarence. "It seems to me that her skills will be needed to help them recover."

"I've alerted her already," Doctor Janice replied, "But they haven't recovered enough to be coherent yet."

"President Harper said he will get you some help," Clarence said a little over an hour later, coming out of his trance. "Some of it may be contact set interface though."

"Thank you," Maryann replied.

"When was the last time you had a good night's sleep, Colonel?" General Gregory asked from the conference room door.

Maryann replied, "It's been a while and I resigned after the revolution."

General Gregory said, "The Senate voted to reactivate you and the President approved it. That's not all, about three days from now a complete army medical evacuation hospital is going to arrive. I understand that two of its doctors have connectors and more of the staff can use contact sets."

"How long will they be here?" Wendy asked.

"They are being assigned here permanently," the General answered. The airfield is going to be upgraded to a full-fledged air force base. In actuality this is going to be the first fully integrated joint forces military installation in the United States. Secretary Treacher will be arriving the day after tomorrow. He says it's to talk to you folks but I've discovered that he has some other plans as well. So Major General Janice, I suggest that you go get some sleep because you're going to need it."

"Major General?" Maryann Janice asked dazed.

"As the hospital director of a multi service hospital," General Gregory told her, "You are going to need the horsepower. That was the other part of the reactivation order. However you are going to be rested when the Secretary arrives to pin it on you."

Wendy asked, "What else did my husband and the President cook up?"

"This facility will be expanded and kept underground," Clarence answered, "But an entirely new facility will be constructed above ground on top of it for the normal care of the military and their families."

"The air base will have the Stilettos and the old B-52s from Minot. The B-52s are going to be run through an upgrade at Boeing and are being reactivated. They have proved so useful that congress decided to ask Boeing to build some new ones as well. In addition, squadrons of Avenger 7s and Stilettos are being assigned here."

Hiro said, "I've heard rumors that the Confederate Air Force is opening a museum at the Des Moines airport. Is there any truth in that?"

General Gregory shrugged and replied, "I haven't heard anything official about that, just rumors."

"Well," Doctor Colonel Maryann Janice said, "Since my concerns are being addressed I think I'll check on my patients and then get some sleep." Her head sank down onto her arms where she had them folded on the conference room table and began to snore softly.

General Gregory grunted softly and said, "I see you remember how to put someone to sleep, Aiko."

Aiko blushed, bowed from her chair, and replied, "The talent has its uses." A gurney and several robots appeared and the Doctor was taken to bed.

"Aside from the hospital, we are also getting some additional ground units from the army, navy, and the marines," the general added. "All of which means that I'm going to be busier than ever managing this three ring circus."

THE GOVERNMENT AT WARP SPEED

After disconnecting from his conversation with Secretary General of the United Nations Jordan and Clarence Stevens, President of the United States, Percival Harper, pressed the intercom button on his desk, his personal secretary entered his office and asked, "Yes sir?"

"Jenny, contact the communications people and set up a joint session of congress and include the cabinet secretaries," President Harper instructed. "I will participate from here and I need to begin an hour from now. Oh, and exclude the press this is to be treated as a state secret for now. Please get the Secretary of defense on the phone for me also."

Startled by the short time requirement, the secretary replied, "Yes sir!" and hurried out. Thirty minutes later a small group of people entered the Oval Office and set up a TV camera and some other equipment.

Exactly one hour after his conversation with Clarence, President Harper began, "Ladies and gentlemen, six months ago I was briefed on a threat approaching the earth. I haven't brought it to you because the Secretary General of the United Nations asked that I keep it secret. After a brief discussion with him and Clarence Stevens I am going to explain that information to you and the Secretary of Defense is going to make some recommendations for you to act upon." The President explained the alien threat and showed what happened to the Pluto observatory and the supply ship then asked Secretary Treacher to explain his recommendations.

"Ladies and gentlemen," Secretary Treacher told his audience, "The main offensive and defensive force to end this threat is again our Psi capable people in Iowa headed by Ms. Wendy Stevens. These same people diverted the Jupiter Body seven years ago. It has been discovered that the aliens have the ability to program humans and turn them into slaves and weapons that they are sending to kill Ms. Stevens and her entire community.

These slaves have not succeeded yet but some of the Psi family members have been injured badly. I am recommending that more forces be sent to General Gregory at Fort Glenn Miller, that the air force station combat aircraft there, and to assist the lone doctor there that connector capable medical people be sent to augment her staff."

A light came on, on the president of the senate's desk and he said, "The chair recognizes the senator from New Jersey."

The senator stood and asked, "Who is the Doctor there now?"

"Former Colonel of the air force Maryann Janice who is both connector capable and Psi capable," Secretary Treacher replied.

Another light blinked and the president of the senate asked, "Is the senator from New Jersey finished?" The senator indicated that he was and the senatorial president said, "The chair recognizes the senator from Idaho."

"I propose a motion," the senator said, "Reactivate Doctor Janice and promote her to a high enough rank to assume command of a multi service medical presence and reassign the needed people from wherever they are currently stationed."

Another senator stood without signaling and yelled, "I second the motion!"

The president of the senate asked, "Is there any discussion?"

"I have a comment," Secretary Treacher said, "Promoting Doctor Janice to a sufficiently high rank to command the recommended medical establishment will require jumping her from colonel to major-general."

"The senator from Idaho responded, "Do it!"

The Vice-President asked, "Does the House concur?"

Over a link from the House chamber the Speaker replied, "The House has voted unanimously in favor of any action that Secretary Treacher recommends pending final approval by the Senate and the President. A second motion has also been voted on to start a federal sales tax. That tax is to expire the day the threat is removed. The money from that tax is to be used to ensure that our Psi resources remain alive and able to accomplish whatever is needed to end this threat."

At the end of Congress's deliberations, President Harper again spoke to saying, "Thank you for your deliberations and I would like the chairpersons of the affected committees and the Secretary of Defense to meet with me as soon as convenient in my office. Mister Vice-President and Mister Speaker of the House I hereby turn your houses back to you so that you may continue your deliberations."

The screens went dark in both houses of congress and in Secretary Treacher's office, he began firing orders at his service chiefs.

At the end of the meeting in Central's main conference room General Gregory had explained the changes that were coming to the area then asked, "Clarence have you worked the bugs out of the detector yet? I'd like to be able to verify that all of the forces coming in are safe."

"Yes but I've been afraid to send it out for manufacture," Clarence replied, "Because of the possibility of leaks in the factories."

"Can we set up a plant here and use soldiers to do the work?" Gregory asked.

"We could but it would take a long time to install the equipment and train the people," Clarence answered. "Longer than what we evidently have available."

General Gregory sighed and said, "I was afraid of that. So we have a problem making sure that everyone coming in hasn't been programmed."

Katherine said thoughtfully, "You know that is the fastest the government has ever done something. Can the forces actually be moved that quickly?"

"The hospital will be here that quickly," the General replied. "Their families will be brought in after we have someplace to put them. The ground units will need somewhat longer and will come the same way, soldiers and equipment now, families later. The marines can move at the same speed as the army units. The air force and navy I don't know about."

"Why navy?" Wendy asked, "There aren't any oceans for ships here."

"Medical, military police, and other services most likely," Clarence answered. "About how many people per day do you expect to descend on us, Tom?"

"The hospital is about four hundred," General Thomas Gregory responded, "An infantry battalion can be upwards of fifteen hundred soldiers. I don't know if other services will arrive at the same time or not."

"Well dear," Clarence said to Wendy, "As much as we'd like to keep our kids out of things, I think we're going to have to use them and have them teach the other triplets how to do it too."

"The others may already know," Aiko said, "Jackie's triplets dealt with the concert crowd the other night and as far as I know none of us adults taught them how."

"That will wear them out pretty badly," Katherine noted. "Will that make them more susceptible to the aliens programming efforts?"

"Maybe we can get this done before a new scout arrives," Hiro put in.

"How would you want to handle new arrivals?" the General asked.

"Get them into some kind of formation is best," Clarence said. "Our oldest did the Guyanan defense forces in about thirty minutes that way."

"I can do that," Gregory replied. "The one thing I don't have yet is arrival dates and times."

"Can you tell them that they need to arrive during daylight?" Katherine asked. "I hate doing things at night when I'm dead tired and I'd like to keep the kids on as regular a schedule as I can."

"I'll do my best," the General responded, "But there are always SNAFUs."

Wendy smiled at Clarence and said, "Then I suggest we go get rested up. Fortunately there aren't any pressing teleports we need to make." With that statement, she rose and headed for the conference room door followed by everyone else.

"Dad," Brenda said as soon as her parents walked in the front door of their home.

"What Kitten?" Clarence asked.

"We were wondering if maybe the robots could set up a small factory to build some of the detectors," Brenda answered. "After all they are doing most of their own construction and repair now."

"They aren't really constructing themselves," Clarence clarified. "They are assembling more robots from parts and assemblies sent here from other places. That does give me an idea though, thanks Kitten." Then to his robot he said, "Jason, meet me in my office." The robot beeped and rolled out of the room.

An hour later several military couriers with guards arrived. Clarence checked everyone to make sure that the aliens hadn't programmed them and sent them out with sealed cases to be delivered to places all over the United States. At supper that evening Wendy asked, "Did you figure out a solution to the problem?"

"I think so," Her husband replied, "But it is going to take a little traveling on my part to make sure that no problems develop."

"That was an awful lot of people, dad," Brenda asked, "How many places are you going to have to go to and how much help are you going to need?"

"What makes you think I'll need help?" her father asked.

"The workers in those plants are going to have to be checked," Arielle responded. "Wouldn't it be best if they didn't know if they were being checked and deprogrammed?"

"Have you kids been eaves dropping?" Wendy asked.

"No momma," Arielle replied, "We asked Jason what was going on and it told us."

Clarence sighed and said, "I've never told Jason to withhold anything from these three. After thinking about it for a moment though, I'm not so sure that they aren't right."

"How would you camouflage your activities," Wendy asked Arielle.

"We think that dad could talk to the bosses about some topic while someone else gives us a tour of the facility," Arielle replied.

"That would cover the shift while you are there," Wendy said, "What about the other shifts?"

"We didn't realize that there could be more than one shift," Sharron replied. "What would you suggest?"

"Actually," Clarence said, "I told the factory owners that I wanted to talk to all of the employees at one time. Most of the businesses are small enough to be able to get all of the employees together."

Brenda said thoughtfully her head tilted to one side as she looked at nothing in particular, "So you broke the device into very small modules to help reduce the chance of theft. You chose small companies to help reduce the number of programmed people in them." Then she looked at her father and asked, "What about housekeeping staff that wouldn't normally be involved in construction but who have access to the construction areas?"

"How about putting an inhibition in the employee's minds about talking about their work as well?" Sharron inquired.

"I hadn't considered the housekeeping staff," Clarence answered Brenda. "A lot of firms use contract housekeeping so I don't know whether something can be done about them or not. What you're suggesting Sharron wouldn't be very ethical but might still be a good idea."

The children's mother said, "A tour of inspection might still be a good idea as camouflage for the scanning operation."

"You sound like this should be a family affair," Clarence said grinning broadly. "Do you realize how much army that is going to take?"

Clarence turned and looked at the robots and Jason beeped, and typed, "I have already notified General Gregory and Colonel Loren."

Clarence said, "Smart aleck."

"Dad," Brenda said, "How many companies are we talking about?"

"Fifteen munchkin, why?" Clarence replied.

"Instead of us visiting all fifteen, wouldn't it be wiser to get the Warrens and Estebans involved too?" Brenda answered. It would be faster and it would help prevent someone from figuring out our itinerary."

"Place the calls please, Robin," Wendy said. Robin beeped.

The phone screen lit and Katherine Warren and Hiro Esteban looked out of it. Katherine as usual asked, "What's up?"

"We've been discussing things and discovered that a meeting would be a good idea," Wendy replied. "When would it be convenient for you all to come over?"

Before either Katherine or Hiro could answer a new window opened and General Gregory said, "Sorry for the interruption, Could we all meet in Central's conference room?"

Clarence responded, "We were just discussing meeting. How about two hours from now and bring the older triplets. Would someone contact Pat and Carroll as well?"

Robin beeped and typed, "I already have."

"That'll give the rest of us time to finish supper before we go," Katherine replied, "See you there."

Two hours later Central's main underground conference room was crowded. General Gregory entered and held a finger to his lips for silence then said, "Robots check this room for bugs."

Jason rolled to where the General could read its screen and typed, "Scanning for bugs requires security robots. I have summoned them."

Two new robots rolled into the room. One stretched its arms out from its sides and began rotating slowly the other moved about the room emitting a beeping sound. The second robot stopped, extended a claw, picked up a book from a corner table. An acrid smoke erupted from the book, the robot put it back on the table, and completed its circuit about the room picking up three other objects and making them smoke like the book did.

Both robots left the room and General Gregory said, "A periodic scan discovered some bugs in my headquarters. Clarence, I gather that you wanted this meeting, suppose you start."

"At my request the General sent me fifteen messengers and guards for them," Clarence addressed the meeting. "I've sent a letter about an electronic assembly I want each company to build without specifics. I specified that I would want to address the entire personnel of each company before the construction information was turned over to them. My family talked me out of doing all fifteen companies on my own. What I'm proposing is for each of our three families visit five companies, deprogram the company's personnel, and then give them the data to construct their module. I own enough interest in each company that there shouldn't be any arguments about their building their piece and shipping them to us and the government. I'd also like to put an inhibition into the employees so that they don't talk about what they are doing to anyone outside of their plant as well as putting the anti-programming block in."

"I take it that you are including Wendy and the oldest triplets," Carroll said, "The same for Aiko and Katherine and you'd like for Pat and I to baby sit the younger kids."

Wendy replied, "That's about it, except that we need security."

"Yes," Katherine said, "In the air as well as on the ground."

"That's where I come into this," General Gregory added. "Each family will leave in its own C-7 and be joined by a squadron of Avengers in the air. I've set things up so that at each location there will be Avengers in the air over you at all times. That and a heavier than normal ground contingent that will travel with you."

"Why heavier than normal?" Katherine asked.

"Clarence asked me to come up with data on how many people in the world have connectors and to see how many of them have been attacked," the General replied. "About forty percent of those with connectors have been attacked and about fifteen percent of those were killed. The result is that I want you all back here as quickly as possible. When were you planning on leaving?"

Clarence answered, "If the planes are ready, tomorrow morning."

Colonel Loren entered the conference room and said, "All three planes will be ready for takeoff at nine in the morning. The Avengers are being refueled now but I would like to have their crews checked before they leave the ground."

"Carroll and I will be there at eight," Pat replied. "If you have them in a formation deprogramming is easier and quicker."

"They'll be ready," Glenn said.

"Anyone have anything else?" General Gregory asked.

Pat said, "Robots have the security teams check every building in Central and all of the rooms here for more bugs. Before destroying them determine their source and send the information to me." All of the robots beeped.

"It'll probably turn out to be a foreign group whose members have been programmed," Carroll said.

"Most likely," Pat agreed, "But if we can discover where they are maybe we can do something about them."

"Dreamer," Wendy said smiling, "Let's go check on Jackie and her tribe then get packed and put ourselves to bed."

The next morning the Dugan's bus and delivery truck arrived at the end of Central's runway where three C-7 Galaxys were parked. Extending along both sides of the runway were three complete squadrons of Avenger aircraft including C-7s for the maintenance people. Their pilots and ground crews were standing at ease in front of their assigned planes. Near the families' cargo planes was a large formation of army soldiers with their equipment. In front of that formation stood General Gregory and Colonel Loren. The bus stopped in front of the officers, Pat stepped out and said, "Good morning."

"Good morning to you as well," Gregory responded, "How do you want to go about this?" Before Pat could answer a captain walked up to the General and spoke to him quietly. "It seems that we have a problem Pat. At the other end of the runway is a very large group of people armed with rockets and other heavy weapons."

"Another witch hunt, huh." "Let's see if we can flush them out. Genghis Kahn come here please." The back of the cargo truck slid open and a robot got out and rolled to the group. Pat asked, "Can your shields handle close range man portable rockets?"

The robot beeped once and typed, "To the limit of our power only. Deflecting each rocket will drain 7% of our usable power."

"I think that will be enough," Pat said. "Drive to the other end of the runway and dismount your team. We will follow a few minutes later. I will get out so the attackers can see me and walk back this way ahead of our bus. Carroll and I will be checking the aircrews as we come back. Captain, Keiyanai Rivera and her team will use the attack on me and my bus as the signal to transport your security forces right behind the attackers. Genghis your job will be to protect me and our bus until the security force is teleported in. Then you will help them break up the attack."

The robot beeped and rolled to the truck. The captain asked, "Can you give me ten minutes to brief my soldiers?"

"Certainly," Pat replied then went into a momentary blank stare. "General, Carroll just told me that she has checked your soldiers so they can begin loading onto the planes. Colonel your crews are checked also." Both men thanked Pat and walked to their places to start things moving. Pat got back on the family bus and Pat asked, "Are you ready kids?" His and Carroll's triplets and Jackie's six-year-old triplets all nodded. Pat added, "When we get to the end of the runway and start back this way, there's going to be some shooting but the robots will block anything aimed at us and the army is going to be sent to stop anything from happening. Our only job is to deprogram any of the army and air force that are programmed. Driver, head for the other end of the runway."

Genghis Khan and its security team had formed a line across the far end of the runway by the time the family bus arrived. The bus turned around, Pat got out and started walking back the way they had come. Behind him the family bus followed closely enough to shield him as much as possible. Behind him he heard several rocket explode and a machine gun begin firing. "Stuff's coming over the robots shield," Carroll yelled. "Get back in the bus!" At that moment an explosion pushed the bus sideways leaving Pat without any protection. Behind them three of the ten robots had been destroyed leaving a hole in the defense shield the robots had running. Rifle fire sliced through the opening hitting Pat. The bus swerved back in between Pat and the hostile fire, Carroll jumped out and dragged her husband back into the bus. The pilots and ground crews at the sides of the runway had taken cover. Two of the pilots had scrambled into their planes and started them up. They moved their planes so that they were facing the attackers and opened fire with their plane's machineguns. Then as suddenly as the attack had begun the only sound was the turbines of the two jets.

"Mom, take dad and teleport to the hospital," Caleb one of her sons said, "We'll finish this then get the driver to take us to the hospital. Driver continue down the runway at walking speed."

Carroll looked at her triplets and Jackie's and asked, "You're sure?" All six children were looking out the bus windows and didn't seem to hear her. She hugged her husband and disappeared with a bang. Along the sides of the runway the pilots and ground crews were standing back up and milling around checking each other out. As the bus drove slowly down the runway an occasional pilot or ground crew would collapse causing those around that person to rush to make sure the person was okay.

When the bus reached where the cargo planes where, it stopped. Caleb stepped off and walked to Colonel Loren and three other family busses stopped there. Wendy asked, "Caleb where are your mother and father?"

"Daddy got hurt when the fighting broke out at the other end of the runway," Caleb replied, "Mom took him to the hospital. Colonel all of the people beside the runway are safe now. Ms. Wendy, mom said she will contact you by telepathy or the robot network. She also said you are to go do your trip not stay here."

Wendy went into a blank stare for a moment then she told Caleb, "She just told me that you are to all go to the hospital to be checked to make sure you are alright. So let's all do as she asked."

"Yes ma'am," Caleb responded and got back in his family's bus, which left the runway.

"Glenn, shall we get loaded?" Wendy asked.

Glenn bowed slightly, waved a hand towards the open cargo ramp of the plane, and said, "After you."

Wendy replied, "Thank you kind sir." She walked into the plane followed by the family bus and the ever-present robot security truck.

Ten minutes after the families boarded their respective cargo planes, the planes pointed their noses down the runway. As each C-150 took off twelve Avenger 7 fighters followed it into the air. A short while later the planes with the maintenance people took off also. Each flight and maintenance plane went in a different direction; one to Las Angeles, one to New York, and the third to Miami.

In the hospital, Pat was taken immediately to surgery and robotic surgeons repaired his wounds. Maryann entered the hospital dining room, which seemed to be the favorite waiting place of the various families, and told Carroll, "He's out of the woods and will be alright in a couple of days. He had some shrapnel in his back and two bullets lodged in his left shoulder. The kids have been checked and are fine. You on the other hand look like you need some rest."

"I don't know how much of that I'll get because we're running out of families to take care of the kids."

"I've taken care of that," Maryann said, "If you'll remember there are fifty PSI families in this town besides yours and the other four. Well I put the word out that we needed some help managing children and got deluged with people willing to help. In fact, your charges and your children are already under other care so you go home and get some sleep. It's either that or I'll do an Aiko on you."

Carroll chuckled and replied as she stood, "You would too, mean souled person that you are."

"Yes I would. Except I don't think I could resist if Aiko were doing it. She's much more powerful than I am."

Carroll walked wearily to the door and said, "Those three are more powerful than any of us except maybe our children. See you later."

Maryann followed Carroll out of the room and went to check on her charges.

EARTHQUAKE

At the Las Angeles airport three hours later the Stevens's C-150 landed and taxied to a restricted area. Nine of the Avenger 7 combat planes followed it to the ground. Three more Avengers continued to fly above the airport and city. The C-150 opened its cargo door and the family bus, their security truck, and several army vehicles departed. More soldiers and robots got off the plane and spread out to secure the plane and its surroundings.

As the bus rolled towards their first destination, Arielle asked, "Dad, which company are we going to, Belkor or Flooke?"

"We're going to go to both of them," Her father answered. "How did you know which companies I have an interest in, Squirt?"

"I asked Jason about electronics companies that could build our device," Arielle answered, "Then I checked them out and discovered that you are a major investor in them."

Suddenly the bus swerved then fell with frightening speed. Around the bus, everything was shaking. Something very large and very hard hit the front of the bus caving its roof in onto the driver robot, Wendy, and Clarence knocking them unconscious. A triple bang occurred as the triplets teleported out of the bus to the ground beside the highway. As suddenly as it began the earthquake stopped leaving an eerie quiet. The area looked as though it had been blasted by bombs. The three girls walked to the edge of a large fissure that had opened and swallowed the section of the freeway that their bus was on. They held hands and a mysterious something reached into the fissure, wrapped around their bus, pulled it from under a large piece of freeway and lifted it out of the crevasse and set it a safe distance from the edge. Then the something lifted the other trapped vehicles one at a time and set them beside the bus. The security robots got out of their truck, which had barely missed falling into the fissure, and began extracting injured people from bent vehicles. The army medics administered what aid they could.

The family robots, Robin and Jason, moved from their storage spaces in the bus towards the front where Wendy and Clarence were trapped and unconscious. Using their scanning powers, they determined that they were still alive. Then they began using tools built into their claw hands to cut the couple free. The noise attracted the soldiers' attention and they rushed to the bus to help. Soon Wendy and Clarence were freed and their wounds were being treated. While they were being treated, they regained consciousness and asked about Arielle, Sharron, and Brenda. A medic told them that the girls were okay and that they were using their powers to rescue people from the fissure that had opened under the freeway.

Wendy grabbed the arm of a sergeant and said with all the urgency she could muster, "Protect my children, hurry!"

Clarence added, "There may be programmed people here. Also if they have been using their powers they will be very hungry so find them something to eat." Then both of them slipped back into unconsciousness.

Somewhat startled by the Steven's urgency the sergeant called for some more soldiers to help. He sent one soldier to a truck to get a box of rations and water can. No sooner, had the soldiers established a security perimeter around the children than the cry of, "Kill the witches," rose from the people in the area. Ten robots appeared among the soldiers as if by magic and the crowd bumped against their force shields unable to reach the girls. The soldier with the box of rations opened it and placed opened ration bars in the hands of the extremely focused trio, which they seemed to eat automatically never losing their concentration on the huge section of concrete freeway they were lifting from the fissure. The soldier gave each girl a drink of water between the bites of ration bar they were so absently eating. The girls had no sooner set the concrete section safely beside the fisher when an aftershock knocked everyone down. Across the freeway, a tank in a chemical plant exploded, shooting burning liquid high into the air. The girls looked at the fire, and as suddenly as it had started, it went out. The girls turned back to the fissure and began lifting more bent and broken vehicles to safety. The crowd regained its feet and milled about uncertain about what had happened. The cry of "Kill the witches!" resumed sporadically, but was crushed by other bystanders with fists and whatever clubs they could find. Soon the crowd was in full riot. The sisters teleported the last vehicle in the fissure to safety, then another aftershock caused a bus to begin sliding backwards towards the fissure. Grimly the sisters linked again and stopped the bus from sliding further but did not have enough energy left to lift it to safety.

Arielle yelled, "Help, we don't have enough power to lift the bus." The sergeant ran to the family bus and knelt beside the two people lying there and then the bus was picked up by a mysterious something and set on level ground. When the bus, which was the last vehicle trapped by the quake, was safe the girls all but collapsed where they had been standing.

Sharron reached wearily into the ration box and pulled three bars out and handed one to each of her sisters. When they finished eating them Sharron asked, "Think we can make it to the bus and see how mom and dad are?"

The sergeant and two other soldiers approached and the sergeant said, "Everyone seems to be safe for now so let's get you and your parents to a hospital and away from the riot. The robots said they are getting low on power too." The girls got shakily to their feet and staggered in the direction of their parents. The soldiers each picked up a girl and carried them to their parents.

When the soldiers put the girls down near their parents, Arielle looked at their bus and asked, "Can our bus be driven?"

Captain Bronson answered, "We haven't checked but we have other vehicles that we can use."

Having regained consciousness again, Wendy said, "I think she's thinking about the arsenal in the back of the bus. We can't leave it here."

"I wasn't aware that you had weapons in the bus," the Captain replied, "Looking at it though, it has less damage than I would have thought it should have considering what crushed the front in."

"It's fairly heavily armored," Clarence, who had come to also, said. "It is the third bus for this family. When Wendy was rescuing kidnapped women her team was fired on by people from a drug factory in Florida."

Captain Bronson nodded, turned to his senior Sergeant and instructed, "See if the bus is still drivable. If it isn't transfer all of the weapons to our vehicles and let's get these people out of here."

"I already checked that sir," Sergeant Mateo replied, "The driver is intact and said it is drivable but because of the open front suggested that it take the van to the airport while we take everyone else to the hospital."

"That sounds like it will work," the Captain said, "Tell the driver to do that and get everyone loaded up. Call Lieutenant Nichols and tell her to expect the bus."

Once everyone was loaded into the army trucks, the security robots began loading into their truck. The rioters seeing a chance to attack surged toward the vehicles. The triplets saw what was happening, joined hands, and the rioters fell to the ground fast asleep. Wendy noticed her girls holding hands and asked, "How long will they sleep?"

Arielle turned to her mother and replied, "We're not sure because we're so tired right now. At least long enough for us to escape."

Arielle's father chuckled weakly and said, "That's all we can ask for, Squirt. Captain, what do you say we get this show on the road?"

Captain Bronson smiled and said, "You heard the man, people. Load up let's move." As the last vehicle drove out of sight of the sleeping rioters, they began waking up. With their targets gone, they turned to helping each other.

At the California Hospital Medical Center, things were definitely a mess. Medical people were trying to organize patients by how badly they were injured. Many with only minor injuries were pushing, shoving, and demanding to be taken care of first. The security robots got out of their truck and charged into the crowd forcing then to back away from the doctors and nurses. No one noticed three girls climb out of one of the army trucks. Suddenly silence reigned and Arielle and her sisters used their powers to freeze every voice box in the crowd. The girls walked to the front of the crowd and Arielle said in a loud angry voice with all of the adult authority she could muster, "You will all keep quiet and follow the instructions of the doctors and nurses or the robots and the army will remove you from the area and place you under arrest."

"What makes you think you can make us little girl?" a man yelled from the crowd. The man floated into the air and was set down between four security robots. When the man attempted to leave that area one of the robots extended its arm and a spark jumped from the robot's claw to the man.

Arielle looked at the crowd and added, "If you behave and follow instructions you will be seen more quickly but the more seriously injured must be taken care of first. Then she turned to one of the hospital's nurses and said, "Please tell the crowd how to sort themselves to be treated. We have some army medics who can treat the minor cuts and scrapes as well as help assess those who need greater care. Our parents are in that truck and they are badly injured."

"Who are you?" the nurse asked in amazed wonder.

"I'm Arielle Stevens," Arielle answered, "And these are my sisters Brenda and Sharron."

"Thank you," the nurse said, "Now if you'll excuse me we'll get things sorted out and check on your parents." The nurse turned to the other medical staff that was standing there looking stunned and continued, "Would you two doctors set up a triage station and you three nurses help them. Use the army medics to help. Jack," she told an orderly, "Get two gurneys and get the injured people out of that truck. The army medics can tell you their condition."

"Captain Bronson," Arielle asked, "Do you have some more of those ration bars?"

The captain reached into a pocket and withdrew six bars and handed each girl two," then said, "I'll see about something to drink to go with those in a minute." The girls thanked the Captain and began eating.

Three hours later in a room on an upper floor Captain Bronson was explaining, "So after the robots cut the front of the van off so we could get to you, your girls rescued the rest of the vehicles trapped in the fissure, put out a fire that ignited in the chemical plant across the highway when an aftershock hit. Then they had to deal with a riot there and another one here. They've been devouring ration bars like there is no tomorrow." He turned and looked at the chairs that had been shoved together which contained three girls who were wrapped in hospital blankets and sound asleep. "The people at the airport contacted me and told me that the damaged bus made it back and that they are having a replacement flown in and that it will be here in the morning."

The hospital room door opened and a nurse asked, "Can I come in?" When permission had been given she continued, "I'm Agnes Brown, your girls were fantastic at helping us straighten out the mess we had downstairs. And your robots with their ability to show us patient medical information. I never imagined anything like it."

"After your girls dumped that first idiot between your robots and they shocked him into behaving things really went well," Captain Bronson inserted.

Clarence chuckled and Wendy said, "Now I understand why they are asleep. I hope they haven't over stressed their minds."

"When will we be able to get out of your hair?" Clarence asked.

"That will be up to Doctor Jordan," the nurse replied. "Probably tomorrow or the day after."

At the door, a beeping sound was heard and a robot rolled into the room. Wendy said, "This is Robin one of our family robots. Jason, our other family robot, probably isn't far and the other ten are our security detail. Robin, have you all gotten recharged?" Robin beeped.

"I do have a question," the nurse said, "With their claws, how do they manage to tie shoelaces together?"

Laughing, Wendy replied, "Robin, show her what your hands have in them." The robot held up one of its claws and suddenly it blossomed into a bouquet of small manipulators and tools. Wendy asked, "How did you discover their propensity for playing tricks on people?"

"We had a guy in ER a couple of hours ago who was driving doctor Bailey nuts. A robot passed by them, paused a moment, then continued on its way. The doctor's pager went off and he told the man to excuse him and walked off. The man tried to follow him and fell flat on his face because his shoes were tied together."

Robin beeped and typed, "There was nothing wrong with the man and the doctor couldn't do his job so I tied his laces together then triggered the doctor's pager."

The nurse laughed, and Wendy said, "We'll forgive you this time Robin, but do try to stay out of trouble."

The robot snapped a fancy salute to Wendy and typed, "Yes ma'am."

"I need to get back to work," the nurse said smiling. "Doctor Jordan should be in to see you in a while. He'll be able to tell you when you can get discharged."

Captain Bronson added, "I'll leave you to rest and get some myself." Both the Captain and the nurse left the room closing the door behind them. Wendy noticed other soldiers and robots in the hall as the door closed.

Wendy grimaced and Clarence said quietly, "They're just doing their jobs. Leave it be."

Wendy looked at her sleeping girls and replied, "I know dear I just hate being wrapped in cotton all of the time. I hope the girls are okay."

Clarence chucked, "Food is going to be in great danger when they wake up from the descriptions of all that they did. I'll bet they burned through those ration bars like they didn't exist."

"I know," Wendy replied softly, "Well we'd better try to sleep too. If only my legs didn't hurt so badly."

"Having a freeway in your lap will do that," Clarence replied, "I hurt too. Thanks to the armor in our bus, at least nothing got broken. Good night love." Both closed their eyes and did manage to sleep.

Nearly a dozen hours later sun streamed in the hospital room windows, the door opened, a doctor stepped in and was confronted by Robin. Robin typed, "Who are you and what do you want?"

The doctor answered, "I'm Doctor Jordan and I'm here to check on my patients. You must be Robin. Don't bother trying to tie my shoe laces, I wore loafers today."

A young and very sleepy sounding girl's voice said, "Let him alone Robin. He needs to check on mom and dad."

Another young voice asked, "Where's the bathroom?"

Doctor Jordan replied, "Over here in the corner by the door."

Brenda climbed out of the chairs she had slept in, went to her mother's bed, shook her to wake her up, and said, "Mom, the doctor is here."

Wendy opened her eyes, looked at her daughter and said, "Thank you." Then she turned her head towards the doctor and said, "Good morning doctor."

"Good morning," Doctor Jordan replied. The door to the room opened and robots laden with trays of food rolled in. Chuckling, the doctor continued, "I won't take long. I just need to check your legs to make sure there won't be any problems. Then I'll leave you alone to eat. What is your robot's name?"

Wendy replied, "This one is Robin. The other family robot which I haven't seen in a while is Jason."

"Jason has been helping in the emergency room all night," Doctor Jordan said. "Robin can you give me an x-ray image of your mistress's left leg at this angle?" The doctor indicated the angle he needed with his pen and an image appeared on Robin's screen. "Thank you," the doctor said, "Now I need the same image angle for the other leg." The robot beeped and rolled to the opposite side of Wendy's bed. "Now let's do the same for your other person," Doctor Jordan continued. He made some notes in Wendy and Clarence's files and told Wendy, "By rights you should have lost both legs and possibly your life. I understand that your bus was reinforced so that it stopped the freeway piece short. You're going to require surgery on your legs, both of you. Where the bruising is the worst, you have dead muscle tissue. If it isn't removed and new muscle grown in it will cripple and then kill you anyhow. I've talked to Doctor Janice and she told us to ship you back to Iowa by the fastest means possible because she has the facilities and surgeons to do the job. So in about two hours your new bus is going to arrive, we're going to put you in it with one of our nurses and get you to the airport as fast as possible."

Robin beeped for attention and typed, "Leave me or Jason, security robots, and the army here with the girls to complete the mission."

"Clarence," Wendy said loudly enough to wake him up, "The Doctor needs to tell you something and Robin has a proposal." Clarence read Robin's screen and the doctor explained the medical problems. Clarence thought for a moment then asked, "Is there a phone line in here?"

"Yes," the Doctor replied, "It's in the panel on the wall by your bed. Let me get you a phone."

"No need," Clarence said quickly to forestall the doctor's efforts. "Robin, please contact Mark James at Belkor and put him on your screen." The robot moved to the head of Clarence's bed, stretched its arm and plugged a connector into the panel. It released a cable from its arm and rolled to where Clarence could see its screen.

After a moment a sandy haired man looked out of the screen and said, "Good morning Clarence. What happened? We expected you yesterday."

"Your little earthquake got me," Clarence replied, "That's why I'm calling." Clarence beckoned his children with a wave of his hand and continued, "Let me introduce Arielle, Brenda, and Sharron my oldest set of triplets. They're going to fill in for me since I was injured and won't be able to make it myself. Can you secure your end of this call?"

Mister James reached out and did something in front of him and said, "My end is secure." Robin beeped and typed, "Secure," across the bottom of its screen.

"Mark the main reason for our visit I can't go into detail about just yet," Clarence continued. "There are people who have been subconsciously programmed to steal information and technology. My kids can detect those people and deprogram them. Don't punish or otherwise single them out because they had no control over or knowledge of being programmed. When my girls arrive they will have robot security, an army detachment, and an additional robot that will have a presentation for you and the members of your company. While it is making the presentation the girls will do their thing. The people who were programmed will go to sleep for about an hour."

"I see one problem," Mark said, "That quake has about a third of my people dealing with home repairs and injuries of their own."

"When do you expect to have all of your people back to work?" Clarence queried.

"Probably about three days," Mister James responded.

Arielle asked, "Can I make a suggestion, dad?"

"If you've got an idea on how to fix this squirt let's have it," Clarence told his daughter.

"Switch the order of the visits around," Arielle replied, "So that we do Belkor and Flooke last."

Clarence looked back at the man on the robot's screen and said, "Mark We'll set a new date so you can get things put back together. I'll send a messenger to you with the details."

"I'll be waiting," Mark James replied and the connection was broken.

"Doctor, what you have just heard is to be treated as highly classified information," Clarence said. "Now if you can give me an hour and send in Captain Bronson, you can ship us back to Iowa."

The doctor replied, "Good that will give me time to coordinate with Doctor Janice." The doctor left the room and a few minutes later Captain Bronson entered the room.

"Captain," Clarence said, "We're changing plans, Wendy and I have to go back to Central for surgery. You, the kids, security robots, and Jason are going to visit the other three companies then come back here at a later date."

"How are you planning to get back to Central?" the Captain asked.

"A second plane brought a new van to replace our broken one," Clarence replied. "The van will come here pick us up and take us to the airport. There Wendy and I will be put in the second plane with a nurse while you and the kids board our plane. We'll be taken to Central and the kids will carry out our mission in revised order."

The room door opened and Jason rolled in, and typed, "The new van has arrived. I have notified the planes of the change in plans. Colonel Loren said he will make sure everything is ready."

Wendy replied, "Thank you Jason. Kids I want you to link with me so I can give you some information on how to go about things."

The four went into a blank stare and after a minute, Arielle said, "Doing those things shouldn't be difficult mostly time consuming." Then Arielle turned and grinned at Captain Bronson and said, "Better make sure that you have a large supply of those ration bars. The three of us are going to be constantly hungry."

"I've restocked on those," Captain Bronson replied, "But I also found a small vehicle that has a refrigerator unit and stocked it with a wider variety of meals for you."

"Thank you," Wendy said, "I know that the ration bars are nutritious but they don't have appetite appeal. That and a constant diet of ration bars can't be good for growing children."

A nurse entered the room and asked, "Are you all ready to go?"

Wendy answered, "Yes we are. You are the nurse who was here earlier but I didn't get your name."

"I'm Kathy Masters," the nurse replied. "There is a new bus downstairs at the ambulance entrance that I figure must be yours. It has a robot driver and the army is guarding it like Fort Knox."

"Then that means it's time for us to be going," Wendy answered, "Are you the nurse that is going with us?"

"Yes ma'am."

"She's safe mom," Brenda said, "We've been checking everyone who has come in."

"Thank you dear," her mother replied. "Captain, what are we waiting for?"

"Actually," Nurse Masters said, "We're waiting on the doctor to bring your files."

A small hole appeared in the hospital window and the Captain was knocked forward, onto Clarence's bed. He gasped for breath and croaked, "Sniper, get down!" Nurse get everyone into the hall."

While the Captain was gasping instructions, Sharron, Arielle, and Brenda joined hands. From the roof of the building across the street, a man with a rifle floated into the air. The rifle was telekinetically pulled from his hands and he began to sink towards the ground. Clarence instructed, "Our kids have the sniper, check Captain Bronson."

The Nurse answered, "Yes sir," and moved to check the Captain who was gasping for breath.

"I'll be alright as soon as I catch my breath," Captain Bronson gasped as he stood up straight. "My vest kept the bullet from penetrating. It just knocked the wind out of me. I'm probably bruised but that can wait. We need to get the blinds closed and then get everyone downstairs and into the van."

"I'll see if the doctor has the records ready," the nurse said and started to leave the room.

When she reached for the door it was opened in front of her and the doctor handed her a record tile saying, "Get these people out of here there is trouble headed this way." There were several orderlies with two gurneys behind the doctor. They entered the room and moved directly to the beds to load Wendy and Clarence for transport. In a few minutes everyone was hurrying down the hospital hall to an elevator that was being held open by soldiers. Security robots appeared from side halls and entered one elevator and the people entered another.

At the ambulance entrance the new family bus was backed up to the door and soldiers had created an aisle from the elevators to the bus. The Stevens family was rushed from the elevator and into the bus, soldiers and robots climbed into their own vehicles and the whole procession of vehicles drove away headed for the airport. Behind them a riot boiled between police and looters.

At the airport, Wendy called her daughters to her and hugged them, then told them, "Be careful and make sure you listen to Captain Bronson, Ivan, and Jason.

Clarence thought to his daughters, "*Contact us telepathically or by robot if and problems occur.*" Aloud he said, "Good luck kids. Make us proud."

WENDY'S RASCALS

The Stevens oldest triplets solemnly watched their parents get loaded into the second cargo plane, and then waved as the plane taxied to the runway and took off.

Captain Bronson said gently, "It's time for us to go too."

The girls walked with the Captain into their plane quietly. When they entered the passenger compartment, Brenda asked, "Jason who is taking care of Samantha, Rodger, and Elizabeth?"

The robot typed, "Ms. Jackie is out of the hospital and taking care of them."

"Contact Virginia and ask it to get Jackie and Doctor Janice to work with them on thinking into mom's and dad's legs to make the muscles grow back and heal themselves."

Jason asked, "Why do you think that will work?"

"She's right," Sharron said, "When I cut myself or get a scrape I think it healed and it goes away."

Arielle added, "Anything that helps mom and dad is worth trying and I think that our sisters and brother would be the best ones to do it."

Jason typed, "I have sent your request to Virginia and to Socrates so it can tell Doctor Janice. We will land in Tucson, Arizona in just over an hour. I suggest that you eat a snack and rest so that you will be ready."

Glenn stepped into the passenger compartment and said, "While Jason finds you something to eat, how about briefing me on what's going on and how I can help."

"When we land in Tucson," Arielle began, "We're supposed to go to Winston Electronics. Jason will make the Holo presentation to the employees while we deprogram anyone who has been suborned by the aliens. Then we are supposed to program a block into all of the employees against the aliens and to prevent any leaks."

"After that the owner or manager should take us on a tour of the facility," Brenda added. "What they don't know is that the tour is supposed to let us check for any stray people who didn't attend the main meeting, check, deprogram and program them also."

Sharron concluded, "We should be finished and headed back to the plane in three hours."

"Where do we go from there?"

"Denver Colorado, Spokane Washington, then back to Las Angeles," Arielle answered.

"Did anyone say anything about layovers? You three are going to need to rest before you do your thing each time."

Sharron answered, "We're doing one a day with day between and we will sleep here in the plane for safety."

Jason rolled into the passenger compartment with meal trays for the girls. It beeped and typed, "Do you have time to eat with the girls? I will bring you a lunch if you do."

"Thanks Jason," the Colonel replied, "But we'll be landing shortly so I need to get back to the cockpit." He looked back at the girls and asked, "When is your birthday?"

Arielle said, "Next month."

"Then I need to remember to get you all presents," Glen said, stood up and went back to the cockpit.

The Galaxy landed at Davis-Monthan air base in Tucson Arizona and was led to a parking area. When the engines had been shut down and the nose of the plane had opened the security robots and Captain Bronson's soldiers set up a perimeter around the plane. The family bus pulled out and stopped because a large truck with pallets containing huge pumps pulled up in front of it and stopped. A staff car bearing a Major General's placard pulled up also. The general got out of his car and stalked towards Colonel Loren and the bus. "Colonel," he said, "I'm General Wellesley and I'm commandeering your plane for a new Mission."

Colonel Loren asked, "Sir are you aware that this plane is assigned to a special Mission and that to change that Mission you have to have the President's authorization?"

"I didn't ask for any hogwash from you Colonel," the General said becoming angry. "That plane belongs to the air force." Several of the Avengers taxied and stopped next to the cargo plane but the General paid them no attention. The triplets had gotten off the bus and joined Colonel Loren and the General, and Wellesley exploded, "Kids! What in the," and let out a stream of invective that would make most adults blush.

Suddenly he stopped and his eyes bulged out as Arielle asked politely, "Would you please refrain from using such language in front of us?"

"General," Colonel Loren explained quietly, "These kids are part of the special Mission. We anticipate being on the ground about five hours then," he waved at the fighters, "We and our escort will be departing for Denver. The mission is need to know unless these children decide that you need the information in the performance of your Duties."

"General," his driver called and held up the handset of a telephone, and continued, "Secure call sir."

The General Wellesley snarled, "Wait here," and stalked to his car. A few minutes later he yelled, "Colonel, get over here!"

Colonel Loren walked to the General's car and asked, "Yes sir?"

The General Wellesley shoved the phone handset at him and said in controlled anger, "The President wants to talk to you."

Colonel Loren accepted the handset and asked, "How can I help you Mister President?" He listened a moment and answered, "Jason is Clarence Stevens' robot and it is with us on the plane. Mr. and Ms. Stevens were injured in the quake in Las Angeles and sent back to Iowa for treatment. Their six year old triplets are completing the mission for their parents." Again he listened and answered, "I'm sorry sir, and there are too many unauthorized people in the area at the moment for me to be able to answer that." The Colonel listened a moment longer and handed the handset to the General and said politely, "The President wishes to speak to you sir."

"Yes Mister President," The General answered the phone respectfully," he listened and after a few moments continued, "I understand sir; I'll see that everything is taken care of." He reached into his staff car and hung the phone up. With a sigh he said, "Well, I guess there are missions that are even higher priority than mine."

"Can I ask what that mission is, General?" Arielle asked. The three girls had quietly joined the General and Colonel Loren.

"There was a mining disaster in Montana," he answered, "And those pallets contain huge pumps because the mine is filling with water."

"Colonel," Sharron asked, "What is the added flight time for a round trip to Malstrom Air Base in Great Falls?"

"It would add about six hours including the time on the ground to unload," Glenn replied.

"General is there an airstrip of some sort near the mine?" Sharron asked. "Or is there a highway or bulldozed strip that can be used to drop the pumps near the mine? That shouldn't affect what we're doing a great deal because we can change crews in the air."

General Wellesley looked from the girls to Colonel Loren and asked, "How old did are these girls and how can you change crews in while in flight?"

"Six going on sixty and we travel with three full crews at all times," Glenn replied. "She has a point too. Those look like drag pallets, so if we can get the people at the mine to bulldoze a clear strip of ground a couple of hundred feet long and arrange a midair refueling when we turn for Denver maybe we can help after all."

General Wellesley sat in his car and picked up a phone handset and instructed, "Major I need a drag chute rigging crew out here at this plane ASAP. I also need you to contact the mine and get them to bulldoze a strip big enough to let a C-150 come in and drop the pumps right at the mine. When you've done that get a refueling plane scheduled for when the C-150 and its escort turns south headed for Denver. Get fuel trucks out here to top this bird and its escorts off." When he hung up his phone he asked, "Why don't all of you come into my office where it is cooler?"

Colonel Loren turned towards the plane and yelled, Sergeant Jenkins!" Then he waved an arm for the sergeant to join them. Sergeant Jenkins trotted over and joined the group and the Colonel continued, "We're going to help with a mine disaster in Montana. As soon as the riggers get here with drag chutes load them for a low level drop."

"Yes sir," Sergeant Jenkins responded and went to the truck to see how the pallets were loaded. A few minutes later he walked back to the General's car, and said, "Sir those pumps can't be drag dropped. Their design is such that their center of gravity is too far off center."

The General sighed and replied, "Thank you Sergeant. Well I guess we're back to waiting on another plane."

Arielle entered the conversation saying, "Sergeant Jenkins, load the pumps on the plane. Colonel, do you remember what mom and the others did at Minot?"

"I remember," Glenn replied, "But I don't think the three of you are strong enough to put a C-150 on the ground someplace."

"We're not going to land the plane, just the pumps," Sharron answered. "General can you get us images of the exact locations where the pumps need to be used?"

"How can three young girls do what you are asking?" the General asked.

Arielle replied sweetly, "Look out your window."

The General looked out his car's side window and swore; looked back at the girls and asked, "Would you put us back on the ground?"

Brenda replied as sweetly as her sister, "We are on the ground?"

Colonel Loren was doing his unsuccessful best not to laugh and General Wellesley demanded, "What's so funny Colonel?"

Colonel Loren took a deep breath to get his laughter under control and replied, "Their mom is Wendy Stevens, formerly Wendy Winston. When they were dealing with President Hillman and his crowd they landed this very C-150 that we're using in the parking lot at the concentration camp north of Minot and about eighteen hours later hoisted it back into the air behind a refueling plane. These girls are probably as strong as their mother was then so I think they could very well place the pumps."

Brenda pulled at the Colonel's sleeve and asked, "Do you have any of Captain Bronson's ration bars on you? I need something to eat."

Glenn said, "I don't but we can get you back to the plane and give you a proper meal once we are in the air. That's the drawback to using their Psi powers they burn calories faster than you or I would in a week of hard continuous exercise."

General Wellesley looked thoughtful for a moment then picked up his car phone again and when it was answered said, "Major I want you to get three large banana splits and put them in a freezer container and get them out here to the C-150. I have some hungry girls who are going to help save a bunch of miners in Montana."

Glenn told Sergeant Jenkins, "Go ahead and load the pallets as they are rigged now and send Jason over here please."

The General asked, "Whose Jason?"

Arielle replied, "Jason is our father's robot."

Jason arrived and Glenn told it, "The girls are going to place those pumps where they are needed when we get over the mining site in Montana. They will need images of the exact locations where the pumps need to be placed. Please get them and contact officials there and have them make sure that the sites are ready and completely clear. When those pumps are placed anything in the way will get hurt."

Jason beeped and typed, "I should have the images in ten minutes." A few minutes later Jason beeped and on its screen was typed, "The mining officials do not believe what they are being told and refuse to cooperate,"

Glenn sighed and asked, "General can I use your secure phone?" Without a word General Wellesley handed Colonel Loren the handset.

When the operator answered the phone he said, "Code Alpha niner, niner, niner Zulu golf. Connect me to the president please." General Wellesley looked at the Colonel clearly stunned by the code he had used. After a few minutes he continued, "Mister President the management at the mine cave in, in Montana is refusing to cooperate with us. Can I suggest that you declare martial law there and get them out of the way? Send in the state police to take over until military people can get on the site. We'll depart here in three hours and have approximately a three hour flight time then the Stevens triplets will place the pumps on the sites where they are needed." He paused then said, "Thank you sir." He handed the phone handset back to the General.

Before the General could say anything a jeep stopped beside the General's car and a lieutenant with a freezer box got out. The General opened his car door and the lieutenant said, "Sir there are six banana splits in here on dry ice. Major Everett said to tell you that when he discovered who they were for he doubled the order because his oldest daughter was one of the captive women in the camp at Minot."

"Colonel," Arielle said, "We need to get on the road to Winston Electronics so we'll eat one on the way and the other later. Thank you General for the treat and please thank the Major for us also."

The General replied, "You're welcome and I'll pass it on to the Major," as the girls and Colonel Loren got out of the General's staff car.

The girls settled into their bus seats and pulled out the airline style trays from the seats in front of them and began eating banana split while the bus and its escorts left the base and traveled to Winston Electronics. The girls were met at the entrance to the company by its president, a middle-aged woman with twinkling green eyes named Edith Hemingway. When the girls stepped off the bus she said, "I understand that you had a little excitement in Las Angeles."

"If you call a magnitude seven earthquake little," Arielle replied, "Then yes ma'am we did."

"You're Arielle, right?" Ms. Hemingway asked.

"Yes ma'am," Arielle replied, "And these are Brenda and Sharron."

"So the robot must be Jason," Ms. Hemingway concluded. Then addressing the robot she said, "If any jokes of any kind get played in my company I had better be the one who did the playing. I have a nice big metal stamping machine for those who don't behave."

Sharron looked at Jason and said, "She's talking to you Jason, behave."

"Your father called and told me what you will be doing so I have a favor to ask," Ms. Hemingway said seriously. "Can you check my security people as we go by so they can stay on the job?"

"I think we can do that," Arielle answered cocking her head to one side thoughtfully.

"Good," Ms. Hemingway said, "Let's get to it then. Captain, do you need to do anything before we start?"

"My soldiers and the security robots," Captain Bronson replied, "Just need to be able to keep the kids safe, so whatever it takes to do that is all."

"Then follow me."

Inside a security officer handed the children visitor's badges and welcomed them to the company. He eyed the robots and soldiers with suspicion but didn't say anything to them. Ms. Hemingway smiled at Lieutenant Carver saying, "I'm escorting this group Tim so you can return to your duties." Another security officer who was sitting behind a counter slumped sound asleep.

Arielle said, "Let him sleep. He will wake up in an hour. Unknown to him, he had been mentally programmed. We just removed the programming. Don't take any discipline action against him because he had no control over what happened to him."

Tim Carver looked at his boss and she said, "She's correct. Please do it her way."

The security Lieutenant responded, "Yes Ma'am." Then he stepped out of the way so that everyone could pass. The group walked to a warehouse that had been cleared for the meeting. The company's employees were sitting in folding chairs set up for the meeting and were talking among themselves when the group arrived.

Ms. Hemingway stepped up to a podium and said, "Ladies and gentlemen let's get started." She paused a moment for her employees to become quiet and continued, "When a major stock holder in this company says that he wants a meeting of all of the employees in this company to introduce a new manufacturing project to us, he gets it. Unfortunately he and his wife were injured in the Las Angeles earthquake but he sent his personal robot and his oldest triplets to deputize for him. The robot will explain the project while his children solve a security leak problem that has been plaguing us so if the person next to you goes to sleep during the presentation, you can tease him when he wakes up." She looked at the robot and said, "Jason would you roll up here and begin?"

Jason rolled up beside the podium and started its holographic projector. Clarence's head appeared in the image field and explained the threat and the project. The girls checked the employees and here and there one went to sleep. Near the back of the group four people stood and walked jerkily to the front and kneeled. Arielle said, "Ivan, arrest mode detain those four." Four robots appeared, rolled behind the four kneeling people, grasped their arms lifted them up and rolled away. Arielle sighed, walked towards Ms. Hemingway and signaled for her to leave the podium and its microphone. When Ms. Hemingway had joined the girls, Arielle said, "The four we just had arrested are wanted criminals. While Jason finishes can we go to your office where we can give you a brain recording for the police?"

"Follow me," Ms. Hemingway answered. In her office she asked, "What do you need to make the record?" A robot knocked on her office door and entered without waiting.

"Let me introduce you to Ivan the Terrible the chief of our robot security team," Sharron said. She asked the robot, "Did you bring our contact sets?" The robot beeped, handed each girl her set and plugged its connector into the contact set interface box. The girls recorded their evidence then Sharron asked, "Can Ivan plug into your computer so it can transfer the data?"

Ms. Hemingway waved the robot to her desk computer and said, "Certainly." She pressed a button on her desk intercom and after a moment Lieutenant Carver entered and she continued, "Lieutenant call the police and have them send some officers here to arrest the people the robots are detaining. The girls tell me that all four are wanted by the law."

"Yes ma'am," the lieutenant responded, "Can I ask what charges to tell the police?"

Brenda replied, "One is a wanted child molester, two are drug dealers, and the fourth is wanted for a string of convenience store robberies."

"Thank you Ms., I'll get the police here immediately," Carver said and left the office.

Arielle's stomach rumbled and Ms. Hemingway pressed a different intercom button, a voice answered and she said, "I need three snacks for some hungry girls in my office. See what the canteen has to offer and bring it here please." The person on the intercom acknowledged the instructions and clicked off. "How long before Jason finishes its presentation," Ms. Hemingway queried, "And do we need to be there when it does?"

Arielle replied, "We finished what we needed to do so we don't need to go back. Ivan, get Jason to send you dad's presentation and put it in Ms. Hemingway's computer so she can see the briefing also."

Ivan beeped and typed, "I already did the file name is Clarence. We must leave in thirty minutes to make the drop in Montana on time."

There was a knock on the office door and Ms. Hemingway called, "come in."

Ms. Hemingway's secretary entered with a cart containing three trays of food followed by Captain Bronson. He said, "The food has been checked girls but don't take too long eating, we have a schedule to keep."

There was another knock on the door and a police officer entered and said, "I was told that you have some evidence for me ma'am."

Ms. Hemingway reached into a desk drawer for a data chip inserted it in her computer, typed for a moment, pulled the chip out of the computer and asked, "Can I have a receipt for this officer?" The officer made out an evidence receipt, handed to Ms. Hemingway, took the data chip and departed.

While that was going on the secretary served the girls large plates of southwestern style Nachos. Sharron tasted one and said, "These are good we'll have to get Jason to add the recipe to its files."

"Glad you like them," the secretary replied watching Arielle fan her mouth, "They aren't too spicy for you are they?"

"No," Arielle replied, "Surprising. Is the chicken marinated first?"

"I don't know," the secretary replied, "They're one of my favorites from our canteen so I thought you might like them too."

Captain Bronson held up a ration bar and said, "In Las Angeles, they were burning so much energy rescuing people that they were eating two of these every fifteen minutes. Just about ran my company out of them keeping them fed before they finished."

The secretary ran a hand over her tummy and responded, "I wish I could eat like that but I'd look like a blimp if I did."

Arielle said, "Ms. Hemingway, your secretary needs to make a trip to Central in Iowa to have a connector installed and be programmed to activate her powers. Since you already have a connector, I'll ask dad if there is a way to get you programmed without you having to go to Central."

"Kim," Ms. Hemingway said, "It sounds like you need to go home and pack."

"That could cause a problem ma'am," Kim Waverly said, "I live out of town on a small farm and I gather stray animals, treat any problems, and then put them up for adoption. Right now I've got about twenty animals there and I'm their only care giver."

Arielle asked, "Captain Bronson, can we detail two people to care for her animals while she's gone? We can tell the General at the base that they are there and ask him to get them transportation back to Fort Miller when Ms. Carver returns."

Captain Bronson replied, "I think we can do that or get the air force to assign some people temporarily."

Having finished eating the girls stood and Arielle said, "Good then we should be leaving. "It has been nice meeting you Ms. Hemingway. Ms. Waverly if you will accompany us to the air base we'll get you connected to the people who will help you and you can take them to your place." Kim looked at her boss who waved her out the door with everyone else.

At the base, General Wellesley was informed of Ms. Waverly's problem and called the base veterinary office and instructed them to detail two people to assist her during her absence. The pumps for the mine had been loaded, the General thanked the triplets for taking on that mission, then everyone boarded the plane, it closed its cargo doors and taxied out to take off.

Once the plane was in the air Arielle said, "Jason please wake us up about forty-five minutes before we need to place the pumps and do you have images of where we are supposed to put them?" The robot beeped, rolled to a power connector and plugged itself in. The girls went each to a different sleeping berth and went to bed.

At the appointed time, the girls were in the C-150's cockpit and Glenn asked, "How much power do you think you'll need?"

Arielle replied, "When we tap your power it should be for just a moment for each pump. We're not really sure how much that will be but shouldn't affect the plane."

"When your mother was doing things she did the same sort of thing. We can fly with three engines so if you're doing it that way draw power from the left inside engine first, okay."

"That should work," Arielle responded, "How long before we're over the mine?"

"About five minutes we're going to go in like as though we were going to do a drag drop to give you time to identify the places on the ground. They're going to mark the corners of each site with red flares to help."

Jason Beeped and typed, "Ivan and his crew are feeding me images of the locations so I can display them for you."

"It sounds like we as ready as we're going to get," Sharron said, "Let's do it."

The plane banked and began to sink towards the ground and Major Lewis the flight engineer said, "Cargo doors are open."

Jason started its projector and displayed a picture of the mining site with three boxes of red flares already burning and the forth was being placed. The cargo pallet anchors on the first pump unlocked seemingly on their own and it rolled out the rear cargo hatch and began to tumble towards the earth. At the last moment it righted itself spun a half turn and landed lightly exactly centered in its location. While that pump was positioned the other three began to fall from the plane two were positioned but the third appeared to be out of control. In the cockpit, the girls screamed in pain, and all of the plane's engines lost power. Glenn grabbed the throttles and shoved them to full power and on the ground several kilometers ahead of the plane a large fireball erupted from the forest. Behind them the fourth pump at the very last moment was corrected its fall and landed in its location. All three girls sat on the cockpit floor completely exhausted. After a moment Arielle asked her sisters, "You guys okay?" Both nodded their heads. Arielle got wearily to her feet leaned on the Colonel's shoulder and said, "Sorry about that, we got attacked while we were putting the last pump down. Please call the authorities on the ground to put the fire out and arrest anyone still alive at their site.

Glenn turned the plane so that he was heading back over the mining sight and asked, "Is that what happened? I hope some are still alive to be interrogated."

The planes radio crackled with the voice of the pilot of the refueling plane who asked, "What happened, I thought you were going to crash for a moment, and what was the explosion we saw?"

Glenn replied, "We almost did and the explosion was the bad guys getting told don't mess with us. We should be at altitude in about two minutes."

On another radio the copilot was telling the people at the mine about the explosion and what they needed to do. The mining company management said they would see to the problem and that the pumps had been place so well that two were already on line."

Arielle said, "Jason I think that it is time to eat those banana splits then we are going back to bed." The robot beeped once and rolled out of the cockpit.

Major Lewis said, "Sleep well kids you look like you need it."

Sharron said, "Thank you Major," then the three left the cockpit also.

"You know George," Glenn said to his copilot, "Those kids are a lot like their mother."

"How's that?" Major George Carson asked.

"Every time an enemy made their mother mad her powers grew, a lot. The kids dealt with a disaster in L.A. and here very probably killed every enemy that tried to kill them just now with an energy burst that took every bit of power our engines were putting out. I doubt they could have done that before L.A."

While Glenn was making his observation, he had eased the big cargo jet into position behind the refueling plane. The boom operator asked over his radio link, "The pilot told me to ask if that is Cowboy Loren flying that truck?"

"Roger," Glenn answered, "Who is the pilot over there?"

"Major Nicholson and he says to ask if you still have that stealth equipment aboard that you used over Minnesota," the boom operator replied as the fueling boom socketed into the C-150's receptacle.

"Tell him it's need to know eyes only."

The boom operator said, "He acknowledges that and says to tell you he was the pilot the other time. Fueling is complete, disconnecting." The fueling boom released from the C-150.

"Roger the other time, catch you later," Glenn said, and turned the plane onto the course for Denver. Watch the store for a little bit, I'm going to check on the kids and talk to Captain Bronson about what happened."

Later the cargo jet settled onto the runway at Denver Colorado's, airport and taxied to a secure area. The security robots and some soldiers got off and set up a safe zone around the plane and fighters. Nothing else occurred in or around the plane until the next morning when a fuel truck and catering truck drove up. The army guards and robots checked the trucks then they were allowed to pass. One of the flight engineers got out of the plane with a test kit, went to the fuel truck, and tested the fuel before he allowed it to be pumped into the planes. The catering truck exchanged empty food warming carts for full ones with the assistance of a robot who checked the food for poisons and a loadmaster who stored the new ones. After a while the family bus, the robots truck, and several army vehicles left the plane. The convoy returned later from the sightseeing trip the girls went on and drove into the plane. Nothing else happened until the next morning when the convoy drove out of the plane a second time to go to Archer Electronics. Like in Arizona, the bus was met by the owner of the company, the presentation was made, and the people were deprogrammed by the girls. The girls ate a snack at the plants lunchroom, then the convoy returned to the plane, it took off without incident for Spokane Washington. The landing in Spokane was very different. A raging thunderstorm kept the plane and its escorts in the air for over an hour. Once the C-150 had landed a small private jet, turned onto the same runway ahead of the plane and accelerated toward it. Glenn turned the cargo jet down a taxiway and the small jet veered towards it and ran off the edge of the runway. In the rain-softened ground, its nose gear broke making it plow a path through the dirt. The plane came to a stop just short of a collision with the C-150. The side door on the cargo plane flew open and robots and soldiers erupted from it. Jason rolled into Colonel Loren's cockpit beeping for attention. On its screen was typed, "Arielle says that the plane is a bomb being operated by remote control. They are going to use its engine power to move it out into the open field before it blows up. She asks that you contact airport security and emergency services and advise them." The little plane's engines, which were running at full throttle, sank to almost a total stop and suddenly the little jet was out in the middle of an open field.

Glenn called the tower and reported what the robot had told him and sirens began to wail all around the airport. Fire and security vehicles left their parking areas and raced towards the doomed plane. When they were halfway across the airport there was a tremendous explosion with a huge fireball that blew soldiers who were outside the cargo jet off their feet. They got up and scrambled back into the plane followed by the robots. A security vehicle veered away from those that were racing towards the explosion. It pulled up in front of the C-150 turned around and the driver waved his arm out a window indicating that the jet should follow him then began driving down the taxiway. The plane followed and was soon parked in a secure area.

When the plane had stopped and been connected to ground services the robots and army set up a secure perimeter around the plane Glenn and Captain Bronson stepped out of the front cargo hatch as an airport official arrived. The family bus and army trucks followed them out and stopped.

The airport official walked towards the Colonel and was stopped by a robot and two soldiers. After searching him he was allowed to continue to the Colonel and said, "I don't know what you're carrying that someone wants to destroy, but no one is to leave this area until the FBI and CAB investigators find out why."

The three girls had gotten off their bus and joined Colonel Loren, Arielle asked, "Is there a problem Colonel?"

"It seems that this airport person doesn't want us to leave until investigators find out why someone wants to kill you," Glenn replied.

"He has a problem doesn't he?" Captain Bronson said. "Hop back in the bus, kids, and let's get you to Microstat and then the sightseeing your parents promised. Colonel, would you entertain this gentleman?"

"Certainly," Glenn replied with a nasty grin on his face. "Attila," Glenn told his security robot, "Escort this gentleman into the plane please."

Attila rolled up to the man and beeped, and waved a claw in the direction of the cargo bay of the plane. "I will not!" the man said indignantly, where upon the robot picked him up and carried him struggling into the plane. While this was happening, the bus and its military escort drove towards the airport exit. At Microstat everything went smoothly. The Triplets were taken to Mobius Kids and the children's Museum of Spokane for some fun. At nearly nine that evening the convoy returned to the plane.

When the girls got out of their bus inside the plane and gone to the passenger compartment, Arielle asked Glenn, "How did that airport person like talking to the President?"

184

He chuckled and replied, "He didn't. But he left in a hurry and we're cleared for takeoff whenever we decide to. Did you have fun sightseeing?"

"I think we drove the manager at Mobius Kids nuts because so much of what he had is way below where we are educationally," Arielle answered. The museum was more fun and the curator was willing to be challenged by us and what we know."

Brenda added, "I think he is going to change the museum to challenge the area kids much more intellectually because of our visit." When she finished saying that Brenda yawned hugely and said, "I'm going to bed."

The next morning the triplets went to the cockpit and Arielle asked, "Are we ready to go back to L.A.?"

"As soon as you three find seats and get buckled in," Lieutenant Colonel Eddy Sanders, pilot for the second flight crew said.

There were three small booms in the cockpit and then Brenda thought to Sanders, *"We're ready."*

Sanders shook his head and told his copilot, "I wish they wouldn't do that. Oh well, let's get going." The copilot nodded for he had received the thought also and the engineer began the startup checklist.

In Las Angeles the visits went off without any problems and five hours after landing the plane was in the air headed for Iowa. When the C-150 and its fighter escort entered Central's air space it was challenged by a flight of recently assigned Thunderbolt IIs. After being identified the plane landed and the family bus took the girls to the hospital to see their parents.

Wendy and Clarence were in the same hospital room sleeping when their daughters entered. They walked up to their parent's beds and Arielle said, "We're home mom." in a soft voice."

Wendy smiled, opened her eyes, and held out her hands, and said, "Come give me a kiss and hug."

"I understand you three did some unscheduled things while you traveled," their father said.

"Such as Dad?" Arielle asked.

"Oh, let's see," their mother replied, "Things like picking up huge mining pumps in Arizona and placing them without landing in Montana. Killing members on an attack team and destroying their generators. Then in Washington moving a small jet that was rigged as a bomb to a safe place before it blew up. Does any of that ring a bell?"

"You left out rescuing you from under a freeway over pass and snuffing most of the bomb when it exploded," Brenda said smiling."

Clarence said, "Of course, how could we forget those. We want you to do a new set of power level tests tomorrow."

"But today we want you to visit with us," Wendy added, "And then catch up on your school work."

"We actually did our school work in the plane," Sharron said, "Jason insisted."

Brenda giggled and said, "It told us that it didn't want us to suffer from boredom or get into mischief."

"How long before you can come home?" Arielle asked her parents.

From the door to the room, Maryann said, "Tomorrow if you three will give me a little help."

Arielle cocked her head and asked, "What do you need us to do?"

"The idea you sent was a good one but your younger brother and sisters don't have the stamina. I can heal your parent's legs by making them grow new tissue but I can't produce powerful enough forces to get the job done. I want you to boost my power."

"We can do that," Arielle replied, "Tell us when you are ready."

The Doctor removed the bandages from Wendy's legs and placed a hand above each wound, then she nodded at the girls and said, "Now." Her hands began to glow, Wendy screamed in pain and fainted. Ten minutes later Maryann Janice withdrew her hands and the wounds were no longer large gashes and had changed to the bright red of new skin. She turned to Clarence and asked, "Are you ready?"

"No, but don't let that stop you," he replied.

She repeated the process on Clarence and shortly he had bright red new skin in place of his injuries as well. Maryann looked at the girls and said, "Thank you. Let's get something to eat."

"How was your trip?" Jackie asked when she joined the four in the dining room. "By the way General, have you seen the mess above ground?"

Brenda looked at Maryann and asked, "When did they reactivate you Doctor?"

"When they decided to enlarge the hospital," Major General Maryann Janice replied, "And if you start calling me General, you'll be in big trouble."

Arielle smiled mischievously and said, "Yes General, of course General, whatever you say General."

When she finished saying that Brenda and Sharron both added their own comments and Sharron concluded with, "Congratulations General." Then all three girls hugged her.

Jackie said, "Let's go so the General can get back to work."

As the four walked out of the dining room, Arielle said, "The trip was interesting and I hope the other families' trips are much more sedate and pastoral."

KATHERINE'S GIRLS

"Mom," Melinda asked as their C-150 took off, "How many cities are we going to?"

"Five," Katherine Warren answered, "We're going to Miami, Atlanta, Nashville, New Orleans, and Dallas. Why do you ask?"

"Will we have any time for sightseeing at any of those places?" Melinda asked.

"The way Clarence set up our schedule we'll have two days in each place," William said. "So I suppose we can get in some fun here and there."

"Won't that make things difficult for the army?" Sarah asked.

"We'll try not to be the source of any problems for them," Katherine replied. "I'd like to see the Grand Old Opry in Nashville."

Katherine went into a blank stare and when she came out, William asked, "What's up?"

"That was a message from Carroll," Katherine answered, "Pat is out of surgery and will be okay."

"Did she say who was taking care of all the younger triplets?" Melinda asked.

"According to Carroll, Doctor Janice put the word out that help was needed," Katherine answered, "And she got an overwhelming response. So everyone's kids are in good hands."

Conversation had continued for just under an hour when Melinda queried, "What was that?" Then there was a triple boom and the three children disappeared from their seats. Katherine and William saw a bright flash through a passenger compartment window and a double boom sounded as they too disappeared. In the cockpit, the triplets had joined hands and the tentacles of a mysterious something were waving around the cargo plane and the fighters destroying rockets that were being fired from the ground.

Katherine said to her husband, "Let's find the launchers and destroy them." Explosions began to spread across several kilometers of low hills. The destruction of the missiles and launchers went on for several minutes.

Sarah asked, "Whew! Where did they get so many missiles?"

Linda answered, "I don't know, but now I'm hungry." She looked at Jennifer, her mother's robot that had followed everyone to the cockpit and asked, "Is there something we can eat available?" Jennifer beeped.

William said, "Let's go back to our seats and get out of the air crew's way."

Lieutenant Colonel Sheffield, the pilot said, "With that kind of help, you can come get in the way any time. I really thought we were going to be shot down. I've also notified General Gregory so he can get some units to go pick up the bodies and other pieces."

"Thank you Alan, but we'll do our best to stay out from under foot," Katherine replied. "How long before we land in Miami?"

"Colonel," Melinda asked, "What state were we over when the attack started?"

The Colonel turned and looked at his copilot and asked, "Where were we, Max?"

Major Max Jefferies replied, "Over the Tennessee Georgia state line and above the southern end of the Appalachian Mountains."

"Why do you want to know that?" her mother asked.

"Think about it mom," Melinda replied, "The bugs in the conference room were killed, and we left the next day yet those missiles were sited to kill us. How and where did they find out our itinerary?"

"That has me wondering how much programming the aliens did before they started in on us," Sarah added.

"Let's walk back to our seats," William said, "See what the robots have to eat and discuss this some more."

As the robots served the five a lunch of spaghetti and salad, Linda said, "Sis, I'm not convinced that all of this is alien programming. After all we still have a large supply of fanatics who may have banded together."

Melinda added, "All of the civil wars haven't been ended either, so we could be dealing with elements from those factions as well."

William said, "Those are enough groups. The question is what can we do about what we come in contact with?"

"Maybe we need to use misdirection," Melinda said, "And change the order of the visits."

"That should help for one or two locations," Linda stated thoughtfully, "But if they have the forces available that they had for this attack we could still have a problem as the sites become fewer."

"Especially if we stay in the air between places," Sarah added.

The cargo plane the family was riding in jerked and dropped suddenly and Katherine asked, "What's going on now?"

The plane jerked upward and lurched sideways then dropped again scattering the remains of the family's meal around the cabin.

Jennifer beeped and typed, "Hurricane Candice changed directions and is hitting Miami which it was supposed to miss entirely."

Melinda and her sisters joined hands and the plane stopped bouncing and gyrating about in the air. Melinda said, "Mom, tell Colonel Sheffield he and the fighters need to land quickly. We can't hold the storm off from us for very long."

Katherine and William both went to the cockpit and William said, "Alan the kids are creating a bubble around us but they won't be able to keep it up very long. Can you get us landed some place real quick?"

"We're going to put down at the Jacksonville airport," Alan replied. "That will be in about ten minutes." At that moment, lightning struck the plane and blinded the cockpit crew, Katherine, and William.

Katherine screamed in pain, closing her eyes but the lightning had already done its dirty work. Bennett, William's robot rolled into the cockpit saw everyone with their hands over their eyes and sent messages to Jennifer, and George Patton, the robot security chief.

Jennifer beeped for attention and the girls opened their eyes briefly to read the message on its monitor. Melinda said in a strained voice, "Tell George to get another crew up here to take over." The robot beeped in acknowledgement.

A couple of minutes later the elevator rose from the cargo bay with Major Kennedy and his copilot who ran into the cockpit. Puffing somewhat from the hurried and steep climb up the stairs two army medics followed the pilots into the cockpit. A little later Major Kennedy landed the C-150 at the Jacksonville, Florida airport. The triplet's parents and Colonel Sheffield, Major Jefferies, and Captain Walters all of whom had their eyes bandaged were helped to the elevator and taken down to the family bus. The girls joined their parents. The bus, the robot security truck, and their army escort drove out of the bus headed for Shands Memorial Hospital in Jacksonville, Florida.

Two hours after arriving at the hospital, Captain Cynthia Stanley led the triplets into their parent's room. Melinda asked, "Mom, are you and dad going to be alright?"

"We don't know right now," Katherine said with a wan smile. "The doctor said our optic nerves were paralyzed by the flash of the lightning."

Sarah put her hands on the bandages over her father's eyes and her hands began to glow. Linda watched her sister a moment and then did the same thing to her mother. Five minutes later Sarah said with satisfaction, "Dad, you can take the bandages off, your eyes are healed."

"You too mom," Linda added.

William didn't move to take his bandages off and asked, "What did you do Minx?"

Captain Stanley said, "The girls put their hands the bandages over your eyes and they began to glow. After a few minutes, the glow died and they told you that you can remove the bandages. While they were doing that Melinda went the room with the plane crew. I think she went to Colonel Sheffield's room and is healing them too."

"Is that what you did Linda," Katherine asked her daughter, "Heal us?"

"Yes mama," Linda answered. "It's safe for you to remove the bandages but your eyes will still hurt until they heal the rest of the way and light will bother you a lot."

A doctor had entered the room while Katherine and William were receiving the explanation about what their girls had done. She said, "I'm Doctor Jackson and I just got off the phone with a Doctor Janice and she said that the girls have that capability. Let me turn off the lights before we remove the bandages. Keep your eyes closed until I tell you to open them."

The bandages were removed and Katherine asked, "I'm seeing red splotches now, is that normal?"

"Seeing red through your eyelids is normal," the doctor replied, "But you will also see everything in a red haze for several weeks. It should gradually fade as your optic nerve heals from the shock."

"Can we open our eyes now?" William asked.

"Go ahead and try," the doctor replied. "You shouldn't be able to see much more than outlines in the dark."

Katherine said, "That's what I see. Come here girls you need a hug." There was a small thunderclap and Melinda rejoined her family and hugged her mother.

After a moment Melinda said, "Mom, dad, please close your eyes and shield them so Jennifer can come in, it has some information. After her parents had closed and covered their eyes, Melinda called, "You can come in Jennifer."

The door opened and a robot rolled in closing the door behind it. Jennifer beeped signaling that is was safe for the girl's parents to uncover their eyes. On its screen was typed, "Doctor Janice wants you back in Iowa and has arranged for a plane to get you there. Wendy and Clarence were hurt in an earthquake in L.A. and their children are going to continue the mission without them."

Katherine asked, "Are Wendy and Clarence going to be alright?" The robot beeped once.

"That's two of the big three out of circulation," William mused, "I wonder what will befall Aiko and Hiro?"

"Sarah, are you okay?" Katherine asked.

Sarah came out of her blank stare and answered, "I was telling Karlita what has happened to us and Ms. Wendy. She told me that they were attacked too."

"Somebody is making a serious effort to put us out of commission," William mused. "Kids, Captain Stanley I think we'll do the same thing. Jennifer would you notify the companies of the change and revise the order so Miami is last so the hurricane can go away."

The robot beeped and typed, "The messages have been sent."

"Girls," Katherine said, "Link with me." The triplets linked with their mother and she passed them the information they would need for their mission.

Jennifer beeped and typed, "All of the companies have acknowledged the change in schedule. The weather bureau states that the hurricane has moved far enough away so that we can take off safely."

"Good," William replied, "Since you have the presentation you will accompany the girls. Girls, make sure you pay attention to Captain Stanley and the robots."

"When is the plane supposed to get here?" Katherine asked Jennifer.

The robot typed, "The plane should be here at nine tomorrow morning."

"Why don't I see about some more chairs and some blankets for your girls," Doctor Jackson said. "I think the Captain would like it better if you all stayed together tonight."

"Thank you, ma'am," Captain Cynthia Stanley replied. "It would make things easier. We'll keep this robot inside to give warning if someone needs to enter so that Mr. and Ms. Warren can shield their eyes."

"I noticed that more robots and your soldiers have stationed themselves to help protect your charges and security has been told to yield to them in an emergency." The Doctor chuckled and continued, "I understand that some of our security people are a little upset about that, but they'll just have to get over it."

William said, "You'll find that our security robots can get into anything they think they need to, including your most secure spaces. They have the ability to display a person's vital signs and a bunch of other things also."

"Interesting," the Doctor replied, "Well, let me get going so you can all get some sleep."

Katherine said, "Before you go check your shoe laces."

The Doctor looked down and Sharron said, "Jennifer you must want mom to reprogram you into a bed pan holder." The robot beeped twice. As the doctor watched, her shoelaces untied themselves and then retied correctly.

Katherine asked, "Which one of you has taken up delicate work?"

"Me, mama," Sharron answered, "It's kinda fun to see if I can do small delicate things with my mind alone."

"Good for you," Katherine said, "Just remember not to give yourself away where it could be someone not understanding what you are doing."

Doctor Jackson said, "Now I understand what happened in the emergency room a couple of hours ago. This storm has driven in the frightened and the crazies. One of the later cornered Grace Hanson our chief ER nurse. He kept talking and shouting at her to help him. A robot passed by the pair and then there was a page for Grace and she told the guy to excuse her and turned to walk away. The guy fell flat on his face because his shoe laces had been tied together."

Jennifer beeped and typed, "That was Bennett. There was nothing physically wrong with the man and the nurse had serious cases to deal with."

"How do you robots tie laces with those big claw hands?" the Doctor asked. Jennifer held up one claw hand and fanned out all of the small manipulators that were built into it. "Oh," the Doctor said.

Jennifer beeped, turned towards the beds, and typed, "Bennett is here and some soldiers with chairs and blankets for the girls to sleep. Please close and cover your eyes so they can come in." Since she could also see the message the Doctor went to the door and when Katherine and William had covered their eyes, she opened it. Just before she closed the door on her way out, she added, "Doctor Shamus will see you before you leave in the morning."

At first light the next morning, the window of the hospital room the Warren family was in was blown in from the exploding of a rocket that had been fired from a building nearby. Those inside the room were not harmed because Jennifer had positioned itself by the window, plugged into the room's power and turned on its shield when everyone had settled down to sleep.

The noise awakened everyone and the girls scrambled to the window to see what was going on. Katherine tried to peek at the window but quickly closed her eyes again and asked, "What's going on girls?"

Captain Stanley heard the noise and entered the room and on the robot's screen was typed, "Someone fired a rocket at this window."

The Captain repeated the message to the Warrens and asked the girls, "Can you see where the rocket came from and can you stop another one from being fired?"

Melinda answered, "Already did, and your people are rounding them and their equipment up right now."

The door opened and the man standing there said, "I'm Doctor Shamus and we need to cover the Warren's eyes for transportation. Can my nurse and I come in?"

Captain Stanley looked at the Doctor and said, "Jennifer check them please."

The robot beeped once and typed, "They are okay. Bennett checked them in the hall." The Captain waved the doctor and nurse into the room.

The Doctor moved into the room and said, "After the damage the hurricane did yesterday we are having problems with looters so we need to get you underway as soon as possible. A robot told me that your plane is waiting at the airport."

Katherine replied while the doctor bandaged her eyes, "Thank you doctor. Captain, that sounds like our marching orders."

"Yes ma'am," Captain Stanley replied, "We're ready to move you as soon as the Doctor gets finished."

"Which is right now," Doctor Shamus interjected.

The hospital room door opened and two army medics pushing wheelchairs entered, one went to each bed, and Katherine and William were assisted into the chairs. A moment later, everyone was moving down a corridor of soldiers to an elevator whose doors were being held open. On the first floor several elevators opened and disgorging robots and people. Stairwell doors flew open and more soldiers came out of them. Everyone was headed for the emergency room exit and as fast as they appeared, they were gone. Patients waiting in the waiting area looked about them in bewildered non-understanding. A nurse at the desk said to no one in particular, "Now that's organization and everything stat."

An intern said in awe, "You got that right." Then he asked, "Who were they to get treatment like that?" The nurse gave the intern a disgusted look and turned to her duties.

At the Jacksonville airport, the triplets watched their parents being helped into a small business jet. Around both planes was a large group of fighters preparing to take off. As the small jet and some of the fighters taxied out to take off the girls waved then turned and walked quietly into the big cargo plane that was their transportation. Once they were airborne and headed for Nashville, Jennifer rolled into the passenger compartment with three meal trays and beeped and typed, "You haven't had breakfast yet and there is no reason for you to get behind in your school work. Eat your breakfast and then class will begin."

Captain Stanley had entered the passenger compartment at that moment, saw the screen and began laughing. "A little mental exercise will help keep your minds off worrying about your parents. Jennifer, do you have another breakfast available? With taking care of my people I haven't had a chance to eat yet."

Major Kennedy entered the passenger compartment, sat in a seat near the girls and said, "We've got a problem. Or perhaps I should say there is a problem on the ground where your powers could really help. It would require that we change our schedule and go to New Orleans first."

"What's the problem?" Melinda asked. "Is the hurricane overloading the levee pumps?"

"Exactly, some of the levees are in danger of collapsing as well."

"What would be our function in this sort of operation," Sarah asked, "And where would we get our power from?"

"How far from your power source can you be and still use it effectively?" Kennedy queried.

"We don't really know," Sarah answered, "We've never tried to tap power that is far away."

"We'll probably have to devise a test to determine that," Melinda added. "The only place that has the equipment to test our power levels is at Central."

Jennifer beeped and typed, "I have contacted Central and the equipment is being sent to New Orleans so we can test this aspect of power. Bennett also notified me that your father said to make the change if you think it is within your abilities. He also said be careful about how tired you get so you don't burn out. Your mother says loves you and she thinks you can do it. I received a message from Robin also that recommends that Captain Stanley lay in an extra supply of ration bars and the airports are to upgrade their catering services to this plane so that you will have the energy you need for the project."

Melinda said, "I guess that means that you should go change course Major."

Major Kennedy replied, "So it would seem." Then with a mischievous smile he continued, "Finish your breakfast so you can do school for today." Then he rose to return to the cockpit.

"Contrary to what you may have heard, Major," Sarah said in her most serious mode, "Some of us actually enjoy learning."

The major burst out laughing and answered, "You win. Let me get back to work."

Linda asked, "Jennifer why can't we make this a working breakfast and learn while we eat?" The robot beeped once and went for the girl's contact sets.

Captain Stanley, who had been quiet during this conversation said, "I guess I need to find my own meal and order the extra ration bars as suggested."

"Sorry Captain," Melinda said, "We did kind of leave you out of things didn't we? We've been in telepathic contact with Ms. Wendy's girls, and they told us that when they were rescuing people from the earthquake in Los Angeles, they were eating two bars every fifteen minutes."

"Hopefully what you are going to do won't be that bad."

Jennifer reappeared with the girl's contact sets and a breakfast for Captain Stanley. The robot beeped and typed, "I didn't forget that you needed breakfast, enjoy. I have placed an order for more ration bars as well."

"Captain," Sarah said, "When we are connected we tend to get somewhat glassy eyed and ignore externals. If something

198

happens that we need to deal with tell Jennifer to make us come up for air." As she told the Captain that, two security robots entered the passenger compartment and rolled to the girls were seated and stopped in front of Melinda and Sarah. Jennifer moved in front of Linda and the girls put on their contact sets while the robots plugged themselves into the interface boxes. The Captain sat back to eat her breakfast and watched the triplets. After finishing eating, she got up and walked behind the girls and looked at the robot's screens. What she saw was nearly a blur of text, diagrams, and mathematical formulas that were scrolling up the screens. She shook her head, went to the stairs, and disappeared to the deck below.

Two hours later the girls came out of their blank stares and rubbed their eyes and Melinda asked, "Are we there yet, Jennifer?"

Jennifer beeped twice and typed, "Another twenty minutes. The plane with the test equipment should land just ahead of us."

"You know," Sarah said, "Ms. Wendy and Mr. Clarence got hurt, our parents have also been hurt. We also know Aiko and Hiro have been attacked. Have they been hurt also?"

Jennifer beeped and typed, "The attack on them injured them."

"As the saying goes," Linda said thoughtfully, "Once is an accident, twice is chance, but three times is enemy action. There has to be another alien scout somewhere close."

"Yeah," Melinda added, "Especially as close together as these attacks have been."

"But they haven't hurt any of us kids yet," Sarah said. "I wonder why?"

Melinda replied, "I hope it's because they are still under estimating what we are capable of. Jennifer, is Ms. Keiyanai's team still okay?" Jennifer beeped.

Sarah instructed, "Contact her and ask her to do a sweep with her team. I think that places that are not directly visible to our telescopes and other surveillance stuff is likely."

Linda added, "The Aliens could have landed on the surface of a planet or moon as well."

Jennifer beeped again and typed, "Message sent, we will be landing in five minutes."

Once the cargo plane and some of the fighters were on the ground, they were escorted to the usual secure area and the family bus, cargo truck, military escort, and a small truck from another plane drove out of the airport and went to the Corps of Engineers headquarters on Leake Avenue in New Orleans.

Mister Gerald Simms met the triplets in his office and asked somewhat dubiously, "Are you the people who are supposed to keep my city from washing away?"

"To determine that we need a lot of information," Melinda replied.

"Such as?" Mister Simms queried skeptically.

"How much water is to be moved from where to where," Linda responded.

"How much electrical generating capability is available and where is it located," Sarah added. "It would also be helpful if the specifications of the generating plants, the distribution network served by each one, and images of the places the water is to be removed from and where it is to be put are available."

Jennifer beeped and Mister Simms looked at it. On its screen was typed, "The girls will need a great deal of food while they are working as well."

Mister Simms looked at Captain Stanley and asked, "What part do you play in all of this Captain?"

"My company and I make sure that these girls stay alive and unharmed," Captain Stanley replied. "There are also ten security robots here as well."

"Alright," Mister Simms said sighing, "Then as soon as the mayor and some electric company reps arrive we can get started. We're going to use the conference room down the hall if that's okay. Do you have any equipment you need to do this?"

Melinda responded, "Because we're going to be using a new technique for tapping power we have some measuring equipment that needs to be set up. Jennifer, would you pass the word to the test equipment truck about where to set up." Jennifer beeped.

Fifteen minutes later the girls and Mister Simms entered the conference room. "Hi Mister Brian," Sarah told the dark haired man who was fussing with some strange equipment.

The man replied, "Hi yourself. You kids have been really stirring things up the last few days."

"How's that?" Melinda queried.

"All of you kids have been doing things that are outside most of our power test ranges," Mr. Ed Brian answered. In fact Ms. Stevens' girls are about three times more powerful than their mother right now."

"Together or separate?" Sarah asked.

"Separate," Ed responded.

Mister Simms asked, "What does that mean in terms of our problem here?"

Before any answer could be given, there was a knock on the conference room door and two men and three women entered. One of the women looked at the girls and snarled, "We have a big problem and all I see is three little girls, why aren't we receiving sand bags and such to protect the generators when the levees breach?" Jennifer rolled silently up behind the woman and grasped her gently with its claws as she suddenly sank towards the floor unconscious.

Melinda said quietly, "Sorry about that but Ms. Callison had been mentally programmed and removing the programming puts the individual to sleep for about an hour. Ms. Burroughs is there a place where Jennifer can put Ms. Callison until she wakes up?"

Mayor David drake asked, "How did she get programmed?"

"Because of national security we're not allowed to say for now," Melinda answered. "Shall we begin?"

Mr. Sims said, "Ladies, gentlemen please be seated. These young ladies have told me that they need the specifications for each of your power plants as part of the solution. According to information I have received they can mentally tap and use that power to move the waters that are about to drown us elsewhere. They can also help us reinforce the weakest levees by putting materials where workers can get to them. Girls, would you explain please."

Melinda looked at Jennifer and said, "Jennifer, do you have our contact sets?" There was a knock on the conference room door and another robot entered the room with three small boxes on its cargo shelf. Melinda continued, "Thank you Patton." The security robot beeped as it handed a box to each girl. The girls put on the contact sets and plugged their connectors into a junction box that Jennifer had already connected itself to. A holographic map of the region around New Orleans appeared above Jennifer and Melinda continued, "The reason we need the power plant specifications is so that we can draw the maximum amount of power from them that we need to without damaging them. Mister Mayor, we can't guarantee that we won't black out those parts of the city so the public should know to expect them."

Mayor Drake replied, "I can get the word out but it will take a couple of hours. What reason should I give them for the outages?"

Mr. Simms answered, "Tell them that the storm has knocked down trees, that a vehicle has crashed into a substation, or that some other disaster has happened."

"You could also tell them that flood waters are shorting out the substations," Sarah added. "The only problem is that we don't know how long it will take us to reduce the water levels."

"I think flooding is probably a more valid reason at this point," the mayor replied. "Mr. Sims, can I use a phone somewhere to get things rolling?"

"See my secretary," Mr. Sims replied. "She'll see that you're taken care of."

In the hallway outside the conference room, the mayor asked, "Captain, how old are those girls?"

Captain Stanley grunted and answered, "Physically they're six. Mentally somewhere around sixty I'd guess." The mayor shook his head and walked down the hall.

"Captain," First Sergeant Jeannette Smith said as she walked towards the captain, "We checked out the lunch room in this place. It has is some vending machines and microwaves so I sent Sergeant Cassidy out to scout the area around here. There are no places open to eat or get food. I contacted Major Kennedy and he is getting the airport's catering service to put together meals for the kids. I've sent Cassidy and two vehicles to pick them up."

A robot beeped for attention and typed, "I am General George Patton #3. Get a box of ration bars for the kids. Jason informed us that in Los Angeles, the Stevens girls were eating two ration bars every fifteen minutes with water while they handled the earthquake aftermath there."

"We'll do as the robot suggests," Captain Stanley said, "But as soon as the meals arrive I want to switch them off the bars."

"Yes Ma'am," the First sergeant acknowledged and retraced her steps.

The Captain stepped quietly into the conference room as Sarah was explaining, "We have the ability to mentally tap the power of your generators. In Iowa, we would go to a special generator station when we need more power than our minds can generate alone. That isn't possible here so we plan that each one of us will tap a different power plant and combine and direct the power where it will perform the work."

"How much of a power gain do you get when you connect to generators?" Ms. Callison, who had awakened and joined the group asked. "Do you get some kind of power multiplication?"

"That's why Mr. Brian is here," Melinda answered. "We get what seems to be an exponential increase in our power and Mr. Brian is going to attempt to measure how much that is with the distances we're talking about."

"At my plant we have two types of generators," Ms. McAffery said. "Four of them are natural gas and the other two are low pressure steam turbines. The plant generates eight hundred and fifty thousand megawatts."

"Mine is a newer plant," Ms. Callison said, "It has six low pressure steam turbines that use geothermal earth taps to heat the water. The plant generates four point three terawatts of power."

"A third of my plant is solar and wind generators," George Nichols put in. "On a sunny day with a five to fifteen kilometer wind that portion alone generates what these other two plants do combined. But that's under good conditions. The rest of the plant is five natural gas turbines generating four hundred and ninety megawatts."

"We should be able to move some water with that kind of power available," Melinda said. "We know which one of us will use which plant. We need for you to tell your plants to stop all load sharing and distribution outside of your immediate service areas." Then she slid a sheet of paper towards Mister Sims and queried, "Can you call this number, please?"

Mister Sims picked up the paper, looked at Melinda and replied, "This is an overseas number, and I don't have the authority to call there."

Melinda took the piece of paper and wrote another number on it and said, "Call this number and they'll give you permission and probably connect you. Use the code I wrote under the number when the phone is answered. Then if you can put it on that screen we can do the talking."

Mister Sims looked at the piece of paper dubiously, then at Melinda and asked, "You're sure?"

"Yes," Melinda replied firmly.

Skeptically Mister Sims dialed the number and when the screen lit gave the code. The look on his face changed to a grin of surprise when the President of the United States looked out of the screen and said, "Good morning girls, is there a problem."

"Good morning sir," Melinda answered, "A small one. Mr. Sims needs the flood waters moved somewhere else and we know that Kenya has been digging a lakebed in the game reserve in an attempt to save the wild life. Army desalinization units are scheduled to fill it next week. We can fill it now and help both places in the process."

"I see," President Harper replied then pressed an intercom button on his desk. When the intercom was answered he continued, "Get Ambassador Larkin in Kenya on the phone and connect him to the call I have now." A moment later the screen in Mr. Sims conference room split and a very dark skinned man said, "Good day Mr. President, to what do I owe the honor?"

"How is the lakebed the Kenyans are digging coming along?" the President asked.

"It is finished," Ambassador Larkin answered, "We're waiting for the Desalinization units to arrive."

Sarah giggled and asked, "Mr. Ambassador how long will it take you to verify that there are no people or animals in the lakebed?"

"Who are you?" Larkin asked.

"Sorry," Sarah replied, "I'm Sarah Warren and these are my sisters Melinda and Linda. Once you tell us the lakebed is clear, we're going to fill it with water from the New Orleans, Louisiana area to prevent flooding here."

The Ambassador's eyes lit with understanding and he asked, "What is your local call combination? I'll verify what you need and call you back within the hour."

"Could you get us the dimensions also?" Melinda asked.

"Certainly," the Ambassador replied, "I suggest you get something to eat while you wait. If I remember my briefings correctly you're going to need it."

Sarah and Linda giggled and Melinda said, "We will. We'll talk to you again soon."

As the screen blanked, there was a knock on the conference room door. When the door opened, First Sergeant Smith entered followed by two soldiers trundling airline meal carts. She asked, "Are you ready for lunch?"

"Did you bring enough for everyone?" Sarah asked in return indicating the adults in the room.

An hour later as everyone finished eating, the phone sounded and when Mr. Sims answered, Ambassador said, "I see my timing was good. The lakebed is clear and here is a diagram with the dimensions."

"The Kenyan's didn't think small did they?" Linda asked. "With that deeper section in the middle we'll need a few billion liters more water."

"Looks to me like the total capacity is around two point three trillion liters," Sarah said. "Mr. Sims how much water can we take from Lake Pontchartrain without affecting the ecology here?"

"The lake is over a meter above flood stage now," Sims replied, "So you can take it down two and a half meters without hurting anything."

"That's more than we'll need for the lake," Melinda responded. Then looking at her sisters she asked, "Where else can we put the rest?"

Sarah looked at Jennifer, the robot, and asked, "Will you get Grandfather on the phone for us?" The robot beeped once.

A moment later the screen brightened and Kenneth Jordan, Secretary General to the United Nations asked, "Is this a grandfather call or business?"

"Business we're afraid," Melinda answered. "We're in the New Orleans, Corps of Engineers headquarters and we're trying to keep the city from being drowned. We're going to reduce the level in Lake Pontchartrain. Part of the water is going to be placed in the new lake bed in Kenya but we need to find useful places to put the other two thirds of it."

A map of Africa appeared on the screen and Kenneth said, "We're trying to derail the government in Sudan so we can get rid of their witchcraft laws. My suggestion is spread about five centimeters or so of rain all around Sudan's borders and top off things like Lake Victoria. The rest can be spread over the rest of the continent. If you still have more after that try the Australian desert. Meanwhile I'll start an advertising campaign in Sudan. When do you plan to start?"

Sarah giggled and said, "That's evil Grandfather."

"When do you plan to start?" Kenneth asked again smiling.

"In about ten or fifteen minutes," Melinda answered, "As soon as Mr. Brian gets us hooked up to his measuring equipment."

"Then have fun," the girls grandfather said, "I'll let you know how the advertising campaign works in a few days."

The phone screen blanked and Sarah said, "It's time to get us hooked up, Mr. Brian."

The much stunned at the political power the triplets had, executives in the room watched in silence as Brian connected them to his equipment. After a few moments of checking Mr. Brian said, "You may begin when you're ready."

An eerie glow formed around the girls that indicated they were using their telekinetic powers appeared. Captain Stanley stepped beside Mister Brian and looked at his instruments. Then he looked at her first sergeant and said, "Bring a case of ration bars, water, and some glasses." The first sergeant left the room quietly and reappeared a few minutes later with the required items. The sergeant opened the case of rations, extracted three bars and unwrapped them while the Captain filled the glasses. These were set near the children and after a few minutes, the girls picked up the bars and began eating.

The phone sounded and when Sims answered, Ambassador Larkin said, "When the girls come up for air, please tell them that the Premier sends his thanks."

Sims replied, "I will and the way the mayor is looking at them they will probably get the keys to the city from him."

Four and a half hours later after a dozen ration bars apiece the glow around the girls faded and Sarah said, "I'm hungry."

Mayor Drake's eyes bulged and he asked amazed, "After a huge meal a dozen ration bars in a little over four hours, how can you be hungry?"

Mr. Brian, Captain Stanley, First Sergeant Smith and the girls all laughed and Brian said, "One of the things that I measure is the amount of calories they burn when they are using their powers. In the last several hours they burned nearly eleven thousand calories each."

Sims secretary entered the room and turned on a media station that was broadcasting pictures of the girl's handiwork in Lake Pontchartrain. She said to the girls, "I thought you might like to see what you accomplished for us." The image in the entertainment device showed a column of water nearly two hundred meters wide going straight up and the level of the lake was dropping visibly.

Captain Stanley said, "Am I to assume that Africa just got very wet?"

Sarah answered, "All except Sudan and a large part of the Australian outback got wet too."

"Good," Captain Stanley said, "Then let's get a meal into you; get you to Southland Electronics, then catch a plane for your next performance."

While the girls were eating, Sarah asked, "Mr. Brian, how did your instruments hold up?"

"I brought several attenuators with me so there were no blown fuses, if that's what you're asking."

Mr. Sims inquired, "Is that what I saw glowing beside your equipment earlier?"

"Yes," Brian replied, "And from the looks of things I'm going to have to use insulated gloves to pick some of them up."

"How long did that take us?" Melinda asked.

"About four and a half hours," Brian answered.

"I take it that it would normally take longer?" Mister Sims asked.

Linda responded, "The generators at home don't provide anywhere near the power we had available here so this would have taken much longer."

While the conversation had been going on Mister Brian examined the readings he had obtained. After a few minutes he said, "Girls I still can't come up with a maximum power range for you. The readings even with the shunts are still maxed out."

"Is the power they use proportional in some way?" Sims asked.

"As far as we know," Linda answered, "It's exponential. What we have not been able to determine is what the multiplication rate is. Ms. Callison, you need to go to Central in Iowa for about three weeks."

"Can I ask why?" Ms. Callison asked.

Melinda replied, "Many adults can be made to have their Psi powers jump started with the installation of a computer connection and programming. Mayor Drake when she comes back you need to create a special department for her to head. She will know what she needs at that time." Then she smiled sweetly at Captain Stanley and finished, "We're ready to leave now."

The visit to Southland Electronics went smoothly and three hours later, the girls and their guards were airborne for Dallas. The trip from the Dallas airport to Multicore Electronics and that visit also went smoothly. On the trip back to the airport, an armored truck pulled up beside the family bus and then slammed into it. At the same time, the girls screamed and the something appeared around them. Jennifer released itself from its storage compartment, rolled to the girl's seats, extended its claw hands into the something. The something immediately grew brighter and then faded out. The girls shook their heads and Melinda said, "Thanks Jennifer. Get plugged in, you can't have much power left after that."

The robot beeped and typed, "Are you all right?" At that moment, the armored truck drove into the side of the family van again knocking it into the right hand lane. Jennifer grabbed an anchor and the driver robot slammed on the brakes. The armored truck surged ahead of the van and swerved right again. Whoever was operating the truck over controlled and the truck tipped onto its side and slid down the freeway. When the truck had slid almost to a stop, it exploded in a huge ball of fire and yellowish green smoke. Jenifer beeped several times and typed, "Chlorine gas, close your eyes and hold your breath."

The robot driver put the bus in reverse and began backing away from the truck and cloud of gas. "Sarah yelled "Teleport to the plane!" A triple boom followed that command. A moment later, it began raining heavily on the armored truck and everything around it even though the sky was clear. Shortly the chlorine had been washed out of the air and the fire extinguished.

Another triple boom occurred and the girls were back. The attack on the girls had also caused a series of chain reaction accidents as other vehicles slammed into one another. Melinda said, "Make sure there are no other fires and then let's separate the vehicles so the army and ambulances can get to the injured." Down the length of the freeway crowded with bent vehicles, were righted and lined up along the sides of the road.

A Texas state trooper walked out from between the vehicles just as Captain Stanley arrived from the other direction. The trooper asked, "Who's moving the vehicles?"

Captain Stanley looked about and replied, "They are," indicating the triplets.

"Great," the trooper said, "The emergency vehicles are stuck about two kilometers back."

"I don't think it will be much longer and they'll be able to get through," Captain Stanley replied as she watched some of her soldiers hand the girls ration bars and canteens of water."

The trooper turned and looked back down the road, grunted, and said, "Then I'll get back to the other end and get the emergency vehicles trough."

"Before you do that," Captain Stanley said, "Check that armored truck and if it has a driver that is still alive put that person under arrest."

Jennifer rolled up to Captain Stanley, beeped for attention and typed, "The armored truck was radio controlled. There is no driver. You will need to contact a HAZMAT team. The truck has the remains of a bomb and chlorine in it."

"Chlorine," the trooper repeated alarmed, "Do we need to evacuate the area?"

The robot beeped twice and Captain Stanley said, "The girls doused everything with water from someplace right when the bomb exploded."

The trooper asked, "What don't those kids do?"

"Stay out of trouble," Captain Stanley replied smiling, "And not because they seek it, it has a way of finding them."

"I understand," the trooper replied, "And it looks like they have things organized so let's get you out of here before the press arrives."

"I can agree with that," Captain Stanley said then commanded, "First Sergeant, get everyone loaded up and let's go."

Everyone climbed into their assigned vehicles and the convoy continued its interrupted trip.

The visits to Atlanta and Nashville went without any hitches. Miami was a different story. The city still had a large contingent of military who were assisting the police in controlling looters and cleaning up the damage hurricane Candice left in its wake. When the convoy arrived at Southern Cross Electronics, everything was badly damaged. Buildings had literally been blown down. Anthony Norwalk the owner met the girls on their bus and told them, "It's going to be six months before my company will be functional again. Please express my sorrow at not being able to build what Mister Stevens wants and ask him to seek another company."

"We've contacted him telepathically," Melinda replied, "And he said to tell you that he understands and has already found a small company in Des Moines to build the module. He also said that he will see what he can do to help your company get back into operation."

"I'd appreciate that," Mister Norwalk said, "Did he indicate what kind of help that might be?"

"No, he said he would get in touch with you personally," Linda responded.

"In that case," Mister Norwalk said, "I guess you should head for home because it isn't very safe in Miami yet because of the looting and stuff going on." Mister Norwalk stepped off the family bus and waved good-bye. The convoy returned to their plane and took off for Central.

AIKO'S ANGELS

The Esteban family had just finished a light meal as they flew over the eastern slope of the Alleghany mountains when two of the fighter escorts below them disappeared in huge fireballs. At nearly the same instant eight tree trunks each about fifteen meters long and sharpened on one end ripped through the Galaxy 7. One of the trees erupted between Aiko and Hiro's seats throwing them and their seats into the ceiling of the plane. Karlita, Mika, and Hana grabbed each other's hands and linked. On the ground a large explosion occurred and as suddenly the now wingless C-150 was gone in a thunderous explosion. A moment later the fuselage appeared between the runways of the Baltimore-Washington International airport. Yoshi and Pecos the family robots righted themselves from where they had been knocked over. Yoshi rolled to the girls and typed, "Go down stairs and get out of the plane in case there is fire."

Karlita replied, "As soon as we get mom and dad untangled so we can take them too."

Several soldiers came up the ladder from the cargo bay below and one of them said, "You three get below we'll get your parents."

The girls went down to the cargo bay and looked at the mess the attack had made. "The other families were attacked with mechanical devices," Karlita told her sisters. "This is the first all Psi attack we've faced."

The girls ducked as a loud roar passed over them and Hana said, "Maybe we should look outside and see if we need to move what's left of our plane."

Karlita answered, "I'm not sure I have the energy. Boy am I hungry."

"Kids," Captain Foley asked, "Can you move us to a bit safer spot? Right now we are between three runways."

A private who had heard Karlita's comment about hunger handed her several ration bars as she asked Captain Foley, "Where should we put it?"

"About two hundred meters southeast of here," the Captain answered pointing in the indicated direction.

The girls joined hands then Karlita said in a mischievous voice, "Okay, it's done."

Captain Foley shook his head and asked, "Just like that huh?"

"Yup," Mika said between bites of ration bar. Do you have some water? These bars are awfully dry."

First Sergeant Reynolds handed each girl a canteen and said, "Drink up. Sir, Colonel Sheridan wants us outside just in case. We're lowering Mr. and Ms. Esteban out through a hole in the side of the upper fuselage. The robots are lowering themselves to the ground by punching holes in the plane with their claws. The Colonel also said that he was able to notify the fighters and they should be here shortly."

Karlita said chuckling, "I'll bet the airport people here are very upset." Then very seriously, "Besides our parents, how many others were hurt?"

"Three here in the plane," Colonel Sheridan said as he joined the group. "We also lost two of the fighters. What did they use on us?"

"Wood," Hana answered, "Or rather trees that had been cut and sharpened on one end."

"We destroyed an enemy Psi team and its generators," Mika added, "Then used the surge of power from the explosion to put us here."

"Where is here?" Captain Foley asked.

"The Baltimore-Washington International airport," Colonel Sheridan replied. "The airport authorities are just a bit miffed at us. Ambulances and other medical people are on the way."

"Can we get either the front or rear opened?" the Captain asked. "Their bus is okay and most of my vehicles as well. I'd rather use our vehicles than unknown ones."

214

"My chief loadmaster is working in the rear now and should have it open soon," the Colonel replied.

"Tell him to get away from the cables and we'll cut them and lower the ramp," Karlita said.

"I heard," the loadmaster said as he walked by the group with a load of tools. "No one is near them now."

Hana asked, "Captain, do you have a large supply of ration bars? If we keep using our powers we're going to stay hungry." When she finished talking the ramp had been lowered.

"If it looks like we're going to run out," the Captain chuckled, "My people will just have to go on a diet for a little while. In the meantime eat up." The Captain turned to his people and called, "Alright people, let's get the vehicles off loaded and get the injured to the hospital."

The sirens of emergency vehicles grew loud as fire, security, and ambulances arrived. The army and robots set up a hasty security perimeter and stopped everything outside of it. An airport security captain got out of his car and stomped towards the battered plane. Two robots and several soldiers confronted him and refused to let him pass. He yelled, "Who's in charge here?"

Captain Foley, Colonel Sheridan, and the triplets walked to the security captain and Karlita answered while smiling at her most mischievous, "My sisters and I are."

"She's correct," Colonel Sheridan said quietly. "No one is allowed past our security perimeter with weapons."

"I was told that you have injured people," the security captain told the Colonel, ignoring the girls, "How are the medical people supposed to get to them to help?"

Karlita answered, "If the medical people allow themselves and their equipment to be searched then they will be allowed to pass." While she said that several medical people were doing just that and being passed to aid the injured.

"Okay," the security officer said, "I see that the injured are being helped." Then he waved at the remains of the plane and asked, "Can someone explain what happened and how that got here?"

"We could," Hana answered, "But because of national security we're not going to."

"And I'm talking to the Colonel not kids," The security Captain snarled.

Colonel Sheridan sighed and said, "If those kids as you called them said we're not going to tell you, then we're not going to tell you. They are in charge here."

One of the robots beeped for attention and typed, "I am Admiral Yamamoto and you are being told the truth, Captain. Captain Foley, Aiko and Hiro are ready to travel. I have instructed that one ambulance person go with each one in the bus with the girls, Yoshi, and Pecos. The other injured are loaded in your vehicles with the company medics and ready to travel as well. The nearest hospital is Harbor Hospital Center."

"Admiral, please instruct eleven through twenty to remain here to help keep things under control. You and two through ten will go with us," Karlita instructed. "Colonel, I suggest that the good Captain here have a telephone conversation."

"I'll see you later, Colonel," Captain Foley said and walked to the Esteban family bus with the girls.

"That sounds like a good idea," Colonel Sheridan mused, "I'll see to it. Go get on the bus with your parents. Then he looked at another robot and asked what number are you?"

The robot typed, "Admiral Yamamoto 12."

"Thank you," Colonel Sheridan said, "Please bring the Captain inside."

The robot beeped twice and typed, "He is armed."

"Captain, you will have to surrender your weapon to me for a little bit," Colonel Sheridan said. When the security Captain tried to back away his arms were clamped to his sides by robotic claws and Colonel Sheridan took his pistol from the captain's holster and said, "Let's go."

In the bus on the way to the hospital, Karlita went into the blank stare of telepathic communication. When she came out a moment later she said, "Yoshi, Pecos we need you to plug into the busses power and feed power to us. Hana, Mika; Dr. Janice sent me the method for starting healing. Put your hands on each side of mom and dad's heads. I will hold onto you. Yoshi, Pecos put a claw on me so I can draw power."

Mika and Hana turned around in their seat and placed their hands as their sister had directed the robots followed suit. Karlita put her hands on her sisters and a glow appeared around her body that ran up her arms surrounding her sisters. The ambulance attendants watched mystified.

Five minutes later the glow stopped and Karlita said, "Would you medics start IVs of saline and glucose on our parents please? Show what you use to the robots first."

The medics looked at Captain Foley and one asked, "Is that alright?" Captain Foley nodded his head.

Aiko opened her eyes and asked weakly, "What happened?"

Mika, who was still turned around backwards by Aiko's head replied, "We got attacked mom. An enemy Psi team shoved big tree trunks through the plane knocking its wings off. We teleported the fuselage to Baltimore and you and dad are being taken to a hospital."

Captain Foley joined the girls and added, "When the attack occurred we lost two of the fighters. The first log to penetrate our plane tore your seats loose and slammed you into the plane's ceiling. These three destroyed the attackers and dumped the fuselage into the Baltimore Washington airport making airport officials very unhappy."

"I'll bet," Hiro said smiling weakly having come to also. Then he asked, "What about us?"

Karlita answered, "When we were linked to you just now Dr. Janice joined us and fixed it so your concussions will heal the rest of the way. She told us that you both have broken bones that the doctors need to put in place before we can make them heal."

Yoshi beeped for attention and typed, "A new C-150 is enroute and Doctor Janice is sending a jet to pick up your parents. The other sets of triplets are finishing their parent's Missions. Doctor Janice recommends that you do the same thing."

Captain Foley who was in the best position to see the screen read the message aloud then added, "Should we change the order around as well?"

Karlita answered, "If the other groups are, it might be better if we don't. Except for New York because I think we're going to be late there unless Yoshi can get our meeting time pushed back."

"Folks," an ambulance attendant, who had accompanied them said, "We're at the hospital. Shall we get your parents fixed so you all can do what you need to do?"

Forty-five minutes later Doctor Mason George was saying to Captain Foley, "I just got off the phone with a Doctor Janice and she told me to get the girls and show them the x-rays on their parents. Why would young girls need to see x-rays?"

The triplets were standing next to Captain Foley and Karlita responded, "Out here in the waiting area we can't tell you. Can we go someplace private?"

"Certainly," Doctor George replied. "This way."

After explaining things to the doctor, the girls were taken to the emergency room where there parents were. "According to Doctor Janice," Karlita told them, "This is going to hurt a lot."

Aiko smiled wanly and said, "We'll feel better afterwards so don't worry." The two beds were put side by side so that the girls could touch each other. Mika and Hana put their hands over the damaged bones in their parents, Karlita put one hand on each of her sisters, and Yoshi and Pecos trailing power cords they had plugged into outlets placed a claw on Karlita. Karlita said as she began to draw power and pass it to her sisters, "Three, two, one, go." Aiko and Hiro screamed in agony then passed out.

The doctor and nurses started to move in to work on the girl's parents when Captain Foley said loudly, "Don't interfere!" Then he waved the staff away.

"We need to check their parents," Doctor George said worriedly.

"See the glow around all five of them and the robots?" Captain Foley asked. The doctor nodded and he continued, "If you enter that field you could kill the girls, or their parents, or all of them including yourself."

A nurse asked, "Just what are they doing?"

The captain responded, "Their causing their parents bodies to heal themselves by mending the broken bones to the point that casts won't be needed." The Captain chuckled and continued, "I can tell you one thing though. When the girls come out of that they are going to be ravenous and want lots to eat. Their parents will be hungry also but not as bad because of the IVs."

As if they had been cued, the girls took deep breaths, the glow died and Karlita asked, "Is there anything around here to eat. I'd even settle for a ration bar right now."

The nurse blinked twice, smiled and said, "I think we can do better than dry old ration bars. I'll be right back."

In a few minutes the nurse was back with three hot packaged meals and said, "These should hold you until you can get to the cafeteria." Yoshi rolled to the nurse then beeped. She asked, "What was that all about?"

"Checking for poisons," Mika answered.

"You'd be surprised at the number of times people have tried to kill our parents and us," Hana added.

In an outraged voice the nurse asked, "Is that why you're here captain?"

"Yes," Captain Foley sighed, then went on, "Remember seven years ago when the Jupiter body threatened to destroy the sun? Ms. Esteban was one of the three women who saved us."

Yoshi beeped for attention and typed, "Colonel Sheridan says that the airport officials are turning purple with rage. The new

C-150 landed and stopped next to our damaged plane. Then a small Jet and fifteen fighters landed and stopped next to the two planes forcing them to close the airport."

"Doctor," Karlita said between bites of food, "Please check that our parents are ready to travel. We need to leave as quickly as possible."

"Right," the doctor answered. Twenty minutes later the Esteban family was back in its bus and the convoy was underway back to the airport. At the airport they were waved past the gate guards and drove out onto the runway. The vehicles stopped and two stretchers were carried from the family bus to the small plane then the vehicles drove into the new C-150 and both planes and the fighters took off. Shortly after the planes took off, a large army transporter and a crane arrived. The remains of the broken C-150 were placed on the truck and then everyone and everything involved in the operation departed.

Aboard the new C-150, Karlita asked, "Yoshi, what is our schedule now?"

"I was able to get the schedule for New York changed for tomorrow morning," Yoshi typed in reply. "After that the schedule is unchanged."

Colonel Sheridan entered the passenger compartment and said, "If you push the arm rests up they'll fold in between the seat backs so you can lie down and sleep."

Captain Foley, who had just come from the cargo bay of the plane said, "That sounds like a very good idea. Let's stay hidden for now and not leave the plane until tomorrow morning. Colonel, can you get airport catering to fix these three up with some decent chow?"

"We transferred everything from the other plane," Colonel Sheridan replied, "But I had to order more because one of the trees took out the refrigerating unit and some of it spoiled. We can feed them a meal now though."

"Good," Mika interjected, "Because I'm hungry. Yoshi would you please?" The robot beeped and rolled to the plane's galley.

"How long before we land in New York?" Karlita asked.

"About forty-five minutes," Colonel Sheridan replied.

"Will there be someplace where we can take a bath?" Mika asked. "I perspired quite a bit while we were doing things."

"We'll see what can be arranged," Captain Foley responded.

Yoshi returned with meals for the girls and typed, "The girls like to swim so I suggest that you get a portable pool and something to heat water with. You will also need to get towels, wash cloths, and soap for them."

"That seems reasonable," Captain Foley said, "And a tarp and some rope so we can make a private space for them downstairs."

"Get with Sergeant Kelly about where to set things up," Colonel Sheridan said. "Enjoy your baths girls." Then he returned to the cockpit. After the plane landed and was parked in the usual secure area, a single military vehicle left it and drove out of the airport. A little over two hours later the vehicle returned. A water truck followed the army vehicle back to the plane. A short time later a hose was run from the water truck into the plane.

Admiral Yamamoto, the robot security chief, rolled up to Captain Foley and typed, "Find me 4 pieces of metal rod and with the help of another robot I will heat the water."

Captain Foley called, "Sergeant Kelly." When the sergeant arrived the Captain pointed at the robot's screen and asked, "Can you fix them up with something to use?"

Sergeant Kelly asked, "How long do you need Admiral?"

"Long enough that we don't put our claws in the water."

"We have some long screw drivers and wrench handles," Sergeant Kelly queried, "Will they work?" Yamamoto beeped. A small swimming pool was set up near the plane's elevator filled with water and heated by the robots that inserted the tools into the water and passed an electric current between them.

The girls wearing robes rode the elevator to the cargo bay and were soon taking a warm bath while Private Marybelle Jones watched just in case. When they finished their baths the girls went back to the passenger compartment where Yoshi had prepared the plane seats to be their beds.

The next morning the family bus, robot van, and several army vehicles rolled out of the plane and left the airport. The visit to Kelly Electronics went smoothly and three hours later the C-150 was taking off for Chicago.

In Chicago, Commander Eddington from the U.S. Coast Guard was waiting for the plane when it stopped in the O'Hare Airport secure area. When the plane opened its rear cargo ramp Captain Foley stepped out and asked, "Can I help you Commander?"

Commander Eddington handed Captain Foley a note and asked, "Can I talk to the girls, I have a problem that their parents feel they can solve for the Coast Guard."

Captain Foley turned and called, "Admiral Yamamoto, can you roll out here and check the Commander?"

A beep sounded from inside the plane's cargo bay and a robot rolled out and joined the two men. A moment later Yamamoto typed, "He can come in."

Commander Eddington stepped into the plane and went with Captain Foley to the passenger compartment where the girls were finishing their breakfast. Captain Foley introduced the Commander and he said, "Girls I've talked to the President and to your parents in Iowa and they feel that you might be able to help with a problem."

"What sort of problem," Karlita asked.

"A tanker and a container ship collided in heavy fog last night," Commander Eddington replied. "The tanker has a mix of chemicals in it and the container ship lost about half of its conexs. Both ships have sunk and if we can't get them out of the water they will irreparably pollute Lake Michigan."

"We would need access to a very large power source to lift something like that out of the water," Hana told the Commander. "Where would we get it and where would we put the ship once we bring it up?"

"How much power would you need?" Commander Eddington queried.

"Some friends of ours had access to three New Orleans power plants," Karlita replied, "With over fifteen terawatts of electricity available to move water out of Lake Ponchartrain."

"That's a lot of power," the Commander stated, "I'll have to see if I can get the Illinois Power and Light Company to cooperate."

"If they don't want to help, call the President," Mika inserted smiling.

Yoshi beeped for attention and typed, "I just received a message from General Lee that the President has already called Illinois Power and told them that if they didn't cooperate he would send in the army to help them."

Karlita said, "That solves that problem. Now we need pictures of the two ships, their exact locations on the lake, and the exact locations for where you want them put. You will also need to make sure that the destination locations are clear of people or animals."

"Could you come to sector Headquarters in an hour and a half?" Commander Eddington asked, "I should have everything set by then."

"Actually," Karlita replied, "If you can just send us the information electronically, and tell the mayor that his city will experience a blackout, we'll do it from here."

"How do I contact you from my headquarters?" the Commander asked.

Yoshi beeped, handed the Commander a piece of paper, and typed, "Call this code from a secure phone when you are ready. Give the code that is typed below the number."

"Then let me get going and get things done," Commander Eddington said as he stood and wave farewell.

As soon as the Commander was out of the plane Karlita said, "Yoshi, please get our contact sets." Yoshi beeped and left to get the contact sets.

Captain Foley asked, "Why don't you want to leave the plane?"

"The Coast Guard district headquarters is on South Lakeshore Drive near the Navy Pier Park," Karlita answered. "To make his timeline we would have to leave at the same time he did and we still need to go to Garland Electronics today."

"And?" Captain Foley asked raising an eyebrow.

"The Commander is under alien control," Karlita continued, "And would have led us into a trap. We're leaving the programming in place for now and doing things so that the trap can't be sprung."

"What about the ships?" Captain Foley asked.

"That's real," Mika answered, "Yoshi, do you have our contact sets yet?" Yoshi beeped and Mika continued, "Good, have you notified the mayor that his city is going to experience a brief blackout and what's available to eat. We'll need food when we're done."

As Yoshi handed each girl her contact set it typed, "There is plenty to eat and the mayor has been notified." Yoshi turned on its holograph projector and it contained an image of a portion of Lake Michigan. There were Coast Guard ships with small craft nearby. The water began to bubble ferociously, then a two hundred and fifty meter long tanker poked its damaged prow out of the water. Slowly the ship continued to slide out of the water until its entire length was in the air. Then it moved through the air to a shipyard dry dock where it settled to the consternation of the dockworkers who watched it land. Back in the lake the other ship with stacks of metal containers in its deck erupted from the water. Around it containers that had fallen off in the collision appeared. The containers settled onto the deck of the ship and then it too floated to the dry dock.

The triplets took a deep breath and took their contacts off. Captain Foley had gotten a food cart and served the girls fried chicken with the trimmings. While pouring drinks for the girls he asked, "Any problems?"

"Just a very angry mayor who didn't get a chance to warn his city," Colonel Sheridan said as he walked into the passenger compartment.

"We never said we would give him time to warn the city," Karlita said between bites of food. "How long did that take us anyhow?"

"Just a little over three hours from the time you put on your contacts until you took them off," Captain Foley replied.

"Good," Hana said, "That should have been long enough for a special team from central to do some serious deprogramming here."

"Special team?" Colonel Sheridan asked.

"Mika replied, "We weren't the only ones drawing power. We were the cover for their operation."

"When did the operation get put together?" Colonel Sheridan asked. "Do we still need to get you to Garland Electronics?"

"The operation was made possible by the two ships sinking because it allowed for enough power to be drawn covering the teams activities," Karlita replied. "Keiyanai's team teleported the team in, in a bus to do the job and pulled them back out again. We still need to go to Garland to make the presentation and implant the security restrictions in the workers."

"Which means, Captain Foley," Hana said, "We should probably get going."

"After you," Captain Foley said waving a hand towards the plane's elevator.

The trip to Garland Electronics was short and they were met by James McPherson, the owner. He greeted them saying, "Hi kids." Then he asked, "Captain, what do you need to do here?"

"Just to make sure that these three stay alive and unharmed," Captain Foley replied. "There are ten robots with us also that have the same mission."

Mr. McPherson nodded his head and asked, "Can we check my security people as we go by?"

"Sure," Karlita responded, "Please lead on."

"This way," Mister McPherson said. At the security office he said, "This is Jim Hardaway my security chief."

Officer Hardaway said, "Welcome to Garland. I see you've brought your own security with you."

"Yes sir, there have been a number of attempts to kill us so we have a large security force that always travels with us." Behind officer Hardaway one of his guards slumped to the floor asleep and Karlita continued, "Don't take any discipline against officer Bixby. She didn't have any control over the programming that had been put in her mind."

Officer Hardaway looked at Mister McPherson and asked, "Programming?"

"Need to know," Mr. McPherson replied, "Do it their way."

"Mika said, "Teasing is allowed if you want to. She'll sleep for about an hour."

Officer Hardaway laughed and replied, "Okay we'll do that. Enjoy your visit."

The group entered a large room with various kinds of machines placed about the floor on an orderly manner. Between the machines were rows of chairs filled with people. Some people were even sitting on top of machines for a better view. McPherson stepped up to a microphone and said, "If I can have everyone's attention please." After a moment the chatter ceased and he continued, "When a major stock holder in this company states that he wants all of the employees present for a briefing on a new project he's going to get it. Many of you know Clarence Stevens from his visits to our place. He was injured in the Las Angeles earthquake and sent the Estebans to give the briefing. They were injured coming here so the family robot and the Esteban's daughters are going to make the presentation instead. Robot, please."

Yoshi rolled to the front of the crowd of workers and started its projector. In the audience several people went to sleep but near the rear door to the room two men began to walk jerkily towards the front of the room. Two robots appeared behind them clamped their arms with their claws, picked them up, and rolled out of the room. Mika who was closest to Mr. McPherson asked, "Our robot can continue the briefing, can we go to your office?" McPherson nodded and waved his hand towards the door.

In his office, McPherson asked, "What do you need?"

"The two men the robots took out are wanted by the Chicago police," Karlita replied, "Could you call them to come collect the men." Turning to Captain Foley she continued, "We'll need our contact sets and if you have one Mr. McPherson, a data chip for us to record our evidence on?"

There was a knock on the office door and a robot entered with the girls contact sets on its tray. The girls donned their contacts, connected to the robot, and after a few minutes Mika asked, "Can Admiral Yamamoto connect to your computer to transfer our information to the data chip?"

McPherson opened a drawer took out a data chip, plugged it into his computer and said, "Go ahead Admiral."

The robot connected to the computer, its screen blurred for a moment, and then, "Please remove the data chip and be sure that the police sign for it as evidence" appeared on the screen.

McPherson said, "I'll do that," then he activated his phone and called the police. While he was waiting for the call to go through he asked, "What do I need to tell them?"

"Mr. Sanchez is wanted for the Navy Pier Park murders," Hana said, "And Mr. Stone is wanted for drug dealing."

The call activated and McPherson passed on the information. After disconnecting he said, "I seem to recall something Clarence said," then he snapped his fingers and activated his office intercom. When it was answered he said, "Judy, I have three very hungry young girls in my office. Can you get them something to eat from our lunchroom and bring it here?"

There was a chuckle and then the intercom clicked followed by a knock on the office door. The door opened and Ms. Judy Davis entered pushing a cart. "These are specialties from our cafeteria. I hope you like them."

Hana said, "When we're hungry we like most anything edible. Mr. McPherson, you need to send Ms. Davis to Central in Iowa for programming to activate her, the rest of the way."

"Activate?" Mr. McPherson asked.

"Yes sir," Karlita said around a bite of deluxe chilidog. "She's had the connector surgery already and she has partially activated her Psi abilities on her own."

"Can I be programmed also?" McPherson asked, "I had the connector surgery about two years ago."

Admiral Yamamoto beeped for attention and typed on its screen, "Doctor Janice is expecting you one at a time two weeks apart. Ms. Davis, you're scheduled to fly to Des Moines tomorrow at 8:00 a.m. You will return in three days."

McPherson asked, "Do we need to go back to the briefing?"

Karlita shook her head no and Mika said, "We already finished what we needed to do and when Yoshi comes we'll have it put the presentation on your computer so you can see it."

As if it had been cued, Yoshi opened the office door and rolled in. It rolled to McPherson's desk, connected itself to his computer, opened a file folder and copied the presentation and some other files into the computer. When it finished a message appeared on the computer screen that said, "I have transferred the presentation, specifications, and diagrams to your computer." Then it disconnected and turned to face the girls and typed on its screen, "We need to be getting back to the plane so we can go to our next destination and you can do school."

Incensed Mika stated, "Contrary to what you may believe, Yoshi, some of us actually like school. So quit the bullying, behave, and allow us to finish eating."

Mr. McPherson laughed, turned to his secretary and said, "I think I understand now, why you always seem to be one step ahead of me. Get a secretary from some place in the building and get him or her up to speed before you leave today, please."

Captain Foley said, "Since you've finished your chili dogs, we should probably get out of Mr. McPherson's hair and take a short plane ride."

The girls set their trays on the cart that Ms. Davis had used, said good bye to Mr. McPherson, the Karlita said sarcastically, "Come on Yoshi, you're the one in a hurry for us to do school today. So let's go."

The journey to the airport was accomplished, and as their plane took off the girls connected to Yoshi and two security robots for school. An hour later the big cargo plane settled onto the runway in St. Paul, Minnesota. The trip to Edmund Electronics and back was uneventful and the girls attended a concert by the Saint Paul Symphony that evening. During the concert Captain Foley noticed that the triplets were holding hands and had a glassy look in their eyes. He patted his pockets checking for ration bars then signaled one of his soldiers and pantomimed drinking from a canteen. The soldier nodded, stepped out of the balcony booth and returned a moment later with three canteens of water. The girls let go of each other's hands and the Captain quietly handed each girl a ration bar and a canteen.

After the concert on the way to the airport, Karlita told Captain Foley, "Thank you for the ration bars."

"How bad was the programming?" the Captain queried.

"The aliens seem to be using large entertainment situations to program groups all at once. I hope they're disappointed that it didn't work in this case."

"I hope they keep underestimating us kids too," Mika added.

"We need dad and Mr. Clarence to look at the power availability situation too," Hana said in thought. "If the aliens figure out that we're tapping it and start sabotaging power plants we could have a problem."

Captain Foley looked at Yoshi and said "Could you pass that on to the appropriate people, please?" Yoshi beeped.

When the vehicles had entered the plane the girls discovered that the swimming pool had been set up for them to take a quick bath after which they rode the elevator to the passenger compartment and went to sleep. The plane left Saint Paul for Great Falls, Montana a short time later.

After the presentation was made at Westholme Electronics the company president took the girls to a working ranch outside of Great Falls where they saw the typical farm animals, milked cows, and went horseback riding in the country for several hours. When they got back to the plane that evening all three complained of soreness from riding. Smiling, Captain Foley sent for Sergeant Alice Rose who had them take a very warm bath and them smeared their behinds with a salve that relieved the pain. Shortly afterwards the C-150 took off for Oklahoma City with the triplets fast asleep on their airplane seat beds.

When the girls left the plane for Sooner Electronics, and headed to the western side of the city, they encountered a huge wild fire that was threatening parts of the city. Smoke made driving hazardous. Hana turned to the family robot and said, "Yoshi, find us a large water source please. It needs to rain here." The robot beeped once and a minute later turned on its holographic projector. The girls looked at the image, joined hands, and it started to rain very heavily over the entire front of the fire.

When the girls let go of each other's hands Captain Foley handed each girl a ration bar and asked, "Where did you get the water from?"

"Yoshi, what was the name of the lake?" Karlita asked.

The robot typed, "Lake Stanley Draper, which is in southeast Oklahoma City."

"Thank you," Karlita said, "Driver, the smoke has cleared can we get underway?"

The driver robot beeped twice and typed, "There is a massive accident and emergency equipment ahead."

Hana growled in disgust and queried, "Yoshi, can you give us a picture of Sooner Electronics parking lot?"

Yoshi's holographic projector came on and with a thunderous explosion the entire convoy disappeared.

A moment later there was a second equally loud explosion in the parking lot at Sooner Electronics. Mika asked, "Have we run you out of ration bars yet Captain Foley?"

The Captain patted various pockets on his uniform and replied, "No, but let's see if we can find you something better to eat."

The large boom from the convoy being teleported to the company parking lot drew many people out of various doors to the building. Among them was Grace Norton the company owner. The Captain, girls, and Yoshi got off the bus as soldiers and more robots erupted from the other vehicles. Ms. Norton asked, "Did you all take a short cut?"

Karlita replied as her tummy growled loudly, "Yes ma'am, there was an accident buried in the smoke from the fire on the west side of the city. We put the fire out then teleported our vehicles here."

"Which means," Captain Foley put in, "That they are all three very hungry at the moment. Using their minds to do things burns calories very fast."

"Then let's get you inside and see what we can find for you to eat," Ms. Norton said. We don't have a canteen but if you can wait about twenty minutes my secretary can make a trip to a local restaurant and get plenty for you to eat."

"Captain," Karlita said, "I think that what Ms. Norton is suggesting is alright, but if we each eat a ration bar now then go do the program, her secretary should be back with real food and we'll be hungry again by that time."

Captain Foley pulled three ration bars out of a pocket and said, "Ms. Norton I think her proposal should be followed."

As the Captain handed the bars to the girls Grace Norton replied, "So be it." Then she turned to the watching crowd and said loudly, "Okay people, back inside. The presentation will start in five minutes." To the triplets and Captain Foley she said,

"I see your security is already attending to their things so shall we go inside?"

While the girls, Captain Foley, Ms. Norton, and her secretary Naomi Green sat in Ms. Norton's office and ate fried chicken with the trimmings. Mika asked, "Ms. Green have you got a computer connector?"

Ms. Green shook her head no and Hana queried, "Ms. Norton does Ms. Green seem to read your mind and do things as or before you ask?"

"All the time," Ms. Norton replied eyeing her secretary quizzically.

"Thought so," Mika said with authority. "Ms. Green your Psi powers are activating naturally. Because of that you are a target and we're not at liberty to say by whom. Ms. Norton she needs to go to Central in Iowa for connector surgery and programming. She will need to be gone about two weeks."

"From what I know about things," Captain Foley commented, "She needs to go immediately."

Yoshi, who had been parked quietly against an office wall beeped and on its screen was typed, "Ms. Green, your flight leaves at 8:00 p.m. tonight."

"Considering what we learned in the presentation," Ms. Norton instructed, "Find me someone in house that can at least answer the phones and then go pack."

An explosion blew in the windows to Ms. Norton's office and a cry of "Kill the witches," could be heard outside the building. The triplets crept up to the window from where they had ducked and peeked over the windowsill, one of the girls said a very un-lady like word and the triplets joined hands. Outside gunfire erupted between the army and some of the rioters. Rioters began to have trouble standing and seemed to become very tired and began sitting or lying down and going to sleep. Ms. Green peeked over the windowsill then turned to Captain Foley and said, "Come on we're going to break a vending machine for these kids. They'll need it while they work this out." Five minutes later the three adults were unwrapping purloined chocolate bars and putting them in the girl's hands. Yoshi had plugged into an outlet and had placed a claw on Karlita's back to feed them electrical power.

Outside the security robots had formed a defensive line between the rioters, the soldiers and the Sooner Electronics building. Two of the robots appeared to have been badly damaged by rockets. Karlita turned to Yoshi and said, "We need some more power or more help, see what you can do." Yoshi beeped.

A loud bang occurred inside the office and three women stood looking out the window with their hands joined. Outside the rioters began dropping like fresh mown wheat. In less than five minutes the riot was over.

"You kids just can't seem to stay out of trouble," Monica Shriver said. "All nine of you seem to have the same problem." Then Monica turned to the others and continued, "I'm Monica Shriver and my partners are Amber Jones and Kira Rostov."

Captain Foley noticed that his charges were still holding hands and asked, "What are they up to now?"

In answer to his query there was a loud clatter outside as every weapon the rioters had was deposited in a pile. The triplets let go of each other's hands, picked up a candy bar apiece, and began eating. Around bites Karlita said, "Thanks for the power boost Ms. Monica. Captain, we've put all the rioters' weapons in a pile outside. We should probably do something with them and then head for the plane."

Ms. Norton instructed, "You head for your plane I'll have my people deal with the weapons. I've got just the machine for all of that ordinance."

Yoshi beeped and typed, "The plane has been notified that we are on the way. Ms. Norton please take the ammunition out of the guns before crushing them so that there are no explosions."

"Are all of your robots such smart alecks," Ms. Norton asked.

Karlita answered, "Practical jokers too. Captain Foley, shall we go. Are you riding back with us Ms. Monica?"

"Yes," Monica replied, "Contrary to what seems to be, becoming the norm at Central, I still prefer the more prosaic methods of travel."

Once everyone had returned to the plane, and it was in the air, Captain Foley asked, "How are the aliens determining where to send people to, to try to kill the girls?"

"As far as we have been able to determine," Monica said, "We still have leaks at home that we haven't gotten plugged yet."

The trip from Oklahoma City to Central was brief and soon the triplets were hugging their father. Mika asked, "Where's mom?"

Hiro answered, "Your mother is in Tank circuit one with Wendy and Katherine. Melinda and her sisters suggested that there had to be another scout some place. Keiyana's team found it and your mom and her partners and Jennifer are dealing with it."

"Good," Hana said emphatically. "Dad did you know that the robots are modifying themselves?"

"Clarence told me about that yesterday," Hiro replied. "It seems that he caught one in the act of modifying another robot. I notice that it is time to eat because your tummies are rumbling let's fix the problem."

As the family walked to the dining room to eat, Hana said, "Did you know that the robots don't seem to require charging as often as normal nor do they need to recharge after a heavy drain like when they feed us power?"

CAPTURING AN ALIEN SCOUT

As Hiro Esteban and his oldest triplets seated themselves at their dining room table, Yoshi beeped and typed, "Wendy is requesting that Clarence, William, and Hiro join them from one of the other tank circuits. You are requested to take me with you."

Hiro asked, "Did Robin say why?"

"Robin told me that they have been able to disable the alien scout without destroying it."

Hiro told his daughters, "See you later kids," then he and the robot disappeared."

In space near the asteroid Ceres, the Clarence/William/Hiro mysterious something appeared and asked the Wendy/Katherine/Aiko something, *"What have you caught?"*

The replying thought was, *"A pest! The problem is if we let the temperature go back up in their ship they'll come back to life."*

The Katherine part of the something continued, *"They have three very high powered fission reactors buried behind some heavy shielding and we can't figure out how to shut them down."*

"What does temperature have to do with it?" the William part of the something asked.

"When we got in and looked at them closely we discovered that they are reptilian," the Wendy part answered, *"So our thought was that they might be cold blooded and not able to function if we froze them."*

"They must be fairly radiation resistant," The Clarence part, said, *"It looks like they are manually damping the reactors. It looks like there are blow out panels on the hull..."* Tendrils reached out from the Clarence/William/Hiro something and three large panels blew away from the sides of the alien scout ship. From inside each opening a large cylindrical object floated out into space. The Clarence/William/Hiro something released the cylinders then the Clarence part continued, *"That should*

solve the power issue. Let's see if they have any other sources of power."

Another something appeared and the Doctor Janice part said. *"I got a message that you have some aliens to study. Are they dead or just cold?"*

"Just cold," was the replying thought.

"So do we make them dead?" the doctor's thought asked.

"Preferably without making a mess," the Clarence/William/ Hiro something thought. *"That way we can send some of them to labs on the moon or Mars for examination. Who are you joined with to get out this far?"*

The Doctor Janice part of her something said, *"I'm joined with Monica and her partners."* A tendril extended from the doctor's something to one of the aliens and flattened out over it. Several minutes later the tendril turned itself into something similar to a chisel and drove itself into the base of the alien's skull. Then in rapid succession, the chisel treated every other alien in the scout ship the same way. The Doctor thought, *"Let one of them warm up so I can make sure that I was successful."*

As it warmed up the alien began to move. The warmer it got the faster it moved with what seemed to be a definite goal. Suddenly a large, very bright something appeared and stabbed the thawed alien three times, each in a different location. After stabbing it the third time, the alien collapsed, obviously dead. Then the something stabbed all of the other aliens in the other locations as well. Arielle's thought to the group of somethings was, *"The robots were keeping us up to date and when the first one started moving we had them consult with Socrates. It told them that there were three things beside what they thought was its brain that it could not identify. We thought that the aliens may have more than one brain so we destroyed all of those organs in each one. Oh, we made brain records of what was in them in case we can figure out how their minds work and decipher more of their language."*

"*The alien did seem to be focused on one machine in particular,*" The Wendy part of her something said thoughtfully.

The Melinda part of the girls something thought, "*General Gregory is here and he says for you to put the ship on the moon at the military installation there. He also said that they have the equipment there to disassemble the ship's equipment. He is also arranging transportation for civilian specialists to be sent there.*"

The Clarence part of the men's something asked, "*So which of us is going to shift that monster to the moon?*"

"*Can I make a suggestion?*" the Mika part of the girl's something asked.

"*What do you suggest?*" the Aiko part of the mother's something asked.

"*Put your three somethings together and do it as a unit,*" Mika thought. "*You're probably going to have to do it when the showdown occurs, so why not practice now?*"

"*Don't we have to be together to do that?*" the Katherine part of her something asked.

"*It seems that you only have to be with your own mind partners,*" the Sarah part of the girl's something answered. "*The trios can be apart. We're actually in our own houses and using power from the generator station.*"

The three adult somethings drifted towards each other and melted into one super something that looked at the alien ship, reached a huge tentacle toward it and suddenly the ship was gone. A minute later there was giggling thoughts from the girl's something and the Melinda part thought, "*The General is in contact with moon base and says that you scared the devil out of the people there when the ship suddenly appeared.*"

Katherine's part of her something thought, "*That was sure easy.*"

Melinda's part of her something admonished, "*Don't get cocky mom. The main event is yet to come.*"

Thoughts of laughter echoed around the somethings and Katherine asked, "*Have you been taking sassy lessons from Jennifer or Bennett?*" Then her thought continued, "*Let's go home.*" All of the somethings disappeared.

An hour later Robin beeped for attention and typed, "Dinner is served and the General Gregory is on the phone."

Wendy instructed, "Put the General on and we'll be in to eat in a minute." The communications screen lit and Wendy asked, "What's up?"

"The people investigating the alien vessel say that it is so radioactive that they need it moved farther away from the colony. They don't know if that's normal of if the aliens triggered something before you got them frozen."

The screen flashed, divided into two images, and Doctor Janice said, "I need everyone who was in that merge here right now for decontamination. Tell your robots to check your houses for radiation on anything you have touched."

Wendy said, "We were about to eat, can we do that and then come in?"

Maryann sad flatly, "No! Get here now eat later."

The General said, "If you've been exposed, don't waste time. Doctor, do I need to send out decontamination people to help?"

"Socrates already called them," Doctor Janice replied. "They're setting up now."

Wendy sighed and said, "Roger, Samantha, and Elizabeth go eat we'll be back later. Arielle, Sharron, Brenda, Let's go." The five walked out the front door to their home and disappeared.

When the families arrived, a large tent had been erected next to the hospital construction site and the families were directed into it. Once inside they were told to undress completely and step onto a conveyer, hang onto the railing that moved with it, and close their mouths and eyes. In the chamber, they were sprayed with a special cleaner mixed with warm water and carwash like brushes washed them from head to toe. At the end of the conveyer, they were blown dry with heated air. As each person stepped off the conveyer he or she was handed a robe and told to walk through a radiation detector to be checked. A robot gave each person a shot designed to treat radiation poisoning.

At the exit everyone was met by Doctor Janice who was also wearing a robe said, "Now you can go home and eat but tomorrow you will stay home because that shot is going to make your body flush out any remaining contamination."

"General Gregory told us that we need to move the alien ship away from the colony because of the radiation," Wendy asked. "How are we going to do that and not get contaminated again?"

"Guess we'll have to figure out how to radiation shield ourselves dear," Clarence answered. "Let's go eat and think about it."

When the rest of the family joined the three youngest at in the family dining room, Roger asked, "Mommy, can the robots shields work when you are put together?"

Clarence chuckled and said, "Out of the mouths of babes."

Wendy asked, "What made you think of that, Roger?"

"The robots can stop bullets and rockets and stuff," Roger replied, "So I wonder if they can stop rad, radi- stuff."

"The word is radiation. Robin," Wendy asked, "Can your shield block high levels of radiation?" Robin beeped and typed, "For as long as it takes to use half of our operating power."

Arielle asked, "Can you join your shield to us when we are merged with our mind partners?"

"We would have to experiment to see if I can," Robin answered. "It might be better if one of the guard robots could do it because they have more powerful shields."

"Ask Ivan to come here, please," Arielle said. Robin beeped.

When the security robot appeared, Clarence asked, "How effective are your shields against alpha, beta, and gamma radiation?"

Ivan the family's head security robot typed, "One hundred percent against alpha and Beta particles but only forty percent against gamma radiation."

"Not so good," Clarence said, "Gamma is the worst one because it causes secondary radiation to be generated where its rays impact."

"Is there any way to shield from just that?" Wendy asked."

"Robin, call the General please," Clarence said.

When the phone screen brightened General Gregory asked, "What can I do for you folks this evening?"

"We're trying to find a way to shield our somethings from radiation," Clarence responded. "We have determined that our security robots can give us protection against alpha and beta radiation but only partially against gamma rays. Does the army have a way to protect against them?"

"How do you get contaminated when it is your something that is what is exposed?"

"Good question. I don't think we know enough about the something's structure and the link that makes it appear and do work."

"It takes about ten meters of good old fashioned dirt to block intense gamma radiation. Has anyone said anything about what the safe distance is from the ship?"

"Safe distance," Wendy asked, "What's that?"

"How close you can get and not receive a high enough dose of radiation to hurt you," Gregory replied.

"Do you have something in mind where that information would be needed?" Clarence asked.

"I was thinking that maybe we could make a sling of some sort to lift it with to move it," the General replied.

"So if the robots can provide even partial shielding for the radiation, Arielle added, "The sling's lifting ends wouldn't need to be as long which should give us better control."

"Robin," Wendy instructed, "See if you can find out what the safe distance is for the ship." Robin beeped once.

The phone screen divided showing a face that was unknown to the Stevens or the General. The person's mouth moved and a minute later her voice said, "I'm Colonel Susan Welch,

Commander of Moon Base. I understand that you all were contaminated when you landed the alien on our doorstep."

Clarence answered, "We're part of the people who landed it, how can we help you?"

After the pause Colonel Welch replied, "I need that thing moved about five kilometers from here to keep the base from being contaminated. I received a query about safe distances for moving it. Was that from you folks?"

"Yes it was," Clarence said.

Welch said, "The safe distance for gamma rays is approximately three hundred and fifty meters but if you take too long moving it that distance will go up. How are you planning to move it?"

"We were thinking of rigging a cable sling of some kind so that we can lift it from outside the safe distance," Wendy responded. "General can we get some rolls of steel cable from somewhere that we can transport to the moon for this."

"I'll call the President as soon as we're done here," Gregory replied.

"Have Keiyanai send them up and begin running them out and then dragging them so that they are under the ship. Tell them to stay at the safe distance to do it," Clarence added.

"General," the Colonel said, "Send up eight thousand meters of eight millimeter steel cable. My people have hard radiation suits and training so I'll have them build a lifting harness and get it run under the ship. I think that would work better because my people know how to rig large objects and we don't need to expose any of our PSI people to any more radiation than can be avoided."

"I'll get on it as soon as we disconnect," General Gregory replied.

While the Colonel was explaining what she needed, Clarence had pulled a cable from the edge of the dining room table, connected himself, and gone into a blank stare. He came out of the stare and said, "General, the Materials should begin arriving at the air field in the morning. The President commandeered the bridge cables for the Trans Lake Michigan Bridge. He said that he is ordering more radiation equipment and qualified personnel sent to you as well Colonel."

"We don't really need more people up here to do the job," Colonel Welch said.

Before Clarence could reply General Gregory said, "Colonel, you will take the people the President is sending and minimize your people's exposure as well. Is that understood?"

Grudgingly the Colonel answered, "I'm not saying I don't want the people, the problem is space to put them in when they need to eat and sleep."

"I'll see that, that is taken care of," the General replied. "Clarence, you and your family better finish eating because you won't want to tomorrow while that anti-radiation medication works on you. I'll also notify Ms. Rivera and Ms. Shriver that their teams will need to transport everything to the moon."

The next morning at breakfast Arielle slumped into her chair at the breakfast table and said, "Mom, I don't feel good."

Wendy replied, "I don't either…"

Before Wendy could complete what she was going to say, Robin beeped for attention and typed, "Doctor Janice said to drink the medication she provided. It will help the upset stomachs. She also said that you will drink the broth that she has had the kitchen robot prepare. Kids when you have finished, it is time for school."

Wendy said, "Robin I think that the family needs a day off. I didn't sleep well because of that shot and I'm sure the girls didn't either. When you finish girls, go take a nap. That's what I'm going to do. Are you coming Clarence?"

"That sounds like a great idea, dear," Clarence replied wearily. The family finished its broth, rose, and went to bed.

Several hours later, Robin and Jason woke everyone up and Robin typed, "Doctor Janice would like for you to contact her."

"We'll call her in a few minutes," Wendy answered, "Let us get woke up first." Robin beeped once and both robots rolled out of the room. A little later Wendy instructed Robin, "Call Maryann for me." When the phone screen brightened, Wendy said, "You called."

Maryann Janice asked, "How are you feeling?"

"We're all still tired but feeling okay," Wendy answered. "Of course all five of us have slept most of the morning."

"Good, that's the best thing you could have done," Doctor Janice replied. "The other families seem to have done the same thing. I need for all of you to come in for a quick check just to make sure that we're taken care of the radiation problems. Could you come in say a couple of hours? That should give you enough time for lunch and a shower or whatever else you may need to do. See you later."

Once the screen darkened Wendy asked, "What's for lunch, Robin, more broth or real food?"

Robin typed, "Mud pies, old tires, scrap metal, and rubber cement for desert."

Wendy chuckled and asked, "If you're in that kind of mood, did the little ones give you a hard time this morning?" Robin beeped and Wendy added with a chuckle, "Good! Get everybody to the table and let's eat." Once everyone was seated and the robots had begun serving baked chicken with rice and mixed vegetables Wendy asked, "Robin told me that you three gave the robots a hard time this morning, what did you do?"

The three young children giggled and Roger answered boastfully, "We played hide and seek and they couldn't find us."

"How did you do that?" Clarence asked.

Roger stood next to his place at the table then faded to invisibility. A moment later, he faded back in standing on top of Jason. He bent down, tapped the robot on its cameras and said, "Peek-a-boo!" The robot tilted its cameras up to look at Roger but he had faded out and was standing next to his chair when he reappeared. There was no give away bang as he made each teleport.

Astonished at the new ability her four-year-old son had just displayed Wendy asked, "How did you figure out how to do that?"

"We can do things while we're invisible to Mom," Samantha said proudly as Roger shrugged his shoulders and resumed eating.

"What kinds of things can you do sis?" Arielle asked.

"Samantha replied, "Whatever I can do visible you just can't see me."

"Can you make whatever you're using invisible too?"

"We haven't tried that so I don't know," Samantha answered.

Clarence asked, "Jason don't you robots have infrared and other sensors?" Jason beeped once and Clarence queried, "Did you try using those to find the kids?"

Again, the robot beeped once and typed, "They do not show up on those sensors."

"Hmm," Clarence said thoughtfully, "Roger, girls, when your big sisters, mother, and I get back from seeing Doctor Janice, I want you to get your connector sets and teach us how to do that. In between now and then stay out of trouble."

With a mischievous grin in his voice and twinkle in his eyes Roger said, "Okay dad."

"Roger," his mother said, "We mean it, stay out of trouble."

Roger answered circumspectly, "Yes mama."

An hour later the in Doctor Janice's office she told them, "All of the radioactivity has been cleared from your systems and you shouldn't develop any secondary effect problems. But that's only going to be true if you don't get contaminated again anytime soon."

Before she could continue Roger faded into view and said excitedly, "Mommy, daddy there's some men in the house and they're hiding boxes."

Wendy squatted down to Roger's level and said, "Show me what they're doing." The two went into blank stares for a moment and she asked, "What are your sisters doing?"

"They're hiding invisible with Robin and Jason and watching where the men are putting things," Roger answered.

Wendy stood up and turned to the Doctor to ask to use a phone and discovered she was already talking to the head of security instructing, "No sirens, there are still two children hiding in the house."

"Shall we go see what we can do about our unwelcome guests, dear," Clarence asked.

"We probably should in case they have been programmed to blow things up if they get caught," Wendy replied. "Kids, stay here and let us handle this. We'll let you know when it's safe to come home."

When Wendy and Clarence arrived at their house, they found eight unconscious people being frisked by Central's security officers. The army's explosives people were there, going through a pile of fifteen or so bombs removing detonators and fuses. An army Captain approached the couple and asked, "Do you have any ideas about how two young girls managed to take out this bunch of terrorists?"

Clarence answered, "Not at the moment. Where are they?"

"The last I saw them they were sitting at your dining room table eating. From what it looked like they were putting away they're probably going to have upset tummies."

Wendy laughed and asked, "Would you care to place a wager on that Captain?"

The Captain tilted his head, looked at Wendy sharply, thought for a moment, and said, "Considering the Cheshire Cat smile on your face, I don't think I'll take that bet."

"That's very wise of you Captain because you would have most likely lost."

"Can I ask why?"

"When we use our powers we burn calories at a phenomenal rate and our girls were protecting themselves and the family robots with a new skill they've developed."

Robin rolled up to Wendy and typed, "The new ability that Samantha, Elizabeth and Roger developed made stopping these terrorists interesting."

"How did it do that?" Wendy asked.

"The girls sat on top of Jason and me and made us invisible with them. Then they would teleport us up to a terrorist and we would knock him out with an electric shock. The last two figured out that something was going on but we got to them before they could escape or set the bombs off."

"There's what, eight terrorists laid out over there," Clarence said. "No wonder they're eating a load of food."

At that moment, four children faded into view and Arielle asked, "Did Sam and Lizzy get them all?"

"Yes they did," their mother answered. "Who told you it was safe to come home?"

"Ms. Maryann said it was okay," Brenda replied.

"Where did you find contact sets from to learn Roger's trick?" Clarence asked.

"We don't need them to share with each other," Arielle replied. "You probably don't either."

"We'll have to try later dear," Wendy replied. "Clarence, have you heard whether we were the only ones to get visitors or not?"

Clarence appeared to be in a blank stare and after a moment asked, "Did you ask me something?"

"Did any of the other families have visitors?"

"We seem to have been the only ones this time so far."

An army truck with several soldiers drove up and four of them got out of the back. An officer got out of the front and gave some instructions to the soldiers then he walked to the Stevens family and said, "Good afternoon, I'm Lieutenant James. We're here to pick up the explosives. Security is on the way with a bus for the terrorists."

Wendy replied, "Thank you that means I need to do a little mind reading. Robin come with me and let's get it done." The robot released its data cable as it followed her to the terrorists. She connected and then placed her fingers on the temple of each terrorist in turn. When she finished she unplugged the cable from the base of her skull and instructed, "Get that information to General Gregory."

"Trouble dear?" Clarence asked.

"They weren't programmed by the aliens. They're part of an Islamic religious fringe group." Wendy replied.

Robin beeped and typed, "The General said thank you and that the ship will be ready to move at eight in the morning."

"Thank you Robin," Wendy responded. "Please round up the kids and let's go eat since it is supper time." The robot beeped and rolled away. Wendy took Clarence's arm leaned on his shoulder and said, "I'll be glad when this is over."

Clarence wrapped her in his arms, hugged her and replied, "Me too." He released her from the hug and arm in arm they went into their home.

"Dad," Arielle asked, "Have they decided where we're supposed to dump the alien ship?"

"Robin," Clarence queried, "Did the General say where we're putting that thing?"

The robot beeped and typed, "In a crater ten kilometers lunar west of where it is now. Congress has authorized the purchase of new earth moving equipment because what is there will be too contaminated when the present landing area is decontaminated."

Arielle twisted her head around to look at Jason and asked, "Jason, can you robots calculate or modify a field that would block the extremely short wavelengths where gamma rays are?"

The robot typed, "I will see if we can do that."

"I think that's enough work talk at the supper table," Wendy said. "Let's finish eating then we can go to your father's office and you can teach us how to teleport without the bang. Roger,

Samantha, Elizabeth what else did you do today besides tease the robots and catch the intruders?"

Samantha replied, the robots taught us about kites so we made some and went outside to fly them."

"I used to do that when I was a little girl," Wendy told her children. "It was fun until the wind would stop blowing."

In due course supper was finished and the family adjourned to the family room. Clarence asked, "Are you kiddos ready to teach us your new trick?"

Elizabeth asked, "Can we link with you and mommy?"

Wendy replied, "Sure." The five went into blank stares and after a moment both of the children's parents faded out. A minute later Arielle started acting very strangely and started laughing. Her father faded back in and the rest of the family discovered that he was tickling her. The rest of the children ran to help their sister and soon a mass of bodies was rolling about the floor in a wrestling match. Wendy faded back in also and smiled as she watched her family play.

A short time later, all six children were laid out on the floor. Clarence sat up and reached to each side of him and tickled the nearest children who began laughing and rolled out of his reach. Robin rolled into the room and typed, "It is time for the children to take their baths and get ready for bed." Clarence started to get up from the floor when all six children jumped up and piled on top of him pushing him back down.

Arielle asked, "Give up yet?"

Clarence answered, "Nope," then faded out and the kids dropped to the floor. He reappeared stretched out in his easy chair. Not willing to let their father escape they also faded out and reappeared piled on top of him in his chair.

Wendy said quietly, "Kids, it's time for you to get ready for bed." The six got off their father, kissed their mother good night, and went to their baths and beds. Wendy faded out from where she sat, reappeared in her husband's lap, and asked, "Care to wrestle some more?"

Clarence pulled her face to his, kissed her, and replied, "I'd rather snuggle." Both of them faded out.

The next morning three of the mysterious somethings appeared above the alien ship. Wendy thought, *"Well since everyone is here should we get this over with?"*

The other somethings agreed and they all flowed together becoming one extra-large something. Tendrils reached from the something and picked up two huge steel rings that had heavy bridge cables connected to them. The cables ran under the alien ship to the other ring. The rings were lifted and brought together. Then the something rose higher and moved sideways, lifting the ship and causing it to swing towards its new home in the designated crater. When they finished the somethings disappeared.

A new something that was very bright appeared with what looked like a huge bulldozer blade. The blade settled into the lunar dirt just outside the danger zone. The something settled behind it wrapping tendrils around two long extensions that protruded from the side that was protected from the radiation. More tendrils anchored themselves in the dirt and the blade began moving forward pushing contaminated dirt into a huge pile that was a safer distance from the moon base. The blade was raised just enough to clear the surface, backed up, dropped back and pushed a new tract of contaminated dirt. The process was repeated twice more then the blade was dropped at the end of the push and the something disappeared.

From Tank Circuit One Wendy thought to everyone who had helped move the ship, *"I think I'm going to see Doctor Janice just to make sure I didn't get contaminated again."*

Keiyanai Rivera thought back, *"It would probably be a good thing for all of us to do. See you there."*

When the adults arrived at the medical facility, they were surprised to discover that their oldest triplets were already there and that Doctor Janice's medical robots were checking them for radiation exposure. Clarence asked, "What's going on here?"

Doctor Janice explained, "They contacted me, the General and the moon base commander about clearing the contaminated soil for them."

"We also called the President about where to get the materials to make a huge bulldozer blade," Arielle added.

The Doctor's phone sounded and when she activated it, the face of the moon base commander looked out of it smiling. She said, "I'm calling to thank whoever built that ingenious bulldozer blade and pushed all that contamination to a safe distance from the base."

Wendy answered, "Our kids did that but we haven't seen what they used. You wouldn't by any chance have a picture or some video of what they did would you?"

"Sure do," the Colonel replied, "Let me switch it in so you can see." The image changed to show a Blade shaped like a capital L laid on its side. As everyone watched the image a very bright something appeared behind the device and a dome shape appeared above it that sealed itself to the edges of the L. The L slid forward pushing a long strip of earth before it. The Colonel continued, "I recognize whatever it is that you folks become when you use your minds, but I have no idea what created the dome."

Arielle responded, "That was the force shields from several of our security robots. They are decontaminating themselves at the decontamination facility."

"Did the children pick up any contamination, Doctor?" Wendy asked concernedly.

"Nope," the Doctor replied, "They're all clean. I suppose that means it's time for them to do school since I see one of the family robots lurking in the hall." A single beep came from the hallway and all nine children faded out. Doctor Janis said into the silence, "Thanks for the call Colonel. Let me get the kids parents checked out so they can go check on their kids."

"From what I just saw I get the feeling that the kids would rather be in school than where their parents can bawl them out," the Colonel replied. "Thanks again."

The screen went blank and Maryann said, "Does bawling them out do any good?"

Clarence chuckled and replied, "Not really, they just find some other hat to pull from a rabbit."

"At least they have been very cautious about what they do so far," Wendy added then sighed, "Let's get us checked out so we can get on with things we need to do."

SPACE SHIPS AND ROBOTS LENDING A CLAW

"Attention," General Gregory's aide called as the General entered the conference room.

"Be seated," the General said, "Let's get started G-1, what have you got for us?"

"We've got the First Marine Brigade tomorrow and the army's Seventh Infantry brigade on Thursday," Brigadier Hanby reported. "I've already given Ms. Stevens the arrival times so they can be checked. I've also messaged both units and told them that their arrival times had to be after eight in the morning even if that meant they had to spend the night somewhere else.

Testing for PSI and connector capable personnel has also begun and is turning up a fair number of people in all ranks. They are being scheduled through the hospital as fast as Socrates's teams of robots can do them. The robots are doing the surgeries around the clock. That's all I have."

"Who's doing the testing?" the General asked.

"There seem to be several new groups of kids getting into the act," the G-1 replied. "I have a feeling that we're about to have an outbreak of PSI active kids other than the three primary sets."

Gregory nodded his head and said, "Good. General Walter, is G-2 as up to date?"

"The information that we received from Ms. Stevens that she got from the bombers at her home indicates that they were part of a company sized group that is attempting to enter the area," General Walter replied. "I contacted Ivan the Terrible and informed it of the problem and asked it to have all of the robots keep watch for strangers entering the area. I got the standard beep in reply. We're starting to see the gadget that Clarence Stevens came up with and it is proving very useful all though we still have to find a PSI capable person to deprogram those affected. That's about all for the moment."

"How many programmed people are you finding?" General Gregory asked.

"It's been running about eight to ten per day."

"Hmm, okay, G-3 what's up?"

"So far integrating the new units into the scheme of things hasn't been a problem," General Granger replied, "But we're going to need to start buying more land or at least get maneuver rights…"

"Excuse me sir," Clara Montgomery the G-5 and only civilian in the room said. "I've been talking to the local farmers and they are willing but they have some concerns. The concerns include crop damage and ground pollution by the vehicles. They've told me that generally from about November to the end of January they wouldn't have a problem if irrigation ditches and such are not damaged."

"You've been busy Clara," General Gregory remarked, "But I think that we also need some dedicated areas."

"I was coming to that sir. We've been able to acquire four adjacent tracts of land where pre Jupiter body farms existed. The Chinese had the families killed and the relatives don't want the farms."

"General Granger, it looks like you need to have a serious conversation about your needs."

"I agree sir," General Granger answered.

Other agenda items were discussed then General Gregory said, "It sounds like everything is mostly under control, let's get out of here."

Late that night every robot in Central rolled onto the parade field in front of the headquarters building and formed in ranks in front of Ivan the terrible. Ten minutes later the robots except for Ivan and his team exploded out of the parade field like the ripples made when a rock is dropped in a pool of water. Just after dawn, several trucks with robot drivers drove onto the parade field. When they stopped robots, who were in the back of the trucks began handing unconscious people to robots on the ground.

The noise from the trucks attracted the attention of the Post Duty Officer and he came out of the front of the headquarters building. Astonished by what he saw he walked across to the nearest robot and asked, "What is going on here?"

The robot's typed response was, "Please wait for Ivan the Terrible. It is on the way."

A different robot rolled up and typed, "I'm Ivan the Terrible. How can I help you?"

"I need to know what is happening," the duty officer answered.

"The G-2 briefed me on a security issue and we robots were able to do something about it," Ivan replied. These are terrorists like the ones who attempted to place bombs in the Stevens' home."

The duty officer asked, "Have you contacted security or the EOD people?"

Ivan beeped then typed, "They are on the way."

General Gregory's staff car drove up and stopped. He got out, walked to the duty officer, and asked, "What's going on Captain?"

"It seems that the G-2 briefed Ivan the Terrible about a problem and it was able to do something about it, sir."

"Is this the group that the Stevens bombers belonged to?" the General asked the robot.

Ivan beeped and typed, "There are over two hundred people here and all of them had bomb materials and weapons."

"Everything's alright Captain, I know about this. I just didn't expect this response," the General said, "You can return to your duties."

The Captain responded, "Yes Sir," and departed.

Turning his attention back to Ivan the General asked, "Have you already contacted security and EOD?"

Ivan beeped and typed, "I also alerted one of the infantry companies to assist with security because most of the robots are grounds keepers, drivers, and such not security robots. I have sent most of the security robots back to their primary assignments."

A convoy of troop-filled trucks led by a jeep drove up to the parade field. A Captain got out of the jeep, approached Ivan and the General, and asked, "What needs to be done sir?"

After reading the Captain's nametag the General instructed, "All of those people Captain Hanson," waving a hand in the direction of the terrorists, "Need to be detained and anything else Ivan tells you that needs to be done."

The Captain keyed a radio he carried and said, "First Sergeant." When the First Sergeant answered he continued, "Secure those that are laid out on the parade field. Don't allow them to talk to each other and follow any instructions from robots." The First Sergeant acknowledged the instructions and soldiers erupted from their vehicles to follow them. "Anything else I need to know from either of you?" he asked.

"I suspect that someone from one or more of the families will be here shortly to interrogate these people, assist them as needed," The General replied then turned and walked into headquarters."

A short while later Jackie, Carroll, and Pat arrived with several sets of triplets. The adults plugged cables from robots into their connectors then watched as the children walked down the rows of prone prisoners placing their fingers on the temples of each one as they went.

Veronica, one of Jackie's triplets, stood up from checking a man looked at an army private nearby and said, "Private Jones, would you take this one to my mother please?"

The private started forward to comply when Caleb, one of Carroll's triplets, stood up and said, "This one too."

Arielle Stevens stood and pointing to a third person said, "Here's another one."

When the third man had been identified, he jumped up grabbed Arielle roughly and yelled, "Everyone up, kill the witches!"

The terrorists started to comply when Captain Hanson fired his rifle into the ground near several of them. Then he yelled,

"Get back down or you will be shot! You!" he continued pointing at the one who had grabbed Arielle, "Let her go!"

Arielle appeared to grow and kept on growing until she was several times larger than the man and he couldn't hold her anymore. One of her huge hands reached down, picked him up like a doll, and set him in front of Jackie. Trying not to laugh at Arielle's use of something her mother, Katherine, and Aiko had used during the Chinese invasion said, "Thank you Arielle."

From across the field a normal sized Arielle replied, "You're welcome," and bent to check the next person.

In short order all of the prisoners had been checked and seven others put where the adults could do a complete interrogation. When they finished, Jackie told Captain Hanson, "These ten are the leaders. Find somewhere to detain the rest and turn these over to security. Tell security to keep them separated from each other for further interrogation.

Captain Hanson replied, "Yes ma'am."

Jackie unplugged the cable from her head and said to the robot, "Ivan, make sure that the G-2 has the information we've discovered so far." Ivan beeped and she turned to the children who had gathered near her and said, "Now that you've had a little exercise, you all need to go do your school for today." All of the children disappeared quietly. "Pat, Carroll, I think we need to have a conference with the big three and their husbands."

Ivan beeped for attention and typed, "I would like to attend also."

"That makes sense to me," Carroll said, "As far as I'm concerned you're invited."

"Please let me know when," Ivan typed then spun and rolled away.

"I wonder what that's about," Pat said thoughtfully as he watched the robot roll away.

"We'll have to wait for the meeting to find out," Carroll answered. "Come on all of this has made me hungry." With that comment she grabbed her husband's hand and they both faded out. Smiling Jackie shook her head and faded out as well.

At home Jackie instructed her robot, Virginia, "Call Wendy for me please."

When the phone activated, Wendy said, "Good morning Jackie. The girls said you had a little fun this morning courtesy of the robots."

"Actually, I think the kids had the fun," Jackie replied. "Did Arielle tell you how she handled the one prisoner?"

"No?" Wendy replied questioningly, "They came in ate a snack and went directly to school. What did she do?"

"When the terrorist grabbed her, she did a Wendy imitation that was about fifteen meters tall and turned the tables on him," Jackie answered. "She plunked him down right in front of me and the army Captain that was there. The Captain put him in some kind of judo hold or something so I could convince him to behave. Ivan gave some added emphasis to it with a spark between its pinchers. The rest of the prisoners behaved themselves after that also."

Chuckling Wendy said, "I bet they did, so what's up?"

"We need to have a conference about what we found out and Ivan wants to be there for some reason."

There was a brief pause then Wendy responded, "Clarence is tied up on some business deals this morning and said to set it up for his office if possible."

Robin beeped for attention and typed, "All adults and children, and the General's staff need to be there so I've reserved the conference room. The army is putting shielding in it now and it will be ready by 2:00 p.m."

"All fifty families or just us five?" Wendy asked the robot.

"Just the five primary families," Robin replied.

"That's enough of a crowd," Wendy told the robot. "Pass the word for us five families to gather at two this afternoon in Central's conference room. Robin says it is being shielded now.

That probably means we need to crowd in a few more robots beside Ivan as well."

"Okay," Jackie replied, "See you then." The call was ended and Jackie asked, "Virginia, what are you robots up too?" Her robot beeped twice. Jackie mumbled disgustedly, "It figures."

That afternoon in a very crowded conference room, General Gregory said, "Shall we get this show on the road, who's first?"

"I am," Jackie answered, "When we were interrogating the terrorists this morning; we found out that the aliens have changed tactics. They are only programming the ringleaders and using our old problem children the religious fanatics. The other change in tactics is the size of the groups involved. They're going to be from company to battalion strength. This will make them harder to deal with especially if they send more than one bunch at a time."

General Gregory sighed and asked, "Clarence, you're the defense idea and construction person here, what do we do now?"

Clarence turned and looked at the gaggle of children siting any place they could find along one wall of the conference room. After a moment he asked, "What have you pint sized geniuses come up with?"

"What bothers me," Arielle said thoughtfully, "Is that the aliens are still able to program people even with the blocking generators running all over everywhere. Is the percentage of programmed people going up or down?"

Melinda asked, "Have we gotten everyone with a connector identified and protected, and has Doctor Janice identified the part of the brain that the connecter uses that stops the programming?"

Karlita queried, "Mom, can you and Ms. Wendy and Ms. Katherine take the nine of us to the tank circuit?"

Startled Aiko answered, "I suppose so what do you have in mind?"

"Something that isn't very nice," Karlita replied, "But I'm tired of having to duck every time I turn around. I think the twelve of us and our fathers need to put 'a behave yourself' compulsion on everyone on this planet."

Mika asked, "General are there any reports of programming or other problems on the moon, Mars, or any of the stations?"

"I haven't heard of any problems," the General replied, "That doesn't mean that there aren't any. The task of identifying connector equipped people isn't finished yet and I haven't heard from the Doctor."

Clarence added, "Population sampling shows that those being programmed is stable at the moment."

Sarah looked at Ivan and asked, "Ivan, if you robots all got together could you combine your power to do something like shoot an assault beam of some sort?"

"We haven't tried anything like that," Ivan typed, "It may be possible. We will have to experiment."

"That would be a very good idea, dad," Arielle inserted. "I just picked up his imperial nastiness ordering some attack ships to take out the tank circuits because he can't figure out what they do and he's thinks they may be weapons. He's also directed them to find and tow the scout back with its crew under arrest for not reporting in on schedule."

"So why do you want the robots to destroy the ships?" Clarence asked.

"The alien society seems to be basically mechanistic with only the mind programming machines for what they consider animals," Arielle answered. "Keeping them as ignorant of our mental powers as much as possible should prove to be very valuable in the final showdown."

"The army has vehicle mounted grasers," General Gregory inserted, "That can puncture over three hundred millimeters of tempered metal from two and a half klicks in the atmosphere."

Clarence frowned a moment and asked, "How hard would it be to mount them in space vehicles and do you think they would be able to penetrate the force shields?"

Yoshi beeped and typed, "I analyzed the shields on the planet bores we destroyed recently. If the pattern is the same, robots can counter them when the grasers are fired."

Clarence pulled a cable from the edge of the conference room table and asked as he plugged it into his skull, "Who makes the grasers?"

"General Dynamics," Gregory answered.

"Contact Soyako in Tokyo," Hiro said. "Arielle, how long before they get here?"

"About three weeks," Arielle replied.

"Clarence, tell Soyako that the new ships they are working on need to be launched next week," Hiro instructed.

"Have you been holding out on us, Hiro?" Wendy asked.

Hiro laughed and responded hugging Aiko, "Not me, my sweet innocent little Japanese doll. She started them on designing and building attack ships right after you three deflected the Jupiter body." Aiko blushed beet red at the praise her husband was heaping on her.

"About six years ago, huh," Katherine said, "I thought I was the only one with clairvoyant tendencies. How many ships have they built and how did you manage to cover that much expense?"

Aiko took a deep breath to regain her composure and said, "Soyako is a family owned business. My father runs the company and we should be able to launch twenty ships with fully trained crews. Or at least as fully trained as crews can be that have never left the ground or actually fired their main armaments."

"Who is crewing them," General Gregory asked, "And how did you protect against mental programming and spies?"

"We have been going to Japan every so often to visit relatives," Hiro replied. "While we're there we go to Soyako and check. The last time we went we took some of Clarence's gadgets with us. The crews are all from the Japanese Defense Forces."

"Can we crowd in?" Secretary General to the United Nations asked from the conference room door. With him was President

Harper, Secretary of Defense Treacher, The Prime Minister of Japan, and Aiko's Father, Isoroku Sato.

Aiko stood and bowed to the men and said, "You honor us with your presence. Please if you can find a space join us."

Mister Sato bowed to his daughter and said in Japanese, "It is you who honor us most illustrious daughter."

General Gregory addressed the Secretary of Defense saying, "Abe, every time you show up I get saddled with something new. So what are you up to now?"

"Saddling you with something new," Secretary Treacher replied straight faced and very seriously. There was a twinkle in his eyes that ruined the effect.

"Which one of you sent a robot after me?" General Loren asked.

"I'm afraid I'm guilty of that also," Secretary Treacher answered.

"Oh lord, Tom, what have they gotten us into now?" General Loren asked.

"They haven't told me yet," General Thomas Gregory said while looking askance at his bosses. "I don't expect it to be good whatever it is."

"Oh, it won't be too painful," Kenneth said. "Since I met Mister Sato and discussed things with Prime Minister Maeda, the scope of the forces you manage are going to increase some is all."

Abe Treacher said with a smile a street urchin who had stolen a cookie would envy, "Both of you Generals are out of uniform. Mister President what should we do about them?"

President Harper sighed and replied, "I guess we'll just have to go ahead and promote them. Ms. Winston, Ms. Warren, Ms. Esteban would you help us get these two properly dressed?"

Impishly Katherine replied, "Most certainly Mister President, we'd be delighted."

"General Gregory," President Harper intoned, "By direction of the United States Senate you are hereby promoted to General of the Army. This rank has not been worn by any military person in the service of the United States since World War II. Congratulations." Katherine and Aiko each accepted a five star cluster from the President and pinned them on Gregory's uniform collar.

"Brigadier General Glen Loren," Secretary Treacher read from a piece of paper he held, "By order of the Senate of the United States Senate you are hereby promoted to the rank of General." Wendy accepted one of the four star insignia and pinned it on Glen's collar while the President pinned its duplicate on the other side.

"Kenneth said, "So much for the candy, now for the vinegar. I have been talking quietly to the leaders of various nations and filling them in on the alien problem. When I sat down to talk to Prime Minister Maeda, I discovered that he already knew about the problem and he introduced me to Aiko's father. The result is that for your sins Tom you are now the United Nations Supreme Military Commander for the defense of the solar system. Glen you are his executive officer. Now that you know what's up, what are you going to do and what is the rest of the solar system going to do?"

"Actually," Gregory retorted, "Before you butted in that's what we were discussing, I think." Then looking at the passel of triplets that were present he asked, "That is what we were doing isn't it kids?"

Arielle said, "After thinking about Karlita's suggestion and in light of what Uncle Kenneth just told us I think we need to end the planetary strife so we aren't fighting a two front war." Then in flawless Japanese she asked, "Honorable Sato, would you describe the capabilities of the ships your company has built please. Don't worry about translating we will do that for you."

Aiko reached into a pocket on the edge of the table, pulled a connector cable out, and handed the end to her father.

Her father accepted the cable with a bow of thanks and connected. A holographic projector turned on with the image of a ship that wasn't really streamlined. It had a sledgehammer head like prow that flowed back into a long body that swelled smoothly to its midpoint then tapered to the engines at the other end. Mister Sato explained the design of the ship and took everyone on a virtual tour of its interior.

At the end of his presentation Clarence asked, "The ship looks like it is more than a kilometer long is it capable of leaving the ground on its own or are we going to need to provide telekinetic help?"

"For the initial launch we planned to fit them with old fashioned JATO units but once they are up shuttles are required to move personnel back and forth," Hiro answered.

"Dad," Sharron said, "We need to get the ships into space today and put them where they can test their weapons and stuff without the aliens seeing them if that's possible."

"I anticipated that telekinetic help might be forth coming," Prime Minister Maeda said, "So I ordered that the ships be fully manned and ready to go without notice."

"Honorable Grandfather, do the ships have any force field shielding?" Mika asked.

Mr. Sato seemed to be taken back at being addressed so formally by a child but answered, "The shields are the same as is in the robots but the generators are considerably more powerful and have windows that can be turned on or off to fire the grasers."

Mika nodded, turned to Clarence and asked, "Mr. Clarence we know the aliens have stolen the secret for constructing the shields, is it possible that they have solved how to penetrate them?"

"We thought about that Munchkin," Hiro answered his daughter, "And we came up with a couple of new tricks. One of them will reflect their beam weapons back at them. The other one uses a gravity idea to deflect beam and projectile weapons and we put both in these ships."

Wendy started to say something then her head snapped towards the children and her eyes widened. After a moment she said, "I think the ships just got launched. I hope they had the hatches closed."

The triplets lost their glassy eyed looks and Clarence asked, "What did you use for power?"

Arielle smugly replied, "Tank circuits one two and three. Robin, could you find us something to eat please."

"Getting good at it aren't they?" Katherine asked.

Gregory instructed, "Since military spaceships seem to fall into my bailiwick, one of you electronic telephones please contact the command ship and tell them to maintain orbit where the earth will be between them and Pluto. More instructions will follow later." One of the robots emitted a sound that was very much like what was heard in the earphone of a very old dial telephone ringing.

"Quit the clowning Yoshi," Hana instructed sternly, "And do what you're told."

The robot made a sound that resembled a raspberry then completed the call. A minute later it typed, "The order has been received and acknowledged."

Glenn asked, "Alright kids, you seem to be the big brains on the aliens, what are we doing next?"

Ivan beeped and typed, "Are the results of the scout ship dissection available yet?"

"I haven't heard from Colonel Welch yet," Gregory replied.

Arielle asked with all the adult authority she could muster, "We seem to have gone somewhat astray, can we go back to Karlita's idea of a 'behave yourself' compulsion?" Gregory waved a hand and nodded to Arielle giving her the floor and she continued, "Robin, please give us a Mercator map of the world showing population densities in relation to having enough technology to cause trouble if they are programmed." She looked at the map that was presented for a moment then asked, "Uncle Kenneth, how hard would it be to literally shut down all transportation on the earth a region at a time?"

Kenneth Jordan looked at the map and said, "Robin, please add national boundaries to the map." He studied the map carefully and then said regretfully, "Without spilling the beans about what we want to do first, I don't see any way to accomplish it."

"Maybe," Hana said thoughtfully, "You adults should use the four tank circuits and we kids should use the generator station and some of the public power sources here on the ground, join up, then sweep around the earth programming whatever population we cross as we come to it."

"Do it one hemisphere at a time," Brenda added. "That should help reduce the amount of time needed and give us time to eat between them.

"That sounds workable to me," Clarence said, "President Harper; can we black out parts of the country unannounced and get away with it?"

"I think that once everyone has been programmed to behave," President Harper replied, "We can probably explain the problem to the general public and not bring too much heat on the government."

"The next question is when do we do it?" Arielle stated.

"Wendy queried, "General, are any new units arriving in the morning?"

"The 7th Infantry is due to arrive tomorrow," he replied, "But I have been informed that Natasha Lane, Laura Manning, and their kids are going to take care of them. We've streamlined the process some too. We set up a couple of tents then have the soldiers enter one end. Inside they are checked for problems and connector acceptability. Once they are processed they either return to their unit or go to the second tent where they are scheduled for surgery and programming."

"So that's taken care of," Wendy said, "Now what about the alien attack ships?"

"What did you kids do now?" Glenn who had been watching the kids asked when he noticed that they gone into a blank stare.

"We moved our fleet to the other side of the solar system and told them to test and practice with their weapons," Hana answered.

"We'll bring them back in time to hopefully be a big surprise to the aliens."

Katherine asked, "Where do you plan to hold the surprise party?"

"Between the orbits of Jupiter and Saturn," Sarah answered.

"What part do we adults play in your plan?" William inquired.

"We're going to let you handle the main attack and feed you power as needed," Brenda responded. "Our thought is that you should mostly solve their force shields so the ships can use their grassers to end the discussion."

"How long before the aliens reach your chosen point?" Aiko asked.

"Fifteen days from now," Arielle responded, "I'm hungry, is there anything else we need to discuss?"

"That sounds like a good place to stop," Thomas Gregory said, "Kenneth, are you gentlemen staying for supper or do you have to leave right away?"

"I think we're going to stay for a couple of days," he answered, "So let's go feed these kids."

EVERYONE BEHAVE

"Ready kids," Wendy thought.

"Ready," came a multiple reply then Arielle continued, *"We'll feed power on your signal."*

"Alright, on three," Wendy thought, *"One Two Three."*

On the East coast of the United States vehicles suddenly stopped moving as Clarence, William, and Hiro with the help of Monica Shriver and Keiyanai's teams stopped them. Right behind them Wendy, Katherine, and Aiko backed up by their oldest sets of triplets began deprogramming people and putting in the behave compulsion. As their efforts passed through the people began moving again. In some places, Freddy or Edna's teams would set a vehicle to the side of a road out of harm's way when the driver went to sleep. In offices and factories, workers thinking that someone had become ill rushed to his or her aid.

Four hours later with the Northern Hemisphere completed, the families stopped for lunch. While they were eating, General Gregory called the Stevens and smiling broadly said, "I have a feeling that this should have been done back when you were deflecting the Jupiter body."

"Why is that?" Wendy asked. "Although, I doubt that we could have done it then."

"I've been receiving some interesting reports from the larger cities around the nation," Gregory replied. "It seems that suddenly crime has stopped. For example in Chicago, the police arrived at a youth gang fight evidently just as you passed through. The next thing the police knew the combatants were shaking hands, being friendly, and cleaning up the area they were set to fight in."

Arielle, Sharron, and Brenda looked at each other and then acted as if they were paying very close attention to stuffing themselves with food. Wendy noticed their reaction, smiled, and said, "Come clean girls what did you do besides feed us power?"

"We were drawing power from the wind generators around New Orleans and had all that extra power so we could do other things at the same time we gave you power," Arielle explained.

"When we discovered them about to fight," Sharron continued, "We made them be friendly and clean up their mess."

"We made them give all of their weapons to the police too," Brenda concluded.

"What other stunts did you kids pull?" Clarence asked.

The three girls looked at each other like they had been caught stealing cookies from a cookie jar then Arielle answered meekly, "The nine of us did the Southern Hemisphere."

"I wonder what stunts the other sets pulled as well," the General said from the com screen as he tried unsuccessfully not to laugh.

Wendy looked at her girls and asked, "Well?"

Brenda answered, "Other than doing the Southern Hemisphere you would have to ask them. We did small things like the fight separately."

"One of these days you kids are going to bite off more than you can chew," the General said from the screen.

"And we may not be available to help," their mother added.

"We all realize that we could end up out on a limb with someone else cutting it off behind us," Arielle told everyone, "But we also know we need all of the mental stress we can find when we're using our skills to develop our abilities to their fullest."

"Brenda added, "We have been testing out ability levels regularly and Mister Brian has told us that individually we are stronger than you were when you were hoisting C-150s around. Our united power without tapping any source is greater than your linked powered ability but we don't have the stamina that you adults do."

"So if we can find ways to stretch ourselves," Sharron finished, "It's to our benefit to do whatever we can to increase our abilities."

Clarence laughed then told Wendy, "They have us there." Then to his children he instructed, "We understand your need to push yourselves, but you also need to keep us advised on what you are up to and I expect more of that so you don't get hurt. Then he pointed his finger at the three and queried, "Do you understand?"

Before the kids could answer Robin beep and typed, "Katherine is on the line."

Wendy instructed, "Split the screen and add her to our conversation."

"Are you ready to do the Southern Hemisphere?"

"We don't have to," Wendy replied.

Shaking her head Katherine said, "They did, huh? Well that explains a couple of things. Like why my three were so hungry and why they went to school so quickly."

"You know if this wasn't so serious," Gregory said, "I'd be busting a gut laughing. Robot you should probably get Aiko into this conversation so she can enjoy the fun also."

Robin beeped once and the screen split again. Aiko asked, "What are we going to do with these kids?"

"Could I make a suggestion?" the General asked.

"Go ahead," Wendy replied.

"In the military we create training problems to test our soldiers and keep them sharp. Perhaps you need to design some games where you adults provide the resistance. Something more strenuous than multi-ball dodge ball."

Katherine chuckled, "Girls, do you think you could catch tank or artillery training rounds?"

"What would we do with them once we've caught them, Ms. Katherine?" Brenda asked. "I don't think the army would want us to throw them back at them."

"No we wouldn't," Gregory responded, "But that doesn't mean that you couldn't do something else with them like stack them someplace so they can be recycled. Another possibility is that you might try blocking the beams of our energy cannons."

"How safe would that be?" Wendy asked concernedly.

"They would not be in the line of fire," Gregory answered, "So it should be safe enough. They should probably start with solid shot."

Clarence said, "This sounds like it should be do able and the kids seem optimistic about it. How long would it take to set up a test for us adults to try out first?"

Gregory shrugged and replied, "An hour or so."

"The kids have school this afternoon," Aiko said, "Can we try it while they are doing that then set up whatever is needed for the rest of the week?"

"For the test no problem," Gregory stated. "However if we go full scale with this and escalate as the kids ability grows I'll need to get the Senate's approval for the expenditures and additional maintenance."

Without a word, Clarence pulled a connector from the table edge and connected. A few minutes later he said, "You've got approval from Secretary Treacher. He said that he'll deal with the politicians."

"In that case I'll see everyone on range seven at two o'clock, if that's okay."

That afternoon a battery of mobile howitzers rolled onto a firing range and lined up on the firing points. General Gregory handed out several pair of binoculars and said, "Look down range at the pair of red flags. That block in between them is a much shot at piece of concrete. The engineers tape rectangle over to our left is where to put the rounds the guns fire. Are you ready to fire Captain Smyth?"

"As soon as everyone puts on these hearing protectors," the captain replied as he handed them out.

Wendy asked, "Can you fire a couple of rounds so that we can get a feel for them before we try to catch them?"

Captain Smyth nodded, keyed his radio, and said, "Guns one and two one round in sequence, fire."

Everyone except the General and Captain jumped as the two howitzers fired. Clarence was looking at the collection area and said, "Those blasted kids! Look!" General Gregory burst out laughing folding double with the effort. The Captain looked bewildered then Clarence ordered, "Kids show yourselves."

As nine children faded into view, General Gregory got his laughter under control and said, "You know, I wasn't serious when I made this suggestion but since they're here, let's see just how good they think they are."

"How do we do that?" Aiko asked.

"Captain," The General ordered, "I want you to battery fire ten rounds per gun just as fast as your crews can load them. When they start firing you children catch the rounds and put them in that square marked with white tape."

The kids nodded and Arielle asked, "Captain have you got some more of those hearing protectors?" Having seen the children arrive a sergeant had walked up with a box of hearing protectors and began passing them out.

After the triplets put on the protectors, Arielle said, "We're ready when you are."

Captain Smyth keyed his radio and said, "Fire Mission, battery fire ten rounds per gun rapid fire. Fire!" The adults watched the impact area expecting to see the target obliterated but when the thunderous roar of eight howitzers ended there was a pile of neatly stacked rounds in the square and nothing had had happened to the target.

Wendy asked the girls, "Did you tap power from anyplace?" All nine girls shook their heads.

Arielle asked, Captain do you still have more ammunition?"

He replied, "Yes ma'am what do you have in mind?"

"That time it was all three sets of us. We want to try one trio by itself and see how we do."

Captain Smyth looked at the adults, Wendy nodded, and Clarence said, "Go ahead."

Captain Smyth asked, "Are you ready?" Arielle and her sisters nodded then he keyed his radio and said, "Repeat."

The howitzers fired and a second pile of training rounds appeared in the square but instead of instantaneously they rippled in, in waves. When they were stacked Sharron said, "I'm hungry."

General Rowe arrived in a jeep. He got out and asked, "Are there any hungry kids here?"

The adults laughed and Wendy replied, "That has just been expressed by one of my children. How did you know we would need to feed them a snack?"

"Jerry and I are telepathic now," Tom Gregory answered as the children all went to the jeep where General Rowe was serving snacks. "I guess that whatever other abilities we will have will develop later."

When he had finished serving the children, General Rowe said, "I have a truck on the way with more ammunition for your guns Captain."

"Thank you sir," the Captain replied, "Some of my people have been checking the stacked rounds and tell me they look like they could be reused right now."

"Let's let the depot folks determine that," Gregory replied. "We've got enough to shoot for now, I think."

"I agree sir," Captain Smyth said, "And it looks like we're about ready for another game of catch. This time I've programmed a variable firing plan so that the kids will have to stay very vigilant. The plan will fire the remaining two hundred fifty rounds each gun has onboard."

"That sounds interesting," Katherine said, "It'll probably make them ravenous and at just about supper time."

"Let's see how many they miss," Aiko added.

William laughed and asked, "You expect them to miss some?"

Aiko smiled and replied, "Not really, but there has to be a limit to their ability somewhere."

"Well we haven't found it yet," Katherine said in a slightly aggravated voice. Then as the children rejoined them queried, "Are you kids ready for round two?"

Arielle in a very cheeky tone asked, "How's the betting going on us missing at least one?"

All of the adults burst out laughing and General Gregory instructed, "Fire at will Captain."

The Captain keyed his radio and said, "Battery fire Mission as planned, Fire."

The Howitzers fired and kept firing sometimes singly other times all of them until their remaining rounds were gone. When the dust settled in the quiet that followed a huge pile of howitzer training bullets was revealed in the taped off deposit area. The target with its red marker flags was completely untouched.

With much satisfaction in her voice Arielle said, "Whoever lost the bet should pay up. General can we try the laser tanks tomorrow?"

Before he could answer, his personal communicator sounded. After a few minutes of quiet discussion with the caller, he disconnected and said, "The alien attack ships will reach optimum range tomorrow afternoon. Did you kids draw any power from anywhere just now?"

"Not electrical power," Arielle answered seriously.

"What did you use for power?" Aiko asked.

"In a way we used wind power," Karlita answered. "When the guns fire and the shell is shoved through the air it leaves a temporary vacuum in its wake. That's where the boom comes from is the air filling the vacuum."

"We changed it into what we can use to do things," Melinda finished.

In an exasperated voice Katherine asked, "How did you figure out how to do that?"

Melinda shrugged her shoulders and responded, "We learned in school that everything is a form of energy. So we thought about what kind of energy was involved and how to change it to what we need."

"We can feel energy," Arielle explained, "And every time a gun fired we felt the kinetic energy pulse set up by the vacuum being momentarily created and collapsing."

Several of the adults shook their heads and Wendy said, "I don't think we're ever going to catch up with our kids. Let's go home. Captain Smyth thank you and your people for all they've done today."

"Any time ma'am," the Captain replied.

Gregory queried, "Do we need to hold a strategy session before we take out the alien fleet?"

Wendy cocked an eyebrow at the children and asked, "Are you going to wait for us and discuss this or are you going to jump in and do it?"

"We need to discuss the best way to defeat the aliens without wearing any of us out," Arielle replied.

"When do you want to have the meeting General?" Sarah asked.

"And in which conference room?" Linda queried.

"Let's meet in the new room at headquarters," General Gregory replied, "It's bigger and we've gotten it shielded as well. How does nine tomorrow morning sound."

"Since we've got a couple of days before we have to take action that sounds fine," Wendy answered for the group.

"You should probably bring the robots too," General Rowe said, then saluting added, "See you all in the morning."

In the headquarters conference room General Gregory asked, "All right kids, how are we going to do this?" Before anyone could give a reply one of the robots beeped and the General added, "Or robots."

A projector started from what turned out to be the medical robot Socrates and General Maryann Janice said, "We've finally identified the contact in the brain that blocks the alien's programming efforts. If you look at the image you'll see that it is the connection made to the occipital lobe."

Wendy added, "When we were deprogramming everyone yesterday we planted a suggestion that they get tested so it would be a good idea to notify the President and Kenneth about setting up testing centers as well."

"I already did," Doctor Janice replied.

General Rowe asked, "So how does having that knowledge help us?"

The constant testing that we do on all of our PSI active people indicates that the occipital lobe is where most of the telepathic reception occurs." Then she added, "It also seems to be one of the first places in the brain that activates when we go active. We looked at the original programming design from the PSI Institute in California, and discovered that it sensitizes that part of the brain first."

"How does that help us to defeat the aliens?" Aiko queried.

"Directly, I don't know," Doctor Janice answered.

"It allows us to find even more people who can be activated," Arielle said, "And incorporate them into our defenses."

"If the aliens give us enough time," Wendy said quietly. "Suppose we just concentrate on the attack ships that are on their way here now."

Ivan, Central's chief of robotic security beeped and typed, "With the help of Yoshi, the other five family robots, and the computers at IASA headquarters we have solved the shields around the enemy ships. If you will teleport one of us to each of our ships we can defeat the enemy shields as our ships fire."

"Will you need any kind of amplifier for whatever signal you use to jam their fields?" General Lowe asked.

"How many ships are our twenty ships going to be facing?" Clarence asked. "In addition how do we keep the aliens from killing our ships while they kill theirs?"

"I really would have liked to try stopping the tank beams yesterday," Sarah said wistfully. "I have a feeling that that information would be extremely helpful."

"General, can you get a tank battalion to the range in say an hour?" Mika asked, "So we can find out how to stop energy beams then finish this meeting this afternoon."

General Rowe consulted a note pad and said, "We have a squadron on the range right now."

General Gregory told everyone, "You will need hearing and vision protection on the range." Then to his Chief of Staff he asked, "Can you get what we need sent to the range?"

General Rowe replied, "I'll meet you all there with what's needed."

On the range, General Rowe distributed hearing protectors and goggles to everyone, the mission was explained to Lieutenant Colonel Evelyn Leclaire who smiled and said, "I think this might be fun. My tankers have been getting cocky because they aren't missing any targets and missing targets with full power bursts will be very good for them."

"So you're not going to tell them what we're up to?" Wendy queried.

Smiling with an urchin's grin the colonel replied, "Nope."

Arielle asked, "Could you have only one tank fire at a time so we can get a feel for the energy involved?"

Keying her com unit the Colonel said, "Alpha six this is Sierra six over," Her radio crackled with a response and she continued, "Have each gun in the platoon that is on the firing line fire one full power shot, one at a time over."

On the firing line a tremendous thunderclap hammered everyone as Thor the Norse God, banged his hammer creating a bright lightning flash. The bolt hit its target down range. The second shot plowed into the ground halfway to the target, the third bent and went straight up, the fourth and last tank fired and its shot faded out into silence as if it had evaporated.

"Now give us a shot from all four tanks at the same time," red headed Brenda instructed.

A stunned and amazed Colonel looked at her then fumbled at the transmit button on her radio and gave the instructions to her troop commander. After a pause, all four tanks fired together and the shots faded out like the last single shot had done.

"I'm hungry," Sarah said to no one in particular.

Colonel Leclaire came to life and asked in awe, "What did you do?"

"They converted the energy to some other form," Wendy replied. I'd like to know where you put the converted energy."

"We turned it into a rain storm in the Australian outback."

A captain approached the group, saluted, and said worriedly, "Colonel we seem to be having a problem with our main guns. After the first round nothing has worked correctly and my troops can't find any faults in their systems."

General Gregory burst out laughing and replied, "There's nothing wrong with your guns Captain. These kids were trying out a new PSI trick. Colonel while we feed them put your entire squadron on the firing line so they can perform another test."

"All thirty eight tanks at once sir?" the Colonel asked, "How are they going to handle that much energy?"

Before the General could answer Arielle said soberly, "That's what we're trying to find out Colonel because the lives of everyone on earth may depend on our being able to handle that much or possibly even more energy."

General Gregory added, "This is need to know, eyes only stuff Colonel."

"Understood sir," The Colonel replied, "And it is always much better to practice and experiment among friends than having to figure it out on the fly when it happens for real. I'll get them lined up. It will probably take me an hour, is that okay?"

"That will be fine," Gregory answered. "General Rowe can I assume that in your usual efficiency that we can feed these bottomless pits?"

"Right this way folks," General said to the group. As he lead the group to the field mess area that had been set up he asked, "Doctor Janice, I understand that you had to hook Wendy and her partners to IVs when they were moving planets around. When the kids were doing things on their travels the officers in charge of their security told me that they kids were consuming ration bars at an enormous rate. What have you planned for this excursion?"

"Socrates and I are planning on doing a combination of the two," Maryann Janice replied. "We're going to hook everyone up and have more flavorful foods and drinks within easy reach. I have a feeling they are going to burn energy at a rate we've never seen before."

"Where are you planning to assemble everyone that won't be in a tank circuit?" Rowe queried.

"I don't think that has been decided yet," General Janice replied, "The adult trios on the tank circuits, possibly the kids at home, and the others in the generator station most likely. Why?"

Rowe explained, "I need to get plans drawn up for security of the whole thing so that we don't get terrorist problems when the battle begins."

"Then we should probably decide on what we're going to do this afternoon," Maryanne stated.

"What are you two plotting?" Wendy asked.

"Feeding you," Maryann answered.

"Keeping you alive," Jerry Rowe added.

"I've been wondering how we're going to make those things work," Wendy stated thoughtfully. "Well that can wait until we finish here and resume our meeting."

Back on the range Arielle said, "Mom, can I link with you to show you something?"

"Certainly dear," Wendy replied. After a moment Wendy smiled widely, waved a hand and said, "Everyone link up. Ivan, give me your connector cable."

"Oh my," Katherine said aloud, "His royal nastiness is really upset. Either his sensors are really good or there is another scout on the other side of the sun."

"Whichever it is, not knowing where the energy blasts came from is sure driving him up the wall," General Gregory said. "What do you kids think should be done about it?"

Sarah smiled sweetly and said, "I want to play with tanks."

"And just what are you going to do with those tanks, Minx," her father asked.

"Mostly blow up asteroids in several other parts of the belt to confuse the old grouch some more," Linda replied.

"And maybe bounce a bolt or two off the attack force shields to help Ivan fine tune what it needs to break them."

"How will that confuse his nibs?" Maryann queried.

"There won't be any evidence as to where the bolt came from mostly," Arielle responded.

"We'll confuse things even more by having different numbers of tanks fire," Mika added.

"Can I join this crowd?" Colonel Leclaire asked as she walked up. "What would you like my tankers to do this afternoon?"

Mischievously Hana replied "Blow up asteroids."

"Confuse the enemy," Brenda added.

"Colonel," Arielle queried, "When are you scheduled for connector surgery?"

"I'm not sure because I have a sleeve around that part of my spine from an old injury and Socrates told me that it had to make a special connector that would incorporate the sleeve," Leclaire replied. A new robot rolled up to the Colonel and beeped. On its shelf was a small contact set box. The Colonel asked, "What's this?"

The robot typed, "It is a contact set so that you can interface with the group until Socrates has your connector ready."

"Connect her up Robin then link through Ivan," Arielle directed. "Ivan can you give us a map of the asteroid belt and feed it to mom and her partners?" The robot beeped once and she continued, "Mom can you and your partners be our gun sight and line us up on asteroids or aliens that we will shoot?" Wendy nodded and Arielle went on, "Dad, General, the rest of you link with us. We'll fire a couple of small charges so you can learn the technique then we'll go for broke. Colonel Leclaire you're our trigger. You tell which units to fire in variations from a platoon to the entire squadron," Grinning broadly Arielle concluded, "The rest of us will make his nastiness wonder what he has gotten into."

Wendy asked, "Colonel, do you need a few minutes to explain the plan to your commanders?"

"They're coming now," the Colonel, who had been sketching on a note pad furiously, replied "So I can do it face to face."

Wendy watched as General Rowe waved his driver over to him and said something to him quietly. The Sergeant hurried away and when the General looked in her direction, she raised an eyebrow in question. He rubbed his stomach and nodded towards the children. Wendy nodded back with an understanding smile.

"The Squadron will be ready to fire in five minutes," Colonel Leclaire announced. Then thirty seconds before firing, she announced, "Thirty seconds to first shot." Then she counted down, "Ten, nine, eight… three, two, one, fire." By the time, she reached one everyone was holding someone else's hand and had taken a deep breath. Four tanks fired and out in the asteroid belt a smallish asteroid disintegrated. Leclaire said, "Ready fire," and a second platoon of tanks fired.

Arielle thought, "*Have you got it dad?*"

His replying thought was, "*It's easy enough on a platoon. How is it going to work for larger units?*"

Colonel Leclaire answered aloud, "You're about to find out." Then over her radio commanded, "Squadron fire, ready, fire!" In space, one of the alien attack ships disappeared in a huge ball of flame from being hit with the energy blast delivered from thirty-eight tanks firing simultaneously. Firing at different levels continued for another fifteen minutes then the Colonel told the group, we've got four shots per vehicle left then they have to be recharged to continue."

Wendy said, "I think that's enough for today kids, let it go."

General Lowe added, "An afternoon snack has been set up over where you ate lunch kids, go eat."

Clarence hugged his wife and said, "Let's join them before they eat it all, I'm hungry too."

While they were eating General Gregory asked, "Have any of you kids had two thoughts worth rubbing together about all of this and what we do next?"

Wendy noticed that Arielle seemed to be in a blank stare so she linked with her daughter to see what she was doing then started laughing and said, "That's the best comedy show I've seen in a while. You really should share that with everyone."

Arielle grinned and suddenly everyone was seeing the scene in the throne room of the alien mother ship where his Exalted Imperial highness was having a fit, ranting about imbecilic underlings, and was throwing or smashing anything that came to hand.

Clarence queried, "Do you think we've pushed him far enough to show his main invasion force to us?"

The Emperor stopped ranting and ordered, "SEND THESE ANIMALS A DEMAND FOR THEIR SURRENDER. I WILL RELISH FEASTING ON THEM."

A moment later a very powerful laser communications beam left the ship for earth.

Hana asked, "Ivan if you link with us can you tap and demodulate their laser?"

Ivan beeped and released its cable connector, which Aiko plugged into herself since she was nearest the robot. After a moment, Ivan started its Holo-projector and an image of the lizard emperor appeared and snarled, "LOWER BEINGS OF THIS SYSTEM SURRENDER. YOU ARE FOR EATING

ONLY. YOU WILL COMPLY IN TWO KEKS OR I WILL SEND FORCES TO HARVEST YOU."

The message repeated until Clarence said, "I think that's enough. Any suggestions on what kind of response we should send?"

Ivan beeped and typed, "Let me and the other robots send a response."

"Ivan are you developing a mean and sadistic streak in your programming?" Mika Asked.

The robot typed, "A kilometer wide where the safety of my humans is concerned."

"I say we let Ivan go ahead and do it," Katherine said thoughtfully. "Being a purely mechanical response should help muddy the alien's concept of what it is tangling with."

"I think I agree," Wendy added, "I get the impression that it still hasn't grasped what we've been using to defend ourselves."

"What about the attack ships and our space borne forces?" General Gregory asked.

"Ivan are you going to deliver a reply tonight while we sleep?" The robot beeped and Arielle continued, "Then let's end that problem after breakfast tomorrow. We'll let our forces do as much as possible and take care of any strays."

Wendy asked, "Ivan do we need to transport robots to our ships to handle the enemy force shields or can they do that from here on the ground?"

Ivan typed, "There is a slight propagation lag so it would be better if the designated robots are in the ships. I will have them on the parade field ready to go at 0800 tomorrow."

General Rowe said, "Since we decided to finish the planning meeting here on the range that just leaves you and me Doctor."

"So it would seem," Maryann replied, "The tank circuits are already set up for IVs and regular food so I just need to send medical people up to keep an eye on things. If General Wallace is as good as I think he is you, kids can use the generator station whether you use its power or power from somewhere else. That way with the help of some nurses, I can keep an eye on you nine rascals."

"And you kids will rest and not jump the gun on this," Clarence instructed. "Do you understand?"

"Would it be possible for us to sleep in a little in the morning, dad?" Arielle asked side stepping her father's question.

Not to be outwitted Clarence repeated, "I asked if you understood that you are not to try anything on your own and I'm waiting for an answer."

Being sassier still, Arielle looked at her sisters and asked, "I don't see stupid stamped on your foreheads, is it stamped on mine?"

"Arielle!" Clarence snapped and his daughter cringed and ducked a little.

"Dad, that's a given," Arielle replied unrepentant, "After the things the aliens have already done to us in small bunches you can count on us not being very adventurous."

"That's probably as close to acquiescence as you're going to get dear," Wendy told Clarence quietly.

ROBOTS MAKE A MESS

During the night, all of Central's security and defense robots and the many sets of family robots gathered on the parade field in rings with Ivan in the center. A glow appeared around them and then a beam of soft white light shot into space from the group. In space, the beam seemed to disappear but then reappeared just outside the alien ship. It struck the ship's shield and clung to it. After a few minutes, the shield failed and the surface of the planet-sized ship began spewing metal, gasses and other materials into space. The beam intensified and the eruption grew into a full volcanic eruption. A minute later the beam stopped leaving a deep glowing crater that was many kilometers deep and wide.

At breakfast the next morning everyone plied themselves with as much food as they could, requesting more as they felt need. Arielle announced, "I don't think his nastiness has had any rest since we teased him yesterday. And what Ivan did last night, has him really upset."

"Why is that dear?" her mother asked.

"He's still demanding that his minions tell him what all of the random energy blast were and where they came from, and he's ordered his invasion fleet to be readied for launch."

"Well I think I've had enough food to at least get started on making his day as miserable as possible," Sharron said, "So if the rest of you are ready let's get hooked up to Doctor Maryann's gadgets."

Brenda asked, "Which one of you robots is going to which tank circuit?"

Wendy answered before either robot, "Jason is staying here with the little ones. Robin is going with you. There are some other PSI adults who are going to be baby sitters for them."

"Jason beeped and typed, "Thank you for the human help. I figured I was in for a really miserable day."

"You may still be because they are bringing their own children as well," Clarence replied.

"Gee thanks for that ray of sunshine."

"However," Clarence said, looking at Roger and his sisters, "I had better hear that you have been on your best behavior you three."

The three chorused, "Yes papa."

"Okay girls," Wendy said quietly, "It's time for you to go to the generator station so Maryann can get you fixed up."

Sharron, Arielle, and Brenda hugged their mother and father and then Arielle said, "Take care up there and don't get hurt." Then the three faded out taking Robin with them.

Wendy sent, *"Don't you three get hurt either."* Then she continued aloud, "Roger, Samantha, Elizabeth, come give me a hug."

The youngest triplets hugged their mother and father then Clarence said, "We'll be back later."

Jason beeped and typed, "It is time for school."

In Tank Circuit One, Wendy asked, "Are you the nurse that is supposed to hook us up?"

"I'm Doctor Abigail Graham and I used to be a nurse," the Doctor replied, "In fact we first met very briefly when we flew here from Japan. I was the nurse that accompanied Doctor Janice."

"Well, it's nice to meet you again," Wendy replied. "Shall we get us all hooked up."

"By all means, as soon as you get on your couches and connect."

Katherine queried, "How do IVs work in zero gravity?"

"We use a clamp and roller system to keep things going," Abigail answered as she worked.

"You act like you've done this in space before," Aiko said as the IV needle was inserted in her arm.

Abigail replied, "Yep, for the last two years off and on. I balked at a long term zero-g assignment because I don't like being away from my family that long."

While the women were being connected, a screen lit revealing their husbands who were in Tank Circuit Two a fourth of the way around the earth. A moment later a screen connected to Tank Circuit Three, lit showing Keiyana's team and tank circuit four's screen came to life showing Monica and her team. Lastly, the generator station appeared on still another monitor showing Freddy and Edna's teams and all of the triplets.

Wendy asked, "You're a little crowded down there aren't you?"

Maryann answered, "Just a little but it should work out alright. I brought plenty of help to keep the IVs going. General Gregory sent a field mess and a company of infantry to keep the bottomless pits fed."

"Are the kids all hooked up and ready?"

"We're ready Mom," Arielle responded with a slight quiver of fear in her voice. "We've already transferred the security robots to the ships so they should be ready also."

General Gregory's image added itself to the view from the generator station and he said, "I've given the order for our ships to move in and begin their assault. They should commence firing in about ten minutes."

"Thank you, General," Wendy replied, "Yoshi is displaying a combat schematic for us."

The General nodded and said quietly, "Now we wait until they fire."

The ten minutes seemed to drag then just outside the asteroid belt, twenty earth ships fired and five alien ships exploded. The aliens returned fire and space blazed with flashes of powerful beams from both sides. The teams snatched alien beams and redirected them back at the ships firing them. In the battle confusion, some of the alien beams got through and one earth ship exploded. As quickly as the battle started, it was over and a lone alien ship was retreating at full speed.

General Gregory told everyone, "Well done." Then he asked, "Arielle as our resident spy, what's his imperial lizardship up to?"

Instead of answering aloud, Arielle sent what was happening in the alien ship telepathically. The Imperial Commander had ordered that all ships, planet bores, and ground forces ships be launched.

Wendy commented, "I wonder how he came up with so many crews for all of those ships." The view Arielle was sending shifted and showed aliens being removed from casket like containers and after a few moments, each one began to move.

"Off hand," Doctor Janice replied, "I'd say they use some form of cold sleep."

"It looks like they're set up in a caste system," Clarence noted. "See how they are marked?"

"What are those?" Nancy Greer, one of Keiyana's partners asked indicating several banks of large machines that were being worked on.

"Oh Lord!" Brenda said in a low voice.

"What is it Kitten?" Clarence asked.

"We can't let them get those machines into operation," Brenda answered, "They're giant sized educator machines."

"You're sure?" Wendy asked.

"Yes mama, they're exactly the same as the ones in the scouts only about a hundred times bigger."

"Can we do anything from this range," Aiko asked, "Ivan's beam only penetrated about fifty kilometers."

"Could our combined something reach that far and be effective?" William asked.

"The other problem is, how large a force are we going to be facing?" Gregory asked.

"I think that if we can bollix the programming machines somehow," Arielle said, "Then dealing with the purely physical forces may be manageable. I certainly don't want to be facing a two front war."

Mika said thoughtfully, "I wonder if we could use sun power and produce a huge beam that would fry the whole ship and everything in it."

"What do you have in mind munchkin?" Hiro asked his daughter.

"Ms. Wendy, do you think the Jupiter body is too far away for us to tap its power and turn it into beams?"

"Why use the Jupiter body, Mika?" Wendy asked.

"I don't want to upset our sun and maybe make it give off things that would kill us anyhow," Mika replied.

"Arielle," General Gregory asked, "Can you determine when they'll have their programming machines running?"

"Pretty soon from what I can determine," Arielle replied.

"Too bad we can't pull their patch plugs out and delay them for a while," Brenda mused.

In the far off spaceship, a cable appeared to fall out of a plug in a patch panel and Arielle said, "We can. Everyone link up and we'll slow them down for now at least."

"If we just pull their patch cables out," Wendy said, "They'll just plug them back in again."

"Is there someplace we can put the cables that will slow them down more?" Clarence asked.

"Do they have some sort of sewage system?" Doctor Janice asked.

"How about their water storage?" Linda asked. Arielle shifted views and row upon row of huge tanks appeared in everyone's minds. Linda continued, "Could we dump water into the machines?"

"I'd like to know Arielle, how you're able to snoop around their ship without being detected," her mother stated.

"It takes a bit of concentration mom," Arielle replied. "I'm using my mind at the very edge of my telepathic frequency range and it seems to be outside anything they've looked for. The problem is I can't do much more than look even with Sharron and Brenda helping."

Naomi asked, "Do they have any of those weapons that they used on me?" As she asked that, the rest could feel the shiver of dread in her thoughts.

Arielle replied, "I haven't seen any of those weapons so I don't know if they have them in the mother ship or just the scout that you destroyed."

"I don't remember seeing any of those weapons in the scout we captured either," Wendy added.

General Gregory asked, "Do they have any armories in the mother ship where such weapons would be stored?"

The view Arielle was showing changed showing rooms with row after row of all Kinds of weapons. Naomi said, "I don't see the weapon they used on us in any of the racks. Is it possible that they have them someplace else?"

The view in the alien mother ship changed rapidly then Arielle said, "I don't see any other storage areas with weapons in them."

"Then with Arielle as our guide," General Gregory said, "Maybe we stand a chance of pulling off a surprise raid on those machines. Ivan, can you robots provide any shielding at this distance?"

Ivan beeped once and typed, "The shield will only be half strength."

"That's better than no shield at all for what I have in mind," Gregory continued. "I suggest we split into two groups, one to pull their plugs and dump them someplace. The other group will fill their machines with water to short them out and give us a couple of days to rest and plan the next phase."

"I can handle viewing alone," Arielle said, "So can Sharron and Brenda. I'll guide the water assault; they can guide the cable attack."

"Then let's do this," Gregory said, "Ladies why don't you join with Arielle and we men will join with Sharron and Brenda and get it over with."

Wendy said, "Give us the views and a countdown Arielle."

The triplets brought up their views and Arielle said, "Three, two, one, go!"

In the alien ship, the sewage system suddenly became clogged with all of the patch cables that were in panels on the programming machines. Just as suddenly, sparks were flying everywhere as the machines exploded from water caused short circuits.

Sarah said with satisfaction, "That should give us enough time to rest and eat before we have to deal with anything else from them."

General Gregory asked, "Wendy, what about the Jupiter body idea? Is it too far away not to try Mika's idea?"

"I'm not sure," Wendy replied, "Let's go eat and rest then try it in the morning when we're fresh."

"Sounds good to me," Gregory responded, "Everybody go home and we'll assemble again at eight in the morning to try Mika's idea out."

Past Pluto's orbit near the Jupiter Body, Wendy thought "*I had forgotten how big this thing is. So does anyone have any suggestions on how we tap its energy?*"

Arielle replied, "*Probably like we were doing with the tanks and alien beams yesterday.*"

"*Those were already formed into beams and all we had to do was steer them, Honey,*" her mother replied, "*There are no beams being fired from the Jupiter Body for us to redirect.*"

Hana answered, "*Light's a form of energy, how do we change it to something we can use?*"

Suddenly a tremendous beam of energy passed by the edge of the group and Mika thought loudly, "*Over there! It's another alien mother ship!*"

"*Look behind it,*" Arielle asked. "*Is that another one?*"

"*Everyone back home,*" General Gregory ordered. "*Meet in the conference room.*" Most of the many somethings disappeared.

Arielle and her sisters turned invisible and went to the nearest alien instead.

Doctor Janice began disconnecting all of her charges in the generator station but when she came to Arielle and her sisters, she stopped then checked because the three were still in the blank stare that indicated they were using their minds. She telepathed, *"Wendy, your kids haven't come back."*

Before Wendy could reply the three came out of their trances and Brenda said, "I'm hungry."

Wendy faded into view and asked, "Where did you three go?"

Arielle replied, "We turned invisible and took a closer look at the new alien. Right now it doesn't have force shields so maybe we can practice by destroying it first."

Brenda added as a soldier handed her a sandwich and drink, "Whatever we decide, we'd better do it quick because it already has its mental training machines turned on. As powerful as they appear to be the blocks we put in may not hold."

"Then finish your sandwich and you can tell the General what you found," their mother replied.

Linda giggled and Sarah asked, "What's up sis?"

"I think I may have just thought of a way to get enough power to do some serious damage to the aliens," Linda replied. "Let's go see the General so I can explain. Oh! We need Yoshi and Mr. Clarence too."

"Then since all of you seem to be finished eating," Doctor Janice replied, "And I've disconnected everyone so let's get over to the conference room like the General ordered."

In the conference room General Gregory asked, "Anyone have any ideas on how we fix this pit of snakes?"

Linda responded, "Yoshi, show the General and Mister Clarence how you tap and use cosmic energy please." The robot's holographic projector started and displayed a peculiar circuit of coils and other components." Linda asked, "Mr. Clarence, do you think that we could tap power from a very large one of these circuits if it was built in space?"

Clarence asked, "Yoshi, What is the maximum power you can draw from your circuit?"

The robot typed, "Unknown, I have not used enough power other than normal for operation to discover the maximum limit. The materials used may be the limiting factor."

Wendy asked, "Linda, Have you determined how we would tap the power from such a device?"

"Not really," Linda replied, "Yoshi, how do you connect to the unit?"

A part of the diagram Yoshi was displaying turned red and the robot typed, "The contacts are connected to my batteries. If you can sense energy the way you were doing on the range you might be able to tap cosmic energy directly."

"On the range we had something to focus on," Sarah said, "What would we use as our focus for cosmic energy?"

"It looks like," Clarence said thoughtfully, "Cosmic energy has a range of frequencies. Maybe all we need to do is learn how to tune ourselves to it like a radio."

Arielle closed her eyes and frowned. After several minutes, she smiled and said, "Link with me everyone." What everyone saw when they linked was a very large Arielle spanking the alien imperial commander while his minions tried to rescue him.

"*Now that you've caught it,*" her mother asked, "*What are you going to do with it?*"

"*Unfortunately,*" Arielle thought, "*I'm going to have it let it go. Even though I'm using cosmic energy, something isn't right and I'm getting tired.*"

"*Okay,*" her father thought, "*Can you just disappear and then let us watch to see what happens?*" The Arielle image blinked out releasing the alien and as the families watched, the alien leader threw a tantrum that amazed the humans and even seemed to give pause to his minions. He even grabbed another alien and ripped its limbs and head from its body. In the conference room Clarence said, "Show us how you tapped cosmic energy and we'll see what we can do to make it more useful."

Arielle replied, "I tried to make a mental image of Yoshi's circuit in my mind. I think the biggest problem was that I couldn't hold that image well enough to pick on old lizard face at the same time." Then she thought, *"Here's what it looked like."*

While Clarence was looking at Arielle's circuit image, Brenda said, "Dad, I just noticed something about the layout of the mother ship."

"What's that, Kitten," he asked.

"Where they've sited all of their reactors. It looks to me like they've put all of their radioactive eggs in one basked right in the very core of the ship and they're the same manually damped design that was in the scout. It looks like they have several hundred that are operating in banks to deliver the power the ship needs."

"We've already determined that the structure of their ship is such that it can't be blown up by anything we can throw at it," General Gregory said.

"In any normal area of the ship, no," Brenda replied. "What do you think the chances are of triggering a chain reaction great enough to blow it up or at least rob it of all of its power? We know that they are using electricity to run things."

"What can they do to us by other means and would we be contaminated in the process?"

Clarence asked, "Arielle, on the range you told us that you could feel energy. How come you need to develop a mental circuit to feel and use cosmic energy?"

"I can feel it but I can't manipulate it the way I could the other energy sources," Arielle replied. "I thought the circuit might help me focus better."

"What is it about cosmic energy that you are having trouble with?"

"It seems to be, I guess you'd say soft energy, because I can't draw enough of it into concentration to do worthwhile work."

"That may be exactly the problem, because it is spread evenly through space. Why don't we let that set for now and look at what Brenda's discovery."

"Okay Dad, Robin, do you think that if you linked with me, you could determine if we would get contaminated in their reactor room?"

Robin typed, "Ivan or Attila would be able to do a better job." Attila was nearest to Arielle. It extended its arm and released its connector. She connected her temple contacts and went into a blank stare. A minute later she disconnected and asked, "Is it hot?"

Attila replied, Very hot, you and I must get decontaminated immediately."

"Then let's get to the hospital right now. Mom and dad can keep us updated." Arielle stood, grasped Attila's claw, and they both faded out.

"Check the area around where they were Ivan," Gregory instructed.

Ivan extended a claw over the area where Arielle and Attila had been, then typed, "They left quickly enough that the area is clear."

The discussion continued until an hour later Arielle, in a hospital robe, and Attila faded back in and she said, "Dad thanks for reminding me about something."

"What's that?" he asked.

"Sensing energy and using the Jupiter sun is the right idea. Light and heat are both forms of energy that we can manipulate. Depending on how much energy conversion our somethings can tolerate, we should be able to destroy the two new ships since they're closest to it and may not have gotten shields running yet."

"Are you up to doing this?" Wendy asked concernedly. "After all you just got decontaminated again."

"Doctor Maryann said that I got decontaminated fast enough to be okay and that what I got was a lower level. But I am hungry."

"Why don't we adjourn and go eat," General Gregory said, "We'll meet back here in two hours and see what we can do with Arielle's idea." The triplets and their parents faded out.

Glenn looked at Tom Gregory and asked, "Think we'll ever get that good?"

"Who knows," Tom replied, "The whole lot including the parents are younger than we are." The two Generals walked out of the conference room.

Two hours later, General Gregory asked, "Arielle, how do we make the Jupiter body work for us?"

"I think or hope at least," Arielle replied, "That the energy from the sun or Jupiter body is a lot like the beams we dealt with, with the attack ships and tanks."

"Have you considered," Wendy asked, "That we might get singed pretty badly trying to handle that much energy?"

"We're going to have to take some risks, mom, or we may as well give up now. I think that we can probably handle large enough amounts of energy to do the job and not get more than a bad sunburn. The question is how much energy is enough?"

Mika asked, "Has anyone made an estimate of how many cubic kilometers those ships are?"

Hanna added, "Is there a temperature that will kill the aliens without having to destroy the entire ship?"

Aiko went into the blank stare of telepathic communication and a moment later said, "Maryann says it would take over three hundred degrees Celsius for over an hour to kill them. I don't think we can sustain things that long."

Maryann entered the conference room and added, "I've discovered that the aliens are not a true water based being like we are. Their systems have large amounts of Francium in them."

"No wonder their environment is so radioactive. Francium is a radioactive element."

"Aside from that their biology is enough like ours to be able to use earthbound life forms for food."

"Then let's go for brute force," William said, "And use the Jupiter body to generate as powerful a beam as we can. Let's work on the two new ships first because if they get shields running we'll be in really hot water."

"We've been at this all day," Aiko said, "And I'm like Wendy I would like the kids on as regular a schedule as I can."

Tom grunted and asked, "Arielle can you spy in the new ships as well?"

Arielle went into a blank stare, then said, "I seem to be able to but they aren't as clear."

Karlita, Mika, and Hana cried in unison, "Got'em!"

"Got what?" Aiko asked.

Karlita answered, "Grumpy ordered message drones sent to the other two ships. He is ordering them to leave this system alone. Evidently, he doesn't want to share. We caught the drones and put them on the moon to be decontaminated."

"If the three ships weren't on opposite sides of the solar system I'd suggest getting them to fight each other," Hiro said thoughtfully.

"I hope that he was stingy about sharing the secrets he's stolen from us," Wendy replied.

"Dad," Brenda asked, "How do reactors work?"

"Basically they use enriched uranium to generate heat. A liquid coolant is used to keep the reactor from going critical and exploding. They use a control rod to start and stop the reactor. The liquid in steam form is used to operate more or less standard turbine generators," Clarence replied. "Are you having a brainstorm?"

"Maybe we don't need to destroy the reactors," Brenda replied. "Sis, have you seen the generators anyplace else?"

Arielle asked, "Dad can you give me an image of what a generator might look like?"

296

Clarence replied, "Generators can take several different forms but basically they are either a coil spinning inside a magnetic field or the magnet spins inside a wire coil. The housing can vary the shape some. Here's a sample," and he sent an image.

All nine children went into blank stares, "Wendy said, "Oh lord, somebody get some food in here. I think one of the aliens just had a power failure. Katherine, Aiko, we'd better go check on them." The three women went into blank stares.

General Rowe opened the conference room door and a stream of soldiers with food trays walked in and put a tray in front of everyone in the room. Gregory said, "Thanks Jerry. Clarence answered a question from one of his girls and all nine of them went blank."

Wendy smiled, and while still in her link said, "Everyone needs to go to their tank circuit and join us. We need more power." In the conference room trios of adults faded out.

In space Clarence thought, *"What do you need us to do, dear?"*

"Let us get to our tank circuit and then we're going to change this ships course for the Jupiter body," Wendy thought in return. *"The kids have depowered it so it won't be able to escape destruction."*

"Where are the kids now?"

"We're here dad," Arielle thought. *"We're tapping the New Orleans wind farms for power."*

While the conversation progressed, Wendy, Katherine, and Aiko had left, gone to their tank circuit, and rejoined the group. Mika thought to the group, *"I contacted IASA and got the angle we need to push at."*

"How do we push without a way to anchor ourselves?" Juanita asked.

Mika thought, *"We're going to use Newton's third law of motion and be a rocket engine."*

Esteban queried, *"What's our fuel, Munchkin?"*

"Electrons, dad. Well electrons and cosmic energy."

Arielle thought, "*We figured out how to make cosmic energy be useful to us in this case. If everybody will link with us we'll show you how. By the way General; we kids are going to need food that is very high energy maybe a combination of protein and banana splits.*"

Wendy asked, "*General, how did you manage to get out here and it doesn't look like you're alone.*"

"*Glenn, Jerry, and I figured out how to join but were not frequency matches for each other,*" Gregory replied. "*We'll figure that out later. Jerry is handling the food things so you should be eating more soon.*"

Wendy asked, "*Arielle, how do we make this work?*"

"*We're going to put ourselves against the ship so that we are shaped like a venturi in a jet engine with intake holes near the hull. Then we'll generate a magnetic field and pull cosmic energy in the holes and force it out the venturi,*" Arielle replied.

"*With cosmic energy being low level,*" Clarence asked, "*How long is this going to take us?*"

"*The biggest advantage to cosmic energy is that there's lots of it so the more we pull in the stronger our engine will be. We think that an hour will be enough.*"

"*After all, Dad,*" Brenda added, "*We don't need to make it go faster only change direction,*"

General Gregory thought, "*I suggest that someone do something quickly because we're under attack by parachute forces.*"

Arielle directed, "*Mom, Dad, why don't you adults take care of the attack and we kids will start pushing the ship where we need for it to go.*"

Brenda added, "*Someone let New Orleans know we're going to tap the wind farm.*"

"*We will,*" Wendy thought, "*You kids all be careful and don't get hurt.*"

The adults disappeared and Mika thought quietly, "*I've got an idea.*"

Arielle asked, "*What's that?*"

"*Two ideas really, first let's push this ship into the one that's following it. Secondly I think I know how to make cosmic energy do what we want it to do.*"

"*Show us and let's see what we can do. We'd better have IVs to do that because we'll get very hot.*"

Sharron thought, "*Doctor Maryanne, can you meet us at the generator station and connect us to IVs?*"

Maryanne's distant thought came back, "*I'll have some nurses there in a couple of minutes, I'm busy with wounded from the attack.*"

Wendy thought, "*What are you kids up to?*"

"*We're going to push this ship into the one that's following it, mom,*" Arielle replied. "*Mika figured out how to boost the amount of thrust we get from the cosmic energy.*"

"*Mom, did the attack get over?*" Brenda asked.

"*No but the Army, Marines, and Air Force seem to have it under control,*" Wendy replied.

"*Then can you stand guard to make sure the other ship doesn't try something while we push this one into it?*" Brenda asked,

"*Are you expecting them to attack?*" Aiko queried.

"*Considering old Sourpusses attitude about our solar system, yes.*" Arielle replied.

"*Alright, start your engine, the nurses have you hooked up.*" Doctor Graham inserted.

The three youthful somethings merged into one large something then changed into a funnel shape that settled broad end against the alien ship. A very bright nearly invisible bluish flame appeared out of the small end of the funnel that extended over a hundred kilometers into space. The disabled ship shuddered and slowed visibly. It came to a stop then began to move towards the third alien ship.

"*What's going on out there?*" Maryanne thought. "*These kids are sweating and very hot.*"

"They're performing the function of a rocket engine and shoving the broken ship into the third one," Wendy replied. *"Are they okay otherwise?"*

"If they get any hotter they will be in danger. We're wrapping them in refrigerator blankets and doubling the IVs."

An hour later, the flame and the funnel disappeared. In the Generator station Arielle queried, "Doctor Maryanne, can I have some lemonade?"

"I think that's a good idea," Maryanne replied, "I also think we can peel you out of the freezer blankets if you're finished being a rocket engine."

"Mom, have the ships collided yet?" Arielle asked.

"Just now," Wendy thought back, *"Link and take a peak."*

"We're finished, Doctor," Arielle said aloud as her mother faded into sight.

"I don't know what we're going to do with you kids," she said smiling.

"Why mom?" Brenda asked.

"You make huge messes then disappear leaving them behind."

Mika asked, "Was there much of an explosion?"

Wendy replied, "Not really but it should be visible for a week or two before it drifts into the Jupiter-body and burns up." Noticing Arielle's blank stare she asked, "Arielle, are you communing with his Imperial Lizardship?"

"He seems to have instructed a whole bunch of message rockets be readied for launch and his minions are getting them ready," Arielle answered. "I think he's finally decided he's bitten off more than he can chew and is calling for help."

"How long before he launches them?"

"Long enough for us to get some rest it looks like. I suggest that we put our space ships out that way to pick off as many rockets as possible if he launches before then."

"That sounds like a reasonable idea," General Gregory said from the generator station door. "In fact I've already asked

Monica and Keiyanai to do just that. Now I suggest that you kids go home, eat and rest, you've had a very long day."

"I can't decide whether I want to swim or soak in a bathtub for a while before I eat," Brenda said to no one in particular.

Jennifer rolled in and typed, "Bennett is preparing bubble baths for you." Katherine's triplets faded out taking Jennifer with them.

"Let's go see what Robin and Jason have for you," Wendy added and she and her children faded out.

Mika, Karlita, and Hana told everyone goodbye and they faded out also.

"Well General," Maryanne said, "Suppose we follow your instructions too." General Gregory grunted and waved at the door for General Janice to precede him from the generator station. Maryanne looked about the room and addressed her nurses and robots, "Ladies, gentlemen thank you for your assistance today. Socrates would and the other robots please straighten things up so we humans can get rest and get ready for the next round?" Socrates beeped once.

ALIENS CALL FOR HELP
AND BUILDING A HIGHWAY

When everyone had gathered in the conference room the next morning General Gregory stated flatly, "We're in big trouble. His imperial nastiness launched his rockets and when our ships moved to intercept them, they were intercepted by a couple of alien fleets."

"How many did we lose?" Clarence asked.

"We lost seven before they could withdraw but took out over twenty thousand rockets and about a third of each attacking fleet."

Maryann noticed that the three sets of triplets were holding hands and staring blankly. She instructed urgently, "Teleport the kids to the generator station. From what I just saw in Arielle's mind, his nib is getting fixed drastically."

The nine kids disappeared and Wendy instructed, "Everyone to your tank circuit or the generator station. I have a feeling that they need help."

All of the adult trios disappeared and General Gregory instructed, "Everyone left ensure that medical people are where they need to be. Jerry, you have food detail again and whatever else turns up. Glenn let's see what we can do to manage this three ring circus."

General Loren replied, "The mental block we put in is being broken all across the earth. I've put our forces on alert. I'm glad that we started that program of shipping non-connector soldiers to other installations."

"*Tell Freddy and the other ground bound trios to support your operations,*" Clarence instructed. "*We're stuck here until our kids get finished cleaning this mess up just in case. They're taking power from everything that puts it out. I think his imperial Lizardship pissed them off beyond belief.*"

"*What's happening?*" Tom Gregory asked.

"Link and we'll show you," Wendy said joining the conversation.

Glenn chuckled and thought, *"They say that red headed women have the hottest tempers and since it's Arielle's image that's doing all of the work she must have really lost it."* With a smile in his thought, he added, *"Kind of like her mother now that I think back."*

"They're multitasking too, look at this image."

"Her image looks like it's tearing his imperial lizard into little tiny pieces from his toes up."

"Now look at this," Clarence added showing them great balls of scrap metal floating in space.

Tom asked, *"Did they do that?"*

Glenn asked amazed, *"What are there nearly two hundred of those balls? Were those the alien fleets?"*

Aiko thought, *"What I'd like to know is how they got through the mother ships shields."*

"Maryanne!" Wendy thought in a scream, *"They've just turned into the rocket engine like they used on the other ship only it's bigger."*

Maryanne chuckled and replied, *"I talked to General Wallace, it seems one of his soldiers was here yesterday and had a brainstorm. Use my eyes and take a peek."*

Clarence observing the refrigeration system that had been constructed chuckled also and thought, *"The General and his soldiers must have been up all night building."*

"I thought that the kids were wrapped in carbon blankets to help reduce the contamination," Katherine thought, *"What happened?"*

Maryanne thought, *"That's more of what General Wallace and his soldiers came up with. Those tanks the kids are in are filled with a chemical that is more effective than carbon. With Glenn's help, he ordered cargo planes out during the night to pick up supplies from all over everywhere. It flows in from the refrigeration units and returns through a scrubber system. Based* on what their body temperature is doing the fluid temperature is adjusted to keep them cool."

Wendy sighed thoughtfully, "*Well, the whole bunch loves to swim so they shouldn't mind being dunked.*"

"*The President and Secretary Jordan just contacted us,*" Gregory thought. "*The President said to pass on that the kids have blacked out almost the entire northern hemisphere with their power demands.*"

"*They've taken all four tank circuits except for life support as well,*" Clarence replied. "*Dear I think that you three had better go to the generator station to be there when the kids finally come up for air and find themselves submerged.*"

"*They just turned their engine off,*" Katherine commented, "*And we have full power back so we'll see you downstairs.*"

"How are our fish fairing," Wendy asked as the three mothers faded into view in the generator station.

"*Doctor Maryanne,*" Arielle thought, "*Can we open our eyes in this soup and can you warm it up some it's cold.*"

"*We sealed your eyes to keep the liquid out because it will damage them,*" Maryanne thought in answer. "*We're warming it up and should be able to decant you pretty soon.*"

"*Good,*" Mika thought, "*I want something sweet; these IVs don't have any flavor.*"

A technician to one side of the room announced, "We're not detecting any radiation on any of them. Starting the drain procedure."

General Rowe asked from the door, "How long do I need to keep these banana splits on ice?"

Maryanne answered, "About fifteen minutes Jerry. Could you send someone after some robes for this bunch to put on when we get them rinsed off?"

"*General,*" Arielle asked, "*Could you ask General Gregory and General Loren to join us? Momma, could you ask Uncle Kenneth and the President to come too?*"

"It's not over is it, Arielle?" her mother asked somberly.

"No momma, it's just starting," she replied as she toweled dry.

"I've told Tom and Glenn," Jerry Rowe said, "Their on the way."

Ten minutes later in another room of the generator station the nine girls were eating banana splits when General Gregory entered and asked, "How much trouble are we in?"

"Trouble," Monica, who had joined them, asked, "I thought that was the end of this."

"Unfortunately, Ms. Monica," Sharron answered between bites, "This was just the first round."

"That ship launched over a hundred thousand messenger rockets," Arielle continued the briefing. "Our fleet destroyed over twenty thousand of them before they were attacked. Once we got the fleet to safety, we destroyed another sixty thousand. The rest are speeding towards their home system, screaming their heads off that someone is a big bully and won't play right. Each ship has an Imperial Commander and they attain rank and prestige by harvesting systems singlehandedly. When something happens, The Imperial Ruler of All, orders several fleets of those planet-sized ships to take care of the problem."

Glenn asked, "How long do we have?"

"Anywhere from next week to about ten years from now," Sharron answered. "Even though you'd like for us to be sweet innocent young girls, mom, you're going to have to put up with us being hardened blood thirsty warriors."

"I think that you can probably be both if you try Sharron," Wendy replied smiling.

"Especially in a few years when you develop an interest in boys," Clarence added as he joined them. "Would you like to tell us what you have planned?"

"Arielle answered yawning, "I think that we'll do that the day after tomorrow after we've slept of the anti-radiation shots and Uncle Kenneth and the President are here."

"I think that's a reasonable idea," Wendy said smiling, "After all you were at that for over eighteen hours."

"What kind of path did you put that alien ship on?" General Loren asked. "We're not going to see it again are we?"

"We put it on a hyperbolic course across the top of the solar system," Mika replied. "It should get to the Jupiter Body about the same time his friends do."

Hana added, "We positioned the fleet to follow and destroy anything that tries to leave the mother ship as well."

Sarah looked around and asked, "Socrates, would you ask Jennifer to start us a bubble bath please?"

Socrates beeped and typed, "I have told all three family's robots to start bath water for you." All nine children faded out. Socrates continued, "All humans go rest we robots will straighten things and secure the building."

"We'll meet in the headquarters conference room at ten day after tomorrow," Gregory said into the quiet then walked out of the room.

Thank you Socrates," Maryann said.

In the conference room two days later, the triplets put on their contact sets and Arielle began, "When we were interrogated his lizardship we hit a bonanza of information, none of it good from our point of view. As I said the other day, he launched nearly a hundred thousand message rockets. Our fleet destroyed twenty thousand or so and we were able to account for approximately sixty thousand. The remaining ones ran off screaming their heads off about us bad animals that won't roll over and die. What that means is we can expect initially single ships to attack, then when they get their act together fleets of ships."

Karlita continued the briefing, "That means that we're going to have to do a bunch of things such as ending strife here on earth, building a bigger fleet, and building more tanks circuits, then find and train people to man and operate them.

"Uncle Kenneth," Brenda added, "We specifically need the brothers Pan brought here for a direct interrogation because we discovered that they were cooperating with the aliens and many of the revolutions and the pirates are under their control. We need to do it here because they are PSI active and are able to block at a distance."

Arielle continued, "General Gregory, there is a new smelting technique for use in space that detoxifies radioactive materials. We left the alien fleets in big balls of junk because we will need all of the metal we can get. Additionally, your tank battalions are going to get a workout because a stress-training program needs to be started for the other PSI active people. We've uploaded everything we gathered so you can get to it for your decision-making." Smiling mischievously she finished, "After all we're kids and aren't supposed to know what to do."

Everyone burst out laughing and after a moment Clarence stated, "That's not stopped you before, why should it now." His reply brought even more laughter.

Regaining his composure Kenneth Jordan said, "I think that's her way of admitting that they don't have answers to everything."

"Why don't you kids go play or swimming or something while we study your data," Wendy instructed the triplets smiling. All nine girls faded out.

"I think that we have nine very afraid girls," Aiko said softly.

"I agree," Katherine added.

"Afraid that they are out on that tree limb they talk about," Wendy completed, "And the aliens have the saw."

Hiro chuckled and said, "Too bad we can't hand them total alien defeat for their birthday party next week."

"Well," Wendy said, "The least we can do is try to figure out how to give them some fun in their lives and maybe take some of the load they've shouldered."

"The problem is," Aiko said, "That even when they're playing they're trying to find solutions. Link with me."

Clarence chuckled, shook his head, and said, "Multitasking seems to have become second nature to them."

"Wendy," General Gregory asked, "Besides you four trios that I know about, how many more adult trios are there in Central?"

"Fifty four youth trios with kids ours ages," Wendy replied, "And fifteen or sixteen adult trios. Very few of them know how to link though."

"Mister President," sighing, General Gregory instructed, "Since she is familiar with the training, I want Colonel Leclaire promoted to Brigadier and put in charge of the stress training program. Jerry, I want you to create a program that will help us frequency match people faster. Get with Doctor Wallace and have her help. Glenn, get with Clarence and General Wallace, and lay out two construction programs that Kenneth and the President can implement. One program for more tank circuits and the second for more ships. Wendy I need you to create a plan to deprogram the world again and to put an end to any kinds of conflicts that are going on. Kenneth, Mister President recruiting campaigns need to start as soon as Wendy completes her project. Alright everyone, if you have questions trot them out."

"We can deprogram the world like we did before," Wendy said. "How do you plan on getting people to cooperate after that? Are you planning on becoming earth's first dictator?"

"I don't want to do that, but if it is the only way to give those kids some of their childhood back…"

Clarence asked, "What was it Arielle told us the kids did in Chicago the first time?"

Tom Gregory replied, "They made some street gangs behave and be friends instead of fighting."

"That might be more than we would like to do dear, but I think we'll need to do just that. Religion and superstition will probably be the biggest problems."

Ivan beeped for attention and typed, "Robin asked me to tell you that the children are in a circle in the pool holding hands."

Wendy queried telepathically, *"What are you kids up to now?"*

The girls let go of each other's hands and Arielle replied, *"We just deprogrammed the world and programmed in the block and a couple of things like religious tolerance and a desire to cooperate for earth's survival. We thought that you might have some qualms so we did it for you."*

Mika added, *"Tell General Gregory that we stopped being kids when this mess started so he doesn't have to become a tyrant for us."*

"At least take some time for a little rest and relaxation while you have the chance and let us grownups worry for a while," Wendy pleaded. *"Let your minds rest."*

Ivan beeped again and typed, "Socrates informed me that Doctor Wallace is on her way to the pool with a group of other children."

At the pool Elana Wallace said, "Girls, I've brought some other fish to swim with you." She turned to the children with her and instructed, "Jump in and introduce yourselves. Have fun." She sat in a chair at the side of the pool.

Wendy came out of her blank stare and said, "I think Elana has the right idea. Shall we continue with what we were discussing? Arielle told me that they deprogrammed the world, built in the programming block, religious tolerance, and a desire to cooperate for our survival."

General Gregory chuckled, "Got out of that didn't you?"

"I'm sure you'll come up with something equally distasteful."

"Hopefully, I won't have to do that." He stood, stretched, and concluded saying, "Let's take a couple of days to rest and think about things. See everyone Monday at eight."

At breakfast the next morning, Arielle, Brenda, and Sharron arrived wearing nice dresses and Wendy asked, "What are you three dressed up for?"

"The Fort Des Moines Museum is hosting a display of First Ladies inaugural gowns and we decided we wanted to go see them," Arielle replied. "The Des Moines Symphony is having a youth concert also."

Brenda added, "We contacted security and our bus and guards should be here shortly."

Jason beeped and typed, "You need to finish breakfast so you can do school."

"We each have two doctorates, Jason, I think that we can take some time off from school once in a while," Arielle shot back. "Especially since our peers only attend school Monday through Friday for six hours a day."

"Jason," Clarence said quietly, "From now on school will conform to the same schedule as is required by Iowa public school law. Don't go increasing what you present because you have less time during the week either."

Jason turned to Clarence and typed, "Understood."

Wendy asked, "Is anyone else going with you besides security?"

"Several of the kids Doctor Elana introduced us too yesterday," Sharron replied.

"Then finish your breakfast and have fun." A horn sounded from the front of the house and Wendy continued, "It sounds like your ride might be here. Jason, would you tell them that the girls will be there in a minute?" Jason rolled out of the room.

"I think that Jason might be upset," Clarence chuckled. "Remember the rules about your powers kids and have fun."

"We will dad," Arielle replied as they left.

Jason rolled back into the dining room near the younger triplets and typed, "You three are late for school."

Wendy said in a no nonsense tone, "Jason, the school rules apply to them too. You are not in charge Clarence and I are. Please get Katherine and Aiko on the phone for me."

The screen brightened and Katherine answered, "Good morning."

Aiko added, "What did Elana do to our children?"

Wendy replied, "I'd say she brought their parents to their senses where school is concerned. Ours are going to a museum and concert today."

Clarence said, "I told our robots that school will conform to Iowa law which seemed to upset them."

"Jennifer is grumpy about that too," Katherine replied, "But I told it that I would wipe its programming if it gave me a reason."

"I hadn't realized how much we've let the robots control our children," Aiko added.

"Well seven year olds with multiple doctorates are a bit much," Wendy said. "Do we know if the other families with robots have had the same things happen?"

The screen split again and Doctor Elana Wallace joined the images. She asked, "Can I be a butinski?"

"Let me be the first to thank you for waking us up to our children," Wendy said, "And yes you can be a butinski."

"You can blame your children on the Boss. When he was playing his games, he instructed the geneticists make the kids insatiable learners. They might take a day off here or there but their need to learn will reassert itself. Think about what they're doing today, a museum and a symphony."

"Learning in a different guise," Clarence said thoughtfully. "I think we'll have to be creative to ensure that they learn to live with the rest of the world."

"Mine were in dresses," Katherine said, "Were either of yours dressed up?"

"They probably were," Elana inserted, "I introduced them to several boys yesterday and they're on the trip also."

"Triplets," Wendy asked, "With the same learning bent as ours I suppose."

"Yes but with different interests. What prompted this trip is that one of the boys sews and makes clothing for himself and his family."

The screen divided again and General Gregory asked, "How's the experiment going Doctor?"

"You're the one with the open communications channels and spies," Elana replied, "Suppose you tell us."

"The way Captain Willard was telling it, they had some of the inaugural gowns labels switched and when Kevin, one of Kyra Rostov's boys pointed it out to a docent. The docent tried to tell him he was wrong so he asked to see the curator. The curator wanted to argue about it also but got the shipping documentation to prove his point and discovered that Nicholas was correct. They're at the symphony now and I understand that the music is educational. It might be interesting to get the kids versions when they get home."

"We'll do that," Wendy replied, "Did you call for something else and get side tracked?"

"Actually yes, two things. A private in one of the infantry companies did a little research and discovered that all fifty-four sets of triplets were born within six weeks of each other. She started asking what was planned for their birthdays and thus has been hatched 'Triplets Day'."

Aiko asked warily, "When?"

Next Friday," Gregory answered. "I've even been rooked in as the Commander of this mess.

Clarence burst out laughing, took a deep breath, and queried, "Parade and all?"

"Yes," Gregory answered sourly.

"So a hundred and sixty-two kids get paraded," Katherine chuckled. "Tell me was there any resistance to the idea or has that private had a quiet burial? What was the other thing you wanted to discuss?"

"Socrates has notified General Leclaire that it has her connector ready and for the two weeks that she's going to be unavailable she would like to borrow your kids as teachers for the range training."

Jason beeped and typed, "That would be a different aspect to learning and a good idea."

"I'm glad you approve," Wendy answered. "I think I agree. Elana, Jason is suggesting that teaching is a different aspect of learning and would be a good idea."

Elana replied, "It sounds good to me too, after all if you can't teach something you haven't learned it yourself."

"We'll talk to the kids and get it set up," Wendy said. "Anything else we need to discuss?"

Tom Gregory answered, "Solar system defense projects and schedules for hoisting materials all over everywhere. I would like to schedule a meeting for Monday morning so you can spend time with your kids."

"About eight on Monday, then?" Katherine asked.

"Sounds good, see you then," Gregory said and disconnected.

"It sounds like we may have some interesting discussions with our kids," Aiko said thoughtfully. "Let's compare notes later, bye." Everyone disconnected.

BUILDING A HIGHWAY
AND LEARNING TO LINK

Several hours later the sisters returned singing and giggling. Wendy queried, "It sounds like you three had fun what did you do besides the museum and concert?"

Arielle walked to the corner where Jason was and began, "Math, science, and such things are interesting but you will adjust what you make available to us to include the humanities, music, and art or dad won't have to disassemble you, we will. That goes for Sam, Lizzy, and Roger as well. You will also seek input for the curriculum from all of us. Do you understand Jason?"

Jason made no response and Brenda who had joined Arielle, said, "We're waiting for you to acknowledge these instructions Jason."

Clarence said, "So am I Jason. I meant what I said earlier."

The word, "Okay," appeared on Jason's screen.

Sharron added, "Sneaky isn't in your programming so don't try."

"Des Moines school districts don't restart for another three weeks, so unless you want to study something, you're on vacation from school," Clarence said.

Arielle looked at her mother and asked, "How long before we eat we're hungry?"

"About a half an hour, "Wendy replied, "What all did you do and see today?"

"Kevin discovered that the labels on two of the First Ladies dresses were switched," Sharron explained. "He told the docent and she wanted to argue so he asked to see the curator. The curator wanted to argue too but Kevin showed the curator and us a mental video image of Mamie Eisenhower in a receiving line the so the curator got the shipping documents. The documents proved Kevin was correct so the curator opened the displays and fixed the labels right then."

"Then he took us into the back rooms and showed us how items are cleaned and restored," Brenda added. "One of the ladies doing restoration showed us some art techniques as well."

Arielle explained, "At the symphony, Maestro Richards recognized us, I guess because he saw the army and sent a message asking us to stay after the concert. The orchestra played a piece of music called, *Young People's Guide to the Orchestra* and he explained what we were hearing. Afterwards, after everyone else had left the orchestra came into the seats and showed us their instruments, and how to play them."

"They even let us try them," Brenda added, "And were surprised that we could play as well as they did. We didn't tell them that we picked their brains."

"Maestro Richards spilled the beans to everyone," Arielle said. "It seems that he met Ms. Katherine when she was at the PSI Institute in California and she told him about it."

"His assistant was putting music on the stands on stage," Brenda added, "And he told the orchestra members to think about how to read music and asked us to study it. Then he asked us to take the musicians instruments on stage and he conducted us in Paul Dukas, *Sorcerer's Apprentice*."

"The orchestra loved our performance," Sharron finished.

Robin rolled into the room beeped and typed, "Supper is ready."

As they ate Clarence asked, "What are you kids planning on doing tomorrow?"

Sharon looked across the table at Robin and asked, "Robin, would you show us a picture of the highway between Central and Des Moines?" The robot beeped and she continued, "What does that stretch of road look like dad?"

Clarence looked at the image, which showed wrecked cars, and all sorts of trash from the several battles fought along the road, and answered, "It does look pretty bad. Are you planning to do something about it?"

"We found out about what General Leclaire wants to do," Arielle answered. "We also discovered that there are only three other trios that can link, the rest can't mostly because they don't know how."

"We asked Captain Willard to contact General Rowe and arrange for cargo trucks and food."

Sharron picked up the briefing saying, "The General called Captain Willard back later and told him that he had contacted the Iowa Highway department and they are going to bring trucks full of bushes, trees, and the stuff to irrigate them."

"I think that the Captain was upset by the last thing the General said," Brenda added.

"What was that?" Wendy asked.

"Prisoners from the state prison are being brought in to plant everything and put the irrigation system in."

Clarence instructed, "Jason, notify Ivan about this."

"We already did dad," Arielle said. "General Rowe said he's sending additional armed security as well."

Wendy asked, "How many sets of triplets and trios are you going to teach linking?"

"Between twenty and sixty, mom. It seems that most of the triplets haven't had the stress we got before the aliens came."

"We slowed the alien ship down some so that when the other teams start shooting tank beams they can punch more holes in it.

Sharron added, "It will give us a chance to try something too,"

"What's that?" her father asked.

"Changing the beam to a flat sheet that can cut slabs off the alien."

"Why do you want to do that?" Clarence asked.

"Recycling," Sharron replied, "We can construct a lot of defense from the materials in that ship. We're thinking of stopping the other two for the same reason. In a way it's what they did to our observatory and the supply ship."

"If what you discovered in His Imperial Commander's minds is true I can see us needing the materials," Wendy said thoughtfully."

"Yes" Arielle acknowledged, "But there has to be a way to stop them without destroying them."

"The trouble is," Brenda added, "They might not see any other species as anything except food."

"The other thing that I keep thinking about," Arielle submitted, "Is that they're egg layers and lay hundreds of eggs at a time."

Jason beeped and typed, "That may be part of their problem, over population."

Arielle instructed, "Look at all of the data we have on the aliens and determine how many eggs are laid at one time, the average number that hatch per clutch, and how often they lay."

Clarence added, "Add to that how many of the aliens are egg layers."

Jason beeped and typed, "Most of that information is in the medical data base and it will take several hours for me to get it from Socrates."

"The meeting on Monday will be soon enough," Arielle replied.

The next morning the girls came to breakfast dressed in jeans, hiking boots, and very bright red shirts. They had wide brimmed straw hats and work gloves, which they set aside to eat.

"You're dressed brightly today," Wendy told them.

"We held a telepathic conference last night," Sharron replied. "The project got expanded and we divided the project into three areas."

Clarence asked, "Are the others in red shirts too?"

Brenda replied, "Melinda and her sisters are wearing green and Karlita and her sisters blue."

"You know," Arielle added, "It turns out that the frequency matching efforts have produced some interesting groupings."

"Such as?" Wendy asked.

"In the military there have been enough matches across the services that General Gregory created a new organization and the matches are being assigned there. The commander, XO, and first sergeant are an army trio."

"I can see that causing problems with the military's laws on fraternization," Clarence interjected.

"The General called the three into his office and they had a long conference," Arielle continued, "When they came out there were reports of the first sergeant who is male having a gleam in his eyes and a smile on his face."

"How long ago was this?" Wendy queried.

"About two weeks ago, momma and the rumor is that both women are pregnant now."

"Not only that," Brenda put in, "General Rowe has a third match also. That story says that Colonel Jenny Landis walked into the personnel office to in process, and Sylvia Rowe was there. Supposedly Ms. Sylvia walked up to the Colonel, kissed her, told the clerk that Colonel Landis was to be assigned as General Rowe's Aid de Camp, then took the Colonel's hand and led her out of the building."

Sharron added, "I've heard rumors that General Gregory and General Glenn are in trios now too."

Brenda finished giggling, "The big three Generals are all having to get used to having two women in their lives."

Smiling Wendy said, "I have a feeling that, that pattern may be something in the activation programming the Boss had created. You three have finished the national budget of food so you should be ready to wrestle minds that aren't sure what to do. Be as gentle as you can."

"Hopefully," Arielle replied as the three picked up their hats and gloves, "All we'll have to do is a little steering."

The three sets of triplets faded into view near a man wearing a hard hat who was studying a map and some blue prints. Arielle introduced herself and the others then continued, "I see we got here enough ahead of everyone else for you to be able to explain the plans to us."

The man leaned on his construction desk and replied, "I'm Eddy and you're just in time. Let me show you what we actually had planned for ten years from now when the state budget focused on this part of the state. Your General was able to get us some financial help so we can do things in grand style."

"Ever do a project this size in one day?" Karlita asked.

"No, and while we will get most of it done today, the concrete that will be laid will have to cure for several days before we can open the road."

"Want to bet on that?" Mika asked.

"How are you planning to cure twenty kilometers of four lane divided highway in a few hours?"

"The curing process is basically allowing the moisture to evaporate out of the cement," Hana answered, "We'll speed up the process without allowing the cement to fracture or powder."

"One of our main goals," Arielle said, "Is to help all of the new trios develop so we'll be guiding them as they do the work. Speaking of the work would you show us the plans so we'll know what's up when we start?"

An hour later large numbers of vehicles began arriving from both directions. From Fort Miller, it was a mixed convoy of staff cars, busses, private vehicles, and heavy trucks. From Des Moines, it was cement mixers, trucks with workers, and trucks with road building materials. General Gregory got out of his staff car followed by two oriental women. He walked to the triplets and asked, "Now that you've got us here how do you plan to make all of this work? Let me introduce my mind partners, these are Nikko and Jasmine."

The women bowed to the girls and Karlita said in mandarin Chinese, "*Welcome to America. May your lives together be complete.*" The women bowed a second time.

Gregory asked, "When you have a moment can you give me Mandarin and them English?"

Karlita smiled and said, "I just did."

Arielle said, "General, We've done some planning and each of us sets is going to take a group of trios for different parts of the work. Karlita and her sisters are going to start with the kids and they will begin loading the wrecks onto the flatbed trucks, behind them; Sharron Brenda and I are going to guide the adults who have learned to link into trios into tapping power and preparing the new roadbed for paving. Melinda and her sisters will take the unlinked trios teach them to link and then lay the new pavement. After that, since everyone will be on the tired side we'll form one massive link to do the landscaping and cure the cement. Your ration trucks need to position themselves as needed to keep everyone fed."

General Glenn walked up with Sally and another woman and asked, "If you haven't met her yet this is Lara Raven, have they got things sorted out?"

"For as late as I worked last night setting things up, they do," General Rowe said, as he, Sylvia, and Colonel Landis joined the crowd.

"Then if everyone is ready let's get started," Arielle said aloud then telepathed, "*If everyone will give us your attention. All of the youth trios please join the blue team leaders. If you've never linked before please join the green leaders. The rest of you join the red leaders.*" There were some loud bangs as people sorted themselves out and moved toward their leaders.

When the sorting finished Karlita and her sisters moved down the road away from the rest and Karlita thought, "*General Rowe, could you instruct the flatbed trucks to begin driving down the road slowly?*"

General Rowe turned to a soldier with a radio and nodded. A short distance away, the large flatbed trucks pulled onto the road and began driving forward. As the first truck drove up even with the first wrecked vehicle, it rose into the air and settled on the truck. A second wreck rose slowly into the air and wobbled before settling onto the truck with the first wreck. General Rowe told the soldier with the radio, "Tell the trucks to go a little faster."

The trucks sped up and suddenly the air filled with wrecks that settled banged and bounced onto the trucks three and four vehicles deep. General Gregory chuckled and said, "I think they got the idea. What do we need to do Arielle?"

"If the red team will link with us we'll show you our part of the project." Then she continued in thought, *"We need to remove the old road then using the survey markers make two dirt strips and pack the dirt. There is a group of steamrollers at the Des Moines end of the road waiting for the signal to roll the length of the strips. They'll roll up their side and back again. Then it will be the green teams turn."*

"What do we do with the old road materials?" Sylvia Rowe thought.

"Put them in a scrap pile at the railroad yard. They'll recycle the material for railroad repairs. It looks like we can start. Basically you all need to tune to us and we'll show you what to do then we'll drop out of the link lead and just feed you all power. Ready, link."

At a place on the road marked by survey markers, the pavement began to peel up followed by the roadbed materials. Behind where the pavement was peeling a strip of bare ground appeared and began to lengthen towards Des Moines. *"Have you got it?"* a thought asked.

The massed mind replied, *"Got it!"*

The first thought said, *"Then here is more power for you to tap."* The strip of road that had been disappearing in meters per minute suddenly began disappearing in tens of meters per second. After a minute the first thought instructed, *"Now pick up the power on your own."* The first thought, which was the Steven's triplets, appeared to drop out of the link. They watched for a minute then wandered to a group of tents that had been set up as shade over a bunch of tables.

"We'll be ready to serve in a few minutes," a sergeant said addressing the triplets. "Are you starved or just hungry?"

"Starved, Sergeant Cassidy," Arielle replied, "But not as bad as they are going to be."

"Why is that?"

"This is their first time linking with a power source and we connected them to the New Orleans wind farm."

"That's a lot of power, are they blacking out a city someplace?"

"It's a possibility, but we haven't turned them completely loose."

"Sis," Brenda injected, "It looks like we're going to have to bring them down the hard way."

Sharron added, "I've notified Doctor Janice."

Doctor Janice and several nurses faded into view and she asked, "Did they go into link thrall like you suggested?"

"Yes ma'am," Arielle answered sorrowfully.

The doctor sighed, nodded her head, and instructed, "Do it." Suddenly everyone who had been in the link with Arielle and her sisters was holding their heads, screaming in pain, or collapsed on the ground. Doctor Janice and the nurses moved among the people placing their hands on the temples of the stricken. The triplets moved to help.

When everyone was back on his or her feet and was lining up to eat General Gregory asked, "What happened?"

Sharron who was closest answered, "The group went into a mental thrall or trance that felt so good you didn't want to come out. If we'd stayed in the group with you we would have been caught too."

"So you dropped out and then forced us to break at the correct time."

"Actually," Brenda inserted, "We never left, just appeared to, to the collective mind. If we'd really left getting back in to break you apart would have killed many of you."

"How do we guard against it happening again?"

"As far as we know," Arielle replied, "It won't happen again. The pain your psyche experienced will prevent you from linking that completely ever again."

"The group was very literally one entity," Doctor Janice said as she joined them. "I had to send three sets to the hospital for over stressed minds, which is the other problem with thrall."

"You sound like you've had problems with this before," Gregory said.

"When Naomi attacked the scout, the three linked that completely. In their case the thrall was based in collective pain not joy and wonder."

Everyone became aware of a rumbling that grew louder moment by moment. The crowd watched as twenty steamrollers rolled along the roadbed that the collective mind had made. Sharron said, "We'd better eat so that we're ready to cure cement once Melinda and her sisters teach the newbies to link."

Eddy the highway engineer approached and asked, "Do I need to have formers laid before the cement arrives?"

"Look," Sharron said pointing at the road where rebar and cement were laying themselves into a perfectly flat and smooth road.

"I guess not," the engineer mused.

"I heard that some of the cement companies couldn't understand why they had to fill their trucks and then not send them out," Sarah said as she and her sisters joined the group.

"I guess they'll be wondering how they got empty," Linda replied.

"How are your charges handling being linked?" Maryanne Janice asked.

"I think they'll survive without the thrall experience, doctor," Melinda replied. "Some of them are still trying to hide their minds from their matches. I'm hungry."

"The eternal curse of the PSI active," Gregory laughed, "So am I. Sergeant is it food yet?"

"Just waiting on you, sir," the sergeant replied.

"Let's eat," the General, instructed waving the girls ahead of him.

After everyone had eaten, they linked and the mysterious something spread out over the new concrete. Several minutes passed then the something disappeared. Arielle told Eddy, "Your new superhighway is finished from the park to Interstates eighty and two-thirty five.

The engineer asked, "Just like that, huh?"

"Yep," Sharron replied, "And here come the heavy trucks that hauled off all of the wrecks."

Brenda asked, "General what do you say, we take the rest of the day off. It is Sunday after all."

General Gregory answered, "Sounds good to me. Everyone help finish whatever needs to be done to get the chow line cleaned and put away then scat."

Three days later, General Gregory was listening to the G-3 give a report when Mika addressed him diffidently in thought, *"General."*

Gregory held up a hand stopping the G-3, and said in thought and aloud, "Go ahead, Mika."

"Sorry to interrupt your meeting. I've been studying the record of third brain of what we think was the scout commander and I found a set of images I think you should see immediately."

"Show me." Mika send the series of images and General Gregory began smiling. *"That's priceless. The aliens were someone else's pets."*

"That's what the record looks like. From the record, they can't gain command rank unless they've been through a ritual where they're shown this evidence. If they don't break down then they advance in rank. That also explains the hodgepodge of their technology. They're thieves not inventors or innovators."

"Let me discuss this with my staff to see if this will help us defeat them and thank you."

"Okay, I'll see if there is any confirmation in any of the other brain records and let you know, bye."

"Ladies and gentlemen," The General said, "I just had my mind blown. Mika was studying one of the alien brains and discovered that they were someone else's pets."

"Pets," General Walter, the G-2, snorted, "Well that explains something but I'm not sure what."

"Ivan," General Gregory addressed the robot that had become a regular at the staff meetings, "Would you lend me your connector and project the image Mika gave me?" Ivan beeped and held out a claw and released its connector. "This is one of the images that Mika sent me. See the leash and collar around the alien's neck."

General Rowe grunted, "I'll bet the masters invented the educators and made slaves from their pets and the pets rebelled."

"That would certainly explain the mixture of technology levels," General Wallace commented. "They're not inventors or scientists, just thieves."

"That was Mika's thought too," Gregory said. "That and their phobia towards any other species makes things interesting at least."

"Downright dangerous," General Loren added.

"Well there isn't much we can do about their inferiority complex at the moment," Gregory said quietly, "So let's finish this up. G-3, you were telling us about General Leclaire's training program."

"From what I understand of things," General Granger, replied, "It isn't really her plan. She told me that she had a conversation with the triplets and they essentially told her what to do."

"I'm not surprised. So what did they arrange?"

"They're going to use three ranges one for the artillery and another for the tanks and the third for a kind of war game. They're running people through the cannons one day and the tanks the next. Then Arielle has turned sadistic and on the third day she and her sisters are going to fight back."

"I could see someone getting hurt," Gregory said, "How have they avoided that?

"The teams in training are going to shoot the alien ship up some more. Or try to at any rate. Arielle and company will be attacking the trios, trying to break them apart or at least slow them enough to miss their shot. Something else too for the partnered command staff. You're first up on Monday and Arielle said that anyone who was too busy didn't have to show up only if they could resist being teleported to the appropriate range. General Leclaire has issued an order for her gunners too. She's going to randomly give a command to fire but tell the trios not to touch the shot. Any gunner who misses will be in big trouble I understand."

General Gregory guffawed and replied, "You know how likely that is, don't you? So what time do we need to be there?"

"Eight in the morning. Clarence decided to make life a little easier for the G-4 and stir the economy some by contracting several catering companies to provide food."

"Considering the amounts of food we eat when we're using our abilities that will more than stir the economy. How is the food being paid for?"

Ms. Montgomery answered, "Clarence ran the contracts himself and got Secretary Treacher to authorize the funding."

"Then we don't need to worry about eating."

"He also arranged for additional acquisitions of ration bars."

"General Loren laughed and said thoughtfully, "I wonder what's going on that they're not telling us about."

"Maybe they think we should keep a supply next to our beds for use during the night," Jerry Rowe said with a big smile on his face.

General Gregory gave his chief of staff a fierce look then asked, "Is there anything else we need to discuss?"

"Triplet's Day," Ms. Montgomery replied.

"I thought that everything was set for that, what now?"

"Hiro scheduled the circus and several of those traveling amusement park companies to be here for several days that week."

"Why is it that things seem to get blown out of proportion around here? Ivan can you help with the increased security needs?"

The robot beeped once and typed, "I was aware that these companies were coming. I have asked the Des Moines police and state police to assist as well. Everything will be set up in the park. The park rangers asked for the extra assistance."

Ms. Montgomery added, "The news media found out about all of this and there has been a lot of coverage so we can expect people from all over."

"Anything else?" Gregory asked. Heads shook no so he continued, "Let's get out of here."

Back at his office, Jenny, his secretary said, "Sir, The White House called. The President will be here for Triplet's day."

Gregory groaned and replied, "I suspected that he wouldn't let the chance to campaign pass."

A BIRTHDAY PARADE AND INTERROGATION

The blue-skied morning had a gentle breeze that made the numerous flags on the parade field snap and pop. Formations of Avenger-7s, Thunderbolt IIs, B-52s, and Stilettos flew overhead. Soldiers snapped to attention as the National Anthem began. Lined up in front of the reviewing stand were fifty-four sets of brightly clothed triplets. When the National Anthem finished the multi-service military band played a very upbeat Happy Birthday. Following Happy Birthday, many officials and nobles from around the world made speeches. Finally, the speeches were finished and the children stood and yelled in unison, "Pass in review!" The band played and the soldiers, sailors, and airmen from all branches of the military marched past the triplets and off the field.

General Gregory joined the triplets to congratulate them. Arielle said, "Thank you for the parade General. I think that you were somewhat mean, making Private Wood commander of troops. Her voice was a little shrill and she sounded like she wasn't too sure of what she was doing."

"She did well enough that tomorrow she will be Corporal Wood. People who prove that can handle tough assignments are promoted in the military. She's scheduled for connector surgery next week."

"Good, I have an idea," Mika said. "How many of the soldiers with connectors, have college degrees?"

"I don't know at the moment but if you're suggesting what I think you are I like the idea," Gregory replied.

Arielle looked around and queried, "Ivan is Jason or Robin near-by?" The robot beeped and typed, "Robin is closest. I have told it to join us."

When Robin joined the group Arielle instructed, "Monday you are to get with General Granger and set up a school for all soldiers with connectors who do not have at least a Bachelor's Degree. You will allow the soldier to choose the institution from which he or she wants a degree and what area they want the degree in. You will use the same methods you use with us."

Gregory asked, "Don't you kids ever take a day off to just play?"

"Because of the education program the robots subjected us to and our genetic design, we never really learned what play is. Our first experience with play was when we went to Florida."

"Mom and dad have tried to ensure that we get involved in some form of recreation," Sharron added, "But we usually end up back to doing things."

Brenda concluded, "Work seems to be a form of play for us and we like the challenges."

"Tom, we gave up trying to turn them into normal kids a long time ago," Clarence said as he and Wendy joined the crowd.

"There's a circus and a whole bunch of new experiences for you to encounter," Wendy told her children. "Go experience them. Maybe you should find the boys you were with last week and compare notes." The girls and their brother faded out.

"Can I join this crowd?" Kenneth Jordan asked.

"What are you doing here," Wendy asked, "And how did you avoid making a speech?"

"I snuck in to bring our triplets. I'm not here officially."

Two oriental women faded into view and one took hold of the General's hand and said, "Please take us to the circus, we have never been to one."

"Everyone these are Nikko Chau and Jasmine Song," Gregory stated. To Nikko he said, "Let me pop home and change out of this uniform. I'll be back in a few minutes."

Nikko asked, "You are so handsome in your uniform, why must you change?"

Clarence chuckled and answered, "That uniform makes him stand out too much and makes him a target. It is better that he change so that he blends into the crowd more. Scat Tom, we'll chat with your ladies while you're gone."

Tom faded out and Wendy asked, "What part of China are you from?"

Nikko answered, I am from Shanghai."

Jasmine added, "I am from Beijing."

"I see a sadness in you, would you tell us if it is not private?" Wendy asked.

Jasmine responded with a savage bitterness, "My cousins are Pan who even in their shame are still evil."

As he faded back into view and hugged Jasmine, General Gregory added, "Tell Arielle that they will be here tomorrow for interrogation. Now you have been sad over those two long enough, let's go to the circus." Holding both of his mates, he faded out.

Clarence asked, "Shall we go see if circuses are as much fun as when we were kids?" Wendy hugged his arm, nodded her head, and they faded out.

At breakfast two days later, Arielle said, "Mom, we're going to interrogate the Brothers Pan this morning."

"Will you need any help?" Wendy asked.

"All nine of us are going to do it, but we would like for the three of you, Ms. Jackie, Ms. Carroll, and General Gregory's ladies but not the General to be there."

"Why not the General?"

"It has to do with attitude and psychology more than anything," Sharron replied, "And we're going to have to do some things to the men to get into their minds that might not be considered nice."

"Like what?" Wendy asked alarmed.

The triplets shook their heads and Arielle replied, "We know you worry about us but it's best if you don't know beforehand."

An hour later, all three sets of triplets, Wendy, Katherine, Aiko, Jackie, Carroll, Nikko, Jasmine, Socrates, Ivan, and the Brothers Pan were assembled in the hospital conference room. Arielle asked, "Ivan would you please connect to my contact kit?" Ivan beeped and complied. Arielle continued, "Socrates, have you completed the sperm collection?" Socrates beeped.

The girls joined hands and began speaking in unison, "Nikko, Jasmine, these are the men who had you captured by the army so that they might rape you and if you didn't become pregnant kill you. We asked you to come here so that you may ease the torments that you are still feeling by watching the interrogation. Lao, Li you will provide complete truthful information about everything we seek."

Lao Pan snarled in defiance, "Children cannot harm us and you will get nothing!"

The collective girl's voice said, "The interrogation will begin now." Suddenly both men were nude and their bodies began to change. Their faces changed from the craggy masculine ones to beautiful feminine ones. Their bodies changed developing large breasts slender waists, wide hips, and that which made them male changed to a woman's. The two screamed and the screams changed from base male voices to soprano feminine ones. Images flashed through the minds of the others present. They saw everything that the Pan Brothers had ever thought, planned, or done in detail. An hour later, the images stopped and where the two men had stood were two very beautiful identical oriental women. The collective voice said, "Socrates take these to surgery and impregnate them with the eggs you have prepared with their sperm." The women were taken out and the voice continued, "Nikko, Jasmine now that you have seen these two punished your minds can refocus to your future with the loving gentle man you are mentally linked with. Ivan see to it that the data is made available to those who need it." The nine girls let go of each other's hands and collapsed unconscious.

As their mothers and others bent to help them the girls recovered and Arielle said in a very exhausted voice, "If Mister Le Bone hadn't been killed by the other inmates in the prison we could have done this to him also. Perhaps this will help of you put this behind you as well."

Mika said, "Let's go home and eat." Showing just how tired they were the girls walked out of the conference room.

After the girls had, gone Wendy asked Carroll and Jackie, "What have we given birth to?"

"A new type of human being," Jackie replied. "Not only more capable but with all humanities interest at heart, thank God,"

"As tired as they were just now I think this is an exception to the things they're willing to do," Carroll added. "We've done our best to raise them with good values so all we can do is continue to support those values."

"Don't worry, this isn't something we liked doing," Arielle thought to the adults. *"We're hosting a dinner for the Pan sisters in the Officer's club at five. Come join us and meet the ladies."*

"Speaking of eating," Wendy said, "It's lunch time." The adults faded out.

That evening in the reception line, the Pan sisters, not dressed in the costuming they had worn as men, but in pastel blue and green cheongsams, were being quietly introduced to the arriving guests. Premier Sang reached the sisters and Arielle said in Chinese, "**Premier Sang, allow me to introduce Lao and Li Pan.**

The Primer looked at the women and asked in English, "I thought that they were men these look like women. Is this a joke?"

"No this is not a joke what was two evil men are now two demure women whose personalities had to be erased and new ones inserted when they were made into women."

"Then they can be set free from the punishment they were assigned?"

"They know what they have done as men and should continue at least until they have their babies. Then I would suggest changing things to a private life away from the public where the current organization can continue to care for them."

"Perhaps, they can find husbands," Sharron added

Premier Sang smiled and said, "Then that's what will happen and I think I will need to announce that they are women now." Then she held her hand to the twins and continued, "It is very nice to meet you." The women smiled and bowed slightly as they shook hands with the Premier.

As the guests milled about and found their seats, Wendy encountered a familiar face and said, "I haven't seen you since we shoved planets around. How have you been Victor?"

"It's great seeing you again too, Wendy," Victor Mason replied. "I'm here to consult on the construction of the new tank circuits. Who are those two beautiful women in the receiving line? I've never seen them before."

"You haven't met our guests of Honor? Come let me introduce you to Lao and Li Pan."

"I thought they were men."

"Until this morning, they were," Wendy replied as a slight frown of worry crossed her face. "Let me introduce you." They walked to the receiving line and Wendy continued, "Lao, Li this is Victor Mason, he built the original tank circuit that we used to divert the Jupiter Body."

The women bowed and Lao said in a soft soprano voice, "We are most happy to meet you."

Mister Mason held out his hand and when Lao extended her hand to shake, he bent and kissed it. He said, "Since the line is breaking up can I escort you to your table?"

Li Pan answered in a voice as soft as her sister's, "Thank you kind sir." Mason held his arms for the women to take and the three walked away.

Arielle said quietly, "Sis, I think you had the right idea because it looks like Mister Mason is on his way to asking one of them tonight."

"Ask what?" Wendy queried.

"One of them to marry him," Sharron answered. "I suggested to Premier Sang that it might be a solution to their future. I wonder where Mister Guthery is. He shouldn't be letting his business partner get all the goodies."

Arielle looked at her mother in surprise and said, "Mom! That's cheating!" Mister Guthery joined his partner and took over escorting one of the twins.

"What?" Wendy replied in feigned surprise, "I didn't do anything."

"So do we tell the Premier she can disband the special unit and that the twins will be staying in the United States?" Sharron asked.

"Let's wait awhile and make sure," Wendy replied.

Later in the evening, Premier Sang, joined Wendy and said, "Should I assume that the Pan's will be staying in the U.S.?"

Wendy held up a hand, went glassy eyed for a moment, then replied, "Yes, Mason and Guthery have both asked, but the twins are reserving their answers because of what they did as men and their sentences. It might help if you dropped a hint to them that if they got married you would cancel the rest of the sentences."

"I'd really like to know how your children were able to affect this change."

"I don't really know. When the nine of them were interrogating the twins, they had their minds locked so tightly that the rest of us present could only see what they showed us."

Robin rolled to Wendy and typed, "The twins have accepted the marriage proposals. Mika told them that she would see about getting the rest of their sentences cancelled if they got married."

"I guess that just got taken out of my hands," Sang said.

Robin typed, "The wedding will be Sunday right before sunset at the tank circuit in the park. Wendy, you and the original five women are to be bridesmaids and your husbands are best men. We will have your dresses and the twins wedding gowns ready."

In a slightly aggravated voice Wendy said, "The boss has been dead for several years. I'd think that, that program should have gone with him."

Sang asked, "What program is that?"

Robin typed, "The Boss put a program in us to dress the original women for public functions such as weddings."

Sunday evening arrived, Wendy and the other brides maids were dressed in lavender dresses, their husbands in grey tuxedoes. When the wedding march started three sets of triplets started forward scattering flower petals. Kenneth Jordan stepped forward with Lao and Li who were dressed in Chinese traditional red gowns with gold embroidered trains. When the three reached the alter, Kenneth presented the women to their prospective husbands. Cardinal Joan Sperling conducted the ceremony. Afterwards Mason and Guthery escorted their wives down the aisle. When they reached the end of the aisle, they threw their bouquets over their shoulders. The reception afterwards lasted well into the night.

At breakfast the next morning, Wendy asked, "What are you kids up to today?"

"Artillery practice on range one," Sharron replied. "Dad, something just occurred to me for when we start lasers. Air traffic, how do we get a no fly zone over Fort Miller so we don't accidently vaporize a plane?"

"That's a good idea" Clarence responded and pulled a cable from the table's edge. Several minutes later he said, "It's taken care of. The FAA is putting the word out now."

"Who are you training today?" their mother asked.

"Thanks, dad. The Generals and command staff, mom," Arielle replied.

"I heard a rumor that you told General Gregory the only way anyone could get out of the training was to be able to resist being teleported to the range."

Sharron giggled and replied, "She did."

"What did the General have to say about that?"

"He said that anyone who failed to show up for training had better be in the hospital dying," Arielle answered.

Clarence chuckled and said, "That sounds like Tom."

Arielle addressed the group of officers and their mind partners before her saying, "Good morning everyone. Today you're going to learn to tap energy sources other than electricity to perform work. When an artillery round is fired, it leaves a vacuum in its wake. We're going to transfer the method to your minds and then you will get to practice what you've learned. Link with your partners, here goes." Several minutes passed where the only noises were the idling of the howitzers and the leaves rustling in trees nearby. Arielle continued, "General Gregory link with us while we have a round fired. Try to imitate what we do with us." The General nodded and joined hands with his mind partners.

Arielle turned to the battery commander and queried, "Would you fire one gun please?"

The Captain keyed his radio and said, "Gun one, one round, fire."

The gun fired and the round wobbled in the air then landed in the taped off area marked for them. General Gregory smiled and accused, "You ducked out of that and we did it ourselves, right?"

Giggling Sharron replied, "Guilty as charged."

"General Loren," Arielle asked, "Are you ready?"

Sally, One of his mind partners and wife responded, "He'd better be or we'll fix him when we get home." Arielle nodded to the battery commander who gave the command for a howitzer to fire.

"Go ahead," General Rowe said, and the Captain ordered the next gun to fire.

The other nine trios took their turn then Arielle said, "Next you're going to handle four guns at a time. Ready General?" The trios finished firing rotations, ate lunch, and then learned to handle mass firing. The day finished and Arielle concluded, "Thank you all for coming. Get a good night's rest and we'll see you on range six tomorrow."

"All nine of you?" General Rowe asked.

"Just me and my sisters," Melinda answered. "Arielle and Karlita are going to introduce a new group to artillery practice tomorrow. You'll see Arielle and her sisters on Wednesday for the fights."

"Fights?" General Glenn asked.

Arielle responded with a smile, "Wait and see." All three sets of triplets faded out.

When the Warren triplets arrived home, Jennifer beeped and typed, "Your mother wants you to contact her telepathically."

Melinda asked, "Do you know why?" The robot beeped twice. Melinda telepathed, *"Mom?"*

"How did things go today?" Katherine asked.

"Some of the trios were wobbly when they started but they caught on fast. Jennifer said to contact you, what's up?"

"More aliens. It looks like two different fleets of them. Check with the Lunar Observatory for whatever details they have. Wendy and Aiko are telling their girls too."

"We'll confer with them and then contact the observatory. Are you going to be home soon?"

"We've still got a couple of loads of stuff to move, probably another hour."

"Okay, see you then," Melinda, concluded. Aloud she asked, "Jennifer, would you find us a light snack, Please?" Jennifer beeped and rolled out of the room. She told her sisters, "Mom said that the Lunar Observatory has found some more aliens. We need to confer with the others and contact the observatory."

"Melinda," Arielle thought, *"Did your mom give you the heads up?"*

"Yes and told me that we need to contact the Lunar Observatory," Melinda replied.

"We got the word too," Karlita thought to the others.

"I've instructed Robin to make the call and to conference it to you guys. Let's find out what is up."

"Jennifer, get General Gregory into the call we're about to get," Sarah said.

The phone screen divided into segments with the triplets, General Gregory, and Doctor Jack Orley, head astronomer at the Lunar Farside Observatory.

Doctor Orley asked, "Are you the ones I was told would be calling?"

Arielle replied, "If you were expecting a call about alien ships, yes. Let me introduce everyone. With me are my sisters Brenda and Sharron. Next is Melinda, Linda, and Sara. The last set of triplets is Karlita, Mika, and Hana. Lastly, this is General Gregory. Please show us what you have found."

"There are two groups of objects of approximately twenty to thirty components in each. Our observations indicate that one group's path will intersect the other at a little over a light year away. One group has the same emission signature that the first ships had. The other group has totally different emissions."

"Is a light-year outside you kid's ability to go look at our visitors?" General Gregory asked.

"We've never tried to go that far," Arielle replied. "I suppose it's possible with generator support."

"If you can, I'd like to find out whom this new bunch is and if they are a problem also. If you're as tired from shooting as I am, I suggest that you look in the morning."

"We'll look into it then," Arielle answered. "Doctor, can you send us the coordinates of both fleets, please."

"Certainly," Doctor Orley replied, "I'll have them to you by eight tomorrow your time."

"Robin," Sharron instructed, "Please alert Doctor Maryanne and the generator station. We'll do this and then go to the range. General, we're going to push the start time back two hours."

"I'll notify the others," Gregory replied.

"Good morning girls," Doctor Janice said. "I understand you're going to try a little astronomy this morning."

"Yes ma'am," Arielle replied. "It seems that the Lunar Observatory found a couple of fleets headed in our general direction."

Karlita added, "We want to use the tanks, because we don't know what we'll encounter."

"Being cautious, huh?" Maryanne asked.

"Actually," Mika answered, "We're far more cautious than most adults seem to want to give us credit for."

The Doctor chuckled and said, "Touché. Okay, climb in and we'll get you hooked up."

Once the girls were connected to the tanks and IVs, they linked and launched their joint something into space. They looked at the fleet that the astronomers had identified as alien lizards; they switched and went to look at the new fleet. There they discovered ships that were arrowhead shaped with heavily reinforced prows. Mika thought, "*I think these guys might be upset with the lizards too.*"

"*I agree,*" Brenda thought, "*Those ships are designed to ram and survive.*"

"*Shall we see what they look like?*" Sharron asked.

The something turned invisible and slid through the wall of one of the ships. Mika thought in amazement, "*Are the pet owners coming to punish the pets?*"

"*They're not happy about something,*" Arielle thought. She sent a thought to Doctor Janice saying, "*Ms. Maryanne, would you ask General Gregory to link with us please.*"

"*What have you kids found?*" the General asked when he joined the girl's something.

"*Remember the image I showed you?*" Mika thought. "*It seems that we've found the pet owners. Take a look.*"

Arielle queried, "*Do we keep hidden, or make contact?*"

Sharron added, "*If we make contact how do we make sure we aren't trading one enemy for another or that they aren't allies of the lizards?*"

"*We should be able to determine one thing now,*" Hana thought.

"*What's that?*" Gregory asked.

"We turn visible looking like a lizard and see what the reaction is."

"Can you do it without getting hurt?"

Rather than answer the General the image of a lizard commander faded into view in the alien ship. It was immediately attacked with several kinds of weapon. The lizard image blinked out.

Linda said, *"Whoosh! They don't like lizards very well do they?"*

"Before we try making contact with them let's try one other thing," Melinda thought.

"What's that?" Hana asked.

"Go to the lizard fleet and do the same thing but as one of these guys."

"It will certainly confirm the relationship between these two groups," Gregory thought.

The composite something moved to the lizard's fleet, entered the lead ship, then became visible as one of the lizards former masters. The reaction was just as instantaneous but it was varied, some cowering and some tried to destroy the image they saw. The image winked out and Arielle thought, *"At least that proves that the other fleet was the masters and that they are on the outs with them."*

Doctor Janice thought to the group, *"You've been out there for six hours. You should come back and take a break."*

"I think that's a good idea kids," Gregory added.

Back in the generator station, Doctor Janice said, "General you need to go to decontamination."

"I'm on my way," he replied and left the room.

Sharron thought, *"Are we safe yet?"*

From the control station a specialist said, "No detectable radiation, beginning drain procedure."

While the girls were drying off, Maryanne said, "There is food in the next room. Did you find anything interesting?"

"You could say that," Arielle replied. "Have you seen Mika's discovery about the lizard aliens?" Maryanne nodded and Arielle continued, "The other fleet is the pet owners and the two groups don't get along."

"Does that make them friendly to us," Maryanne asked, "Or just a different enemy to deal with?"

"We don't know that yet. Next time out we'll see if we can figure it out. We haven't seen your triplets in a while what are they up to?"

Maryanne smiled broadly and answered, "Mischief most likely just like you nine."

Mika said matter of factly, "You need a husband. We'll see what we can do."

"What makes you think I need or want a husband?"

"It shows on your face whenever you see our parents together," Karlita responded. "Besides your children need a man to set a good example for them since two of them are boys."

"They also need more interaction with humans," Sharron added. "The robots have their own ideas of how to raise children that isn't always the best."

"I heard that Jason was a little upset when Clarence and Arielle cornered it," Maryanne said.

"I think we caused its circuits to freeze for a moment," Arielle said. "Let's go eat the food you said is in the next room, I'm hungry."

"General Gregory said that since this took longer than intended he rescheduled the training for tomorrow," Maryann added as the kids walked to the next room.

"*Kids,*" General Gregory thought, "*Doctor Orley sent a message. It seems that one of the pet owner ships has left its fleet and is headed directly for us. I've called a command and staff for eight tomorrow morning, please attend.*"

A NEW ENEMY

The adjutant called, "Attention," as General Gregory entered the conference room.

He said, "Be seated." As he was sitting, the girls all faded into view and found seats. The General continued, "The day before yesterday, the Farside Observatory reported that there are two fleets of aliens headed our way. The girls and I went and looked. We discovered that one fleet is more of our old friends the lizards. The other group if you've all been keeping up with the intelligence is the lizard's pet owners. We were able to verify this by appearing in a ship in each fleet in the image of the other alien. Late yesterday Doctor Orley from the observatory notified us that a ship from the pet owner fleet has changed course directly here. Any ideas on how we handle the single ship?"

"Is it possible that this ship was sent because of our visit?" Brenda asked.

"I wish I knew, anyone else?" Gregory replied.

"Could we put a part of our fleet in front of them and try to signal them by radio etc.," General Glenn asked.

"Possibly have the girls put a satellite in front of it to attempt communications," General Granger stated.

"How long would it take to get something like that ready?" Arielle queried.

"Do a combination," General Rowe said, "Put the satellite on one of the ships then put them in range of the alien and have them launch it. Ships suddenly appearing will definitely draw their attention. That should ensure that they notice the satellite when it's launched."

General Gregory looked at the girls and asked, "You're the ones that will have to sling things around, is this doable?"

Arielle asked, "General Wallace, how long would it take for you to double the generator stations output?"

"If the generators are available someplace in the nation, about two days," he replied.

"I just talked to dad," Brenda said, "He's talking to NASA about a welcome and ID satellite and also about a camera probe. He should have an answer about them this afternoon or evening."

"In the meantime if you don't have anything further, General," Karlita concluded, "We could get in a little gunnery practice."

"Since we're not going to get any instant answers," Gregory said with a chuckle, "That sounds like a wonderful idea. Those of you with partners get them and report to the appropriate range. Spread the word to anyone else who should attend."

At dinner that night, Wendy asked her daughters, "How was your day?"

"Varied," Sharron answered, "But interesting."

"What all did you do?"

"Went to a staff meeting," Arielle replied, "Then went to the ranges."

"Jason," Brenda instructed, "Please prepare classes on gardening to include Japanese and Chinese classical gardens."

Wendy queried, "Have you decided to become a gardener?"

"At lunch we were discussing them with Ms. Nikko and Ms. Jasmine. They were describing the gardens they had and saw in China. They sounded like wonderful places."

"They showed us mind images of their family gardens," Arielle added. "They are very beautiful."

"Very peaceful places to rest and relax in," Sharron concluded. "They were a little sad that they didn't have much garden of any kind here."

Clarence asked, "Do I sense a construction project in the making?"

"I don't think that we've thought that far ahead, Dad," Arielle responded. "After all we've been busy dealing with aliens a great deal. We can probably get the grounds robots to build some of them."

Once the family had finished eating, Sharron asked, "Have you heard back from NASA yet, Dad?"

"They are still investigating things to see if they can adapt something they already have to fill the missions, Squirt," Clarence replied.

"How long would it take to build something new?" Brenda asked.

"Probably a couple of years because of design and construction time," her father answered.

Sharron queried, "What characteristics would a welcome and ID satellite need?"

"What would a reconnaissance drone need?" Arielle added.

Before Clarence could answer, Brenda looked at her mother and said in an astonished voice, "Mom, you're pregnant!"

Wendy asked curiously, "How can you tell?"

"I can sense their auras."

"Auras, plural, triplets?"

"That's what I'm sensing and your aura has changed too."

"She's right mom," Arielle added, "I can sense them too and you're glowing."

The phone panel brightened, and General Gregory asked, "Hi everyone. Girls, can you come to the conference room? My staff thinks it has come up with a plan that might work." Then he looked at Wendy and asked, "Wendy are you pregnant?"

"That's what the girls are telling me," Wendy replied. "I'll visit Maryanne tomorrow to find out for sure."

Chuckling Gregory added, "Where their talents are concerned, I'd be willing to wager that they are correct. Girls, can you come now?" Wendy nodded approval and the triplets faded out.

In the headquarters conference room, General Gregory said, "General Granger, would you explain what you have in mind."

"According to Mister Sato, the shuttles onboard our fleet ships can be remotely controlled from their mother ship," General Granger reported. "We propose putting the fleet in place then remotely launching a shuttle from one of the ships that will have been modified with some equipment that we would need to establish communications."

"We think we have the lizard's language figured out," Arielle said. "From the quick look we took the pet owners don't have the same three brain structure. I wonder…" Arielle went glassy eyed and thought, *"Mom, Dad, could you join is in the conference room?"*

Wendy and Clarence faded into view and Wendy asked, "How can we help Arielle?"

"When we captured the scout we were able to extract enough from the triple brains to reconstruct a large part of their language and history. We killed them doing it which wasn't an issue," Arielle stated. "Can we pull the same sort of thing with a pet owner without killing it and while possibly under attack from the rest of the crew?"

"You kids always seem to come up with the toughest questions," Clarence responded.

"It should be possible," Wendy said thoughtfully, "If some of us interrogate the alien while the rest provide defensive shielding."

"How about this, General," Arielle asked, "We kids will provide the defensive part while mom, dad and their partners interrogate the alien captain. Then you can build its language into the shuttles equipment."

General Granger responded, "Mister Sato has a shuttle at the right point in construction for us to use after modification. When the mods are finished, we would need to have it shipped to the fleet. It will take about a week to do that."

"That should be enough time for us, shouldn't it mom?"

"I don't see why not," Wendy answered.

"Alright," General Gregory said, "You kids scat and get to bed. General Wallace, Get with Clarence about the generator station. Two days from now you triplets and your parents make your raid. I will want to launch the shuttle four days after that. Do any of the rest of you have anything?"

"While we were shooting lasers," General Loren responded, "We shot down a drone cargo plane that entered the no fly zone. We reported it to the FAA."

"So the company is suing the army?" Gregory asked.

"Actually the plane's owners were arrested by the FBI. When the FAA investigated the crash site they found illegal narcotics in the remains."

"Then they're in good hands, anything else?" After a pause, General Gregory continued, "Good, let's go home."

Hana said to no one in particular, "How are the aliens able to cover interstellar distances so quickly? I think our scientists need to look into that."

"Since your mother is into the space business," Clarence suggested, "Why don't you ask her to get that area checked."

General Gregory asked with a huge grin, "Why are you all still here?" Then he faded out. A moment later the room was totally empty of people.

Two days later Arielle thought from the generator station, *"Okay mom, Ms. Maryann has us hooked up, shall we get this done?"*

Her mother replied, *"We're ready to so go ahead."*

A large mysterious something appeared on the command deck of the pet owner ship and settled around what appeared to be the commander. The other aliens tried to rescue their commander and destroy the something by any means they could. Nothing worked and fifteen minutes later, the something disappeared.

Wendy thought, *"We've got their language and history, we'll upload it to the system as soon as we get down."*

"See you at lunch," Arielle replied and continued, *"Doctor are we safe yet?"*

"With all of the weapons you nine were stopping you're still a little hot. Probably about five more minutes," Maryann thought. *"You're also going to need the anti-radiation shots this time too."*

"They were certainly upset about us. At least we should be able to talk to them if the something didn't end the possibly."

Twenty minutes later the tank technician said, "Radiation is zero beginning drain procedure."

Maryann thought, "*You're being uncorked now. Food is in the usual place.*"

While the girls were eating Wendy faded in and Arielle asked, "Hi mom, do you glow in the dark too?"

"Actually you kept us so well protected," Wendy replied, "We only had to shower. How about you?"

"Bad enough that they've had to have the anti-radiation injections," Maryann said as she entered the room. "We've been studying the mysterious something, looking for ways to protect it from radiation. We haven't come up with anything yet. What I find amazing is that something with as short a half-life as Francium can be part of the alien's makeup."

Melinda asked, "Could their bodies be manufacturing it?"

"That's what I'm beginning to think," Maryann said, "Is happening but I can't prove it."

"We have a problem," Sharron queried, "Don't we, Mom?"

Wendy sighed answered, "Unfortunately."

Maryann said, "Don't tell me we have to fight both groups."

"That's exactly what we're going to have to do."

"They don't get along with each other and we still have to fight both of them, how come?"

"Resources," Arielle answered, "Natural and otherwise to include us as food."

"Are we going to have time to build enough defenses to defeat them?" Maryann asked.

Wendy replied bleakly, "No," as the others shook their heads.

General Gregory faded into view and asked, "Did you find out anything worthwhile?"

"Just that we now have two enemies," Wendy replied.

"So do we still send the modified shuttle?"

"No!" Brenda said emphatically. "They're extremely good reverse engineers."

"No chance of any kind of alliance or peace, from what we got from the commander's minds. The lizards are actually a programmed proxy for their owners unless something like us occurs where we defeat them."

"General," Arielle asked, "Could you ask General Wallace to come here?"

General Gregory took out his phone and made a call, then asked, "What do you have in mind?"

"Doctor Janice," Arielle asked formally, "How cold can you get us and not kill us?"

Before Maryanne could answer, General Wallace came in and said, "You called?"

Maryann answered, "I can put you into hyperthermia but that usually puts the person into a coma."

"General Wallace," Arielle queried, "We're going to use the Jupiter body to take out the majority of both fleets before they get joined up. Doing that means our bodies are going to become extremely hot if that liquid can't cool us enough. How cold can you get the fluid before it freezes?"

Wendy sat up straight and gasped, "You can't! You'll die!"

"Mom," Sharron answered with the same finality in her voice as her sister, "We don't want to die either, but we will not let then have our solar system, our planet, our families, or anything else. We will kill them first!"

Katherine and Aiko faded in and so did the girl's fathers. Wendy said, "But you can't, we love you too much to let you go. There has to be another way. There has to!"

"I wish there were," General Gregory said very sadly. "I asked Monica to send a shuttle out toward the solo ship. The aliens blew it up when its programming tried to contact it."

Sarah asked, "General Wallace, do you have a contact set?" He sighed, reached into a pocket withdrew his contact set put them on and connected to a connector in the table.

Sarah connected to a set as well and Brenda asked, "Dad, you're aware that all of us have read your Lensmen[1], novels, how did Thorndyke defeat Boscone in the battle of Tellus?"

Clarence grunted and answered, "So that's why those books are so dog-eared. As I recall he used a sunbeam, but that was an electromechanical set of devices."

"General Wallace, How long with help from the fleet and all of us, would it take to build what Sarah sent to you?"

"I'll have to get with Mister Mason," Wallace replied. "I can probably answer that by the day after tomorrow."

"Good enough," Arielle said nodding, "We've got to sleep the anti-radiation shots off anyway."

William asked gently, "Sarah would you share your idea with me, please?" Sarah blanked for a moment then William continued, "Generals, Clarence, Hiro I think that we need to put our heads together and see if there isn't some way to protect our girls better than what they have planned."

General Wallace said thoughtfully, "I haven't read the Lensmen books but an author named Hogan[2] described a powerful beam weapon in one of his books. The people who used it were alive afterwards so there has to be a way to shield the girls as well as using the tanks."

Maryann said gently, "Girls go get a bath and something to eat and let us figure out how to help with this." Without any discussion, all nine girls faded out. Maryann continued, "So, does anyone have any ideas?"

Wendy slumped in her chair and said, "Too bad we can't go in their places."

Clarence sat beside her, put his arm around her and replied, "You know it has to be them, dear. We're not anywhere nearly as powerful as they are. General Wallace, How long would it take to build two more sets of tanks and generators in a different location say a block away?"

"How long before the fleets merge and how many generators per station?" Wallace asked.

"If they're the same size as what's being used now, I'd say ten for each station may work."

General Gregory asked, "What do you have in mind?"

"Cooling the kids by diverting as much heat as we can into the three biggest heat sinks in the solar system Jupiter, Saturn, and Neptune."

"We've never done anything like that, dear," Wendy injected, "How would we go about doing it?"

"How did Pat do it in El Paso when you were rescuing kidnapped women?"

Wendy turned to face her husband with a shocked look on her face and said, "That's right, we know how, I'd forgotten about that."

"It's been so long," Katherine said, "We'll need to practice."

"I guess that means I need to contact President Harper and Secretary Jordan," Gregory muttered to himself.

"That comes with the territory Tom," Hiro told him smiling.

Before the General could comment Katherine said, "I just told my father. He said he'll come tomorrow and bring the President with him."

"Since that's taken care of let's follow your kids example and go home and sleep on all of this," Gregory suggested.

Two days later, everyone gathered in the headquarters conference room and General Gregory asked, "Okay, who's first?"

Second Stage Lensman by E. E. Doc Smith Pyramid Books 1953
Voyage From Yesteryear by James P. Hogan Del Rey / Ballantine Book 1982

"I'll start," Arielle said. "What we plan to do is use our combined something and all of the power we can find to create a huge cannon in space. Our ammunition will be energy from the Jupiter body. It will be an electromagnetic gun we'll draw energy from the body into the barrel and accelerate it towards the fleets. We anticipate using all of the tank circuits and all of the power sources worldwide to accomplish this. That means that when we start anything using alternating current power will be blacked out."

General Wallace spoke next saying, "It will take three to four weeks for the construction projects you've all requested. Mason says that in that time using the fleet he can get your trigger device built and also get four more tank circuits online. Clarence, it will take three weeks to build and install stations for you and your wives will use. Most of that is to construct more generators."

"That will probably be enough time," Clarence said, "As long as the alien training machines can be kept at bay. Girls, when you start snatching power from everywhere we need for you to leave the twenty generators General Wallace mentioned alone. With our mind partners, we're going to keep you cool by using them to transfer heat from you to the gas giant planets. With remote sensors that Maryann will hook up to you, we should be able to control your body heat levels enough to allow you to live through what's coming."

"So you need me and President Harper here to whip up an advertising campaign to prepare the worlds populations for living in the dark ages," Kenneth Jordan said. "How long a period of blackout are we talking about?"

Sarah replied, "We anticipate that it will take us about twelve to eighteen hours to generate and fire the beam. Doctor, Is it possible to provide us with IVs that will not be destroyed by the heat we're expecting to have to deal with?"

"General Wallace," Maryann answered, "You and I need to get together and design a special IV system. The glucose we use won't be any good above eighty degrees."

"What happens to it?" Wallace asked.

"Under the right conditions it can ferment and become a very powerful alcohol. The other problem is that hot fluids will raise their body temperatures."

"We certainly don't want them drunk or cooking from the inside out."

"How are you planning to take care of them once they start?" Wendy asked.

"That's part of what I need to work out with General Wallace," Maryann replied.

"Tom," General Wallace asked, "Can we put the Corps on alert and use them to help build and construct?"

"I just told Jerry," Tom Gregory replied. "I also asked Glenn to get the fleet into close orbit to provide workers for the space borne projects."

"Doctor," Arielle said, "When we get into the tanks you'll need to light proof our eyes as well as seal them from the chemicals."

"I'll get a construction timeline drawn up and have it ready for us to start tomorrow," General Wallace concluded.

"We're going to do you nine like the Boss did us," Aiko said, "Three days before the big show you will take a vacation and do nothing but rest and play."

"And I'm going to sick Doctor Wallace on you to make sure that you follow instructions."

GARDENING AND OTHER PROJECTS

When the girls arrived at the generator station the next morning, Chief Kennedy told them that the station was closed for the modifications to be made. The girls turned and discovered that the boys they had gone to the museum with standing there.

"Doctor Wallace sent us to fetch you to go to General Gregory's house," Nicholas Rostov said. "She also said we were to walk there."

Arielle quizzed, "Did she give any reasons?"

"No," Nicholas replied, "Not even a hint."

"Then let's go see what she has on her mind, walking of course."

When they arrived at General Gregory's quarters, Doctor Wallace greeted them with, "Good morning to you all. The General's mates had to return to China. They are attending a funeral for one of their family. They will be gone for a week. During that time, you kids are going to build them a Japanese garden, by hand. The robots and I will be watching."

"We really should be helping to build what we need to defeat the aliens," Arielle said.

"The adults are handling all of the construction requirements for that," Elana Wallace told them. "Next week however you nine, well eighteen will be hoisting fifteen new ships into space, without generator assistance because modifications and such will still be going on. In the meantime, you will be doing those things I arrange for you to do. Got that?"

Hana asked, "Did our moms put you up to this?"

"Nope," Elana answered, "I figured this out all on my own. Now suppose you consult Robin for the layout plan and get to work."

"You're enjoying this aren't you?" Brenda asked.

Elana replied, "Yep, now quit stalling and get busy." She watched for a while then the kids hats appeared on their heads without someone bringing them to them. She chuckled and let the use of their powers pass. At lunchtime, an army vehicle pulled up and set out a picnic style lunch for the kids under a tent that had been erected for shade. Elana asked, "Anyone got sore muscles?"

Arielle responded, "Contrary to what you might think of our using our powers, we all exercise regularly and do strenuous things for fun."

Mika asked, "Where are they getting the crews for the new ships?"

"From what I've been told the commanders were the executive officers from several of the current ships and the crews are from all over the world," Elana replied.

"How did they choose which people to use?" Stephen Rostov queried.

"I don't know for sure but the rumor is that they took mostly military people who already had the needed skills."

Justin stated, "That makes sense, it would certainly cut down on training time. How did they get around the language problem?"

"I heard that they mostly took people who could use connectors or temple contacts," Elana answered. "Do you kids eat like this all of the time?"

Arielle answered, "Actually this is light compared to when we're using our powers. Then we might eat two or three times as much."

The sergeant in charge of the food asked, "Anyone need more?"

Heads shook no and Hana said, "I think we're good for now but we'll probably need a snack and cold drinks in a couple of hours."

The sergeant said, "I'll see what we can do," and then signaled to his people to pack things up.

The kids went back to work and an hour later one of the boys tossed a shovel full of dirt at a mound that was being built and missed. The dirt landed on Sharron's back, she turned and asked, "Why did you do that?"

Kevin Jones sassed, "I felt like it."

Sharron responded, "You felt like it! Why you," and suddenly Kevin was dirt covered too.

The other kids stopped to watch, then started laughing. Suddenly dirt was flying everywhere. Robin and the other robots started to move in and restore peace but Elana instructed, "Robin, don't interfere." Soon the children were laughing and hanging onto each other unable to continue their battle.

Alexander Shriver gasped between bouts of laughter, "I'm thirsty."

Elana said, "You should be, you've probably swallowed a kilo of dirt." That comment set everyone to laughing again.

An army truck drove up and the same sergeant asked, "Anyone thirsty?" That question set the kids laughing a third time.

Elana smiled and replied, "That sentiment has just been expressed by one of them. Now if they can stop laughing long enough, you can serve them."

The kids had drinks and a snack and went back to making the garden. Later Wendy, Katherine, and Aiko arrived to take their children home and Aiko asked, "How did they get so dirty?"

Elana replied, "They had a dirt fight and I wouldn't let the robots interfere. Get the robots to show you later."

"Did they come out friends or enemies?" Katherine asked.

"Friends," Elana answered.

"Still trying to make normal children out of them, Elana?" Wendy asked.

"I made pretty good progress in that direction today too," Elana replied.

Wendy shook her head and said loudly, "Come on kids, you need baths before you can eat supper."

At the end of the week, Nikko and Jasmine returned from China. The children met them at the airstrip and they all teleported into the middle of the garden they had built. Arielle told them,

"We heard that you missed a garden in which to find peace for yourselves. Please accept this garden to help you through life."

General Gregory faded into view and said, "So this is where you dragged my ladies to. This is beautiful." He hugged Nikko and Jasmine and continued, "Welcome home."

"This is now more home than it was before," Nikko said addressing the children, "Thank you for such a peaceful place to sooth our minds."

All eighteen children bowed and said, "Búyóng xie[3]."

Arielle added, "Enjoy your garden," then the children faded out.

The General, Nikko, and Jasmine looked about then he said, "I must remember to thank Doctor Wallace for getting the kids to do this for us. Shall we explore a little and see what surprises they have hidden here?"

At breakfast Monday morning Aiko asked her girls, "You three are eating an awful lot of food what are you doing today?"

"We're meeting in the headquarters conference room to hoist the new ships into space," Karlita answered. "We're introducing the guys to high powered unassisted teleports."

"Unassisted?" Hiro asked. "Can you hoist all fifteen ships that way?"

"If we can't, New Orleans has been alerted that we may be using the wind farm again," Mika replied.

"Aren't they getting upset with you taking their power all of the time," Aiko queried.

"President Harper told them that if they had a problem with it," Mika answered, "He would be happy to send in the army to help them understand."

(3) Mandarin Chinese for "Your welcome."

"And the Mayor told the electric company president that if any electric company official objected, he would have them arrested until the crisis is over," Hana concluded.

"Well it looks like it's time for you to go," Aiko said, "Come give me a hug."

In the conference room, Arielle asked, "Ready, guys?" The boys nodded their heads or mumbled that they were ready. Arielle continued, "For the first two ships we'll lead and you feed us power, then we'll switch. After that we'll alternate a ship at a time." To the lieutenant sitting at a communications station in a corner of the room she asked, "Lieutenant, would you give is a view of the Sato ship yards in Japan, please."

A wall panel brightened showing a row of space ships and Brenda asked, "Are those ships bigger than the first fleet?"

Karlita inquired, "Lieutenant, can you get Mister Sato on the screen for us?"

The Lieutenant nodded and a window opened showing Mister Sato. Karlita asked, "<u>Honorable Grandfather, how much larger are these ships than the first fleet?</u>"

Mister Sato replied in English, "They are about one third larger, granddaughter. Here are the mass figures. The crews are onboard and the hatches are sealed."

A row of numbers appeared at the bottom of Mister Sato's window and Arielle said, "Lieutenant, please notify New Orleans that were going to use the wind farm for about two hours. Also could you get a large size snack sent in for us? Mister Sato we will begin lifting the ships in five minutes. Would you please warn the commanders? Change in plan guys, we're all linking and tapping the wind farm for all fifteen ships. We'll do eight of them, eat, and then do the other seven. Mister Sato when we have teleported the first eight we will be taking a thirty minute break, then we will do the rest of the ships."

"I will notify the captains," Mister Sato replied, "Good luck."

Arielle said, "Thank you," and held out her hands to those next to her.

In the Sato shipyards, the first ship rose majestically into the air. When it had cleared all of the gantries it disappeared. The second ship floated up, disappeared, followed by six more in succession. The kids let go of each other's hands and Rodney Jones, who was the heaviest of the group, said, "Now I know how you girls stay so slender, I'm starving." That brought laughter form the rest.

Before anyone could reply the conference room door opened and six robots rolled in with food cocoons on their shelves and distributed them. Sarah said, "Thank you, Jennifer."

Jennifer beeped and typed, "You're welcome. When you finish lifting the other ships, your mothers would like a report on how things went. Arielle, your mother said that someone in New Orleans complained about the blackout you caused and the mayor kept his promise. The official is under arrest."

After eating they finished hoisting the other ships into space, then Arielle thought, "*Mom.*"

"*Go ahead dear,*" Wendy answered.

"*It would have been nice if someone had told us these new ships were a third larger than the originals.*"

"*I wasn't aware that they were, did that pose any problems?*"

"*We used the New Orleans wind farm instead of just our minds. Other than that there were no problems.*"

"*See you at lunch then, we've still got a couple of loads to move this morning.*"

"Mom said she wasn't aware that the new ships were bigger," Arielle told the other kids. "We'll probably get any details at lunch. Guys, thanks for the help. Lieutenant, thank you for your assistance too. Let's go home."

At lunch, Wendy told the girls, "Aiko wasn't even aware that the new ships were larger than the originals. She said she'll have to ask her father what's different about them."

"They weren't enough larger to be a problem with power support," Arielle replied, "But there's no way we could have lifted them without power. Not only were they a third larger they were nearly fifty percent heavier which was the problem."

Sharron asked, "How are the magnetic rings coming?"

Wendy chuckled, "The engineers were a bit confused over how they are to be powered but I think that Mason and Guthrie got them set straight. They say that the first one should be ready to orbit the day after tomorrow."

"Good," Arielle said, "So what does Doctor Wallace have lined up for us next?"

"She hasn't told you?" Clarence asked.

"Not a word, papa," Brenda answered.

Sharron asked Robin, "Robin, do you know what we're going to be doing tomorrow?" The robot beeped once and Brenda continued, "Can you tell us what we will be doing?"

Robin beeped twice, then typed, "Dr. Wallace asked us not to reveal what you will be doing tomorrow."

"I guess you'll just have to die of curiosity," Wendy told her oldest girls.

"It would at least be nice to know how to dress," Brenda lamented.

Robin beeped and typed, "I will lay out your clothing in the morning."

The next morning all six children appeared dressed in jeans and t-shirts and carried hats.

Wendy greeted them with, "It looks like you're either going to work hard or play hard dressed that way."

Robin rolled to where the children could not see its screen beeped and typed, "Play."

Wendy smiled and said, "Okay." Robin blanked its screen.

When they had finished eating Arielle asked, "Where are we supposed to meet, Robin?"

The robot typed, "The family bus will take you where you are going."

Clarence chuckled and said, you're not giving away anything are you, Robin?"

Robin typed, "They are also supposed to be blindfolded before the bus leaves the house."

The family bus arrived in front of the Steven's home followed by an army security detachment the kids got on and put on blindfolds provided by Robin, and the bus pulled away.

At Saylorville Lake north of Des Moines, Doctor Wallace and a group of men and women who were festooned with rods, reels, and various types of fishing tackle met the children. The children were assisted off the various family busses, put into pairs, and handed to an angler, who led them to an assortment of small boats. When everyone was out on the lake the anglers told their charges that they could remove the blindfolds and introduced them to the art of fishing. Six hours later the boats returned to shore. On shore, tents with tables and chairs, and some large grills had been erected. The anglers explained how to clean the fish and soon the air was filled with the odor of cooking fish. Several hours later, the trios bade their fishing partners farewell, boarded their busses and returned home.

Wendy asked, "What have you kids been doing, you reek."

"Fishing, momma," Roger answered proudly. Then demonstrating with his hands, he continued, "And I caught one this big."

Arielle sent an image of Roger holding a fish that was just over half the size he had indicated. Wendy asked, "Are you sure it was that big?"

Roger nodded emphatically and Clarence telepathed to his wife and older daughters, "*To someone his size and age it probably seems that big. Let's not destroy his illusion after all you're only five once in your life.*" Aloud he said, "Scatter and take a bath I'm hungry." The children left the room to comply.

At dinner, Wendy asked, "Has Doctor Wallace revealed what you will be doing tomorrow?"

"She told us to wear athletic cloths and running shoes," Arielle replied.

"She said that she had contacted the Des Moines School District and several of the schools are sending track and field teams to compete with us," Brenda added.

The next day dawned clear and bright and at Fort Miller's Athletics Center nearly a hundred kids were preparing to challenge each other in various sports. More kids and adults were watching and cheering their teams. An hour later the games were well under way and the triplets were holding their own against the other teams when suddenly the older trios were in the middle of the field facing each other holding hands. Doctor Wallace took one look turned to Captain Stanley and yelled, "Get food, something's happened!"

Captain Cynthia Stanley turned to her First Sergeant and said, "Break out the rations and water; it looks like we have some customers."

First Sergeant Jeannette Smith replied, "Yes Ma'am, I'll see about some real food for when they get done as well." Then she keyed her radio and said, "Bravo sixteen, Bravo three, over." When the call was acknowledged, she added, "Drive the ration truck over where the triplets are gathered and start feeding them." The truck began moving and then she called, Bravo Twelve, Bravo Three over." The call was answered and she instructed, "Get to the dining facility and pick up a hot meal for two hundred kids ASAP."

Doctor Wallace queried, "How did you know food might be needed?"

Captain Stanley replied, "We were the family security team when they went to Las Angeles and the earthquake hit. Whoever gets assigned to anything involving the families has a truck with ration bars and water. After all, we never know what mischief will find them."

General Gregory appeared and said, "There was an explosion on the moon and several tunnels have had cave-ins. I expect that they will be at this for a while."

Captain Stanley turned to the First Sergeant and instructed, "You get to try that idea you've had the company practicing."

The First Sergeant replied, "Yes Ma'am," and trotted to where the rest of the company was sitting in the bleachers.

"What is she going to do?" Gregory asked.

"Watch sir," the Captain replied smiling mischievously.

Another truck drove onto the field and stopped next to the first one. A large bale of something was pushed from it and as everyone watched, the B Company soldiers erected a large tent over the linked triplets without touching or disturbing them.

Five minutes later, Gregory wondered, "Who came up with that idea?"

"My First Sergeant came up with it then drilled the company in how to get it done until they had it down cold. They practiced for PT several times a week."

"She needs a medal for that idea," Doctor Elana Wallace said, "I was wondering how to keep them from being sunburned."

Changing the subject Gregory asked, "How are the boys progressing with their abilities?"

"They still don't have the girl's stamina, but they have higher power levels than the girls while they last," Elana replied. "I've noticed that the girls take the lead and the guys feed them power in situations like this."

"I wonder if New Orleans is experiencing a blackout again," Gregory mused. "The army has contracted to build a wind farm here specifically for them to draw power when they need it. We'll sell power to the grid in between times."

Four hours later three trucks drove onto the field. One began handing cases of rations to those feeding the trios and the others began setting up a serving line to feed hungry children. Elana excused herself and told the other competitors what was going on and invited them to go eat. When she returned she asked, "How is the lunar hospital handling the injured?"

"They aren't," Gregory replied, "Right now General Janice and every medical person except the ones here is treating them over by the hospital construction site."

"What were their parents doing during all of this?"

"Putting the first ring in space and helping to dig people out of the damage on the moon, I suppose."

The children let go of each other's hands and they got in line to get something to eat. Clarence, Hiro, and William faded in and looked around. Clarence asked, "How come the kids are just now breaking up?"

"I guess because they finally got everyone rescued that needed it," Gregory replied.

"They were done with that three hours ago."

General Doctor Maryann Janice faded into view and said, "Those kids all need a great big hug for what they've spent the last three hours doing."

Hiro asked, "What were they doing?"

"Let's put it this way, I've only got a dozen injury cases left in the hospital. Between them and my robots the others have all been healed and are ready to go back to the moon."

"How many patients did you have?" Captain Stanley asked.

"Nearly three hundred," Maryann replied.

"And you've got a dozen left!"

"That's why those kids need a great big hug."

Wendy, Katherine, and Aiko, faded in and Aiko asked, "I thought the kids would be home by now, what have they been up to?"

"Playing doctor," Maryann replied smiling.

"Did you get the first ring positioned in space with everything else going on?" General Gregory asked.

"Yes," Wendy replied, "And barring any more disasters we'll launch number two tomorrow and three Wednesday. Playing doctor?"

"My robots would display what was wrong," Maryann replied, "And part of the something cloud that hovered over us would wrap around the patient and his or her wounds would go away. Now the trick will be to get them all back to the moon."

With plates of food in one hand and a fork in the other, Arielle and her sisters joined the group. Arielle asked, "Dad, how long would it take to build an air tight bus like vehicle that could hold fifty to a hundred people that can be coupled to the moon base's airlocks?"

"If the airlock components are on hand probably a couple of days," Clarence responded. "I think that's a workable idea, Tom, can you house all of them while I get it built?"

"As a matter of fact, yes," Tom replied, "General Wallace just notified me that he has some new billets ready to occupy and the units going into them won't be here until next week."

"Doctor Wallace," Arielle asked, "Since we didn't get to participate in the track and field stuff, can we get it rescheduled and shouldn't we explain to our guests and say good bye?"

"I think that's an excellent idea," Elana replied waving the kids in the general direction of their guests.

"Shall we do the same and go home," Clarence asked.

"That sounds wonderful," Gregory replied and faded out.

FIRING THE SUN GUN

"Good morning," Brenda greeted her family as slid into her seat at the breakfast table.

"Good morning to you too," Wendy replied. "How come you're trailing the others to breakfast?"

"I was checking on our unwelcome guests with the Lunar Observatory."

"What did you find out?" her father asked.

"The single ship has altered course for the first ring," Brenda replied, "And the two fleets are moving in that direction and have converging courses."

Arielle asked, "How long before we have to act?"

"Day after tomorrow at the latest," Brenda answered. "They may not know for sure what it is, but the lead ship is accelerating to get to it."

"Is the course change going to make it harder or easier to deal with them?" Wendy asked.

"Both actually," Sharron answered, "Easier in that they will be closer together and harder because the congregation of ships will be denser. Sis, I think we should do it tomorrow, just to make sure so we better confer with the others."

Arielle went glassy eyed for a moment then she said, "General Gregory says the big conference room is available. Mom, dad would you come to and bring your partners?"

"What time?" Wendy asked, "We're scheduled to make some deliveries this morning and help clean up some of the explosion and cave in mess on the moon."

"Would one o'clock be okay? We need to discuss some things with the Generals and Uncle Kenneth as well."

"That should work if nothing else happens. What about you dear?"

"What time are you meeting with the Generals?" Clarence asked.

Arielle replied, "At nine, dad."

"I'll be there. Do I need to notify Hiro and Esteban?"

Arielle shook her head and answered, "They got the word from Melinda and Karlita."

"Then you'd better finish your breakfast so you won't be late," Wendy said smiling.

In the conference room, General Gregory started, "Okay girls what are you going to do and what are the rest of us going to do while you're busy?"

Arielle stood and queried, "General Wallace, What is the status of the generator station reconstruction and the construction of the other stations?"

"Undergoing testing," Wallace replied, "If no problems arise then you should be able to use them all tomorrow."

A screen on one side of the room lit, split in two and showed the faces of Kenneth Jordan and President Harper. Arielle said, "Good morning gentlemen, essentially it is time for us to go on the offensive. Tomorrow we're going to the generator station and activate the sunbeam gun. Dad, you and your partners are going to need to hold the rings in alignment and aim them. Mom and her partners are going to have to help keep the nine of us cool."

General Wallace raised his hand and said, "The new cooling system was designed to allow us to vary the speed at which the chemical moves through the tanks as well as cool them a great deal more than we could before. We've also received a set of special suits from a company that has been following your activities. The suits provide electronic cooling for your bodies, and will protect you from the new anti-radiation coolant."

"Where does the electricity to power them come from?" Brenda asked. "We'll need to make sure we don't take that power while we're working."

"Your mothers will feed some special receptors on the suits and route the heat to a lake we built that has some large heat sinks in it."

"Are there any things we need to know about them once we have them on?" Sarah asked.

"The few features that you need to know about are best explained as you put them on," Wallace replied.

Melinda picked up the briefing with, "Grandfather, Mister President, You need to let the world know that if it is on an alternating current source, it will not have any electricity once we start, not even generators, unless we know where they are beforehand. You'll need to get the information to the General staff so they can plot them on a map for us."

General Loren asked, "Can you give us an idea of how your weapon works and how can the rest of us PSI capable people help?"

"Certainly," Arielle responded and paused to gather her thoughts. "We're going to do something akin to the cosmic engine we used to push alien ships around. We will get our joint something as close to the Jupiter Body as we can, then give it a blast of cosmic energy and cause it to erupt. The plasma that is ejected will be shoved through the engine towards the rings. The rings are magnetic accelerators each somewhat smaller than the previous one. They have cosmic and solar energy collectors built into them so that as the plasma beam passes through them they will get a huge pulse of energy, which will increase the beams power and focus. Anything in the beams way will get just a bit crisp around the edges at a minimum."

Melinda continued, "Our fathers will be linked to the Lunar Observatory and will align the rings so that the beam passes through them and is headed the direction that will produce the greatest destruction in the alien fleets."

Karlita finished, "Every other PSI person will transport our fleets to positions that will allow them to destroy the remaining aliens in a pop them in, they fire, and are moved immediately to a new location. This should capitalize on their disorganization from our efforts and help conserve our people and ships."

Doctor Janice asked, "What are the chances of you nine being hurt or killed in your encounter with the Jupiter Body?"

Mika answered. "We've attempted to ensure that everything that can help us survive has been done and you've all added your own efforts and ideas. Hopefully that will be enough."

Silence reigned after Mika's statement, then shaking himself back to life General Gregory asked, "What time does everyone and everything need to be in place and ready to go?"

"We will arrive at the generator station at nine to put on the suits and get hooked to IVs and such," Arielle replied, "We plan to begin the assault at about ten after Ms. Maryann tells us that everything is set and monitoring is okay."

In the three families homes the next morning breakfast was a very somber affair. The girls ate enough food to make most people ill then hugged their parents as if they would not return and teleported to the generator station. In the generator station they were met by Doctor Janice, several other doctors and a company's worth of nurses and technicians who helped the girls don the special suits and get connected to the cooling tanks. When the connecting procedures were completed and testing done, Maryann thought, *"Okay kids we've got you as ready as we can, go do it and good luck."*

Arielle replied, *"Thank you, mom, are you ready?"*

Wendy replied, *"We're ready, be careful."*

Arielle replied, *"We'll try, dad are you ready?"*

"The astronomers say that we have the rings oriented and locked into position," Clarence answered.

"I have the fleets positioned and the rest of us are ready," General Gregory reported. *"Good hunting."*

The triplets launched their somethings and they joined near the Jupiter Body. There they formed into a tunnel shape similar to the cosmic energy engines they had used before. Arielle thought to everyone, *"On five,"* and began counting down. When she reached one, the Jupiter Body dimmed almost to extinction and a rod of energy erupted from their mysterious something weapon. The beam passed through the three rings. As it went through each ring, it went faster. When it touched the leading alien ship, the ship vanished, the energy of its destruction made no ripples in the beam. In the distance between the last ring and the Pet Owner's fleet, it had begun to spread slightly. As it passed through that fleet, the ships sparkled like fire flies as they died. The beam was wider still and the lizard fleet was completely destroyed.

The beam winked out and the Jupiter body flamed back to full brilliance with hundreds of sunspots and solar storms. Prominences reached for the girls something in apparent revenge. As that happened an energy beam from deep space part way around the Jupiter body barely missed them and Sarah thought, *"Dad, there's three more fleets coming from behind the Jupiter Body,"*

Clarence thought despairingly, *"We can't move the rings fast enough to help."*

Karlita thought, *"Let them go and surround us and aim us at the fleets, Hurry."* The girls father's something surrounded the girls something and moved it in the correct direction.

Wendy thought, *"Girls we're having trouble keeping you cool. Your tanks have nearly a meter of ice around them and Maryann says your body temperature is very high."*

"We still have to do this or everything we know and love gets destroyed, mom. We'll try to hurry. Ready dad?" Arielle asked.

Clarence replied, *"You're lined up on the nearest fleet, fire."*

The Jupiter Body dimmed again and the storms on its surface became more violent. The sun blinked back up to full brightness as the sunbeam destroyed most of the fleet. The Clarence something moved the girl's something to line up on the second fleet and the girls fired again. The process was repeated a third time but when the Jupiter Body brightened this time it suddenly expanded in a nova.

Wendy thought, *"Clarence get out of there the Body exploded! General help them!"*

General Gregory thought, "*All adults join with me.*" A huge something appeared in space and raced towards the nova. When it arrived a second later it extended a tendril into the maelstrom, wrapped around a disintegrating something and pulled it out of the fire. Gregory instructed, "*Doctor Janice we have them, start getting them out of those tanks.*"

"*We're working on it,*" Maryann replied, "*Several robots are breaking the ice for us. I have medical people checking their parents. Wendy, Aiko, and Katherine are okay. Clarence, Hiro, and Esteban appear to be badly sunburned but are alive.*"

"*Clarence's trio's something just left. The kids something is twisting and curling like it is in extreme pain. Do you think we should bring it to the girls?*"

"*Do it, I think that being closer might help the somethings separate and join their girl.*"

In the command conference room two weeks later, Doctor Janice briefed those assembled there saying, "Clarence, William, and Hiro received mostly first and second degree burns when the Jupiter body went nova. The girls were drawing the Body's energy through their somethings; they have very extensive third degree burns over ninety-five percent of their bodies. Those of you in the link that pulled them out of the flames received bad sunburns. The problem is that the girl's somethings haven't separated and reentered their bodies. The somethings are still that big roiling mess that was pulled out of the nova. Lao and Lin have been visiting the girls every day. They walk up to each tank, bow and speak in Mandarin for a couple of minutes then move to the next tank. The girls bodies are responding to whatever they say because they but they still aren't healing."

The Doctor continued her explanation and on the Fort Miller Parade field Nicholas Rostov and his brothers, Alexander Shriver and his brothers, and Kevin Jones and his brothers sat in the bleacher discussing their friend's plight. Nicholas said, "We know that we can identify the something of each girl, the question is, are we strong enough to pull them apart?"

"I think that we can do it but we'll need external power to do it," Alexander replied. "The last I heard was that the New Orleans wind farm was still being repaired from the drain they put on it."

"I discovered that there is another wind farm out in west Texas, near El Paso," Jesse Rostov inserted, "It isn't quite as large as New Orleans, but it should be enough for our needs."

"Is that why you've been going off into the stares lately," Nicholas asked teasingly.

Jesse grinned and Kevin asked, "Do we need to be at the generator station near the girls to do this and should we let someone know what we're going to do first?"

Mathew Jones replied, "I'd like to be close to what we're going to do and if we announce what we plan we may get stopped. I say that we just appear and do it."

"When?" Alexander Shriver asked.

"We've all eaten recently," Nicholas replied, "How about now?"

"Which one of us grabs which one of them?" Matthew Jones queried.

"You mean to say that you don't know which one of them you want to help?" Nicholas teased.

"I just want to make sure no one wants to switch for some reason."

"Mika give you a hard time?" Justin asked.

"No," Matthew replied, "I think she's probably the funniest of them all even if she is the quietest."

"Then we should be set," Nicholas said, "Let's go." The nine boys faded out. In the generator station, each boy appeared beside the tank of one of the girls. Their somethings reached into space to the orbit where Keiyanai's team was containing the girl's somethings to keep them from dissipating away and allowing the girls to die. The boy's something pierced the adults shell and each part of it grasped a part of the girls somethings and pulled them apart. In the generator station cum hospital ward, the boys reached into the tanks and put their hands on each side of the girl's heads. The somethings dove into the respective girls and pushed. Around the world, anyone with even a vestige of PSI ability cringed and held their heads screaming in pain, pain the girls felt and projected unconsciously.

The girls temperature's shot upward and a technician operating the console reacted by turning the tanks refrigeration systems on and cooling the chemical baths the girls were in down.

The boy's somethings fought the girls and their something as the girls tried to escape their own super-hot something. Still holding her head Maryann appeared and saw what was happening. A pair of surgical gloves appeared on her hands and she went to each tank, put her hands on the girl's temples and the girl stopped struggling her something settling into her body. When she finished the last girl she instructed, "Boys, you can let go now."

The boys withdrew their hands from the girls and tanks and began blowing and shaking them. A nurse noticed that the boy's hands were severely burned, picked up a sterile pan poured some fresh healing chemical like the girls were in into it took it to Nicholas. She said, "Sit on the floor and put your hands in this." The other nurses present followed her example and a few minutes later all of the boys were seated on the floor with their hands in a pan of chemical.

Maryann asked, "Just what did you boys think you were up to?"

Nicholas answered defiantly, "We were putting our friends back together so they can get well."

A nurse who had been checking the girls said, "Doctor, look, their healing."

Maryann looked into the tank nearest her and the burns on Mika's body were reducing noticeably. Keiyanai followed by General Gregory faded into view and he asked, "What happened?"

Maryann replied, "These boys decided to try a damn fool stunt and it worked."

"So that's what happened," Keiyanai responded. "Boys, do you realize that you could have hurt me and my partners when you broke us up to get at the girls?"

"I don't think we had thought things out that well," Nicholas answered, "We just knew that we had to help our friends somehow."

Gregory asked Doctor Janice, "Did it work?"

Maryann replied, "Their bodies are healing very rapidly but I don't know what their mental states will be when all is said and done. All right boys, we'll let you off the hook this time." Then continued fiercely, "If you ever pull another stunt like this again, I'll skin you alive."

Nicholas gulped and answered respectfully, "Yes ma'am."

Maryann said, "Let me see your hands," Nine pairs of hands were held up so that she could see them and she continued, "Your hands will be tender for a few days but you're healed, get out of here." The three sets of triplet boys faded out.

The boys reappeared in the parade field bleachers and Rodney Jones said, "I think that we're still needed to help our friends recover."

"I agree and I'd like to cook up some kind of surprise for their parents when our friends recover," Jerome Shriver added.

"Without letting their parents in on it beforehand," Jesse Rostov concluded.

Nicholas Rostov went into a blank stare and thought diffidently, *"Doctor Janice, are you free that you can come talk with us?"*

Sensing the concern in his thought she replied, *"Give me a few minutes. Where are you, the parade field?"*

"Yes ma'am." Aloud Nicholas said, "Ms. Maryann will be her in a few minutes."

Fading into view five minutes later Maryann asked, "Getting into trouble once wasn't enough, what are you plotting now?"

Nicholas queried, "Have you told anyone about this yet?"

"No, not yet."

"Please don't tell their parents yet," Kevin pleaded, "We'd like to surprise them by having a banquet to return our friends to their parents."

"Besides," Justin Shriver added, "Our friends are going to need our help to come back. We saw that in their minds when we forced their somethings back into them."

"What do you have in mind?" Maryann questioned sensing their concern and need to help.

Nicholas answered, "It would be best if we could show you. Can we link with you?"

Maryann agreed with a nod, the boys joined her into their something and she saw and felt what they had discovered in the girls minds. Afterwards she said, "We'll have to get Doctor Wallace involved to help you fix the problem but I agree that you nine need to be the agents of their recovery. The surprise I'll have to think about."

"That's all we ask," Nicholas said. "Can we see Doctor Wallace and get started tomorrow?"

"Are you that eager to be in that kind of pain again so soon?"

"The sooner our friends get well the better it will be for them," Nicholas answered. The other boys all nodded in agreement.

"All right, I'll brief Doctor Wallace this evening and she will let you know where to meet her tomorrow." Everyone faded out.

That evening, General Gregory, General Loren, Maryann, and Doctor Wallace sat in Gregory's office and Maryann explained, "During a conversation with Keiyanai earlier, I discovered that the boys' daring was the correct thing. The reason the girls weren't healing was that some of the nova was in their something with them and continually burning them and they were unable to separate on their own. Keiyanai said that she and her partners were sunburned before they could escape. The pain we all felt was the boys forcing the girl's somethings back into their girl."

"You're saying that the boys could tell the somethings apart?" Glen Loren asked.

"Yes, exactly. Doctor Wallace's machinations before the attack saw to that. This brings us to what the boys want to do. Elana, would you explain?"

"The girls need coaches," Doctor Elana Wallace explained, "And because of their association with the boys they are the best coaches available and before this is over will probably wish they'd never gotten involved. I'm meeting with them in the morning to explain what needs to be done. As for their idea of a cover up, I think that it is the best for all concerned now but I want you three present tomorrow to discuss with them what they have in mind.

HEALING

Early the next morning the boys, the Generals, and Doctor Wallace were assembled in the command conference room. Nicholas opened the meeting with, "We began to help our friends yesterday and with Doctor Wallace's help are going to continue. We know that their parents have been kept away from the generator station and subtly redirected to their other children. Because of the uncertainties in helping our friends recover, we don't want that to change. When our friends are well enough to be removed from the tanks we don't want that fact to be discovered until we spring the surprise and present them to their parents healed."

General Gregory leaned forward, pressed a button on an intercom on the table. The intercom speaker said, "Yes sir," in the voice of his secretary.

"Find General Wallace and tell him we need him in the conference room immediately," the General replied.

The discussion continued for ten minutes and then General Wallace arrived and asked, "You sent for me?"

Gregory waved and said, "Grab a chair; we need some more of your magic."

As the General sat, Nicholas picked up the discussion saying, "We've started the girls on the road to healing but we need to keep it a secret from their parents because of possible complications. When they can be taken out of the tanks, we need to have bodies of some sort put in place and the nurses to continue their routine until we're sure that the girls are healed."

"Can you create what we need?" Gregory asked.

"How much time do I have," Wallace queried. "How many people can I involve?"

"I'd say you can use what you need as long as the girl's families don't find out," Gregory replied.

"Okay," Wallace responded, "I'll get the rubber dummies and tanks assembled. Do I have at least a week?"

Kevin asked, "How will rubber dummies and tanks camouflage anything?"

"Read about World War II particularly about the deception that kept Hitler from moving forces to block the allied invasion of Europe 1944."

"Are you planning to involve Hollywood?" General Glen Loren asked.

"Not if I don't have to. I think I have some pretty good special effects people in my units."

A week later, Doctor Wallace walked into the room that Arielle had been transferred to and asked, "Are you ready to do this?"

Kevin answered, "As I'll ever be. I got General Wallace to make us some special stools so that we don't have to stand while we're working."

"I noticed, that should help," Elana said as she sat in a regular chair and put on her contact set. "Go ahead and link with her so I can get in to see what is going on in her mind."

When they connected, "Arielle thought, *"I can't breathe. I feel like I'm suffocating. Please help, I can't breathe!"*

Doctor Wallace picked up a phone and dialed a number. When it was answered she said, "I think the girls may have lung damage. I'm in Arielle's room."

Doctor Janice faded in and said, "Let's see what is going on here." She put her hands on Arielle's chest over her lungs, looked at Kevin and continued, "Help her control the pain while I fix her lungs and wind pipe." Maryann's hands began to glow and Arielle croaked a scream and passed out. A moment later she took a very deep ragged breath, then a second one and her breathing settled to normal. Maryann's hands stopped glowing and she said to Nicholas, "Let her rest a little and go get something eat. You burned more energy than you think you did.

"Yes ma'am," Nicholas answered, "Should I pass on what I did to the other guys so they'll know what to expect?"

"Yes do that, now go eat. Elana, she should respond better to you now also. Give it a try when he's eaten something." Kevin went into a blank stare then faded out while Maryann was talking.

Twenty minutes later, Kevin faded back in, noted that Arielle was awake and asked, "Feeling better?"

Arielle nodded and telepathed, "*My throat is still very sore and Ms. Maryann said not to talk out loud. Doctor Wallace went to get me some ice cream to help sooth it. Do mom and dad know I'm awake?*"

"No they don't. At the request of us guys, you're being kept under wraps until you're all well then we're going to get you into pretty evening dresses and take you to a formal dance in the officer's club and surprise them. If you're still speaking to me by then I'd like to escort you."

Elana returned with Arielle's ice cream and asked Kevin, "Do you need some ice cream too?"

"Thank you ma'am, no, I just finished a banana split."

"Okay, Arielle, Are you ready to let me poke around in your mind to make sure you're not going to have any post trauma problems?"

Arielle nodded yes and thought, "*Would you ask if I can finish this first?*"

Kevin said, "She asked if she could finish the ice cream first."

Elana replied, "I don't see why not."

"Did Ms. Maryann fix the other girls too?" Kevin asked.

"Yes, they're all resting much better now," Elana replied, "Which as soon as I take a peek inside your head, Ms. Arielle, you should be able to do also,"

Arielle handed the empty ice cream dish to Kevin layback in her bed and waved come on to Doctor Wallace. Kevin took his position; put his fingers on Arielle's temples and Elana connected to them through her contact set. In Arielle's mind, Elana and Kevin found the trauma and shock and helped Arielle understand them and eliminate them so that they would never bother her again. Two hours later Nicholas removed his fingers from Arielle's temples then he and Elana quietly left the sleeping girl's room.

In the hall Elana told Kevin, "You did very well. I don't think that I would have had the power to help her by myself. Her mind is just too strong.

Kevin replied, "I don't think I would have had the power by myself either. I was tapping the wind farm out by El Paso, Texas for the extra energy. I've passed everything I did to the others so maybe they will go all little smoother."

"I hope so. Go get some rest, you start swimming lessons tomorrow."

The next morning Kevin was in Arielle's room when a nurse entered with a brand new swimsuit for her. Kevin said, "It looks like I need to step out for a moment or two."

"Actually," Nurse Masters replied, "If Arielle doesn't mind a boy in the room while we get her into her suit; I could use a little telekinetic help."

Arielle smiled and whispered, "Stay, help."

Kevin sighed and asked, "What do you need for me to do?"

"Lift her up and hold her in the standing position a few inches above the floor," Masters replied. Then I can get her disconnected from the plumbing and slip this suit on her."

Arielle floated above her bed then as she moved to the upright position beside it. Nurse Masters remove Arielle's gown and the various tubes and wires. Then she bent and slipped a bright green one-piece swimsuit onto her limp body.

Masters finished dressing Arielle and instructed, "Okay, lay her back down." Arielle moved back onto the bed. When Arielle was back on the bed, Masters continued, "Let me get a wheelchair," and left the room, returning a moment later with a chair and an orderly.

The orderly set the chair up and moved toward the bed but Kevin forestalled him with, "Let me," and Arielle began to float towards the chair and changing to a sitting position.

Maryann appeared and said, "Neatly done. Now let me check Arielle out then you can take her swimming."

At the underground hospital swimming pool, they met the rest of the girls and boys. Some of the boys looked a little sleepy from a late night. Doctor Janice said, "I know that some of you boys and girls had a very late night waiting on Doctor Wallace. Because of you girls physical condition this will be a short session but they will get longer and more strenuous in the coming days. My goal is to have you all able to walk into the officers club under your own power."

Kevin Jones said, "Doesn't the Officer's Club have a dance floor in the main ball room?"

"Yes it does," Maryann replied smiling, "And you kids could use the fun."

"I don't know how to dance," Arielle said, "I've always been too busy."

Nicholas asked, "I don't think very many of us can dance. Can we learn to dance in the water?"

The physical therapist, George Hampton replied, "I think that's a reasonable request but let's get your friends to where you don't have to hold them up first. Go ahead and get them into the pool." He stepped into the pool and moved to the middle then continued, "Girls I want you to hold your arms straight out and then move them in big arcs in the water. Boys anchor their bodies so that all that moves is their arms."

The girls began waving their arms and after a minute, Sarah asked, "This is hard, how come we're so weak."

Maryann answered, "The Jupiter Body's plasma that was trapped with your somethings burned and destroyed a great deal of your muscle. What you are working on now is brand new muscle that has grown through a combination of something General Wallace found and mine and some other's mental abilities."

"Kind of like we did with mom and dad," Arielle said, "When they were hurt in Las Angeles."

"Yep, same idea."

While this conversation continued, the girls had been waving their arms in the water. Now George said, "Let your arms rest and scissors your legs back and forth like your walking stiff legged."

A week after the girl's rehabilitation had begun Wendy faded into view in General Gregory's office and asked, "What are you hiding?"

Thomas Gregory leaned back in his chair and replied, "And good morning to you. I'm hiding classified information of all sorts, it's part of my job."

"You're dodging, what have you got the boys doing?"

"I don't have them doing anything. Elana caught them hanging around the generator station and dragged them off somewhere. I think she's been occupying their time constructively."

"Then how come their parents haven't been able to get anything out of them about what they've been doing?"

Tom shrugged, waved at his computer and replied, "I don't have the faintest idea and if you'll excuse me I have a meeting with my staff in a few minutes and I need to finish this." Wendy growled but faded out. Tom Gregory sighed and thought, *"Doctor."* Doctor Janice responded and Gregory continued, *"Times just about up I just had Wendy in my office wanting to know what the boys were up to."*

"What did you tell her?"

"That Elana had caught them moping around the generator station and is occupying their time. That didn't go over too well because the boys haven't had anything to tell their parents about their days."

"There's always a SNAFU in any plan isn't there? The girls are walking now," she paused then continued, *"And learning to dance."*

"Dance?" Tom asked surprised.

"Yes, the foxtrot and some other slow couples type dancing. They've been doing it in the pool with the boys." With a sigh

in her thought she finished, *"I guess we'd better schedule the celebration."*

"I'll alert the club for next Saturday and see about invitations. Have the girls got dresses?"

"That's been a lot of fun for me and Elana. The boys have tuxedos also. What time, about nineteen hundred?"

"That's sounds about right. You'll let the boys and girls know?"

"Yep, anything else?"

"No, talk to you later."

Gregory keyed his intercom and when it was answered, said, "Would you bring the invitations I had you get ready for my signature. It's time to send them out." His secretary brought the invitations; the General signed them and instructed, "I'd like officers in full dress uniform to formally deliver these to the addressees." His secretary acknowledged the instructions took the invitations and left his office.

Major Southerland arrived at the Warren residence and rang the bell. Bennett answered the door and the Major asked, "May I speak with Katherine Warren for a moment please." The robot beeped and allowed the Major to enter. In the Family room, the Major saluted the Warrens and said, "I have been sent by General Gregory to deliver an invitation to a formal ball Saturday evening." Handing the invitation to Katherine, he continued, "A limousine will arrive at eighteen thirty to take you to the banquet."

Katherine asked, "I don't really feel like celebrating anything do I really have to attend?"

"Ma'am, the General said to tell you that you had moped enough and that if you didn't attend he would send his and General Loren's ladies to ensure that you do."

"I think we'd better attend dear," William told his wife.

"Wendy told me that Tom was up to something and that it involved Keiyanai's and the other boys that Elana had with the girls. Now I know he's up to something."

The phone panel lit and Wendy said, "I see you've got a visitor from the army too. Did he give you an invitation?"

"Yes," Katherine relied, "And said that the General threatened to send his and Glen's wives after any one of us that didn't want to attend."

"I got the same threat, so I guess we'd better go. I'd sure like to figure out what he's up to. Okay, see you in the morning." The screen blanked and the officer bade the couple farewell and left. "Have you heard of anything going on that would turn Tom into a sneaky person?" William shook his head no.

Saturday arrived and that afternoon, Robin, Jennifer, and Yoshi, family robots disappeared from their family's homes and went to the hospital where they spent several hours styling the girl's now snow-white hair. They arrived back home in time to dress their mistresses according to their programing.

Wendy, Katherine, Aiko and their husbands arrived at the Officer's club at the same time. When they got out of their vehicles and greeted each other, they discovered that their dresses were exactly the same style but different colors. Wendy's was blue, Katherine's Green, and Aiko's rose pink. Wendy asked, "I wonder if the robots style sense has any significance tonight?"

Aiko answered, "I guess we'll have to go inside to see."

"Knowing our robots," Katherine added, "There's probably an ulterior motive. Shall we go in?"

At the entrance to the clubs grand ballroom a marine in full dress uniform took their invitations and checked them against a list then handed them to other marines who escorted them to their tables near a large dance floor.

The three tables were set for eight people, and Katherine commented, "I guess were the first ones here for this table." She examined the table and noted that there were only two place cards, one for her and one for William.

He seated his wife in her seat and mused, "From the looks of this room there should be some other people here."

The Generals and their wives and mind partners and others came in and were seated. No one else seemed to be arriving then the marine sergeant who had checked invitations stood at attention inside the ballroom door and called, "Ladies and Gentlemen, The guests of honor!" The army band that had been playing changed to a new piece of music that was just right for people who needed to walk slowly.

Nine girls in dresses that were the same colors as their mother's stepped into the ballroom with their escorts and walked slowly towards their parents. When they were half way across the room, Wendy's eyes grew wide with astonishment. She looked at Clarence who was clearly stunned then back at the girls. Her hands flew up covering her mouth and tears rolled down her cheeks. She looked at Katherine and Aiko who were crying too. As the girls neared their parents, their mothers moved to the head of the aisle.

When their daughters stopped, Arielle said, "Hi mom, we're back."

Wendy sobbed and rushed forward gathering her daughters in a loving embrace. Beside her, Katherine and Aiko were doing the same completely oblivious to the clapping and cheering going on around them. A few minutes later Wendy regained enough composure to ask, "What happened to your hair?"

Arielle responded, "Let's sit down and we'll explain."

When everyone had been seated and the noise died down. General Gregory stood and began, "Ladies and gentlemen, tonight we are honoring nine young ladies who we would have lost if it weren't for the actions of nine young men. You're all aware of the destruction of five alien fleets bent on destroying us." The General told the rest of the story, then looked at Wendy and concluded, "Because no one was sure whether the girls would heal or not, Doctor Janice kept the parents from visiting them. As General Loren says, 'There's a SNAFU in every plan and Wendy Winston discovered that the boys were being secretive and dropped by my office. I checked with the doctor and we decided that it was time for a party. I've talked enough, let's eat." There was scattered laughter around the room as the stewards began serving.

After everyone had finished eating, the band started playing Glenn Miller's, *Moonlight Serenade*. Kevin leaned to Arielle and asked, "Shall we show them what you've been doing for therapy?" Arielle nodded, the two stood up stepped onto the dance floor and began dancing. A few moments later the rest of the boys and girls were whirling about the dance floor.

Clarence asked Wendy, "Shall we join them or just watch?" Wendy jumped and she looked at her belly and Clarence asked, "Are you all right?"

"I think that the babies want to dance, so perhaps we'd better," she replied.

The couple rose stepped onto the dance floor and began to dance. A moment later, Katherine and Aiko with their husbands were dancing also. When the band began the next song, others joined the families. The dancing and socializing continued until Maryann thought quietly to the girls, "*You have physical therapy in the morning so you should go rest.*"

Kevin and Arielle were near the bandleader. They stopped and Kevin whispered something to him. When the song ended he turned to the dancers and others and announced, "Ladies and gentlemen, "Our honored guests are still receiving medical care and their physician has reminded them that they need to rest before tomorrow. They have asked that you join them in a final dance with them and then continue your celebration after they've gone." He turned to the band and gave the downbeat for *Fascination*. As the waltz progressed, the girls and boys danced to the applause of the other guests, down the main aisle and out the ballroom door.

At the entrance to the Officers Club, the girls bade goodnight to the boys and all eighteen, seven-year-old children faded out, reappeared in their own bedrooms, where they went to bed. The next morning they arrived at breakfast wearing exercise outfits and Wendy asked, "How are you three today?"

"I feel better than I thought I would," Sharron answered.

"I've got some sore muscles," Brenda added.

"Me too," Arielle concluded, "In places I didn't know could get sore muscles. Robin please find me a large canvas, a set of acrylic paints, an easel, and such."

"You're thinking of what Doctor Wallace told us?" Sharron asked. Arielle nodded and she chewed a bite of breakfast. "Me to Robin but I want a computer program that will let me design cross stitch patterns and apply them to cloth. Please get the needles, a hoop, threads, scissors, and anything else needed."

Robin beeped and typed, "Brenda, what materials do you need?

"I haven't decided what medium I want to use," Brenda explained.

"What are you thinking of making?" Clarence asked.

"Chinese puzzles, but I can't decide whether to make them from wood, plastic, or marble."

"I think that are traditionally made from teak or some other very hard wood," Wendy said. "Robin get her a jig saw, a pen type electric drill with an assortment of cutters, bits, and polishers."

Clarence added, "Locate a basic lapidary set up so that she can try marble as well. See about converting the room that was added to the back of the house into a studio for them."

Robin beeped and typed, "That was intended to be a nursery for Wendy's babies."

"I want them to have their own rooms upstairs with the rest of my children," Wendy said. "Tell the construction robots to add three rooms over the studio." Robin beeped acknowledgement.

"Girls, has Maryann said whether your hair will turn red again or not?"

Arielle answered, "She said that it is possible but considering the trauma we experienced, not likely."

Wendy sighed and said, "Well if you decide on a different color there are lots of hair color kits on the market."

"One of the nurses commented that after all of the burning we received, she was surprised that we aren't bald," Brenda replied.

Clarence chuckled, "I know what she means. I think that the shielding our something gave yours helped. My partners and I did have some singed hairs before we were snatched out that maelstrom. You need to finish your breakfasts and go see George for your therapy."

"Arielle sighed and pushed her plate away saying, "It seems strange not to be able to eat everything in sight."

"I'm sure you'll regain your appetites before long," Wendy replied. The girls hugged their parents and faded out.

EPILOGUE

For the next eight months the girls continued to heal physically. They each worked in their chosen art medium creating fantastically beautiful works of art and at the insistence of the Des Moines Art Gallery held an art show. During that time each girl also had the psychological trauma release that Doctor Wallace new would happen when the girls began expressing themselves. Their mothers gave birth to three new sets of triplets who were all red headed girls.

Because more lizard and pet owner fleets could be expected, one of the adult trios was always scanning the heavens. When a new space ship entered the solar system it was spotted and earth fleet ships were sent to intercept it. This ship was only a little larger that earth's largest ships. Unlike the lizards and pet owners' ships this one came in with its running lights on and using searchlights to attract attention. When the fleet arrived, it stopped and waited. General Gregory was notified about the new comer and he notified Wendy who with Aiko and Katherine went to look at the new aliens.